ENDORSEMENT

"This novel struck multiple chords with me, being at once sadly poignant and beautifully romantic. From the book's first couple of pages, the perceptive reader discovers that Alzheimer's disease will play at least a supporting role in the book. In the final part of the novel, Alzheimer's is clearly the solo performer of a piece every audience dreads hearing. Ms. Elam Dauw's excellent narrative paints a vivid and endearing portrait of each one of her characters. I wanted to be *in love* and *be loved* in exactly the same way as Ellie (in Part 3). This is a very moving novel."

—Wendy M. Hershey,
CFA, CFP, CIMA, CAIA

"A travel through generations interconnected by the love of music, *If Music be the Food of Love* is a story that defines the true meaning of love at first sight. Ms. Elam Dauw gives us an intelligent male character who fights for what he believes is right through patience, self-determination, and affection: a male protagonist who truly goes above the call of duty to fight for love. This is a story that charms audiences by the growth of pure love and proves that true love is worth fighting and waiting for!"

—Andrew Westerman,
Language Arts Teacher

"Ms. Elam Dauw taps her personal experience with a family member's dementia to guide us through a musical, multigenerational tale of love and commitment where even a cure for the despicable Alzheimer's disease seems like a believable possibility. Let us hope that as this book depicts the characters' life stories, its hope for a future without Alzheimer's may be fully realized."

—Janis McGillick,
MSW, LNHA, Education Director
Alzheimer's Association St. Louis Chapter

IF MUSIC

BE THE FOOD OF

LOVE

Best Wishes,

IF MUSIC

BE THE FOOD OF

LOVE

DENISE ELAM DAUW

TATE PUBLISHING
AND ENTERPRISES, LLC

Published by Tate Publishing & Enterprises, LLC
127 E. Trade Center Terrace | Mustang, Oklahoma 73064 USA
1.888.361.9473 | www.tatepublishing.com

Tate Publishing is committed to excellence in the publishing industry. The company reflects the philosophy established by the founders, based on Psalm 68:11,
"The Lord gave the word and great was the company of those who published it."

Book design copyright © 2013 by Tate Publishing, LLC. All rights reserved.
Cover design by Samson Lim
Interior design by Caypeeline Casas

Published in the United States of America

ISBN: 978-1-62563-940-0
1. Fiction / Romance / Historical
2. Fiction / Contemporary Women
13.06.14

Dedication

*To my grandmother
and all those who hope*

If music be the food of love, play on;
Give me excess of it, that, surfeiting,
The appetite may sicken, and so die.
That strain again! It had a dying fall:
O, it came o'er my ear like the sweet sound,
That breathes upon a bank of violets,
Stealing and giving odour! Enough; no more;
'Tis not so sweet now as it was before.
O spirit of love, how quick and fresh art thou!
That, notwithstanding thy capacity
Receiveth as the sea, naught enters there,
Of what validity and pitch soe'er,
But falls into abatement and low price,
Even in a minute! so full of shapes is fancy,
That it alone is high fantastical.

— William Shakespeare, *Twelfth Night*

PREFACE

It is happening. She can feel it. Every day she inches closer toward the inevitable feeling, like a raindrop falling into an abyss of water, lost forever. She is her mother's daughter, at least in this way, and it looms like a dark cloud. Waiting. Down in the fabric of her bones and gene deep...

PART 1

MAE

CHAPTER

1

nock! Knock!

She faintly hears two taps on the oversized solid oak door to her room from the main hallway, drowning out the typical sounds she desperately tries to block from day to day. Raising her head slowly to peer at the man in the doorway, she attempts to recall his face. Like usual, her mind turns blank, but she smiles and waits. The tall beautiful man gracefully and gently crosses the room to touch the back of her wheelchair. He grins before leaning down to steal a quick kiss from her wrinkled cheek with a small hug, then sits down on the cushioned floral-fabric chair at her side.

When her head finally follows where he sat down, she gradually finds his face and eyes. "Good morning, Mae," he greets her. "I haven't heard one of your great stories in a while. Would you do me the honor today?" The man speaks in a tender voice reminiscent of mannerisms from an older era.

Mae glances over his features, trying to decipher his present attributes. That he is handsome is an understatement. The man is dressed in a deep-brown suit over an ivory button-up shirt and no tie. His brown shoes are broken in and need a polish, though one would never notice; his face is unequivocally breathtaking. With piercing blue eyes gleaming underneath thick brows and the sharp downward angle of his nose to balance a full set of perfectly sculpted lips, it is difficult to notice anything else about his clothing. "You look like my husband," Mae states. "He has the same hair color."

"Really?" The man smiles with a set of straight white teeth.

Slightly delirious from his gleaming face, Mae takes a moment to regain her thoughts and looks down to hide her subtle blush.

As a woman of meticulous dedication to personal hygiene, Mae visits the salon once a week in the assisted-living facility to freshen the large soft curls in her hair. The pigment previously held a bright golden-blond hue but now resembles a silvery gray. Her eyes are vibrant, deep blue behind plastic glasses. With help from the staff, Mae manages to find a small portion of her jewelry, allowing for the half-inch gold necklace and matching bracelet to be worn daily. She briefly fidgets with the zipper of her red loose-fit sweatsuit jacket before looking back up.

"My Henry and I were so in love," she begins, taking in shallow bits of air, slightly breathless as she slowly speaks. "He was always trying to speak with me, but I was busy taking care of other patients." Mae turns to gaze out the window, descending into her reflection of another time.

"Other patients?"

"I was seventeen years old when I graduated from high school. My parents knew I was bound for nursing school before I did." Mae pauses to catch her breath a moment while admiring the pale-pink roses just outside the window. "The day after graduation, my father drove me directly to Boonville. He convinced the nuns to accept me straight away into their program. I was top of my class in the US Cadet Corps." She glances back at him with a crooked smile.

The handsome man reciprocates a surprised expression, raising one eyebrow, and proceeds with a gentle grin. Mae's frail heart flutters with palpitations a number of moments in an attempt to decipher whether she is imagining his presence in her room. She feels a connection with him in a way she cannot describe; however, the various medications forced down her throat on a daily basis leads to second-guessing every thought.

Turning back to the window, Mae lets her words drift to a whisper and become inaudible as she focuses on the memory she tries to see clearly.

Certain days, thoughts are just flickers and flashes of time, but on occasion, she can make a few memories come into perspective long enough to recount pieces of her story. In her mind, though, a margin of error is inevitable with conjured details and probable mistakes. This particular memory is quite lucid, picturing this beatific and radiant spirit next to her in the chair as *her Henry*.

Just before sunset on Christmas Eve in 1946, Mae is one of nearly twenty nurses gathering in the foyer of the Mount St. Rose Sanatorium in St. Louis where she is carrying out a portion of her hospital residency. Dressed in standard-issue United States Cadet Corps uniforms, the nurses are a sea of formal white button-down dresses, complete with navy blue capes lined in red satin. White head caps are pinned to the women's wavy, rolled hair.

The entire hospital is decorated beautifully for Christmas. A ten-foot Fraser Fir, laced with colored lights, popcorn garland, metallic tinsel, and handcrafted ornaments made by the nurses send a warm greeting to visitors in the typically drab front lobby. The hospitality counter is overflowing with pine trimming accompanied by red bows. Christmas cards, crafted with care by parish family children close to the sanatorium, cover the hallway walls. Pinned up in every high corner between two adjoining walls, shiny garlands hang in wide dips near the ceiling.

"We need to make two lines, ladies," the head nurse states while passing out a single sheet of manuscript paper. "Mae, Josephine, and Beth, you three need to switch with someone taller and stand up here in the front row, please. I cannot see you. Ladies, let us practice quickly before we head into the first room. Please begin at the top of the page with 'Joy to the World,' then down to 'It Came upon a Midnight Clear,' and end with 'God Rest Ye Merry Gentleman.' Lucy, would you sing a C for us, please?"

Reflexively and in perfect recall, Lucy sings the C reference pitch before the head nurse counts the group off at an allegro tempo, "One, two, ready, and."

A mixture of timbres resonates in the foyer, descending down the C major scale for "Joy to the World." The practice session continues for five minutes until the head nurse waves the lines forward down the hallway, heading into the first patient's room. Each time the nurses rotate through all three songs, the harmony expands. After arriving on the second floor of the sanatorium, only a few of the twenty nurses keep a tight grip on their manuscript for reference.

The ladies enter yet another room. Mae becomes apathetic, lost to distraction while singing the repetitive music with thoughts of holidays spent with her family at home in Versailles. Seventy acres of farmland with rolling hills, sycamores, and oak trees decorate an indigenous landscape of predominantly barren land in central Missouri.

As the youngest nurse in training, born in 1928, she misses the comforts of home and the safe haven of her parents' shelter. Mae reminisces the feeling of holidays at the farm, sister to eight siblings; two now married. Even when snow left little to do outside, Mae's mother gathered all the children around the piano, singing carols and church hymns to pass the time. Mae's earliest and most coveted memories are from around their piano. Her mother initiated teaching her the art of piano performance, just as her siblings learned early in childhood. But within a few years, Mae's principal focus shifted to private violin studies instead. Refusing to give up time on the piano, she remained committed to her hymnal practicing. Playing made her feel at peace, as if she were in worship whenever she sat on the piano bench.

Music became the perfect escape from her intense household duties. As the second-oldest living daughter and perpetual recipient of the remnants of her older sister's play clothes, Mae was the primary caregiver in the house while her sister dressed up to impress suitors. Her short, petite frame often held one baby as she fed, changed, and bathed her three youngest siblings. While completing her chores around the farm, she cared for up to four children much of the time. Mae's mother concerned herself with farm duties and educating her eldest daughter when she was not teaching piano.

Mae sighs between songs, staring down at the tiles lining the floor, transitioning to thoughts of her father. Appreciation flows thick in her chest. Growing up, he taught her everything about raising, breeding, and mastering care of the horses on their farm. His persistence in speaking with the nuns who ran the nursing school north of Versailles in Boonville, Missouri, opened the doors to her future. *Mae will be a natural at nursing*, her father insisted to the nuns. Considering the descending long line of doctors and physicians in various specialties in her family, his intuition is validated in Mae's daily quality of work.

It is her voice, however, now initiating the next chapter in Mae's life as an adult.

She is unaware of an admirer.

Engrossed in her Christmas memoirs, Mae completely misses the intense gaze from Henry, a patient in the room. First, he begins staring with utmost awe then diligent focus, attempting to memorize the lines of her high cheekbones, beautiful golden hair, and gorgeous mouth outlined in red lipstick as she sings like no one he has ever heard.

Henry loves music. His knowledge of singing and pitch perception is kinesthetic and practiced, beginning with his mother, whose yodeling technique was a known art form having grow up in Switzerland. Although today he fears he may as well have been deaf, never hearing anyone with a voice like the angel standing before him.

The last song ends. Mae never looks up to bring Henry into view, consumed in her thoughts. The nurses exit the room and move on to the next, leaving Henry floundering for the name of the nurse who just captured his affections. He focuses on his breathing, attempting to slow down his pulse.

Henry lies in bed, thinking of the many months spent in the sanatorium with this bout of tuberculosis. He is frustrated that he has not had one glimpse before at the woman singing to him with this beautiful voice. *Who is she? Where is she from? She must work on the women's floor.*

Henry is admittedly a flirt as he enjoys talking with the ladies…*any* lady. The nurses are all aware of his energy. Being in and out of hospitals since he first caught tuberculosis at the age of fourteen, his excitable personality is somewhat understandable. Just following his sixteenth birthday, a doctor visiting from Brazil told him he would not live past the age of thirty-five. Henry was depressed and restless for weeks, truly compromising the healing process. A tuberculosis patient's only job is to rest, taking all the longer for Henry's lesions to disappear during that occurrence. He is justifiably ready to start his life at eighteen.

Who is this nurse with the beautiful voice?

For hours that night, he is in a daze.

"Werner, you've been here longer than me. Do you know the names of all the nurses?" He finally breaks the silence to his roommate before bedtime.

"Yes, many, I suppose. Why?"

"I think I just lost my heart," Henry replies, dropping his head back to the pillow.

"Oh, boy," Werner utters. The two exchange a brief chuckle and smile. Moments pass. Werner sighs, looking out the window from his bed.

"Do you miss her every day?" Henry inquires.

"Yes. I've been here nearly a year now, and not a minute goes by that I don't think of her. I haven't even held our son yet. He's six months now just last week." Werner takes the picture of his wife and baby boy off his nightstand and strokes the front of the print.

"I am really sorry to hear that, Werner. Real sorry."

"Thank you, Henry. I know they tell us we can be up for two hours a day, but I'm doing my best to cut it down to a half hour. Hopefully, I can get home sooner that way. The doc says my lungs sound good this week. No fluid drained yet," Werner states, feeling hopeful.

"Oh, that's swell, Werner. That is something."

The two sit in silence for several seconds.

"Merry Christmas, Werner," Henry offers.

"Merry Christmas to you," Werner replies. He turns on his side, shuts his eyes, and folds his hand under his pillow to sleep.

Snow softly falls outside the window. Henry watches it come down, and gradually, his lids begin to droop. He lays his head back on the pillow and shuts his eyes.

The next day, numerous nurses are absent for Christmas celebrations with their families. Lucy is filling in on the floor for Marilynn, Henry's regular nurse. "Good morning, Henry. Merry Christmas to you both," Lucy addresses the gentlemen.

"Merry Christmas, Lucy," Werner replies with a smile, sitting up in his bed.

"Lucy, do you know the nurses on the women's floor?" Henry asks while she completes her morning cleaning duties in the room.

"Sure, I do. We all get together after work on occasion."

"Oh, well *we* were wondering about this nurse we heard singing the other night. She had the most beautiful voice. Could you help us out with a name?" Henry throws a wink over at Werner, who is smiling back at him.

Lucy stops in the middle of the room with fresh towels in her hands.

"You mean *you* were wondering if I could help you with a name?" Lucy's eyes tighten slightly, understanding his motive.

"Well, if you wouldn't mind, that would be grand," Henry says, trying to maintain his charm.

"Henry, I don't think you fully realize what all the nurses say about you."

"What do you mean? I just like to have a good time," Henry defends with an edge of fake innocence.

"Yes, unfortunately, you've given the women here an entirely new definition of *fun* in their off hours."

"Playing cards is a harmless activity," Henry states in a straight-forward tone, glancing directly at Werner across the room.

"Except when it involves betting the removal of clothing when the girls lose, among other appalling wagers."

"I didn't make anyone do anything they didn't want to do," Henry insists with a wink and crooked smile. Lucy sighs with a growl in agitation, continuing her tasks in the room. His face drops to a different expression altogether, realizing his angle is amiss. "Well, wait a second. You've got this all wrong, Lucy. I feel completely different about this girl. When I saw her, I just knew, you know?"

Lucy stops and turns to speak to him. "Knew what, Henry? Knew you wanted to *play cards* with her?" Her tone is smug.

"No, not at all. Something about her presence—a glow." Henry stares off. "She just seemed like a dream. I can't imagine even speaking to her, to be honest." He finds Lucy's disbelieving eyes looking right back at him, and resorts to pleading. "Please, Lucy? Just a name? Come on, I don't even want to play cards with her. I promise." His eyes beckon with every last ounce of charm.

Lucy sighs and rolls her eyes. "The lady you're speaking of, does she have soft golden curls?"

"That's her! What's her name?" Henry beseeches.

"Her name is Mae. She not only has the best voice, but she is probably the brightest nurse of us all. I doubt she would give you a second look, so I would not bother at all if I were you." With her lips pressed in a hard line and a final look at Henry in disproval, Lucy exits the room.

For the next twenty-four hours, the name *Mae* consumes Henry's thoughts. His visions of her take on a dreamlike quality, and he is not sure whether he is awake as the hours drone on relentlessly.

He registers sound in the early morning when a few nurses outside the door snap him out of his reverie. He immediately grabs the black comb off his nightstand and dips it in his glass of water, quickly smoothing out his dark-brown hair to a standard comb-over.

"No, I do not know where she is. You may want to check in a few of her patients' rooms," a nurse suggests.

"Okay, thank you," Henry overhears another woman reply.

Henry looks to the door in anticipation and miraculously, there she is, looking like a vision of angelic light, grace, and beauty. His heart thuds in his chest as he speaks quickly.

"Hello, Mae," he says instinctively with a shaky voice. From out in the hall, Mae looks up to the sound of his call. She wonders why he is speaking to her but decides to walk in the room in search of the nurse she needs to locate.

"Hello, Henry," she replies courteously, but with slight agitation.

"You know my name?" Henry asks, shocked.

"Of course. You do have a chart, and your reputation precedes you," she says with a crooked, pressed smile. Mae is familiar with Henry's flirtatious leisure activities, in addition to his persistent requests for personal information from the nurses. He wants to know what each one is doing all the time and what their plans are for the evening.

"Have you seen Marilynn?" Mae questions.

"I think she went that way." He points. "May I walk you down?"

"It's not necessary, but thank you."

"Please. I insist." Henry stands from his bed.

"I suppose."

Henry is having two adequate days in a row since first seeing Mae, and he is eager to know her. Henry slowly walks to the doorway and begins escorting her down. As soon as they are alone, he freezes up. He is uncertain Marilynn actually went this direction at all, but he longed to speak with Mae badly enough and acted impulsively. Adrenaline pumps in his veins. He desperately wants to open his mouth to speak but cannot assemble his words properly. He looks at her, takes in a breath of air, and closes his mouth again. Looking up, he realizes they are somehow already at the end of the hall.

"Thank you, Henry," she says while continuing down the opposite adjacent hallway.

The sign in front of him has an arrow pointing back in the direction from where they came, stating "Men's Tuberculosis Treatment: Quarantine." Henry still cannot speak and instead gestures good-bye with a small wave as Mae glances back quickly with a curious look on her face.

Henry is frozen in place, disbelieving the sequence of events. He somberly turns to walk back to his room. Once there, he lies back down in silence. Frustrated, he sighs. On his exhalation, Henry starts to cough. He knows the doctor will be in soon to check on his lungs, but the coughing persists. He can hear and feel the slight burn in his body from excess fluid. *Oh God, it's starting.*

Over the following week, Henry is tortured. Like other tuberculosis patients, the illness is never constant, and the symptoms contain minimal gray areas. Patients either feel well enough to briefly journey outside for fresh air or are frequently on bed rest. Hoping this was the last of the worst, he yearned to finally go home to his loving mother and aunts who helped raise him since his father's premature death from a massive coronary five years ago.

Henry's mother runs a banquet hall and motel with her sisters in west St. Louis called Dreamland. The location is a common resting point for travelers to stop for a fresh shower and enjoy lively music entertainment. Due to the fact it sits along Route 66, the famous path of the Lewis and Clark Trail, it is a popular attraction for unique guests and residents all around town. Henry frequently washes dishes but does serve now and then. The regulars feel it is a magical place; he fancies watching them come in to eat and dance every night, typically to polka music.

Two houses are within walking distance of Dreamland, one shared by Henry and his mother, and the other occupied by his two aunts. Large stones outline the front foundation of his home with white siding trailing up to the slanted roof. A small porch yields a short landing with stairs leading down to a limestone path to the main road, Barrett Station. Henry misses his home with fond memories of his own room, the small bed he slept in, and sweet sounds of laughter shared with a younger child he loved. Henry once carried a unique bond with his only sister, Charlotte, before she tragically and suddenly passed away at the age of six. Her tuberculosis met a disastrous strain of meningitis, and she slipped away quickly. He misses Charlotte enormously but sometimes sees her in his dreams. In his mind, Henry pictures her as an older, mature teenager and a friend to talk to, sharing different matters. As he drifts in and out of consciousness, he feels her presence there with him, holding his hand through the worst parts.

Henry is growing tired of having needles in him every day. Needles so painful at times he would rather die than go on, and then times he could feel barely a pinch. The needles function to drain fluid or to perform the often fatal pneumothorax. Partially collapsing the lung is always dangerous, but because some doctors manage to walk around with little experience and less than desirable credentials, the results can be grim. It is always a gamble.

Henry is distraught physically and emotionally but decides to take the opportunity to ask Marilynn a question or two. He sits by the window looking lost and fidgets slightly while she tends to Werner with her stethoscope, checking his lungs.

"Marilynn, would you tell me about Mae? What's she like?"

Marilynn pauses, looking up at Henry, who is looking away and out the window.

"You let her do her work, Henry. She's got a long ways to go yet, and she doesn't need distractions," she states with a firm voice.

Henry looks down and sighs. "Yes, ma'am," Henry answers, feeling defeated.

Marilynn turns to look at Werner as she pulls the stethoscope from her ears, feeling awful about her findings.

"Werner, you're going to need a drain today. Lay back, and I will get the doctor." Marilynn is somber with an apologetic expression.

"Oh, of all the rotten luck!" Werner exclaims, pounding the mattress as Marilynn walks out of the room. He rests his head back on the pillow, irate.

"I'm sorry." Henry walks over to console him. "I can't say I've never been there. It feels like that doctor we had last week was trying to torture me. Dr. Rossling, I think? I don't know who they have here this week."

"Great," Werner responds, annoyed.

Marilynn walks in with another nurse and the doctor. Henry notices it is not Dr. Rossling and sighs in relief for his friend.

"Henry, you need to be seated in your bed for a little while." Marilynn glances at him and points to his bed.

Henry nods and walks slowly across the room to sit down. Werner looks at Henry as the doctor prepares the syringe and tray of other small medical equipment. Marilynn then closes the partition curtain, shutting Werner off from Henry's view. Henry lies back on his bed, closing his eyes. He covers his ears with the pillow and cries softly to himself.

Henry does his best to leave the image of Mae in his head alone, spending some time reading to pass the hours. Nights are harder. His eyes are often open wide, unable to sleep. On occasion, he squeezes them closed, attempting to hear Mae's lovely singing voice ringing in his ears. Longing and torture remain his constant companions.

The days pass. Henry starts feeling better physically. Not one pneumothorax all week, and he is able to walk the halls frequently. Even with the bitterly cold weather, the nurses suggest taking in fresh air, even if for a few moments through the windows.

On the sunrise of January 18, Henry hears two unexpected knocks on his door. He wakes up suddenly, confused by the time of day or hour. Werner is not in sight. After focusing on the voice in the room, he is surprised and disoriented, nearly falling out of his bed upon discovering who is walking across the room with graceful precision. "I'll be covering Marilynn's patients today while she is out sick. How's your breathing today, Henry?" Mae quickly approaches his bedside.

Marilynn out sick? Thank you, Lord! I have a second chance. Don't screw it up, Henry. Still recovering from her entrance, he finishes smoothing out his hair from the night's sleep.

"Oh, my lungs are fine," Henry concedes with a pause. "But I tend to be short of breath around you."

Mae fluffs and rearranges his pillow, allowing him to sit upright. She removes the stethoscope draping around her neck to place the ear tips in her ears. She listens to his chest. "Why's that?" Mae asks, moving the chest piece of the stethoscope around to his back.

"You make me nervous," Henry replies with a whimsical smile, turning to find her eyes just over his shoulder. Mae stops and looks down into Henry's eyes for the first time. She removes the ear tips slowly.

"Is that so?" A soft pink blush graces her cheeks.

"Would you pull up that chair and sit down for a few minutes?"

"I'm sorry, Henry. I can't do that," Mae replies firmly, looking down.

"Please, Mae. I'd really like to speak with you," Henry pleads, finding purchase on her blue eyes.

Mae sighs, slightly agitated. "If you insist, but I can't stay long," Mae warns. She turns briefly to find the metal chair beside the bed and scoots it up just inches from his bedside. She sits down with perfect posture.

"Please tell me about yourself," Henry insists.

"What would you like to know?"

"What does your father do?" Henry inquires candidly.

"Well, he breeds and raises horses on our farm back in Versailles," Mae replies.

"Tell me more," Henry persists.

Mae gently crosses her ankles and shifts her feet to the side, a proper lady. She looks out the window, assimilating her response. "All right. I have eight siblings. Annie is the oldest and lives with her family in Jefferson City. Then there is Francis with his family in Sedalia. Rosemary came next, but she passed away at fourteen with appendicitis. After me, there's Irene finishing up high school, and then the twins Roy and Ronald, Joyce, then Lily," Mae finishes.

"And, you're here." Henry nods once with a wistful grin, full of charm.

"Yes." Mae returns his energy, locking eyes with Henry. The moment somehow lingers on in slow motion, frozen in a trance. Mae tries to pull herself away, but her will is lost. Consumed by the depth of his warm stare, she sees something in his face. She gasps subtly as a bit of information she fears missing all this time hits her; like finding the last piece of a puzzle, an alignment snaps into place. *I have to go. What am I doing?* Mae blinks, initializing the movements to stand while still bewildered.

Henry hesitantly speaks. "Mae, I have something important to ask you."

Shocked by her revelation, Mae nods for him to proceed before she has a moment to think it through completely.

"Will you marry me?" Henry proposes.

Mae lets out a laugh, snapping out of her daze. She waits for the punch line of his joke, continuing to smile back at his steadfast gaze. He is not laughing. *He is serious,* she realizes as she tries to swallow her next laugh. Her smile relaxes, and she deliberates, looking down and back at his face over again. *Why in the world would I even consider this?* Her heart pounds forcefully in her chest, a wrinkle developing over her brow, while a tidal wave of thoughts rush through her mind. It seems like an eternity is passing within a matter of seconds.

Finally, she comprehends.

Every question she would ever need to ask is inconsequential. It made no sense for his answers matter little.

"Yes," she replies simply.

Henry is beaming in response to her reply, and Mae cannot contain the energy flowing from her bones. It feels like an electronic transfer from him to her. She smiles with a blush in return before substituting it with her serious and professional face. "Now, I have to get back to my work." Mae is stern.

"Yes, ma'am! See you soon." Henry speaks energetically, bringing his hand to his brow for a mock salute. Mae chuckles as she stands and turns for the exit. She stops at the doorframe, allowing a quick parting wave and smile before leaving the room.

Within approximately five of her steps, Mae is startled as a loud "Woo-hoo!" erupts from the doorway two yards behind. A large grin graces her lovely face. She shakes her head side to side with a slight chuckle beneath her exhale. *What am I thinking?*

Mae diligently completes her work every day over the next several weeks. The patients she cares for continue to be her first priority, but her sense of balance seems off since agreeing to marry Henry. Her energy and patience is abundant, as if she could work a whole week straight without stopping, resting, eating, or drinking and be completely well. It reminds her of taking care of all her siblings at home. She had no choice but to keep going.

While Mae is off duty from work, she frequently visits Henry's room. The two spend time talking, getting to know one another while Werner is away making phone calls to his wife. When Werner returns to the room and without any initial prodding, Mae suggests cards to Henry knowing his devious record. However, the joke becomes her own while consistently beating the boys at games like rummy. When one of Mae's friends is available, they make teams to play bridge or pinochle. Card games are practically the only source of release for tuberculosis patients, especially in the winter.

February flies by as Henry's health continues to improve and his lungs remain clear. Mae sweetly stops at the local bakery multiple times throughout the week to purchase Henry's favorite indulgence, doughnuts. The two begin their mornings together with the local paper and coffee.

In the spring, Mae accompanies Henry outside. The two walk slowly in the fresh air, holding hands as they lap around the main entrance roundabout. White and yellow lily buds appear around the garden beds amidst fresh green grass.

"How did you become such a beautiful singer?" Henry poses.

Mae rolls her eyes. "Henry, my voice is not anything special."

"I wish you could hear yourself when you sing. It's so amazing and beautiful to me."

"Are you on some different medication?" Mae laughs lightly.

"I'm serious. Did someone teach you?"

"Well, my mother sings, and as you know, she taught all of us to play instruments. I always heard her singing to my older sister, Annie. Of course, Annie had the nicest things too, from the newest fashions to shoes and all the authority from my mother to do anything. She was always visiting family or traveling and getting dolled up just to step outside it seemed."

"Well that doesn't seem fair."

"No, but that's how things are when you raise a girl. Annie's married to a wealthy banker now, and I'm sure my mother thinks her hard work paid off. Anyhow, I suppose I picked up singing from my mother but used it to help all the babies get to sleep or keep them distracted from crying."

"Didn't your mother help with them?" Henry's brows angle down in anger.

"She did at times, but Mother was busy with the farm."

"No wonder you're such an outstanding nurse, Mae. You've been doing this since you could walk and talk." He is filled with surprise.

"I suppose you're right. It's funny when I think about how small I was as a child back then, carrying two babies half my size at times." Mae chuckles in a puff.

"It seems downright crazy to me," Henry states, shaking his head.

"You say that because you were raised with just your sister. You two didn't have to share clothes. I'll bet she didn't wear your rags around to work in either."

Henry stops and turns to look at her face in shock. "Oh, Mae, that's awful. When we are married, you will never have anything less than the finest fashions or anything else you desire."

She shrugs once and looks into his eyes. "It's all right, Henry. Besides, it's not about what you possess. It's about how you cherish what you've got. I learned a great deal by having very little. When I do decide to spend some of my own saved earnings, I'll truly appreciate and take good care of what I purchase."

Mae and Henry continue their walk on the gravel of the roundabout.

"Henry, there is something I've wanted to share with you for quite a while," Mae prefaces, sighing as she looks down at the ground.

"What is it, Mae? You can tell me anything." He takes both her hands in his and faces her squarely in the drive.

"Henry, the nurses are due to rotate soon to other hospitals. I am not sure where they will place me next."

"When will you know?" Henry is concerned.

"I hope to know by the end of the week."

"I will take whatever comes. We are in this together, and I'm not letting you go, Mae," Henry conveys, placing his palm to the side of her smooth face, gently tracing her cheekbone with his thumb. Mae looks up into his eyes, feeling a break in the regular rhythm of her heart. "I love you, Mae. From the first moment I saw you and heard you sing, I've loved you, and nothing will ever change that. Nothing at all." Henry gazes deeply into her gorgeous deep-sapphire eyes and brings his other hand up to cup her face, smiling now. He gracefully moves a curly strand of hair back in place behind her small ear. Bringing her petite frame into his chest, he holds her tightly for several minutes, leaning into her hair.

Though content to remain in his arms all day, Mae's sense of responsibility brings her to reality. "I have to get back to my patients now."

"I know. I miss you already," Henry admits.

"Shall I come after work for cards?" Mae inquires.

"Yes, though I hope Werner is feeling better tonight. He's been so unhappy about his sputum checks. None of them have been coming back clean." He pauses. "I feel even worse that he knows mine have been clear. If they continue, I'll be out in a few weeks."

Not wanting to think about any change taking her away from Henry, she decides to address the former topic.

"Well, maybe a game of rummy will cheer him up," Mae replies. "I'll let him win this one," she grants with a devious smile.

"That's very kind of you." Henry chuckles, taking Mae's hand once again.

The couple walks slowly up the front steps of the sanatorium, making their way back to his floor. Before turning the corner for Henry's hallway, a commotion erupts down the hall toward his room.

"We've got to call someone now!" Dr. Rossling instructs to the nurses. "Now! Call anyone close by, even the fire department! He needs to be transported immediately!" Mae and Henry see the familiar doctor frantically run out of the room toward the supply cabinet. At the same time, two nurses run the opposite direction for the phone room.

Mae and Henry glance at each other and quickly rush down to his room. Werner is lying on his bed, head cocked back, receiving oxygen from Marilynn. His naked torso and face are purple. As the nurse vigorously works over him, Mae runs to his bedside to help.

Henry stands there, motionless, looking on at Werner in shock. *He's gone.* He knows the doctor just killed his friend. Mae takes over resuscitation while Marilynn tearfully steps back.

"I don't know what happened," Marilynn whimpers through her tears. "He sounded clear yesterday. The doctor started on the front for the collapse, and when he went to his back, I thought the needle was off. He was too low! Why didn't I say something?"

Marilynn is in hysterics, snapping Henry out of his shocked state. He walks over and guides her gently by the shoulders to sit on his bed. She can barely walk, sinking into his side. After a minute of sobbing, Marilynn starts to slow her tears with some deep breathing.

"He's gone," Mae claims moments later. Henry and Marilynn look over at her. "I'm so sorry, Henry. Marilynn." Mae turns to look down at Werner. After a moment, she takes both Werner's hands and crosses them at the stomach then leans forward to close the small gap of his eyelids.

Henry quickly strides over to his lost friend, not knowing what to do, and freezes, staring down at him while his own body quivers in shock.

Dr. Rossling enters the room again, breathless from running back down the hall. "We've gotten hold of the fire department! They're on their way," he says.

"It's too late," Henry declares somberly, gazing blankly at Werner. "You've killed him."

The doctor takes a deep breath, placing his hands on his face. He pushes his hair back, grabbing onto the follicles in earnest, and walks over to Werner. He checks his pulse one last time. After thirty seconds, he glances at his watch and claims, "Time of death, 3:02 p.m." He walks somberly out of the door.

Marilynn tearfully approaches Werner's bedside, taking hold of the sheet at the bottom of the bed. Mae sees what she wants to do and helps her gently bring the bedsheet over his legs to his waist and finally over his head to rest.

"I'll call his wife," Marilynn manages. "I know she was planning a visit for tomorrow." Sorrowfully, she exits the room.

Mae turns to Henry, who is still looking at Werner in disbelief. After giving him several moments, she gently speaks. "Henry, I am so sorry. I know you're in shock right now, but I need you to lie down. Please?"

Henry is immobile. Mae rounds the corner of the bed and touches his back, attempting to ease him into turning around. He gasps, snapping into reality.

"Oh god. Werner." Henry breaks down and sobs.

Mae gets him to plant his feet well enough to make the two and a half yards to his bedside, softly assisting him onto the mattress. She pats his head lovingly. "I'm right here, Henry."

Moments later, three nurses enter the room to remove Werner's body. Henry does not open his eyes to watch.

Mae remains with him as he sobs in spurts for hours. She strokes his hair and face, holds his hand, and spends time rubbing his back until he finally falls asleep in the evening. Mae wishes to stay in case he wakes, but after such an emotional day, she decides it best to get rest.

The next day, Mae visits Henry before her shift begins in the morning, bringing him breakfast. "Hello, Henry." She walks over to his bedside.

Henry is unresponsive to her positive energy.

"I brought you a few things from the little store around the corner. I know you don't care for the food here. Here, I even picked up your favorite doughnuts." Mae pauses briefly, waiting for him to respond while laying a few items on the tray by his bed.

Nothing.

"I-I'm sorry I have to work a full shift today. I won't be able to stop by until lat—"

"Don't worry about stopping by. Please, I want to be alone," Henry interrupts softly, gazing out the window opposite from Mae.

Mae's stomach twists and turns in knots as Henry's words cut inside her deeply. "Henry, I know it will take some time for you to—" Mae starts.

"Please, would you just go?"

Her thick inhalation feels razor sharp in her throat, permeating down through her chest like shards of shrapnel invading her system. "Certainly," Mae says quietly, looking on at his gaze directed out the window. She hesitates briefly while watching his profile, waiting to see if he will come around, but then turns slowly and walks out of the room.

Henry puts his face in his hands, refusing more tears, then resumes his blank stare out the window.

While in a catatonic state of mourning, Henry's sputum remains clear as his health improves daily. The painful cough disappears, taking with it the night sweats, fevers, and chills. He is genuinely thankful the needles keep a distance. With the perpetual emotional grieving process for Werner's sudden passing, he is physically unable to take further pain. Marilynn imparts positive feedback to Henry and believes he should be clear for release in the next two weeks. Nowhere near as optimistic as Marilynn, he feels drained in every way and remains in his room.

Embarrassment creeps in for the fear he feels going back to his former life after half a year away from home. Facing the societal vulnerabilities, all the elements and the return of responsibility for work feels like a pressing weight, nearly as forceful as a ton of bricks on his chest. *What were my plans?* He tries hard to remember but is simply lost. His perfect vision and path for the future is a blurry, muddied mess.

Mae checks on Henry's progress through Marilynn but refuses to allow herself permission back over to see him. She remains professional and studious at work, keeping her time preoccupied.

To maintain her strong façade, she steps out for multiple evenings with friends, but she is desolate. She grieves for the happy life she is missing with Henry and the future they envisioned together. At night, she floats through dinner, her shower, and other routines in a withdrawn state. Her eyes lack the ability to bring objects in focus outside of work. Numbness consumes her body and mind, a default coping mechanism for which she is grateful. In bed, she lies awake. Her disorientation buckles frequently, sending her into short bursts of crying, but the tears halt quickly. Now and then, she turns her face to feel a pool of water on her pillow, realizing the tears escaped without her knowledge. Mae hopes Henry will come around by her last day before residency rotation the following week, but she is doubtful.

2

"How are you, Mae?" Marilynn questions while strolling down South Broadway en route to work.

"Oh, just fine." She returns a smile briefly, diverting her eyes.

Marilynn sees through her pitiful attempt at normalcy. "You know, we should take you out again before you transfer. I know this amazing place to go dancing. Last month all the girls went together and had such a grand time. The men were real swell and danced with us the whole night!" Marilynn's voice rises with excitement. "What do you say, honey?"

Mae ponders her response, knowing she hardly feels up to it but will never say as much. "Sure, Marilynn. Sounds peachy."

"Say, you know what?" Marilynn says softly.

"Hmm?" She replies absentmindedly.

"Mae, I just wanted you to know the other girls have been keeping an eye on Henry."

Mae stops walking and turns to see her face. "Oh?"

"You know, he never has anyone to his room anymore. He is quite changed, and I just thought you should know," Marilynn states in a serious tone.

A massive piece of Mae is content to hear this information, but she puts off her interest aloud, attempting to believe the false response. "You don't have to share anything about Henry with me. I've moved on, and he should as well."

"Is that so?"

"Sure. In fact, I just received a letter from my parents this morning saying a nice-looking fella from back home was even asking about me the other day. We've been acquainted since grade school. I think he had an eye for me, but he's a bit shy."

"Sounds like you're ready for some dancing then," Marilynn offers with a wide grin.

"Let's plan on it," Mae counters, feigning her mood.

As promised, Marilynn spends the following days planning the outing with her closest friends. Mae loathes the idea but solidly fakes excitement for the adventure. One of Marilynn's friends suggests the four of them meet beforehand to dress and put on their makeup. Within an hour, the quartet is driving across town to Casa Loma, a popular dance spot in South St. Louis. Upon entry, she peruses the crowded dance floor with the other girls, who quickly disperse in the mass of people. Mae finds solace in an open chair along the perimeter of the floor and pretends to watch the dancers.

"Say, honey, you care to dance?"

Mae looks up from her sitting position to see a young clean-shaven man with a tender smile holding out his hand. The man's dimples accentuate a nice set of lips and white teeth. His dark gelled hair hangs loose from a full evening of dancing in his black wide-leg trousers attached to matching suspenders wrapped around a white cotton button-down dress shirt. The two-tone patent leather wingtip spectator shoes, along with his overall appearance, gives Mae a sinking feeling of incompetence. She registers the band's superior performance of a jive dance before answering.

"You know, I'm not too familiar with this style yet. I'll just sit this one out," she projects over the music, smiling at him politely.

"Oh, no worries. I'm happy to teach you, come on!" He takes her right hand, pulling her out to the floor with him. Mae is unsure whether to be elated or angry at his persistence, but his monumental energy captivates her interest. He pulls her off to the corner to create space for error. "Okay, so the basic pattern is similar to East Coast, but you start with the rock step on the one-two count. Then flow into the two triple steps on three-four and five-six." As he speaks to Mae, he shows her the dance concepts. He steps away from Mae, gesturing for her to imitate the moves.

Mae shakes her head and shouts over the music, "It's too fast. I won't be able to keep up!"

"You'll be great! Just give it a try."

Mae sighs in response, half-rolling her eyes. She listens to the music for her cue to begin the six-beat progression. Nodding her head as she counts, she rocks her right foot back on count one then shifts right to chassé on three and to the left on five.

"That's it!" The gentleman shouts with a smile. "You're no dead hoofer. Are you holding out on me?"

Mae's beaming smile in response brings on a blush. "I-I don't think so."

"What's your name, doll?"

"It's Mae. Yours?" She requests.

"I'm Charlie. It's nice to make your acquaintance, Mae. Are you rationed, though?" He looks around while inquiring.

"No, I'm just here with some friends." Mae is reminded she is not single by choice, looking away to respond.

"Well, let's see what you can do, Mae!" Charlie smiles at her and takes her hands.

The jive dance begins simply, keeping their hands in front of their bodies for ease. Mae gets more comfortable every six beats, predicting his larger movements as he sweeps her around to cover more space. Charlie is ecstatic to learn of her natural talent, teaching her many difficult moves like variations of the American spin, throwaways, chicken walks, and arm breakers through the course of the evening's jive tunes. He spends the rest of the night dancing with Mae, captivated by her sweet smile and apparent lack of interest.

Mae comprehends the joy of her newfound talent is only temporary, but the escape from reality provides needed relief. Marilynn and the other nurses from Mount St. Rose wave to her frequently from the dance floor, finding their new partners just as entertaining. When the band finally stops after midnight, her friends are disappointed she declines to stay out late with their new acquaintances for snacks at a nearby diner. Mae is stern with the girls regarding their duties the next day at work, although she is packed to leave for her new hospital. Despite being the youngest, her friends decide her instincts are always accurate and depart for their residences.

In the morning, the nurses gather around the Mount St. Rose foyer to bid her and three other residents a parting farewell on their last day. Mae is more emotional than she anticipates, giving hugs to the friends made during her residency. Slowly, she walks down the steps toward the waiting car. Just before reaching the door, she peers up at Henry's window one last time and slides into the backseat.

⚜

Two days later before lunch, Dr. Thompson and Marilynn enter Henry's room for the final prerelease checkup. He is dressed in newly pressed business casual clothing, sized just for his build. Upon sanatorium registration, patients are required to surrender their personal attire due to bacterial contamination concerns.

"Looking like a respectable stranger in your new outfit, aren't you, Henry?" Marilynn poses, smiling.

"Yes, these will do just fine," Henry responds, working hard for a minimal grin.

Dr. Thompson crosses the room to speak. "Henry, be careful. Be sure to look over all the discharge information. Do not try to get right back into your routine at home. Do very little work, and be sure it is not strenuous. You don't want to come back here, I'm certain, but should you require care, I guarantee that Dr. Rossling will no longer be overseeing it. He stopped practicing altogether. I just thought you should know. Take care now," the doctor says, patting his arm gently. He exits the room.

Marilynn begins humming a flowing ballad while cleaning his side of the room; the other portion is still vacant. Registering sound for the first time in weeks, his sensory follicles stretch to absorb the music through his ear canals. The high and low mixture of frequencies wash over the residue from weeks without stimulation, awakening his mind like an electric bolt. Suddenly, Henry snaps his head up. The reason for his attachment to this place is quite profound. Sorting through his thoughts, he realizes he does want to be there, but why? He does not wish to be ill, of course, but there is a pull to this building and the time spent in his room. *Why?* He stands immobile, listening to the melody of her song. Gradually, he begins to sway and close his eyes, humming with her to the tune.

Marilynn looks over at him in confusion. "Henry, are you all right?" She moves over to strip his bedding.

His eyes flash open, seeing the outline of her white nursing uniform. Instantly, it hits him. *Mae. Mae. Mae!* His vision is perfectly clear.

"Marilynn, is she here today?"

Marilynn stops removing the sheets and turns to look at his face. "Don't...don't you know? I'm sorry. I thought she would have come to tell you."

"Tell me what?"

"Henry, she's gone," Marilynn replies quickly.

"Gone? Gone where?" He questions with heightened distress.

"Mae's residency was transferred. She starts at a new hospital today."

"No! Well, where Marilynn?" He steps toward her.

"I can't recall the name of it right now, Henry, but if she didn't come to tell you, then maybe it's best you let her alone. You put her in quite a mess the last two weeks, so please think of what's best for her."

Henry takes a deep breath, deeply concerned for Mae. "I am, and what's best for her is me. I need her, Marilynn. I have to find her. Please help me?" The resolve of his revelation is in flawless clarity now.

"Are you sure?"

"Yes, never been more sure of anything," Henry affirms with certainty.

"Well, first, I would start by asking the head nurse. See whether she can tell you, but you need to be casual about it."

"Okay. How?"

"Tell her you have something of Mae's and need to return it to her. If she thinks you're being overly emotional, then she won't tell you anything to protect Mae," Marilynn warns.

"Got it." He turns to head out the door and stops in his tracks. He turns back around and crosses the room to give Marilynn a hug. "Thank you, Marilynn, for everything." He pulls away to look at her and smiles.

"You are quite welcome. You take care, and I don't ever want to see you in here again," Marilynn says with a grin. Henry sends her a parting wave and exits the room.

Gripping the dozen pale-pink roses he purchased in his hand, Henry makes his way toward the front inquiry desk of St. Mary's Hospital in Clayton. Amazingly, this is the closest hospital to his St. Louis home at Dreamland in Manchester. *Of all the places Mae*

could have been transferred, she was sent here. God must be helping me. First, with the head nurse answering my questions easily, and now, with the hospital location.

"Excuse me, ma'am. Do you think you could help me track down a beautiful young lady who works here?"

The desk receptionist chuckles. "We have a number of those, but who might I be able to help you find?"

"Her name is Mae Sh—"

"Oh, Mae! Yes, I just met her two days ago when she started here. She certainly is a doll, isn't she? Let me see if I can find her for you." The receptionist picks up the receiver as she scrolls through her reference phone number cards.

"Well, thank you so much. I appreciate it." Henry smiles.

He wanders around the lobby for a few minutes, mulling over his mother's advise during the ride home from Mount St. Rose the previous day. Henry spent every moment in the car talking her ears off about Mae, also describing how he acted when Werner passed. Like every mother, she knows him well, responding gently. "Henry, you're still so young, but if she makes you happy, then you tell her absolutely everything. No more holding back one thought or emotion…nothing. You be certain you do what it takes because it sounds like she is a smart, classy young lady. You should tell her how you feel and where you went wrong. Apologize."

"Henry?" Mae breaks into his reverie. He turns to gaze upon the beautiful young woman he loves, who is standing across the hospital lobby.

"Mae!" Henry happily crosses the distance to her. She takes a step back, looking cautious of his presence. Seeing her apprehension, he slows down. "Mae, I'm so sorry. I was so upset about Werner that I just froze up," he says with a shrug. "I said some things I didn't mean. I'm not even sure of what I said, but I do know it was hurtful, and I most certainly did not want to hurt you. Ever." Henry holds up the flowers toward Mae. She stands there, not accepting the roses, looking away from him. He lowers his hands, fearful.

"You hurt me, Henry. You've no concept of your own strength in that regard. So how do I know you won't do it again?"

"Simple. You know I want to marry you. Marry me, Mae."

"Henry, I ca—"

"Mae, I've hurt you, I know, but I promise I will never hold anything back from you ever again. I will always tell you what I'm thinking, feeling, everything. I'm not sure what happened when Werner passed. It felt like everything I envisioned for myself, for us together, was snipped into little pieces. Suddenly, I saw nothing. I felt nothing. I remembered nothing. My whole life felt like it was hanging on a thread, and I suppose, subconsciously, I didn't want to pull you into something so frail. Our lives are so frail, Mae, and I don't ever want to see you hurt because of me." Henry pauses and steps closer to her.

"Please. I know it's hard to trust me, but do give me one more chance. Our life together is all I see. It's all I care to see. Please," Henry pleads to her, his blue eyes piercing straight to her heart as he raises the roses one more time.

Looking into his eyes, Mae sees everything she fell in love with from the beginning. She knows he means it but is not prepared to give her heart again so easily. Slowly, she lifts her hand from her side to reach for the flowers. He walks closer to her, placing the wrapped stems in her hands. He encloses his hands lightly around hers as she leans in to smell their sweet, blossom scent.

Mae looks up into his eyes again. "Henry, I must complete my exams first. You'll have to wait for me until after graduation. Do you think you can—"

He silences her with one finger over her even lips. "You don't even need to ask. I will wait as long as it takes," he replies.

She beams at him in return. He takes the other hand away from hers to bring her petite body in for a warm embrace. Standing there, the two lose track of time, obligations, and everyone else in the room.

Henry and Mae exchange information, determined to spend a great deal of time together while off work. After one week at home, Henry returns to moderate dishwashing duty. He is eager to start saving money for their future.

Mae's schedule at St. Mary's is an afternoon to late evening shift, which works well for Henry and his primary duty of cleaning up after dinners at Dreamland. He has just enough time to watch people dance most nights before he picks Mae up at the hospital. He routinely takes her out late for burgers and shakes at the Parkmoor Café in Clayton, located near the hospital and close to Mae's residence. Their conversations always lead to stimulating topics, frequently realizing interests they have in common, like watching baseball. Adversely, heated discussions make it clear a trivial number of topics should be avoided, such as opinions of past presidents and miscellaneous politically charged discussions.

The pair discovers another significant passion by spending many of Mae's nights off dancing together at Dreamland. One of the small ensembles to frequent the ballroom includes steel guitar, piano, drums, German squeezebox, and a cornet. On rare occasions, a few extra players will sit in with the group. The band plays polka, big band, and popular dance music. Circle dances are Henry's favorite as it involves everyone on the floor, sending ample energy radiating throughout the room. Mae loves dancing to the jive music when the larger ensembles come in to perform but also enjoys slowing down with the jazz ballads and standards.

Through the remainder of the summer, fall, and winter months, Mae works diligently as a nurse at St. Mary's. Irrevocably attached to her work in the labor and delivery department, she feels it is where she belongs, assisting the doctors delivering babies. Her favorite aspect, however, is caring for the women during and after their labor, nursing each individual back to optimal health.

Seeing the joy on a mother's face when placing a new baby in her arms is a wonderful feeling.

Inseparable in their time off work, Henry and Mae venture on a road trip or two when the weather breaks in early March. Henry's new 1948 Plymouth is his first purchase as an adult. With money down and an agreement for financing, he feels he is on his way to being the responsible man Mae deserves. She feels a sense of pride for Henry having his priorities in line.

Both are equally sanguine until mid-March when Mae receives notification of her impending return to Boonville to begin studies for the state board exams. Her presence is required on the first of April until after graduation in May.

The two dance to an arrangement of "Stardust" on her last night in St. Louis. Henry sings the lyrics against Mae's cheek as he moves with her across the floor, "You wander down the lane and far away, leaving me a song that will not die. Love is now the stardust of yesterday, the music of the years gone by."

She pulls away from his cheek to look into his eyes. "Henry, I need you to be patient. I'm certain the nuns will not let any of us be distracted while studying for our exams. Are you going to be all right?"

"Mae, we've danced to this song before, and you know I'll be waiting for you." Then, with slight hesitation, he adds, "I have something for you."

Mae's eyes are curious. Henry eases their dancing to a stop at the back of the dance floor and gently takes both of her hands.

"It's something I've wanted to give you for quite some time, but there's no time like the present for us." Henry reaches into his pocket and retrieves a small box. He opens the lid and removes a thin gold band, turning it to show the diamond on the other side. Holding the diamond side up, he kneels down on the dance floor in front of her.

Mae catches her breath, placing her small hand to her chest, looking at the luminous ring sparkling under the ballroom lights.

"Mae, would you do me the honor of becoming my wife?" Henry smiles.

"Henry," she replies in a sigh. "Of course," she manages, wiping away an escaping tear.

Henry ecstatically places the band on her left ring finger before jumping from the floor to pick her up, whirling in a quick circle. The couple takes a number of moments to hold each other before spinning off around the dance floor to finish out their favorite song with more power and liveliness than ever.

The evening ends too quickly with her imminent departure to Boonville the following morning. Henry drives Mae back to Clayton for the last time. Their departure lingers on as both fail to stay strong for the other. A final hug and wave good-bye seals the end of a perfect day together.

When Mae arrives in Boonville the next night, she unpacks her clothing and basic necessities, feeling ready to begin her studies. She then writes to Henry, announcing their safe arrival. After the initial greeting, she takes two to three sentences to reminisce the previous night together but ends reminding Henry to be patient and how much she cares for him.

Within days, Henry is elated to receive Mae's letter in the mail. Upon the hour of arrival, Henry responds, describing how much he misses her already. He feels his hand cannot match the speed and vigor of his mind in putting words to paper. He sends his letter the same day.

After Mae's first correspondence, no others arrive for Henry. He writes her again after seven days, then waits two weeks to hear back. Nothing. He tries to call her at Boonville, but she is unavailable. Every nun on the phone insists all the nurses in their program are well, and unless his call is of an urgent nature, they will not interrupt their studies.

The entire month of April leaves Henry floundering for ground to stand upon every night. Watching other couples from behind the bar at Dreamland is torture. He is sad, often closing his eyes, imagining her in his arms. He feels her small fingers in his open palm as he holds his left hand high in the air, sweeping smoothly across the dance floor for a waltz. When the band moves onto tunes like "Stardust" and "Paper Doll," Henry can no longer stand it. The dishes are complete; he leaves for the night.

⚜

Weeks pass. Henry attempts to call Mae every few days, thinking she must be finished soon considering the days rolling by in May. He feels weak, and then pain surfaces. Not certain at first whether heartache is simply the culprit, Henry blows off the slight agitation in his chest. With no coughing to accompany the heavy pressure in his lungs, he deduces that it must be the changing weather throwing his body into hyperactive. His breathing is strenuous at night, causing him to lose massive amounts of sleep. Noticing the deep circles under his eyes, Henry's uncle Albert, who is a houseguest for two weeks, notices his unresponsive behavior one morning prior to breakfast.

"Hey, Henry. Snap out of it, kid!" Uncle Albert tries to gain Henry's attention. He blinks just once before looking over at his uncle, mouth gaping open and hand wrapped around his glass of milk.

"You all right, Henry?"

"Oh. Yeah, I guess," Henry responds complacently, still staring blankly off at the tiles across the room.

Uncle Albert looks slightly agitated. "You don't seem all right. Do we need to get you to a doctor or somethin'?"

"No, I'm fine. I'll be just fine," Henry assures his uncle, gulping down the rest of his milk before heading out of the kitchen to complete his daily house chores before work.

The same night, Henry lies awake in his bed. With each passing minute, he feels like cinder blocks are being set onto his chest one by one. He cannot move nor breathe. His body stiffens and locks into place. The pain is unbearable as his lungs refuse to function. Henry can bear it no longer.

Gasping for air, Henry finally yells out, "Help! H-help!"

He knows his mother is still at Dreamland at this hour, closing down the ballroom. Shutting his eyes, he prays in his mind. *Our Father, who art in heaven, hallowed be thy name, thy kingdom come, thy will be done…Oh god, Mae! No! This can't be it!*

"He-elp!" Henry musters his last ounces of fight and oxygen left. Panting for the remaining bits of air, he hears the thunderous advance of feet up the narrow wooden stairs to his bedroom. Before Henry can blink and reopen his eyes, two strong hands pull his head and upper shoulders away from his flat pillow. Delirious from lack of oxygen, Henry brings the side of Uncle Albert's face into view and turns his head to look at him, grateful for a savior. Shaking and sweating, Henry takes in his first clean pull of air. The bottom of his ribs writhe with each expansion, like one-ton steel cables, pulling on open nerve endings. He is still gasping loudly.

"Yeah. I'd say it's time to visit the doc, kid," Uncle Albert remarks.

Henry continues to focus on his breathing, ironing out the shakes in process. He is positive this man just saved his life. His uncle props him up, staying until Henry's mother returns home. She watches him the remainder of the night as every pillow she owns supports her only son.

CHAPTER

3

O n May 21, Mae stands in front of her room's mirror in Boonville. She resets her nurse cap, smoothing out the strands of stray curls for a moment. After one final adjustment of her navy and red satin cape, she exits her room for the last time.

The nuns greet the nurses with warm smiles while each woman files through the foyer to take those last steps toward their graduation ceremony outside in the open quad.

"Mae, would you come here, dear?" Sister Carrie greets Mae, palms up with an invitation to approach.

"Yes, Sister Carrie." Mae holds a sincere smile, wondering what she could possibly need before the big event.

She takes a tender hold of Mae's arm and speaks softly. "I wanted to let you know how proud we are to tell you that your state board exam scores came through this morning, and they were the highest of all the young ladies at Boonville. Not only that, a letter from the director of placement services for the Cadet Corps came to us as well, stating that you were also the highest scoring nurse in the entire Corps this year! The director's letter claims you have the opportunity to pick any hospital in the region to serve as a permanent staff member. Congratulations, Mae!" Sister Carrie says with a tempered gentleness.

Mae is shocked and completely elated inside her petite frame.

"We are so proud of you, Mae. God has blessed you with many gifts, child. Serve Him through those gifts, always." She cups Mae's face in her hands briefly before giving her a quick and final parting hug.

"Thank you, Sister Carrie," Mae manages to utter with tears streaming freely down her cheek. The two women exit the doors to the event.

Mae glows through the ceremony, intensely relieved. She is more confident than ever as she affirms her commitment at the end of graduation with all the nurses standing at attention and reciting in unison:

> At this moment of my induction into the United States Cadet Nurse Corps of the United States Public Health Service, I am solemnly aware of the obligations I assume toward my country and toward my chosen profession. I will follow faithfully the teachings of my instructors and the guidance of the physicians with whom I work. I will hold in trust the finest traditions of nursing and the spirit of the Corps. I will keep my body strong, my mind alert, and my heart steadfast. I will be kind, tolerant, and understanding. Above all, I will dedicate myself now and forever to the triumph of life over death. As a Cadet nurse, I pledge to my country my service in essential nursing for the duration of the war.

Mae is finally done.

She spends time saying farewell to friends then rushes to the phone just inside the building. She waits in line for ten minutes while other graduates make calls for final transportation arrangements. Dialing zero for the operator, she waits to be put through to Dreamland. The phone rings, but no one answers. *Where is everyone?* Mae assumes Henry and his family are busy with customers due to an increase in spring travelers. She finally steps aside to allow the next woman in line to use the telephone. The car to take her home to Versailles is due to arrive any moment, but she aches to try once more. Before she can, Sister Carrie informs Mae that the car is outside. She looks back at the phone and the three girls in line, picks up her bag, and walks down the steps to the waiting car.

Mae's parents welcome her home with plentiful questions about her residency, studies, and the exams. The conversation flows quickly at the kitchen table, and within the hour, Mae relays the nature of the plans she made with Henry. Aware of their engagement for many months through letters sent during her time in St. Louis, Mae announces their plan to be married as soon as possible before assuming her position at a hospital. Confident of Mae's intelligence, they know she will be happy and successful no matter the circumstance.

"Mae, you've always carried your own weather with you. I'm not sure of much, but I am certain you will always make good decisions. We're proud of you," her father conveys, standing up from the table.

Mae feels his words down in the pit of her stomach, as if he has imparted the most vital piece of information of her whole existence. She never realized she was waiting to hear these words or the depth and weight of her response when she heard them, and it floored her.

Mae stands up, still winded from her revelation, and finds purchase on her target. She lunges forward at her father, wrapping her small arms around his tall frame. "Thank you…for everything," Mae breathes. The destiny of her whole life was entirely dependent upon his persistence in believing in her. Mildly stated, she is intensely grateful.

Her father gently wraps his arms around her shoulders, softly kissing the top of her head.

"When is the last time you spoke with him?" Mae's mother questions.

"Well, I suppose it was the night before I left for Boonville, but we wrote letters."

"And when was his last letter?"

Mae is annoyed with her mother's obvious pessimism. "It's been since April, but I asked him to be patient while I studied, and I wrote to him the day I arrived home. Why do you ask?"

"It's been over a week. You don't seem to know his whereabouts, you can't get a hold of him, and you're supposed to be getting married?" Her voice rings with a condescending tone.

"Mother, you don't know Henry."

"Well, if I were you, I'd consider my other options."

Mae is confused. "What do you mean?"

"Buddy's been asking about you. His father still runs the main grocery store in town, and they do very well." She smiles over at Mae while preparing the green beans for dinner.

"I am not interested in Buddy," Mae retorts with conviction.

"Well, if you don't hear from Henry in two days, I'm telling his father you'll see him."

"You truly want me to be courted by Buddy?" Mae is appalled.

"Don't you remember playing together?"

"I remember Buddy, Mother, but it was a long time ago. I was completely focused in school." Mae stares her mother down without blinking.

Her mother is the first to look away, turning back to her food preparations. "Well, I think it would be good to know all your options."

"I'm sure Henry will write or call by then." Her voice is full of confidence, but the inner lining of her stomach screams otherwise.

Mae places the phone receiver back down to hang up. She is stumped, feeling incredibly heartbroken. Again. Uncertain what to make of the circumstance and without the means to travel to St. Louis herself, she gives in to her mother's timeline.

"Buddy will be picking you up at six o'clock, Mae. Do you have something nice to put on? I think he's taking you to the Royal Theater for a show." The higher timbre to her mother's voice knowing she has succeeded annoys Mae profusely today.

Mae growls under her breath in response. "Yes," she replies, kicking her feet up the wooden steps of the house.

"Oh, and I laid a pair of my nylon stockings for you to borrow on your bed, dear," she calls up the stairs from the kitchen.

Mae retreats to the room she originally shared with older sisters, Annie and Rosemary. After Annie's marriage and Rosemary's passing just after her fourteenth birthday, her younger sister, Irene, consumed the empty living space. She closes the door with a huff and presses her back against it to calm her temper. Looking around the room, she recalls Rosemary's last night in the bedroom eight years ago at age twelve:

> Complaining of a stomachache, Rosemary is still awake in the dim light of the evening, lying down on her bed and gripping the area of pain on her lower right side. Mae refreshes her ginger tea and mint from the garden and sits beside her, though her symptoms worsen by the hour. Mae brushes her long sand-colored hair back from her sweating face and replenishes the wet, cold rags on her forehead every five minutes.

> "Mae," Rosemary breathes in a pant quietly. "Your heart is as big as your intelligent mind, isn't it." It is not a question.

> Mae smiles in embarrassment, squeezing the fresh wet cloth from the cold-water bucket along the bed. "Oh, I don't think so. You just rest so you start feeling better tomorrow."

Rosemary grins. "You know what I wish?"

"What's that?" Mae folds the cold washcloth and exchanges it with the warm one on her forehead.

"I wish I could go dancing." She pauses briefly from the pings of pain shooting through her lower abdomen. "I've always wanted to meet a nice boy and go dancing."

Mae smiles with a puff. "Well, you will, Rosemary. Just give it some time." Her intuition senses an ill feeling, but her optimism overrides it, knowing her parents agreed to take Rosemary to the doctor in the morning. Rosemary's hot hand grabs her wrist while stroking her hair.

"Thank you, Mae. I love you," Rosemary says sweetly in exhaustion.

"You're welcome, Rose. I love you too. Get some rest now. It will feel better soon," Mae soothes.

"Mm. Would you sing to me, Mae? That new hymn we sang in church a few weeks ago. Please?"

"Okay." Mae takes a moment to hear the notes in her head. "I come to the garden alone, while the dew is still on the roses, and the voice I hear falling on my ear, the Son of God discloses. And He walks with me, and He talks with me, And He tells me I am His own, And the joy we share as we tarry there, None other has ever known." Mae continues singing the lyrics to "In the Garden," watching Rosemary close her eyes gently.

Tears of sadness and frustration stream down Mae's cheeks as she reminisces her sweet sister, pure in spirit and kind grace. Grieving brings Mae into a disposition for which she is familiar.

The numbness consumes her body while sauntering over to the closet. She pulls out her calf-length maroon cotton wrap dress with subtle pinstripes before donning her undergarments. She slips her dress on after touching up her makeup and hair then straps on her brown suede wedge shoes. Her perceptive mind slips farther away from conscious reality, sheltering the onslaught of any attacks from her memory.

She gives up.

Without looking at her hand, she removes the diamond ring from her finger and places it in her jewelry box. She walks down the stairs to greet her company at six in the evening.

"Mae, you remember Buddy?" her mother introduces.

"Good evening, Mae," Buddy greets with a soft smile.

"Hello," Mae replies, offering her hand politely. She does not see his face but watches her hand extend from her body as if in slow motion.

"It's nice to see you again." He shakes her hand gently.

Mae's eyes only extend the height of his shoulders and neck, nodding in response. From her unfocused view, she sees a powder-blue dress shirt covered partially by a black tightly tailored suit vest and matching tie. His slim-leg black trousers are pleated in front and accompanied by freshly shined, black Oxford shoes.

"Well, you two should be on your way. You don't want to miss the show."

"Certainly." Buddy properly holds out his hand, inviting Mae to exit first.

His mannerisms are perfect, arriving to the passenger side early to open the car door to his blue 1948 Cadillac Series 62 convertible with a V8 engine. The tender smile he displays is wasted while chauffeuring Mae down the long stretch of road toward town. Mae stares out her window, watching the landscape pass; she makes no eye contact.

"So how have you been, Mae? It's been a long time." He makes conversation uneasily with his shy personality. He waits nearly a minute, attempting to overcome his wounded ego, and tries again. "I hope you don't mind the diner in town. I suppose the choices are fairly limited here compared to St. Louis."

Mae feels a slash of pain rip across her chest. Her gut reaction relies upon distraction. "The diner will be suitable. No worries," she responds, still refusing to meet his eyes.

"Good. I-I hope you like the show too. It's called *The Lady from Shanghai*. Have you heard of it?"

"No."

"It opened over a week ago. It has Rita Hayworth and one of my favorites, Orson Welles, too." He smiles.

"Hmm." Mae nods, acknowledging the talented actors.

"Do you like movies?"

"Of course, but I don't have time to sit down when I'm working."

"I hear you're quite a nurse. Getting to choose a workplace sounds like a rare opportunity for any lady."

Mae puffs out a smirk, looking down.

"I guess I'm not surprised about you being at the top of your game. I knew you were a natural way back when we were kids." Buddy is embarrassed to compliment her even indirectly, focusing on the road. "I remember falling out of a maple tree once. I banged up my legs pretty bad, and you fixed me right up. Got the bleeding to stop without batting an eye. I knew back then you were a real gem." Buddy realizes he said more than intended, attempting to change the subject. "Eh, you probably don't remember any of that though."

Mae reflects on the incident, recalling how his hysterical disposition turned babyish at the sight of blood, calming quickly when it stopped. "On the contrary, I do remember it now. Vaguely."

Buddy pulls into the diner parking lot. "Well, here we are. This place hasn't changed a whole lot since you left." He exits the car to walk around to her side and opens the door.

"Thank you."

Buddy escorts Mae to the front entrance and walks through the doors to the hostess. "Booth for two, please, Eleanor."

"Right this way," Eleanor offers with a smile. She guides them back to a two-person booth at the rear of the diner, quiet and intimate.

"Thank you."

"You're welcome, Buddy. Menus are on the side there. You two enjoy."

"So what's your favorite meal? What do you like?" Buddy pulls out the menus and hands her one.

Mae's mind cuts to her many late nights out with Henry at the Parkmoor Café, eating a glorious entrée of hamburgers and fries never to be matched in taste at the present diner. She hesitates while viewing the menu. Knowing her selection of food will ultimately contradict her reply, she opts to lie and avoid explanation. "Oh, I like steaks and baked potatoes, I suppose."

"Ah, they have a great baked potato here, remember?"

"Good." She closes her menu, shoving it off to the side.

"What can I get for you two?" A brunette waitress stands close, holding her pencil and pad of paper.

"Ladies first." Buddy gestures to Mae.

"I'll have a glass of water and the steak cooked medium with a baked potato, butter on the side."

"And you, Buddy?"

"I'll have a water with hamburger and fries, please, Helen."

Mae glances at him from the corner of her eye.

"You got it!" Helen says with a smile, walking away.

Buddy places his menu back in the table holder. "It must be nice to come home and people question your identity. They always want to know each other's business in small towns like Versailles, but I guess I have no choice being the next in line to run the store."

Mae evaluates how her own achievements were catapulted by her father's belief in her skills. "Buddy, we haven't spoken much since before grade school, but I do know everyone deserves to follow their own path."

"That seems like a nice thought, Mae, but I've been told this is the way it will be since the beginning. After a while, I felt there wasn't a point to having my own dreams," Buddy concludes dismally.

Mae looks up from under her lashes for the first time, assessing his face as he looks away. His features are attractive with high cheekbones, a narrow yet masculine face with green eyes, and thin dark-blonde hair parted down the middle. The front of his bangs wrap around to frame his forehead while the back is trimmed in short layers, stopping just above his shirt collar. A wide set of thin rose-colored lips accompany white teeth, few of which are crooked. He turns his attention back in her direction.

"If I may, Buddy, you should still hold on to your dreams. Circumstances can change any moment unexpectedly." Mae's eyes break away from his line of sight. "What would you like to do?"

Buddy sighs, choosing his words. "My father's success with the store has opened my eyes to great places. Cities with bustling life, nonstop news, and constant attractions with things to explore…It's the life. I want to see it all and live in the thick of the high traffic and action. I'd love to work right in the city. Any big city. I'd even run a store, so long as it sits downtown." Buddy gestures with his hands open, picturing his dream.

"Where would you go?"

"Well, I liked Chicago, but I think if it ever worked out, I'd probably keep running to New York City, you know? I'd just go all the way." Buddy envisions his plan. "Eh, my father would have me bumped off if I did that, though. It's silly to even think of it."

"It's good to just say it aloud, no matter what," Mae consoles.

"Can I ask you something, Mae?"

Mae looks up with a nod to proceed.

"Your mother twisted your arm to come out with me tonight." Buddy looks straight into her sapphire eyes, waiting for a response.

Mae clears her throat with a blush. "That was not a question," she states.

He smiles at her wit. "I suppose it wasn't, but did she?"

Mae looks down, smiling under her lashes. "No. Not physically," she puffs out with a slight chuckle.

"Hah!" Buddy laughs with her briefly.

"Here we go." Helen places the two hot plates on the table.

"Thank you," Buddy and Mae respond in unison. They look at one another, grinning momentarily.

"You're welcome! I'll be back to refill your waters in just a few minutes."

Buddy and Mae continue moderate discussions of mixed categories while eating, from stories of old teachers and classmates to small-town scandals and favorite moments in St. Louis Cardinals' baseball. Unsurprisingly, their favorite Most Valuable Player is Stan Musial, but honorable mention goes to player Enos Slaughter, whose unexpected dash to home plate and winning game 7 of the 1946 World Series places him in every fan's high regard.

The evening runs smoothly over to another venue at the Royal Theater in town. Mae is thankful the movie is filled with crime and mystery rather than romance and is happy to find it entertaining. Buddy suggests a stroll around the block after the film. Mae agrees, yearning to stretch her legs before the car ride home. Buddy is curious how she enjoyed the film, dissecting her intelligent answers. They arrive back to the car and at the passenger-side door.

"Mae, I really enjoyed the evening. I hope you did too." Buddy hesitates, opening the door for her as he speaks.

"I had a pleasant time."

"Can I ask you something else? I-I promise it will be a question this time," he adds humorously.

Mae chortles. "Certainly."

"Where are you planning to work as a nurse right now, Mae?"

Mae looks at him, curious and defensive. "Why do you ask?"

Buddy directs his attention down, his shy personality making another appearance. "Because I'd like to take you out again."

"Oh." Mae sighs, scratching her head with an uneasy expression of regret. "Buddy," she breaks, taking in a breath. "My life is complicated at the moment."

His green eyes are coated in sadness, staring off. "I see. I'll just get you home then." He opens the convertible car door for Mae.

"I'm truly sorry, Buddy. You've become such a nice man, but—" She is interrupted.

"It's all right, Mae. I'll drive you back." He avoids her eyes.

Mae slowly sits down in the car. He shuts the door gently, walks around, and slides into the vehicle before starting the ignition. The drive to her home is silent. She feels awful for him and angry with her mother for putting them both in this situation. *What did she expect?*

Buddy places the Cadillac in park upon arriving at Mae's house. He opens the car door for her in the dim moonlight. "Good night, Mae."

"Thank you, Buddy. Good night," she replies softly.

⁘⁘⁘

The next afternoon, Mae sits down at her bedroom desk to compose a letter to Marilynn. She misses her friends at the sanatorium but is also curious to know whether she has heard from Henry. A fraction of her thoughts veer to the worst scenario of his tuberculosis relapsing, hoping the reason for his absence is not due to a return to Mount St. Rose. Her letter reaches *Dear Marilynn* when she hears three taps on the door. She crosses the room to open it.

"Mother wants you," Irene states unemotionally and walks away.

Mae sighs and reflects. *I miss my privacy.* She walks down the steps to the kitchen, seeing her mother sitting in a chair at the table.

"Yes, Mother?"

"That was Buddy on the phone, Mae. He said you two had a nice time last night." The timbre of her mother's voice sends a wave of nausea through her stomach.

"He is nice, but I'm not interested."

"Well, why not?"

"You know why not, Mother." Mae begins to turn for the stairs.

"I told him you would go on out with him tomorrow night," she states in a matter-of-fact tone.

Mae turns around sharply. "Pardon me?"

"You need to remember to keep your options open, that's all. Trust me." Mae's mother gets up and patronizingly pats Mae on the shoulder two times before turning away.

"Mother, do you not understand at all? Do you even care to understand me or what I want?"

She turns back around, "Well, of course I care, and that's why you're going to spend some time with Buddy."

"Does Father know about this?" Mae knows he would take her more logistically sound side on the matter.

Her mother stops in place and turns around to glare into her eyes. "Your father has more pressing concerns than worrying about all this nonsense. You leave him alone."

Mae pulls together what little gumption she has left. "Perhaps he does, but I am not one of your possessions you can *marry off* like Annie, Mother. Do not forget that I have an education and can leave at any time. Now, out of courtesy, I will see Buddy tomorrow night and clarify, once more, that I am not interested, but you will no longer answer for me. I will make the decisions in my own life." Mae bolts immediately for the stairs, avoiding the stunned expression on her mother's face. After her first two steps, she turns to add another comment. "Oh, and Mother? Welcome to the forties." Mae continues her quick ascent up the stairs to finish her letter.

Buddy picks Mae up at six o'clock, escorts her to his Cadillac to open the door, and starts the car. As soon as the car is in motion, Mae starts the conversation.

"Buddy, I thought I was fairly clear the other evening. It's not you. I hope you will understand."

"Understand what?" Buddy responds playfully. Mae's appalled expression quickly turns to anger. Seeing her face contort makes him nervous. "I'm just kidding, Mae. Don't flip your wig!"

"Please don't do that. I feel badly enough as it stands."

"About what? Look, I appreciate your honesty. I just enjoyed your company the other night and thought we could be friends."

"Friends?"

"Friends, I promise." He raises his right hand, making a sign as if taking an oath.

"So long as you understand the expectations and guidelines for proper behavior."

"Mae, it's all right. We started as friends, remember?" He smiles at her from the driver's seat.

"That was a very different scenario in another time."

"Eh, try to relax, Mae."

Mae glances over at him, now seeing remnants of the baby face she recalls from Buddy's childhood features. With the perimeter walls down of proper courting expectations, she feels comfortable assessing his appearance whether good or bad.

Buddy pulls into the diner. Having established terms of friendship, the instinctual hesitations of conversing disappears altogether while enjoying their meal of hamburgers and fries at the diner. Mae finds the open and honest aspects of her character refreshing through the evening, even while speaking of some of her resident experiences with patients and other nurses. The two then stroll down the street for ice cream at the local parlor. "This right here is why I love summer." Buddy finishes his last bite of vanilla.

"I have to agree. It is certainly a perk to offset the heat," Mae responds, only three-quarters of the way through her ice cream.

Buddy tosses his cup and spoon in the trash and sits back down on the bench facing Mae. "Mae, I have another question for you."

"All right," she responds quickly, predicting he will continue their debate on Stan Musial's current batting average for the 1948 season. She takes another bite while waiting.

"The other night you said your life was complicated right now." He watches her face freeze midbite.

She gulps conspicuously. "That's not a question," she replies slowly, looking down at her cup.

"I was just thinking…Would you like to talk about it?"

"About what?" She leaves her spoon in the leftover ice cream and crosses her arms.

His expression is incredulous. "Look, I don't have to know, and you have every right to keep it to yourself, but by my observations, some *Joe* has certainly done a number on you, doll."

"You're right." Mae stands abruptly. "You don't need to know, and it is my business." She swiftly takes her ice cream cup and walks to the trash can to throw it away. Buddy follows her fast-paced trail back to the car down the block.

"Hey, slow down." Buddy jogs to keep up with her quick stride. "Slow down, Mae." His eyes cut away to her legs, which are proportioned to her petite frame. "How can you go so fast?" He is genuinely impressed.

Mae stops midstride to face Buddy, surprising him. "Let me ask *you* a question. Why do you care to know? Did my mother put you up to this?" Mae is hotheaded and red with anger.

"No, nothing like that!" He puts his hands up in a surrendering pose.

"Then why? Why do you care?" She leans toward his face.

Buddy relaxes his posture, phrasing his thoughts. "I just thought, you know, so long as we were friends that you might want someone to talk to. That's all."

Mae relaxes her posture in turn. She sighs, looking away. "Am I really *that* obvious?" Her voice is completely defeated.

"Oh, of course not. No worries, Mae." He touches her arm with one hand. "I'm sorry I asked. I didn't mean to upset you."

She nods, acknowledging his apology. "Like I said, things are complicated, and it doesn't seem to take a great deal to upset me these days. I only have a few weeks left before I have to report for work, but I don't know where I'm going now."

"I had no idea," he replies, consoling her.

"Henry and I had big plans, and now...now I feel like I have nothing."

"Ah, try not to think like that, Mae. You've got your education, you're smart as a whip, beautiful, and have the opportunity to work almost anywhere. The sky's the limit!" The excitement he exudes helps Mae pull herself together. Buddy feels an unfamiliar part of his personality shine through for the first time. Around Mae, an alternate character exuding boyish, outgoing, and care-free traits breaks overtly into play. He fears nothing.

"Thank you, Buddy."

"Come on!" He offers Mae his arm.

"Where are we going?" she questions, placing her hand under his elbow and around his forearm.

"Let's go have some fun!" Buddy takes off in a quick pace.

"What? Where?" Mae pants, trying to keep up in her wedge shoes.

"You'll see! It's time for a drive," he replies with a wink and a smile.

Buddy keeps Mae completely preoccupied over the next week. Fortunately, it is his vacation at the store, and with his father's permission, he escorts Mae all over central Missouri, planning daylong excursions. He drives northwest to Sedalia, Missouri, home of the State Fair and Scott Joplin Festival, where they explore the Katy Depot and various parks and scenic attractions in the area for two days. Then the two travel south three consecutive days to Lake of the Ozarks to hike, scout out caves, swim, and fly across the lake on Buddy's family boat, a wooden 1946 Chris-Craft Runabout. Monumental time is spent enjoying picnics and taking recreational walks and bike rides along the parks in and around Versailles as well. Finally, Buddy tops off the week with a drive northeast to Columbia, Missouri, for a surprise matinee performance of *Oklahoma!* at the Missouri Theatre. Mae is elated to watch the superior performance, finding the musical to be her new personal favorite. Buddy's kind gesture tops off the end of a wonderful week—the greatest of times since her trips with Henry. Mae begins to feel more at ease with him through the course of their adventures, even in moments of silence.

Buddy accompanies Mae to the front of the ice cream parlor upon their arrival back in town from Columbia.

"Hmm, shall I guess what you will order?" Buddy questions playfully, knowing she orders the same thing each time.

Mae puffs a smile. "Are you suggesting that I am dull?"

"Not at all, but if the same shoe fits, then…"

Mae jabs him in the arm as he bounces away, chuckling. "Actually"—she looks straight at the parlor worker—"I will have a chocolate cone, please." She turns around to Buddy and sticks out her tongue.

He laughs and steps up to order. "Whatever this lovely dame is having along with a vanilla cone for me, please." He turns to see her expression as he pulls out his wallet, flaunting and trumping her ability to choose differently as well. He sticks out his tongue at her and smiles.

Sitting on the same bench facing each other, they enjoy their post-dinner treats. "I bet you can't get halfway done with yours before I finish mine," Buddy wagers with a crooked grin.

"I'll take that challenge!" she responds with energy. Mae takes a massive bite of her ice cream, holding it inside her mouth momentarily to melt the bulk of it. She repeats the action, getting a tasteful. Buddy nonchalantly takes his time, making a neat dome with his ice cream, pretending not to watch. "You're going to lose, you know," she mentions in between bites.

"We'll see."

"Ah! Ouch!" She grips her forehead with one hand.

Buddy bursts out laughing, holding his chest as he projects deep chortles from his gut. His outburst lasts over thirty seconds. Still beside his own cleverness, he comments, "I can't believe you fell for that trick, Mae! Hah!"

"Why, you!" Mae holds in the next number of words, attempting to retain her Christian disposition while massaging her head. "I never get these headaches." She looks up at him. He is happily eating his ice cream and gloating. Annoyed, she becomes vindictive, narrowing her eyes down to slits. Rapidly, Mae takes her cone and thrusts it into his face, lodging it into his nose, splattering ice cream all around his cheeks.

"Aw, Mae!" Buddy shouts at her. She erupts with laughter as he scoops a huge portion off his face.

"You think that's funny, huh?" He asks, peering out through his messy cheeks.

Mae continues giggling and pointing. "Yes. I win because it's all gone now!" She cups her mouth to laugh breathlessly, closing her eyes to savor the moment.

He smiles at her through the dripping ooze and jams what little is left of his vanilla cone onto her nose. "There! Now that's funny!" Her shocked expression breaks quickly, seeing the humor in their current and considerably messy status. Both of them enjoy exhibiting moments of heaving chuckles, even ignoring the funny looks from patrons appreciating their ice cream. Still smiling, they rise from the bench simultaneously, walking over to the parlor counter to grab napkins to wipe off the sticky remnants. Mae tosses her used napkins in the trash first, then Buddy. The two look at one another in the dim light and see ice cream spots remaining on their faces.

"You missed some," Mae and Buddy say in unison. They break out in laughter once more before Buddy moves over to the ordering counter.

"Hey, Bobby. Do you have a clean wet rag we could borrow?"

"Sure, Buddy." He reaches over to the dry pile of washcloths in the corner, wets it in the sink, and hands it to him through the window. "Here you go, kid."

"Thanks, Bobby." Buddy steps over to the side of the parlor with Mae. "Please, allow me," he offers. Mae nods for him to proceed. Buddy uses the end of the cloth to gently wipe off the bridge and tip of Mae's nose.

"Thank you. Your turn." She takes the rag in her hand. The chocolate left a dark impression around the perimeter of his face like scrapped-off dirt. Bobby turns up his radio volume from behind the counter, streaming the smooth and silky voice of Frank Sinatra singing "Always." The last two weeks, Mae worked diligently to avoid beautiful songs like the piece flowing through her ears, but the simplicity of Sinatra's effortless timbre saturates her mind and shoots warmth into her body.

"Thank you," he says softly. She takes hold of his square masculine chin and makes a path around his nose, above his mouth, and then down below his lips. Staring at the set of his lips, Mae eases her movements to a halt. Buddy sees her deep-blue eyes gloss over and takes her wrist gently. "May I have this dance?"

Mae glances up, entranced by the melody and his tender green eyes; she nods to accept. Buddy gently takes the rag from her hand to toss it on the counter. His opposite hand encircles her small fingers, escorting her a short distance away. He turns slowly to wrap his hand around her back and holds her right hand high up, initiating a subtle step-off. The motions remain delicate, knowing Mae is vulnerable. "You look really pretty today, Mae."

She looks away in a blush. "Thank you. You look nice too."

Buddy gently squeezes her right hand, rotating her along in a refined circle. "This whole week has been, well, the best of my life, Mae," he speaks sincerely.

Mae's glazed-over expression of surprise is not from Buddy's words but for her own mixed thoughts and feelings, she realizes. She denies the occurrence of giving access into her heart—a heart she has not owned for some time. She did not willfully give him permission to enter it. *How did this happen?* Mae is stupefied.

Buddy strengthens his hold from the small of her back, bringing her closer. The height of his chin just meets the top of her forehead. Closer still, he bends his head down gently and kisses her high cheekbone slowly. She shuts her eyes and does not flinch. She accepts that she wants him to continue and therefore must stop. The song comes to an end, and her eyes open gradually, waking from the trance. Mae pulls away in disbelief of her own actions. "I'm sorry. I have to go." She hurriedly turns and bolts to the car.

Buddy leisurely makes his way back, figuring she needs a moment. He is disappointed, but understands. He sits down in the driver's seat and sighs. "I'm sorry too, Mae. I'm not sorry for my actions or how I feel, but I am sorry you're still hurting." He turns the ignition and drives her back home to the farm.

Mae's face is turned toward the passenger-side glass for the ride back, crying gentle tears she wipes away discreetly. She pulls herself together in time to bid him good night after exiting the car. "Buddy, thank you for everything this week. Good night." She closes the door before he can respond and moves to the house promptly.

Once in her bedroom, she shuts the door to see Irene reading a book on her bed. "Hello, Irene," Mae greets her, crossing over to the closet to undress.

"Hi, Mae. A letter came for you today. I put it on your bed," Irene resumes her reading.

Mae practically lunges over to see it. "Thank you, Irene. It's from Marilynn!" She speaks with excitement, ripping open the envelope stamped from earlier in the week:

Dear Mae,   *10 June 1948*

I was so happy to hear from you! Things haven't been the same without you at Mount St. Rose. Everything was too calm for my liking, which is why I decided to spice things up. Do you remember the night we went dancing at Casa Loma? The man I was dancing with was there again just a few months ago. We spent the whole night on the floor together, and he could not wait to take me out again. After our date, he wanted to see me again, then again...He is sweet, has a steady job as a banker, and already introduced me to his family.

I am sorry to hear about Henry. Although, I am happy to report he has not been readmitted to St. Rose for any relapses. I hope he is okay and you hear from him soon. I know a girl who frequents Dreamland for dancing and asked her to inquire his whereabouts and report back. Mae, try not to worry. A man like Henry does not simply change overnight for any dame. He loves you.

It was so lovely to hear from you. Stay in touch, and let me know when you are in St. Louis soon.

Sincerely,
Marilynn

Mae drops the letter on her bed instantly. She lets her dress fall to the floor as a reminder to scrub off the ice cream stains and grabs the robe in her closet. Mae folds it around her body quickly and makes her way down the steps to the phone. She dials zero for the operator, provides the long-distance number, and waits. The line rings and rings. Nothing. Mae hangs up the phone and retreats somberly to her room.

She completes her nightly routine before crawling in bed for sleep. Irene is already passed out on her side of the bedroom, book in hand. Mae closes her eyes but feels the onslaught of information and emotions she refused to sift through make an appearance. The day's events slam into her chest. She covers her eyes and nose with her hands, allowing her mistakes an opportunity to wash over her brave façade. *I am an awful, evil person.* Mae is uncertain how much longer she can wait for Henry but knows she must avoid Buddy. Her tears come to an end. She is exhausted, but her mind is conscious for a majority of the night.

4

Mae clears and washes the dishes after breakfast the next morning. She makes her routine phone call to Dreamland with no success as usual and then grabs her worn hardback of *The Grapes of Wrath*, retreating to the porch chair. Though Mae enjoys the book, she pretends to read it, completely exhausted from no sleep. She breathes in the mild June breeze.

After thirty minutes of staring blankly, contemplating using some of her savings for a train ticket to St. Louis, Mae registers the rolling of tires at the entrance to the farm. Buddy's blue Cadillac convertible is casually approaching the house. She stands in response, tucking her golden hair back into place out of habit and uncertain she wants him to know of her presence. *It's not like you can run anywhere, Mae. Sit down.* She finds her chair again and takes a deep breath as he opens the door.

"Good morning, Mae."

"Good morning, Buddy." She holds her book to her chest.

"I'd like to speak with you, if that's all right." Buddy walks up the steps to the porch.

"I'm right here. Go ahead."

Buddy looks up to see Mae's teenage twin brothers poking their heads out from the window. "Alone, please. Would you mind taking a walk with me?"

"Well, I told my father I'd help him in the stables soon," she retorts.

"Mae, please," he pleads. His eyes reveal a lack of sleep.

"Certainly." Mae places her book on the chair, descends the stairs, and heads down the path to the main entrance to the farm.

Within twenty yards from the house, Buddy starts the conversation. "I'm sorry to barge in unexpected like this, Mae. It's just, I can't stop thinking about last night." He turns to view her face.

Embarrassed, Mae keeps her eyes down. "About that, I didn't mean to give you the wrong impression. The music...I just got carried away, I suppose."

He stops walking to speak directly to her. "But that's the thing, Mae. Whether we intended it to happen or not, we *both* got carried away. You felt it. I felt it. It's not just last night I can't let go of either. It's you. You're all I think about every minute of every day."

Mae covers her eyes. She shoves back the sorrow in her mind and trades it for anger. "No! You promised we could just be friends." She raises her voice.

"That's the thing, Mae. People change. I've changed, and I think you have too." He steps closer, reaching out to take her hand.

"No, Buddy!" She pulls her hand away. "You have no idea what I've been through lately."

"I would if you just tell me!"

"It's not my story to tell. It's our story. Henry and I. Don't you see?"

Buddy sighs. "Mae, how long are you going to wait for him?"

She turns to glare at him. "That is none of your business, Buddy."

"Oh, come on! I can give you all he can and more."

"You're wrong," she explains, soberly and deliberately. "Because when you wake up one morning and realize all your giving still won't earn you the kind of love you deserve in return, you'll realize you just scattered little pieces of yourself all over and lost everything." She puffs out a sigh, looking at his anguished face. "And you don't want that, Buddy. Nobody does."

"Why are you so fearful of what you *feel*?"

"Excuse me?"

"You think you've given away your heart and that you're betraying him, don't you? That's why you won't let yourself believe in what you're feeling." She looks at him in shock.

"Buddy, I *know* I am betraying him. Up until a week and a half ago, I had a diamond ring around my finger."

"Well, where is it now?"

"Safe in a box."

"Then what? Are you going to work and wait for him to come slip it back on your finger every day for the rest of your life?"

"Maybe. I made a promise."

"And so did he, but again, people change."

Mae's eyes narrow. "Is this what you came here to say, Buddy? And infuriate me in the process?" She turns away from him and crosses her arms in anger.

"No, Mae. I didn't come over to make you angry. I came here to make you an offer," he replies in a calm voice.

"Which is what, exactly?" Mae turns in surprise to see his face.

"I know this might be crazy, but considering all the foolish things we did to have fun this past week in our travels, I think it's a brilliant plan."

Mae is confused. "What plan?"

His face livens to a wide smile. "Picture it, Mae. City life, running my own store in a bustling downtown area, and you working at a top-notch hospital right in the heart of New York City!"

"What?"

"Mae." He takes her hands, holding them close to his chest. "Your heart is twice the size of everyone else's, so don't be afraid that you can't make room. They say time can heal all wounds, so let's just get out of here. Together. I promise I'll be patient, care for you." He brushes a loose strand away from her face. "And I won't ever take you away from what you love to do." He cups her face in one hand then adds the other. Again, she does not flinch from his touch and the shock of his previous submission. She looks up into his green eyes, feeling a rush boil through her veins, igniting heat in her muscles. He pulls her swiftly into his body and kisses her deeply. The battle of emotions from the night before unleashes a full attack inside her mind, and though she needs to stop the kiss, she wants to continue.

"Stop." She speaks the moment she thinks it, breaking away. Mae is overwhelmed with guilt, letting the tears flow immediately in a wave of emotion. She stares at him, knowing what she needs to do now. She takes off in a delicate sprint toward the house, leaving Buddy puzzled. Mae runs into the house and picks up the phone to call Dreamland one last time.

"Hello? Hello? Who am I speaking with?" A man questions through the phone.

Mae is confused, having not heard the phone ring. Suddenly, she vaguely recognizes the voice. "H-Henry? Is that you?" Mae questions hesitantly.

"Mae?" Henry asks in shock.

"Yes, it's me!"

"Is it really you?" Henry is ecstatic with relief.

"Yes, I'm here," Mae says, confused by his excitement.

"I've missed you, Mae. Are you finished? Are you all done?"

"Yes, of course I'm finished. Didn't you receive my letters?"

"What letters?"

"I've been trying to call Dreamland every day the last three weeks. I also wrote you two letters since arriving home."

"No one brought me any mail, but I've been held hostage at home, Mae. I was sick."

"What was wrong?"

"My lungs, of course. I wouldn't let my mom take me back to Mount St. Rose, so she made a few calls, and the doctor visited frequently. I had to stay still. It was so awful. I've missed you so much."

"I'm so relieved. I've been trying to call, but no one answered."

"Yes, no one answers when I'm not there. I didn't have your home address to write a letter either. I'm so sorry, Mae."

Mae feels sick, leaving silence between responses.

"When can I come to Versailles? Have you made all the wedding arrangements?" Henry is upbeat.

"I..." Mae is speechless.

"What's the matter?"

Mae snaps up. "Oh, I'm just happy you're better, but I haven't had time to make the arrangements."

"All right, just tell me the date you and your parents worked out, and I'll be there with a few family members."

"We haven't had time to look at the calendar, Henry."

Henry is surprised. "Oh. Should we set up a time for me to call after you speak with them?"

"Sure." Mae uses every ounce of power to sound normal.

"How about tomorrow at the same time?"

"That sounds good."

"I can't wait to see you, Mae!"

"Me too, Henry." Mae smiles through her concern.

"I'll ask around for those letters and speak with you tomorrow then."

"All right."

"I love you so much." Henry is sincere.

Mae pauses. "I love you too," she says softly. Henry hangs up while Mae drops the receiver down in the hallway of their home. A burst of nausea rolls through her upper frame; it feels as if he is back from the dead.

Mae saunters gradually into the stable, debriefing her thoughts of all that happened in the last hour. She picks up the rubber curry, soft brush, and comb off the wooden table just inside the door and walks over to the Arabian mare she bathed five days prior. She sets the brush and comb off to the side of the pregnant horse, pets its neck down to her shoulder, and begins stroking the liver chestnut hair with the curry toward her crest. Moving the curry in large circles, she extracts extra hair, dirt, and dust from nose to haunches. She sets it down and picks up the brush to wipe down any excess. With her fingers first and then a comb, she gently detangles the mane from bottom to top for the length of the horse's neck. Mae moves to the tail, repeating the process. She uses the brush once more to massage the mare into a beautiful summer shine. When finished, she pats down the side of the peaceful creature. "You have a lot of work ahead of you soon, so you may as well look amazing while doing it."

"You in here, Mae?" her father questions.

"Yes, I was just cleaning her up."

"You want to take her out for a bit while I get the other two?"

"I'm getting ready to," she replies from behind the stable gate.

"Well, saddle her up, but no more than a trot. Take breaks and lead her around the fence line."

"Still no grazing, right?"

"She can, but watch where she eats. We don't want her getting sick before delivery." He rounds the corner to see her face.

"I remember," Mae replies with a gentle smile.

"I'm sure you do, sweetheart. You okay? I noticed Buddy stopped by."

"I am just fine, but thank you."

"Mae, you never were much of a fibber," he says to her with a crooked grin.

She looks down in a blush. "I know. I just have some sorting to do, that's all."

"Well, I find horses can often help, so I'll leave you to it then," he comments, placing his hat back on his head before exiting the stable with two other Arabian mares at his sides.

"Hmm." Mae smiles.

While saddling up the horse and preparing her for exercise, she sifts through her plan before Henry called, intending to phone Mount St. Rose for Marilynn and ask her to deliver a message to Dreamland. The reality is that she considered Buddy's offer, but only because she cared for him. She did not want to live in a fast city; in fact, she is certain he neglected to think through raising children. *How naïve to believe I could let my own kids grow up with all those people! The denser the population, the more people to quarrel.* Her thoughts lead her to the most important conclusion and justification: Buddy is immature.

With Henry, she trusts his intuitive experience and open personality. She knows he will never let her down and keep their love the priority. Henry's solid foundation of family sold her on his maturity, and somehow, she knew he was the right one from the beginning—blind love.

Mae's choice is clear. Though she is sad Henry's sickness guided the development of their friendship and, in the end, a hurtful relationship, she will have no contact with Buddy. The door is closed. Permanently.

⚜

The next morning, Henry and Mae discuss details for their upcoming nuptials, set for the twenty-seventh of June.

"Mae, I'm sorry. No one around Dreamland seems to know what happened to your letters. I am so furious I can't see straight," Henry puffs into the phone.

"It's okay, Henry. We are here together on the phone now, and that's all that matters."

"You are certainly correct, though I would love to know what you wrote." He speaks more peacefully.

"Well, I suppose you don't know the biggest news yet." Mae is energetic.

"What's that?"

"Sister Carrie told me that the director of placement services for the Cadet Corps is allowing me to select any hospital staff to serve that is sanctioned by the Corps. Isn't that grand?"

"Anywhere?" he asks in disbelief.

"Yes, anywhere. I'll finally be a paid official nurse now. I decided the moment she informed me where I'd like to be, Henry."

"And where is that, my darling?" Henry inquires playfully.

Mae giggles in response to his humorous tone. "Oh, I don't know. I suppose it doesn't matter all that much," she states in a passively whimsical manner.

Henry laughs loudly, thankful she is finally on the other end of the phone.

Under two weeks later, Henry arrives at the Versailles farmhouse. He is dressed in a pressed black suit and black-and-white casual dress spectator shoes. Nervously, Henry knocks on the front wooden screen door of their home. After a distressing six seconds, Mae's father walks to the door, pushes it open gently, and walks slowly over the threshold onto the porch to face Henry. Henry's nerves do not allow him a detailed look at his features or time to assess which of Mae's attributes resemble him. He anxiously backs up, attempting to relax, but is certain Mae's father notices his trembling.

"Hello, sir. My name is Henry Williams," he offers his hand for a shake. Mae's father gradually takes it and squeezes it assertively. "I'm sure Mae's already told you everything, but it's a pleasure to meet you, sir."

Mae's father does not respond or seem at all welcoming. Henry comprehends he is a man of few words, creating further apprehensive agony.

"I-I'm sorry I couldn't meet you before today, but I want you to know how much I love your daughter. She means the world to me, and I never want to live without her, sir. I realize this is a little backward, but it would ease my heart and conscience if I could have your blessing to marry her today." Drops of sweat begin to form on Henry's forehead.

Mae's father crosses his arms and lets out a long sigh, looking away. He pretends to ponder it thoughtfully, enjoying the tortured expression on Henry's face, sensing the internal turmoil he feels. Like any respectable father, he makes Henry sweat for nearly an entire minute. Henry pulls out the white handkerchief from his suit coat and wipes the beads of sweat off his forehead, trying to keep his breath even.

"Well, I suppose it won't change anything, but yes, you have my blessing," Mae's father finally replies. "Just do me a favor," he continues.

"Yes, sir. Anything, sir."

"My daughter will be using her gifts to take care of people, nursing them to health, all day long. I expect that you do your best to make sure she's taken care of when she gets home. You understand? You keep your ducks in a row," he insists, looking straight into Henry's eyes.

"Yes, sir. I will," Henry says with a nervous smile. "Thank you, sir." Henry feels relief as he returns inside to change for the wedding. He takes a few moments to calm down from the bubble of anxiety boiling in his skin.

Henry pauses his pacing on the porch to see a car approaching the house. He deduces it is Mae's older brother, Francis, arriving after dropping his wife and children off at the church. Mae, her mother, and sisters had been at the church since early that morning, preparing for the ceremony.

Francis exits the 1947 Chrysler Town & Country Convertible in a fitted gray two-piece suit and matching fedora hat. As he approaches the porch smiling, he speaks to Henry. "You must be the lucky groom!"

"Yes. Hello! Francis, right?" Henry holds out his hand at the same time Francis reaches for it.

"That's me. How are you holding up?"

"Oh, just fine. Relieved your father decided not to shoot me about five minutes ago when I got here," Henry says with a chuckle, looking away.

Francis scoffs while removing his fedora. "Well, the day's not over yet."

Henry glances up, relieved to see him grinning back. "That's funny," he remarks, attempting to brush off his serious undertone.

Francis chuckles in return. "Have you seen the boys?"

"No, I haven't. I assumed they were getting ready when I arrived ten minutes ago."

"I see. Hmm. Well, I'll go see what's keeping them."

"All right."

Francis helps himself inside the front door.

Henry knows little of the twins, Ronald and Royce. Mae described them once as "all boy, starving for attention most of the time." As a young girl, Mae fed and changed them when they were babies, but other than their high school status, Henry's information is limited.

Ten minutes go by when four pairs of feet travel down the wooden boards of the steps. Francis is first out the door, then presumably Ronald and Royce follow, and finally, Mae's father. The later three gentlemen head toward the Studebaker sitting on the other side of the drive.

"Well, Henry, why don't you ride with the boys and my father. I was just sent here to get something for my mom." He holds up a small dark wooden box with a golden latch. "We'll be making our way back to Sedalia just after the reception, so I'll see you at the church."

"Sure. Nice meeting you, Francis." Henry politely bids farewell.

"Likewise, Henry." He opens his car door.

Henry hears the engine of the Studebaker start and heads for his Plymouth to retrieve his tuxedo from the backseat.

Ronald and Royce graciously slide in the back of the Studebaker, allowing Henry the front. Henry opens the door and gets in the car. Mae's father takes off down the drive toward the main road. The vehicle is silent while traveling to town.

"Beautiful day for a wedding, isn't it?" Henry attempts to break the silence. He glances to his left for a response, but seeing none, he awkwardly shies away to peer out his car window. The scenery passing by begins to slow down. Henry looks forward to see the railroad crossing lights flashing but void of signal crossing barriers, typical for a small intersection. Hoping the train is traveling fast, Henry feels anxious to get to the church now.

Mae's father approaches the intersection, braking later than Henry anticipates for a safe stop from the tracks. Gripping on the handle of the door, Henry realizes he is not stopping before the tracks at all. Looking out the windows and searching for the approaching train, Henry is in a panic. "What are you doing?"

Mae's father slows the car directly on top of the tracks, a smirk on his face, placing it in park. Ronald and Royce grab a tight hold of Henry's shoulders from behind, pinning them to the seat so he is unable to move at all.

"Stop this! Let go of me now!" Henry looks down the tracks toward the passenger engine approaching quickly. His assessment is five hundred yards. "You have to move. Now!"

Mae's father hears the strain in his voice and peeks over his shoulder at the train as the twins laugh hysterically at Henry's discomfort. Three hundred yards away, the train's whistle bellows out a monstrous noise.

"Please. Stop this now! Move!"

Royce and Ronald's laughter reach higher decibels, covering up the train whistle, as Mae's father glances one last time toward the approaching train. At one hundred and fifty yards, he looks up at Henry, places his hand slowly on the gearshift, and draws it into drive. The car moves slowly across the back half of the tracks at the moment the twins release Henry's shoulders.

"What in the hell is wrong with you people!" Henry yells as the train passes behind the Studebaker now, missing them by just forty yards.

"Calm down, Henry." Mae's father finally speaks, accelerating down the road.

"Calm down? Do you realize how close I've been to death on an involuntarily basis throughout my life? And you want me to calm down when my life is being voluntarily threatened?"

"Yes." Mae's father is stern. "Because if you made it through that without messing yourself, we figure you can make it through just about anything." He chuckles. "The boys just wanted to welcome you, and I wanted you to remember to be grateful as you stand up there with my daughter today."

"What have I gotten myself into?" Henry exhales, shaking his head.

"We were just making the day memorable, Henry. We like you." Mae's father is sincere. He gently punches his upper arm.

"Well, I'd hate to know what would happen if you didn't then," Henry responds, still agitated.

"Ha." Mae's father is contrastingly full of lighthearted energy now as they reach the church.

Henry quickly exits the vehicle, passing Francis on the way inside. Francis is grinning. "Did you have a nice trip here then, Henry?" Henry, still extremely disconcerted, attempts to keep his walking stride fluid past Francis, ignoring that he and the others obviously set him up. He finds a restroom inside the church to change into his black double-breasted tuxedo with matching tie and cummerbund.

Twenty minutes later, the service begins. Henry stands near the minister, seeing Mae for the first time in months. She is gloriously breathtaking, dressed in a full-length satin gown fit to her slender waist and a long train with a veil to match its measurements. A small amount of intricately woven lace lies around the collar and short sleeves. Her makeup is light and luminous, with the exception of her signature red lipstick. Her hair still sits above her shoulders, rolled in large golden curls away from her face. Henry is thankful for his patience as she walks down the aisle. She was worth waiting for, and he knows he would do it infinitely over again.

Henry is studiously dapper with a daisy tucked in his jacket pocket to match Mae's bouquet. Two of Henry's cousins are groomsmen, walking with Irene and Mae's next younger sister, Joyce. The couple exchanges traditional wedding vows followed by a short reception in the chapel's fellowship hall. The Studebaker is nicely decorated to commemorate the day, but now serves as a reminder of the pre-wedding nightmare Henry would like to forget. Mae's father drives them off as they wave good-bye to family and friends from the backseat. After arriving back at the family farm, Henry and Mae change clothes, share a farewell with Mae's father, and depart in Henry's Plymouth.

The couple finally attains their marriage license in Jefferson City the same day in 1948, only after driving through a series of dangerous thunderstorms. Instead of traveling to their Kansas City honeymoon destination, the two laughingly decide not to push their luck any further that stormy day and remain in Jefferson City. They are together now; the location is irrelevant.

After returning to St. Louis from the honeymoon, Henry's mother graciously offers to move into her sister's house, closer in proximity to Dreamland, allowing Henry and Mae to rent his childhood home while settling into married life.

Happy to receive her back, Mae assumes the head nursing position for the Labor and Delivery Department at St. Mary's Hospital on July 1.

Just before Christmas the same year, Mae receives a blank post card in the mail of the New York City skyline. She smiles in understanding and tucks it into the bottom of her dresser drawer, thankful for the life she lives every day.

Henry finds a position in realty and, with the charm acquired over the years, becomes a successful businessman. After saving up enough money, the couple purchase a new home down the road from Dreamland, where Mae delivers twins in 1949.

Close to lunch, Mae awakes from her reverie to see a nurse shifting her weight by propping a pillow underneath her right hip from the left.

"Henry?" Mae lifts her frail head to search the room. "Where did that man go?" she asks the nurse in confusion.

"What man? It's been only me in here, Mae," the nurse replies.

Mae turns her head the other direction, already realizing what the nurse's response implies, and allows one tear to escape down her creased cheek.

PART 2

JEAN

CHAPTER

5

"Hello, Jean," the slender man greets. He bends down to swiftly kiss Jean on the cheek. She looks up to find his face, smiles, and lifts her arms with an invitation for a hug. The man, still nicely dressed in his brown suit and ivory shirt, leans over and tilts his head aside to give Jean a warm embrace with a gentle squeeze. "How are you today?" He pulls back to view her face.

Jean quickly draws her eyes, squinting from the brightness of the sun, to the yellow tea roses lined up across the courtyard from where she sits on a cushioned iron bench. "It's just lovely outside today, and the smell coming from those flowers is wonderful." Her bright blue eyes hold all the genuine excitement of a five-year-old child, though she is sixty-two now. Like her father, her long hair is naturally dark and well kept from frequent visits to the salon every month. She chills easily with the breeze as older adults often do. The warmth of the spring midmorning sun makes her happy, but wearing only her long relaxed-fit sweats and long-sleeved shirt in combination with her pale skin, her time outside will be limited.

"My husband used to plant all kinds of flowers in our back-yard patio garden," she continues. The polite man offers Jean his arm and gently escorts her closer to the tea roses and a nearby bench in the soft shimmer of sun-spotted shade. He assists her soft landing onto the bench and sits next to her.

"I love to be in the garden as well, Jean," he offers, smiling angelically.

"You remind me of my husband, so tall and skinny, just like you." The man grins back at her while she continues, "I always tell people he looks like Harrison Ford, but everyone thinks I'm crazy." She half chuckles. "You're even more handsome than him, I think. What's your name again?"

"Jean, I come to see you most days. We like to share stories," the man replies with tender charm.

Jean lights up in response to his statement. "You know, I thought you looked familiar. This place makes me feel a little crazy sometimes, but I knew you were special to me. Thank you so much for coming to see me today."

"You're quite welcome."

While staring into this man's eloquent smile and soft blue eyes, she feels her connection with him too deep to be true. *Is he really here with me?* She feels his presence to be surreal. Jean drifts in thought while the chill of the shade creates goose bumps over her skin. Flickers of a potential distant memory come to the forefront of her mind, which she welcomes. She reflects back on a cool fall evening surrounded by new friends.

"That little breeze just reminded me of one of the *best* nights of my life in high school. It's nice to know I can think back that far, even if I still miss details at times." She turns to view the man's expectant eyes, giving her heart a subtle palpitation. "My family had just moved to Decatur, Illinois. I was so upset to have left my other high school friends back home, but as long as I had my guitar, I knew I would be okay."

Jean, thrilled to have some source of entertainment to cling to today, is beaming about her oncoming reverie. As it shapes itself into a dreamlike quality, the faces of the people she pictures begins to blur. While this angelic man's face next to her is fresh,

Jean feels the significance of his presence take over this flashback. *Is this my James?*

"I was nearly seventeen and thrilled to be invited to a party as the *new girl.* Warrensburg-Latham High School wasn't exactly the epicenter of all things trendy in 1966, but we managed to get by with many of the farmer's kids and those mixed in from the soybean, tractor, or tire factories in town." Jean speaks fluidly, turning away to lock her eyes on the bush of pale-yellow roses across the garden. "Of course, I brought my guitar that night. I don't remember leaving home without it much at all then." She slows her word pacing and drifts deeper into her memory.

It is Friday night. Jean sits alongside a number of people all circled around a small bonfire in Lisa Maxwell's backyard. Lisa is in the popular crowd at school, and Jean is thrilled to be sitting at an invitation-only event as a junior, new to the area.

Jean is chatting with the girl next to her about their social studies project due on Monday. Clear on their expectations at home, her parents would never let her out of the house to attend a football game or party without completing her homework. She feels relief knowing her perseverance pays off tonight.

Despite her age, Jean is mature, which is partly why people respond to her quickly. She exudes a presence that is eager and yearning to start life. Extremely comfortable making music, Jean hopes a career path in music or entertainment will be in her future. She feels a sense of freedom being a performer, but does not throw herself into opportunities as a young woman with a sense of humility. With an impressive relative ear, she is able to decipher chords without reference but never grasped note reading concepts; therefore, she naturally leans toward the entertainment route.

"Hey, Jean, you brought your guitar. Why don't you play us a song?" Lisa suggests enthusiastically from the other side of the fire.

"Oh, sure. What would you like to hear?" Jean responds with a smile.

"Hmm. How about...'House of the Rising Sun'? Can you play that?"

"Sure! I just learned that. It's one of my favorites right now." Jean is ecstatic as she bends down to pull the guitar out of her black hard case. After the football team's win tonight, she feels sharing music will make people even happier.

Sitting around the bonfire in the chill of the air, she figures her guitar needs a tuning check. When possible, Jean prefers not to use a pick when she plays, gently plucking the low E string with her thumb to check the pitch. The low E rings correctly in her relative ear from her practice session earlier in the evening, then she presses the low E at the fifth fret to cross-check the A string. Pressing down the fifth fret of the A to check the D, she adjusts the peg slightly. After the D is in tune, Jean moves onto G. The G is precisely synced to the reference string, then she moves down a fret to test the B and slides back to the fifth-fret B string to check the high E string. The entire tuning process only takes her seven seconds.

Jean forms her A minor chord shape and starts the first of the arpeggiated chords to the popular tune. She begins to sing after the seven-and-a-half-measure introduction. "There is... a house...in New Orleans..." While she continues with the rest of the song, people start singing along with her on the refrains. She plays louder and nods her head to help keep time. Others close to the house decide to walk up around the fire to listen to Jean sing and play. When the song finishes, Jean opens her eyes to a crowd of clapping and cheering people.

As the noise starts to die down, a young man calls out from the back, "Play another one!"

Jean is thrilled to oblige, thinking to herself one quick moment before starting on the chords for the next tune. "Yesterday...all my troubles seemed so far away..." Jean sings on as more people continue to crowd around the circle, enjoying the sweet melodic sound of the Beatles.

Being the third of four children leaves an incredibly unique view on the general makeup of life. Jean has two older sisters in college and a brother two years younger. Her father was elated to finally have a boy, ultimately creating the sense of neglect in Jean's subconscious. Like any child in a homogenous line, the hand-me-downs are a given, along with the notorious understanding younger siblings fend for themselves. However, adding the opposite gender at the end of the ranks automatically deems one less than desirable in the middle of the chain. Jean's position necessitated an open personality, guiding her ability to step out of the box and into the spotlight. Making people happy feeds her contentment in life.

Of the few individuals Jean does see out in the crowd, James is not one of those people. He stumbles up, slightly inebriated, to the back of the crowd with another girl and out of Jean's peripheral view. He is clueless as to the name of the petite sophomore girl under his arm, but it is draped around her neck, regardless. Tall with a slight build from football training, his attire includes faded bell-bottoms, a white T-shirt, and his leather maroon-and-gold letterman jacket. His long sand-colored bangs come down to his eyelashes just below the rim of his thick black glasses. He forces gravity to toss his hair to the side with persistent head jolts to his left. Because he is tipsy from chugging three cans of beer in celebration of his football team's win tonight, he uses his fingers to smooth his hair back instead, preventing further dizziness.

When James hears Jean, he stops immediately to see the face behind the guitar. The girl under his arm attempts to claim his attention, but James shushes her and looks on at Jean. The slight teenager shrugs out from under his heavy arm. "You jerk!" She offends before storming off.

James then freely walks forward, finding a post next to his close friend, Elliot, from the football team. "Hey, who is that singing?" James asks.

"Oh, that's the new girl, Jean. She's pretty good, idn't she?" Elliot compliments with a thick Decatur accent. James merely looks on and nods, affirming as he smiles, seemingly sober now.

James always exudes confidence, usually landing him into trouble. As a child, his father was a monumental disciplinarian. Incredibly intelligent and a former navy medic in the South Pacific, James's father could spot a lie before it started. With impeccable senses, his father anticipated the mischief James might instigate before it came to his mind. However, at times he did not predict James's behavior, his father required no extra incentive to apply a firm and brutally physical reminder for him to follow his rules. At times, the physical consequences were severe. James suffered a number of broken bones, including a broken nose, after setting a small part of their horse barn on fire with firecrackers. Attempting to show off for friends never landed James into such hot water before, but his father's hard nature and style was handed down from his parents.

For James, following rules and guidelines is a crucial aspect of helping his parents run and maintain their farm on the west side of Decatur. He is tough, having to put down horses, dogs, and other animals with which he formed attachments. With a firm, fatherly hand keeping him in line and a no-nonsense yet loving mother, James grew to be a man quickly. He is overly confident; however, no amount of assurance will land him success where Jean is concerned. He is immediately enamored with her talent; the long and silky black wavy hair with bright-blue eyes in contrast ignite heated desire throughout his body. Though she plays sitting down, he notices her shorter frame, only measuring five foot four to his six-foot-three height, but stature is inconsequential to him now.

James stands still, listening and watching Jean. He is entranced. Uncertain why he feels this way, he understands simply by looking at her that she is too good for him. He needs a plan and patience, a quality he lacks, admittedly. James starts plotting his introduction to her in school as creativity is key for acquiring Jean's attention.

Jean finishes "Yesterday." The people around the bonfire cheer and applaud, but it is time for more excitement. She starts the chords for Van Morrison's "Gloria." As confirmation of the crowd's approval, the whole party sings "G-L-O-R-I-A" in the underlying refrain by the end. Jean is on a high as it is the best day of her life thus far.

⁕⊹⊱⊰⊹⁕

Monday at school, James finds Jean's locker in the junior hallway first thing in the morning. He decides to wait to approach her until after school to avoid feeling rushed.

After a full day of classes, one hand carries his books, and in the other, an electric guitar. He is hopeful his plan will work out. As James advances, his heart starts to flutter slightly.

"Hi, Jean?"

She turns to look up at James's face and takes a step back. James realizes he is too close, and with the eagerness he feels to know her, he decidedly moves back.

"Yes?"

"Hi, I'm James. I saw you at the bonfire the other night and thought I could ask you a few questions about this guitar here." James draws his eyes down to the black case in his hand.

"I know who you are, James." Jean turns back to organize her items. She gathers up the last of her books, places them in her bag, and shuts her locker. "Doesn't everyone?" She turns to look up at him again.

"Oh. Well, I suppose. Is that bad?" James replies with a smile.

"I guess it depends on your definition of *bad*. If bad means using and disposing of girls like tissues, then yes, that is bad."

"Huh, never thought my reputation would precede me *that* much." A slight smirk of humor touches his face.

"Sometimes you don't have a choice anymore. Character is everything, and we are defined by *all* our actions."

Jean turns the other way and begins walking at a medium pace down the hallway. It takes one second for James to regain his train of thought. "Hey, wait! Can you help me out with this guitar?" James attempts to catch up with Jean.

She stops, lets out one big sigh looking to the sky, and turns to meet his desperate eyes. "Okay, fine. *What* is the problem?"

"Well, I've been playing this guitar for a while, but the problem is I'm just not sure if the strings are still good. I can't seem to tune them right."

"Okay, I'll look at it. Let's go out to the courtyard," Jean suggests and turns for the school exit.

"Thanks so much for taking your time to do this. If I keep you late, I apologize," James says with a wistful grin.

Jean knows he is likely up to no good based on what she has heard about James, but she gives him the benefit of her trust regardless. "It's okay," she yields.

"May I drive you home after this?" James follows her out the door.

Apparently, Jean gave her trust too soon, stifling a scoff in response. "No, that's okay. My friends will wait."

Jean sits down on a short limestone flower-bed retaining wall in the courtyard and waits for James to hand her the guitar. He stands there, blanking slightly about his next course of action. "Oh...sorry," he says, handing her the black case. She lays it down flat on the pavement, lifts the latches, then the lid. Jean gasps slightly when she sees the make and brand of the guitar.

"What? What's wrong with it?" James questions anxiously.

"Oh…um, nothing." James waits while looking at her expression. "It's just a really nice guitar, that's all."

"Oh, thanks," James answers as he watches Jean pick up the sunburst-colored 1960 Fender Stratocaster electric guitar. She quickly studies the body, neck, and craftsmanship then places the slender instrument in playing position to begin the relative tuning process. Jean assumes it takes longer being void of recent playtime, but that morning James moved the pegs around to capture a few extra moments together.

"So where did your family move from again?" James asks.

"We've lived in a few different places, but most recently a little town named Mexico. Ever heard of it?"

"No, I haven't. Is it nice?"

"Not really. There's not a whole lot to do there, which I guess is okay because I had more time to learn tunes."

"You are really good," James compliments.

"Thanks, and that should do it. Here you go." Jean hands James the guitar back sooner than expected. He takes it slowly. Jean gathers her things as James stands there, debating on blowing his cover.

"I have a confession," he admits.

"Really?" Jean sounds only half-surprised.

"Well, I really don't know how to play guitar at all. I was hoping you would teach me?" He inflects his statement into a question.

"James, anyone can teach you, I'm sure."

"But you're so great. Please? I will be good, I promise. We can meet in public, here at school, or wherever. I'd really love to learn to play." James never speaks to anyone like this but is amazed at how it sounds, coming out gracefully. *What's wrong with me?*

Jean stares at his face, perceptively aware of his ulterior motive, but against her better judgment decides he should be harmless enough in a public place. "Fine, but don't expect anything out of it. You'll be lucky to gain my friendship considering your lack of honesty from the beginning."

"Yes, I'm sorry about that. You make me a bit nervous," James admits, looking away.

"Hah! I make you nervous? Well, these lessons should be interesting then," Jean replies. "See you later."

James stands there a moment, smiling while he watches her walk away. He bends down to place the guitar in the case and latches the guitar closed. *Is it tomorrow yet?*

⁘

Over the next month, Jean and James meet two times per week before school in front of the building or in the courtyard. James works nearly every day in his father's convenience store after football practice, leaving little extra time. Because of dropping temperatures moving into late fall, the two then meet in the quiet cafeteria, unbothered. James commits to asking Jean one personal question every time, attempting to know her better. He is surprised she always poses inquiries in return.

"What do you want to do when you graduate? Do you know?" Jean probes.

"Actually, I'd like to become an architect. For some reason, I've always been interested in the artistic aspects of building a home, figuring out the design dimensions, or the makeup of churches and buildings. It would be nice to create my own works of art as a designer, but I'd love to manage building projects as well."

"That's really something, James. Good for you."

"How about you?"

"Well, I've always been pretty good at science, and I enjoy taking care of people, so we'll see if that leads anywhere. I really love making music, but it's always just other people's music. I've never really felt an urge to create my own. I guess that element is fairly important when you want to entertain people for a living." Jean drops her head slightly, feeling defeated.

James reads her body language. "Well, hey, I'm sure there are plenty of people out there who want to hear your version of those songs. I mean, everywhere you go around here it seems like people know you. That says something."

"I guess so," Jean returns and sits up slightly at the thought. "All right, well, let's get these chords down," Jean encourages. "It's a newer Beatles tune with only three primary chords. We'll keep it simple with the downward strum we talked about, but you'll sound great."

James gets his left hand shape set for a C chord on the acoustic guitar Jean loaned to him for beginner lessons and practice. James's massive hands benefit from the wider guitar neck, not to mention eliminating the need for amplification. Jean counts off the song.

"One, two, ready, go! Ah, look at all the lonely people...Ah, look at all the lonely people..." Jean sings on while James focuses on his change from C major to E minor, back and forth. When he finally gets the awkward shifting down midphrase, he is pleased with himself, smiling while he plays. Reaching the refrain, James is animated, remembering the shift to E minor seven in the correct place. Admittedly, he is not musically coordinated. He has a hard enough time keeping a steady handclapping beat, let alone switching chords, but Jean keeps him on track all the way to the end on the downbeats.

"Yeah!" James calls out, pleased with his work when he finishes the last chord.

"Nice job, James," Jean offers with a genuine expression.

"Thanks, and thank you for teaching me too. You know, at first I was really just doing this for the wrong reasons, but now I'm really glad I did it."

"For the wrong reasons?" Jean inquires, the center of her brow pointing decidedly down.

"Well, I'm sure you know, but I'd really like to ask you out, Jean. Would you go out on a date with me?" James questions softly.

Jean deliberates for a moment and begins shaking her head. "James, you just admitted you were dishonest again. That's two strikes. At some point, you will have to earn it back." Jean looks away.

"Earn what back?"

"My trust. Let's start with being friends, and if you prove yourself a good friend, I will consider your offer." Jean smiles.

James returns a grin but feels defeated, unaccustomed to disappointment with girls.

· ⚬❧⚬ ·

James is committed to understanding Jean and developing a friendship with her over several months. He phones frequently, resulting in pleasant conversations on multiple topics. Jean senses how weary he is from protecting his façade of popularity, enabling himself to play petty high school games to fit into a mold. She feels her barrier walls come down, especially when learning his avoidance of opportunities to be with other girls making advances. He decides to ditch his high school peers to be with Jean on numerous occasions. Naturally, she enjoys his friendship, even introducing him to her parents over winter break.

"Hello. It's a pleasure to finally meet you both." James first shakes the hand of Jean's father firmly and moves to gently take her mother's hand.

"So you're the boy keeping Jean so preoccupied," Jean's mother remarks.

"Yes, ma'am. Jean is an amazing girl and a great friend. One heck of a guitar teacher too," James compliments.

"I'd say she comes by her talent quite honestly, wouldn't you, dear?" Jean's father smiles as he sidesteps closers to his wife, wrapping his arm around her.

"Well, it's from both sides, really," Jean's mother offers.

"That's nice. Well, I'm sure Jean has told you how hard it's been for me to even keep a steady beat," James responds, chuckling. Jean and her parents laugh briefly with him. He notices the Christmas tree set up just behind the couple. "Is that a spruce there?"

"Yes, a black spruce, actually. Do you know trees, James?" Jean's father inquires.

"A little, but I'm no expert. It looks great."

"Well, here, son. Let me show you around the rest of the house," he suggests to James.

"Thank you, sir."

Jean and her mother exchange a pleasant glance watching the two men disappear into the kitchen.

Rolling into the spring, Jean and James are enthusiastic to head outdoors. After a break in the weather, the two catch a gorgeous day and decide to take a walk in nearby Fairview Park. Several minutes go by of peaceful silence as James contemplates an issue in his head. Jean notices how at ease and comfortable she feels, even in the calm and quiet. She enjoys the green and colorful presence of the tall oak trees towering over the paved pathway. Abruptly, James stops and turns to Jean. He hesitates a brief moment when she turns to peer up at him in response. Noticing his unease, Jean's forehead creases with confusion.

"Jean, can I take you to dinner Friday night?" James breathes.

Jean is surprised by his nervous energy but appreciates his endearing sincerity. "As in…an official date?" Jean knowingly toys with her reply.

"Yes. Please?" James says slowly, laying down the power of his gaze with fervent passion.

Jean ponders for a moment and looks away. "James, you're graduating soon. I still have another year. How wou—" Jean is stopped by one finger pressed gently to her lips. She draws her eyes up to his face.

"Don't even worry about that right now. Do you want to go on a date with me? Yes or no?" James throws her a crooked smile.

In spite of her initial hesitations, she can feel her willpower break with him standing so close. "Yes," she mutters against his finger humorously. James laughs and removes his finger.

"Okay, can I pick you up at seven?" James turns to continue their walk, but he is elated, barely containing his excitement.

"I'll have to check with my parents, but that should be okay," Jean replies with a soft smile. She searches his face for an underlying emotion while he walks but sees a decent poker face.

⋅⊙⊛⊙⋅

James picks Jean up for their first date in his 1959 Ford Fairlane, a bright china-blue perimeter with a white hood. Handed down from his grandfather as a gift, the car is a means to an end, merely assisting him to destinations. Admittedly, James is fascinated with driving fast. The adrenaline of a race is hard for him to pass up, but he feels his time burning up engines may be over as he turns onto Jean's street. Sitting on the porch bench strumming her guitar, she stands to place the instrument inside her house, offering a quick good-bye message to her parents. James opens the car door for Jean, who slides easily onto the seat.

With a high metabolism, James needs little help polishing off the last of the large pizza the two are sharing at Monical's Pizza. The pair has enough time to relax before heading to a drive-in movie to see *Thoroughly Modern Millie*, a perfect blend of music and comedy to entertain both of them.

At the table, the conversation topics are extremely light until after dinner.

"What's the scariest thing you've been through?" James questions, taking a sip from his soda.

Jean deliberates her honest answer for a moment, sighs anxiously, and presses slowly forward with her response. "When I was five, my mother and I were struck by an oncoming car at a popular intersection. Our light turned green, my mother accelerated, but the other driver didn't stop. The car hit us on our side with me sitting behind my mother. I wasn't wearing my seat belt." Jean pauses briefly, reflecting her next thoughts. "I remember bits and pieces. I was panicked and frozen in shock, wondering where my mother was taken. The doctors had to put my face back together a little." She breaks another moment, contemplating. "I try to hide the scars, but they reconstructed my nose and upper lip." Jean ducks her head down to shy away from James's piercing stare.

He watches her face, seeing now how she truly feels about herself for the first time. He cannot fathom her insecurities. "Jean, I know you think your scars are noticeable, but all I see when I look into your beautiful blue eyes is your kind heart," James consoles.

Jean looks up to return his gaze.

"Hey, they're just lines, Jean. We all have lines on our faces. You are *gorgeous*. Believe me," he asserts.

Jean breaks away from his stare for a moment and nervously swallows, glancing to the side with a soft smile. Attempting to hide her blush, she takes a sip of her water and initiates the same question for a diversion. "How about you?"

"Oh, I've seen some pretty awful things happen at our farm with the animals. Real scary stuff, but I'm not sure I've really been through anything all that bad myself. Thank God."

Jean regains her posture at the thought. "Yes, thank goodness," she states with a smile. "Would you do me a favor, James?" Jean poses softly.

"Okay, what is it?"

Jean sighs, wondering how to phrase her needs. "I know you enjoy driving fast, but I want you to remember to slow down and be careful, that's all. Please?"

James lays his arm across the now cleared empty table and stretches his hand, palm up, over to Jean. He looks into her eyes with an unspoken invitation to take his hand. She grins, laying her small hand in the open large palm. He wraps his fingers around hers. "I promise I'll try. Now are you ready for a movie?" James invites.

"Always."

No part of the evening feels awkward or forced. The pair carries on conversations easily without having to think ahead, laughing freely at each other's jokes. By the end of the movie, James feels at ease reaching over the middle of the long car seat to take her hand. Lacing her fingers with his, Jean looks up into his eyes. Within the same moment, they both can feel their hearts start to pound within their own chests. Blood rushes through their veins and pounds inside their ears. James gives Jean's hand the slightest squeeze. He invites her with a gentle pull of her hand to come closer. Moving subtly to the middle of the seat, James releases his hand to wrap around the back of her shoulders and cradle her upper arm. Jean leans in to rest her head at the crook of his neck, pretending to gaze up at the drive-in screen. James presses his cheek to the top of her smooth black hair. Slowly, he eases the angle of his nose down gradually to smell her scent, closing his eyes on the inhalation.

In an attempt to slow down his racing heartbeat, James internally decides to try to concentrate on the film in front of his eyes. The movie is highly entertaining, but the screen is a blur as he tries to keep a sense of stability in focus. James understands Jean embraces propriety, refusing to push too far.

During the ride to Jean's home after the movie, James holds her hand, often stealing glances of her profile during the drive. They arrive at Jean's house. James opens the car door for her, assisting with balance while she exits. He holds one hand to escort her up to the porch, but short of it, he turns to face Jean and takes both her hands. "Jean, you know how deeply I care for you. Since the first time I heard you and saw your face, I felt something I don't even know how to describe. I wanted to know if you'd go steady with me?"

Jean blushes as she looks down at her fingers enclosed in his rough hands, feeling warm, protected, and at peace. James graciously soothes her cold hands, raising them up to gently kiss the top of each one. She is overwhelmed by the massive evolution in character he has seemingly made and is humbled he would even try. "Of course I will, James," Jean answers, seeing James sigh in relief. "I do feel what you're feeling too, but I want to be sure we always put our friendship first. You've become my closest friend, James, and I think we should remember that's where we started."

"You are absolutely right."

"I've really had the best time tonight. Thank you," Jean states with a soft coy smile.

"Thank *you*," he replies, squeezing her hands slightly with excitement. "Can I call you tomorrow?"

"Yes. I can't wait," Jean replies. "Good-bye for now." She gently pulls away while backing up to the door.

"Good night." James speaks softly.

"Good night." Jean steps inside the house, waving gently with a smile before closing the door.

James and Jean walk down the school hallway holding hands. News spreads quickly of their steady relationship, but the couple could not be happier. Lost in a different world, James sees no other girls in his mind nor is he interested in changing that vision. He spoils her with natural and unforced affections, reflective of the inner peace he feels in Jean's presence. Jean finds a new level of confidence from her relationship with James. She still values her alone time after school to remain true to her individuality and music while James continues employment at his father's store. He insists on driving her home after school before work every day.

"Jean, I have something to tell you. Exciting news, or at least I hope you will be excited," James announces as he escorts Jean to his car to take her home for the day.

"What is it, James?" She turns to face him with eager anticipation once they reach his Ford.

"I sent out a few applications to colleges a couple months ago, not really remembering I had until I heard back from one yesterday. It's the one place I never thought would take a look at me, but I suppose they must have liked my essays."

"That's great, James! Which school?"

"The Illinois Institute of Technology up in Chicago accepted me into their architecture program. I start this fall," James proclaims with a halfhearted grin.

"That's wonderful news! What a great school! Congratulations," Jean exclaims, jumping up to wrap her arms around his neck for a hug.

James's response is mixed. He gently holds her in his arms, uncertain she will understand his mood. Jean feels the unusual feather-light touch and releases her hold, pulling away to look into his eyes.

"What's wrong, James? I thought IIT was your dream."

"It is my dream. It has been for a long time. I mean, just the thought of surrounding myself with people who've worked with Mies van der Rohe would be surreal. I can't even wrap my head around it quite yet."

"Then what's wrong?"

"Jean, I…I'm just having a hard time also wrapping my head around not being with you every day. Not seeing your face, holding you in my arms." He brings her into his chest for an embrace. "I just can't even think about it," he says with a sigh.

Jean breaks away from his hold and looks him square in the eyes, slightly agitated. "Listen, James. This is what you've always wanted, and now it's what I want for you, too. You will never convince me that sticking around Decatur is what's best for you. Think about it, James. As long as you want me in your life, I will be here, but this is a once-in-a-lifetime shot. You have to take it because I don't want to see you waste your talent," Jean reaches up to take his face in her small hands. "God gave you these gifts. It's what you do with them that matters most. Please. For me." She lays down the full gaze of her ocean-blue eyes.

James lets out a sigh, feeling torn. He takes her hands from his face into his own. "I know you're right, Jean. I'm just…already dreading being away from you."

Jean moves back into his arms, squeezing him tight around the waist from her short stature. "I will miss you too, but we'll write and probably run up the phone bills on occasion. Plus, we still have all summer together."

James rubs her back with his large hands in soothing circles. She always makes him feel better, no matter what the circumstance. Jean's positive nature is a force of epic proportions.

✦⟋☙☙⟍✦

James and Jean are inseparable the entire months of June and July in 1967. For his nineteenth birthday, she throws him a small party with all his friends and family. When August hits, Jean helps James pick out items for his dormitory, East Hall, a newer residential building on campus. He is happy about his placement in East, having heard of opportunities for recreation and fitness offered through the IIT student groups. He predicts staying active will help him remain focused in school and distracted enough to bear being away from Jean.

The day James is set to leave for Chicago with his parents, Jean drives over to James's house off Sunnyside Road to bid him farewell. She maintains a happy face while tapping on the door, standing on the maroon-colored cement steps of their front

107

porch. James's mother answers the door. "Good morning, Jean," she greets with a smile, inviting her in with an open-hand gesture.

"Good morning. How are you today?" Jean replies courteously, walking through the door to the living room.

"I'm just fine, thank you. Although that's probably a better question for you. Are you all right?"

"It's a big day," Jean offers. "How is he?"

"Oh, he'll be fine. He's just being James. You know, trying to plan everything with too much attention to details at the moment," she states with a slight chuckle. "With the way he is, I have no doubt he will be successful in architecture, but goodness, he's stubborn." She leans in closer, bringing her voice down in volume. "It's that German blood from his father's side."

Jean lets a soft chuckle slip out her mouth.

"Jean, is that you?" James projects from his bedroom upstairs in the attic.

"Yes, I'm here."

"Mom, can Jean come up?"

"Sure," she replies, escorting Jean down the hallway to the steps.

Jean begins the steep ascent up the stairs to his bright-blue room with windows on both sides of the long space. The slanted ceiling carries one two-foot-wide flat panel at seven feet tall down the middle and angles downward on each side, stopping four feet in height to house a number of small closet doors for storage space. James frequently hits his head from his tall stature.

Jean reaches the top step. Flanking left, she sees three large unmatched suitcases. Across the awkward-shaped room, James sits at the end of his twin bed, hunched over with his face in his hands, one of which holds a white handkerchief. Jean feels her stomach twist, doubting her resolve to keep her composure together today.

"James," she breathes, walking swiftly across the hardwood floor to kneel down in front of him. Jean attempts to pull his hands from his face, but he will not budge or look up. He feels inferior, weak, and does not want her pity. "James, look at me," she pleads, touching his shoulders, then reaching to stroke the back of his neck. "Hey, look at me. Please? It's going to be all right. We will be just fine. I promise, you're not going to lose me. I'm sure we'll write to each other so often it will feel like no time apart at all. Okay?" Jean comforts him, stroking his hair away from his face. His glasses are off, lying on the bed at his side.

"I brought you something," Jean states, hoping to cheer him up. James sniffs, wipes his nose and eyes briefly with his handkerchief, and grabs his glasses. Jean looks down to grab her canvas purse wrapped around her shoulder; she reaches in to pull out a dark wooden frame. James places his black glasses on his face, making his puffy eyes look worse. "Remember those pictures my parents had taken of me for senior year?" Jean turns the frame around, revealing the headshot of her looking like she is painted directly on the canvas inside the glass. With a soft smile, her deep-blue blouse illuminates the bright eyes James loves underneath the gentle arch of her dark-brown brows. Her smooth and wavy brunette hair has a luminous shine, complementing the thin gold chain glowing around her neck like a subtle halo.

"It's beautiful, Jean. I couldn't have asked for a better gift. Thank you." James finally looks her in the eyes, slightly ashamed of the current state of his disposition. Always exuding confidence, Jean has never seen him in this manner before.

She reaches up, placing both her hands around his thin cheeks. "Nothing's going to change. I will wait for you, but this is your life now. You need to grab on to it and don't let go," Jean insists, keeping her willpower in complete check.

James closes his eyes and gently leans into her forehead, pausing there as he enjoys the last of their time. He rises slowly from the bed and takes hold of her hands. He pulls them around his waist and encircles her with his long arms, squeezing her frame with his strong hands. They hold each other, unmoving for ten minutes before James hears his father calling him to the car.

CHAPTER

6

ithin weeks of James's departure, Jean begins her senior year at Warrensburg-Latham High School. As a singer in the Glee Club, Jean's loveable personality is appreciated and respected among faculty and peers at school. She finds time to daydream, thinking of all the vast knowledge James is gaining at school, and is immensely happy for him. She vows never to write a letter when she is lonesome or pining for his return, realizing he feels bad already. However, in the multiple times she is tempted to write longingly, Jean turns to her music. On average, she learns one to three songs per week, depending on the difficulty level, but has an obligation to keep schoolwork a priority. Jean's parents feel she has varying abilities to warrant success in several career paths, wanting her to keep all desired pathways an option.

Eager to keep in touch, James writes Jean often during orientation week at IIT. Each correspondence he shares carries detail, conveying his yearning to be close and feel her in his arms. When fortunate, he sees Jean in his dreams at night.

Classes begin, and the course work is heavy. Architecture students are typically required to complete fifteen to eighteen hours within first semester on average. A monumental amount of time is work on projects in several areas of architecture studio, geometry, and freehand drawing. With James's inherent appetence to pay attention to details, he obsesses over perfection, with organization playing a key role in his every move. He never procrastinates on any assignment. Each minute of his day is perpetually calculated, including the allotted time he spends writing Jean. He allows his writing five minutes per day over three days, with three additional minutes each third day to address, stamp, and walk the letter downstairs to outgoing mail in his dormitory.

For an hour in the early evening every other day, James exercises alone or with friends outside in the nearby quads on campus. Through James's love of football, he gains friendships easily with other men in the architecture program and those in East Hall. His roommate and fellow architecture major, Gary, has a number of acquaintances from the engineering program through his high school best friend, also attending IIT. Gary's best friend brings them along for games. With the large group, it is easy for James to become distracted for over an hour every other day. He mingles with the same gentlemen on occasion during supper, if he sits down to eat a meal.

Jean begins school every morning chatting with her best friend, Julia. The previous year, the two met in social studies where Julia's sweet nature made Jean feel welcome. After spending time chatting at the bonfire, the two girlfriends quickly realized the commonality of their interests. Julia and Jean enjoy the same movies, music, and being entertained. It is a relief to have a wonderful friend in Julia to distract Jean in the spare moments of weakness, daydreaming about James. Julia and Jean are both positive deterrents for one another and, being musicians, support each other's interests. Upon Julia's insistence, Jean joined Glee Club.

On September 15, Jean sees Ms. Baldwin, her Glee Club teacher, approaching her in the hallway before school. "Good morning, Jean."

"Good morning, Ms. Baldwin. How are you?" Jean asks politely.

"Just peachy, dear. Thank you. I'm leading the committee of students in charge of this year's homecoming activities, and we were wondering if you would be interested in performing for the big football game. Just one song, singing and playing guitar during halftime, and I promise it doesn't have to be anything too stressful or fancy. Would you be interested? We hope you are because everyone just loves to hear you." Ms. Baldwin gently squeezes one side of Jean's shoulder with her hand, releasing a full grin to match the intensity of her desperate stare behind thick-framed glasses.

"What would you like me to sing?" Jean asks, hesitating.

"Well, our homecoming theme is 'Happy Together,' so we were hoping you could sing that by the T—"

"The Turtles, sure. Yes, I know that song."

"Oh, perfect!" Ms. Baldwin exclaims excitedly.

"Actually, that tune's easy enough. I could play it on my twelve-string. It only has four or five chords, and it would sound fuller on the field. Is that where I'm performing?" Jean is slightly shocked.

"Is that all right, dear?"

Jean swallows loudly, realizing her mouth is hanging open. "Um, sure. I'll have to alter the lyrics a little. I also need to be close enough to have amplification for my guitar and voice. I don't think I could carry the whole stadium, Ms. Baldwin."

"We will take care of you. Don't worry. It will be perfect! Thanks so much, Jean," she finishes, walking away to her classroom.

Jean turns to Julia with her mouth still gaping open. Julia is beaming at Jean with her large white teeth blinding her in the eyes. "Eek!" Julia exclaims, wrapping her arms around Jean. She shakes her side to side to break the shock.

"What...just happened?" Jean poses. Julia lets her escape from the bear hug.

"You're going to be the star of the show for homecoming, that's what just happened!" Julia pronounces aloud to her friend with pride.

"Oh my..." Jean is speechless.

"Come on, let's go to class," Julia gently pulls her along.

"Oh, that's great!" James reads the last paragraph from Jean's letter once again, just to be certain his eyes are telling his brain the correct information. He walks over to the wall calendar hanging in his dorm room, flips up the page, and zeroes in on October 4. Nothing is written down the day before or after the Saturday in question. As it stands one week away, he also has no projects due the following Monday through Wednesday. He is decided. Somehow, James will get home.

James starts with Gary, who is reading his *Introduction to Architecture* textbook on his bed. "Gary, do you know of anyone from Decatur in our program?"

Gary ponders. "Hmm, let me think. You know, possibly. I remember speaking with this guy who says his old man works at Caterpillar, I believe, but now I can't remember. Who was that?" Gary focuses.

"Please. Try to remember," James encourages.

"Yeah, let me run through the people in my classes a second in my head."

Thinking about seeing Jean, his stomach is already full of butterflies. James misses her entirely. To be able to make it Friday night to surprise her would be a dream.

"You know, I think I remember who it is now. He's in our drawing class. His name is Mike, I believe."

"Yeah, I know him. Shorter guy with dark hair, right?" James inquires.

"That's him," Gary replies.

"Great. Thank you." James articulates abundant fervor in his appreciative voice.

The next day, James enters his drawing class, scanning students to find the hopeful savior of his loneliness.

"Mike, right?" James stands behind his drawing easel.

"Yes, and you're James," he states, looking up from his desk.

"That's right. Hey, I hear you're from Decatur?"

"Yes, I am."

"I'm surprised we've never met. It seems like such a small place compared to Chicago." James offers his hand.

Mike takes his hand for a brief firm shake. "Yep, I'm still not used to the city. My father warned me it would be this way though. We moved to Decatur my sophomore year when he took the position with Caterpillar."

"Where did you go to high school then, St. Teresa?"

"Yes, sir." Mike nods with a proud edge in his character.

James suppresses a chuckle. "I was kicked out of St. Teresa after my freshman year, which is why we never met."

"What did you do?" Mike asks, looking humorously impressed. He has an understanding for the esteemed patience the nuns convey daily at St. Teresa.

"Let's just say they didn't appreciate some of my vocabulary. Specifically, the art teacher who didn't have any idea how to teach art. It's a long story, which I'd love to tell you sometime, but I need to ask you something else first, if that's all right."

"Okay. Shoot," Mike invites.

"Well, I was wondering whether you had a car on campus?" James inflects his tone, turning it into a question.

"Actually, I do. Can I help you get somewhere?"

"Well, it's a bit more complicated. Did you have plans to get back home soon?"

"Wow. Not really this soon, but I suppose I could be up for a road trip."

"Really? Would this coming weekend work? Could we leave Friday, early afternoon? It's homecoming, and I wanted to get back for the game."

"I'll check my calendar, but I'm sure that'd be fine. If your schedule's clear, then mine should be as well. Now that I think about it, St. Teresa should be having a small homecoming dinner planned as well. I remember my parents writing about it in a previous letter."

"Oh, good," James adds, relieved.

James starts to walk back to his desk when Mike stops him. "Hey, James?"

"Yeah?"

"This is about a girl, isn't it." Mike presents his question as a statement.

James smiles, allowing a quick muted sigh before answering, "It always is, isn't it?"

Mike grins back, shaking his head downward in response. "I guess you're right."

◦⟨⟩◦

"Jean, you look great," Julia states, brushing lint off the back of Jean's short sapphire jumper dress. In the ladies' restroom closest to the football field, Jean straightens the thin headband separating the bulk of her voluminous brown hair should the wind pick up while performing. Julia hands her the lipstick on the counter for a last touch-up. Looking in the mirror, Jean takes a deep breath and decides she is ready. She bends down to claim her twelve-string acoustic guitar by the neck and places the shoulder strap behind her head, heaving her hair from underneath it out of the way.

Jean turns to look at Julia. "How do I look?"

"Amazing, Jean. Truly great," Julia compliments, picking up Jean's black guitar case to carry to the field.

"Okay. Let's go."

Jean and Julia make their way to the track, spotting Ms. Baldwin waving her arms at Jean, slightly anxious and awkward. The football teams are still huddled in their two-minute warning time-out.

"What's she so nervous about? There's still two minutes left, which everyone knows could turn into ten minutes," Julia complains.

"That's Ms. Baldwin," Jean answers with a smile, still fifteen yards from the center field track.

Ms. Baldwin meets the two halfway. "Hello, ladies! Jean, we've got your amps, cords, and microphones all set right here. Everything's been checked to make sure it's just as we rehearsed this afternoon. Julia, thank you again for volunteering to help carry the microphones."

"No problem."

"It's too bad I don't have a patch in for this twelve-string, but I'm just lucky to have it at all. Dad bought it for himself but never learned to really play," Jean states casually while tuning the guitar one last time.

"You are going to sound perfect, just like you did this afternoon," Julia encourages.

"Thanks, Julia. You are a wonderful friend, and that's an understatement."

The two hug as the halftime horn blows from the press box. "Oh, it's time. Let's go," Ms. Baldwin states.

Jean, Julia, Ms. Baldwin, and two other homecoming committee students help move the equipment carefully out to the field. Jean finds her mark at the center fifty, turns, and plants her feet ten yards behind the front line. She deliberately avoids looking up, ignoring the audience in lieu of checking that everything is set up correctly.

"Jean, are you on? Can you hear?" Ms. Baldwin questions.

Jean plays a few chords, listening for the playback reverb from the bouncing acoustics of the stadium she became accustomed to earlier that afternoon.

"Test, test," she speaks into the microphone.

"I've got a thumbs-up from the press box, so they can hear you. Are you okay to start?" Ms. Baldwin inquires.

"Yes, I'm great. Thanks, everyone!" Jean whispers, setting her fingers for the first chord while her helpers scurry off the field.

The announcer in the press box introduces Jean. "In honor of Warrensburg's homecoming dance theme tomorrow night, we have a special guest to entertain us with the WLHS homecoming theme 'Happy Together' by the Turtles. Please give a warm Warrensburg welcome to our very own musician in residence, Jean!"

The crowd—filled with alumni, staff, and fellow students with their family members—erupts with applause for Jean. She looks up for the first time, finding her center of focus for the performance, and locks in just below the press box. Ignoring her audience, she begins the soft chords and starts singing with the substituted gender-neutral lyrics. "Imagine me and you, I do, I think about you day and night, it's only right, to think about the one you love and hold them tight, so happy together." Jean continues with the tune, focusing on the sound of the guitar below her fingers. The crowd is loud and supportive as several sing along during the chorus respectively. With the syncopated shuffle upstrokes, it is difficult to remain on task hearing the audience behind her pulse, but she is diligent in maintaining a steady tempo.

When the overlapping chorus is through, ending the song, the crowd explodes. A standing ovation takes over the bleachers. "Thank you so much!" Jean moves her guitar to her back, grabbing one of the two microphone stands, careful not to step or trip over the attached wire. She hands the heavy stand to Julia, who is beaming, as the two helpers run back to grab the other equipment.

"Jean, that was fantastic! It was perfect. How did you drown out all that noise?"

"I'm not sure, but I just had to." She walks back to the track, seeing Ms. Baldwin approach with gleaming exhilaration.

"Jean, that was simply phenomenal! What a great way to kick off our homecoming celebration. Thank you so much for playing. It sounded great!"

"Thank you for asking me, Ms. Baldwin. I really enjoyed it," Jean states with a smile.

She places her guitar back in the black case on the track but wipes it down to avoid condensation before closing the lid. Then Julia pulls her down the track, rushing now. "Julia, why are we walking so fast? Your legs are longer than mine, remember?"

Julia chuckles under her labored breath briefly. "I just remembered something, that's all."

"What is it?"

"Nothing. Well, not nothing, but I'll tell you soon."

"What? You've never kept one secret from me," Jean is slightly breathless, attempting to keep up with her through the crowd to the exit. "Julia, wait. Hang on a second. My parents gave me permission to watch the whole game. Why are we heading to the exit?"

"I just, uh, want to talk with you up here in private. That's all."

"Oh, okay." Jean looks down at the pavement as the crowd clears. No one is headed to the exit at the moment. The band is still setting up to perform on the field during the remainder of halftime. Julia stops and turns to speak to Jean.

"Jean, I've been keeping a secret from you. A big one," Julia admits.

"Oh, really? What is it, Julia? You can tell me anything."

Julia smiles, stealing a quick glance over Jean's shoulder.

"Hi, Jean," a deep voice booms from behind.

Jean freezes. Butterflies immediately fill her stomach from the sound of a voice she can recognize anywhere. Her breath catches, dragging loudly through her open mouth, as she turns to see James. He is wearing his letterman jacket, a maroon plaid shirt underneath, and jeans. She is unable to pinpoint why, but he looks different somehow in only two months apart.

"James? Oh, what a surprise!" Jean sets her guitar down swiftly and leaps into his arms. He wraps his hands around her torso, easily picking her off the ground.

"I've missed you so much, Jean. I'm so happy right now. You've no idea how amazing it feels to be here." James sets her back down on her feet.

"I think I know exactly how you feel." Embracing once again, James kisses the top of her head, overjoyed to hold Jean.

"Jean, you were sheer perfection tonight. Just incredible. I've never been so proud of anyone or anything in my life."

"I wish I'd known you were here."

"Do you? I wasn't sure if I'd ruin your concentration, and I didn't want to take the chance," James admits.

"I guess you're right, but I've just missed you and wouldn't have wanted to miss one more moment with you. How long have you been here?"

"I think we made record time. I've been here since about four thirty. I spent some time with my parents before coming tonight but let Julia know I was here before she left for the game earlier."

"Julia, you little stinker," Jean looks back at her friend.

"Sorry, honey. I was sworn to secrecy," Julia responds.

"Yes, don't blame her, Jean. I wanted your performance to be great, and it was better than I could have expected."

"Thank you for coming," Jean says.

"Well, you know what this means, Jean," Julia says.

"What?" Jean looks to her with a puzzled expression.

"You need a homecoming dress! Shopping tomorrow morning?"

"Julia, I don't expect James to go to our high school dance. He's in college now. I'm sure he doesn't want to—"

"I'd love to come to the dance with you. The chance to hold you all night is far too tempting to pass up," James states with a smile.

Jean's returning grin is like staring at the sun. "Really? You want to go?"

"Absolutely, I'd love to take you," James replies with a genuine and eager expression. "So long as you can handle my two left feet."

James and Jean gaze into each other's eyes, rememorizing each other's features in the light as the band finishes their half-time show.

⁂

"Now, you need to have her back by midnight, James," Jean's father reminds him.

"Yes, sir. Not one moment past, I promise," James vows, waiting expectantly on the front porch for Jean to appear. The front door opens, and James turns eagerly to look.

"All right, here she is," Jean's mother announces, walking through the doorframe with Jean following behind. The dress is a floor-length hunter green empire waist with slightly cuffed short sleeves in satin to contrast the chiffon overlay. Jean's hair is twisted up and tucked into itself in the back with wavy strands draping in front to outline each side of her face, and rhinestone bobby clips to keep the layers of her hair in place.

James catches his breath. "Jean, wow. Anything I say will be an understatement, but you look wonderful."

"Thank you." She coyly smiles.

"You two have a nice time." Her mother hands her the matching wrap to cover her arms and a small clutch purse full of makeup.

"Thank you," she kisses her mother on the cheek.

"Sir." James offers his hand to Jean's father as a farewell.

"Be careful," her father returns, shaking his hand firmly.

James assists Jean gently into the car and drives her to a quiet romantic restaurant for dinner just outside the perimeter of Decatur in Pana. James knew he would have privacy with Jean by picking a less popular location, but with excellent steaks, both enjoy the meal. After dinner, James drives directly to the high school.

"James, are you sure you want to go?" James escorts Jean up the walkway to the front doors of the gym. "I mean, I'm happy you're here, but—"

"Jean, you know I want to be where you are. Plus, I owe you a dance. I know being away from each other has been rough on both of us, so I think we deserve a little time celebrating being together. Not only that, but..." James stops just before reaching the double doors, pulling out a small delicate box from his pocket. "Happy birthday," he offers with a smile.

Jean's eyes light up at the words. In the midst of her celebrating James's return to see her, she nearly forgot the date altogether. "Oh my goodness, I totally forgot."

"You forgot it was your eighteenth birthday?"

"I did. I am completely hopeless," Jean adds with a worried half grin on her face.

"Not hopeless. Just selfless, which makes you more irresistible," he replies, stroking her soft cheek with his thumb. "I know it's not until tomorrow, but all through dinner and this morning during our walk through the park, I've wanted to give this to you. I just can't wait one more minute. Please, open it."

"Okay." She gently takes the white box from his hands. Jean slides the elastic golden bow from either side of the corners and opens the small lid.

"Do you like them?" James inquires, impatient for her response to the opal earrings encased in an intricate circle of tiny diamonds, set in gold casing.

"Oh, James. How beautiful. They're just gorgeous. I... I can't accept them though."

"Why ever not?"

"I know how hard you worked to buy these, that's why, and I will not allow you to throw your money at jewelry for me. It's unnecessary."

"Please accept these as a gift, Jean," James retorts, unleashing the weight of his gaze into her eyes. "Putting money toward a gift like this may not carry the same weight as you think. The money I've made means nothing to me, so please accept this for your birthday? I promise, the next one will be lighter," he offers with a crooked smile.

Jean deliberates for a moment, questioning if he truly means what he is pledging, dissecting his features. She decides he inevitably wants to believe what he says but is sure his good-hearted nature will never change. "Well then, thank you," she concedes, looking down with a subtle blush.

James removes the case from her open hands, placing the lid back on the box.

"What are you doing?"

"I figured you would want to save these for another day, so I was placing them back in my pocket for you." James halts his progress, seeing her horrified expression.

"Actually, I'd love to wear them now."

"All right." James removes the lid once again while Jean quickly swaps out her borrowed diamond earrings on loan from her mother with the new opals.

Once in place, Jean looks up. "Well, how do I look?"

James looks at her total face and beams from the emotions he feels for her in this moment. "You are always perfection to me. You look stunning," James compliments. He offers Jean his arm and escorts her inside the building.

The evening runs smoothly between the coronation and the band's energetic balance of ballads and fast songs. James and Jean never leave each other's side.

"All right, guys and gals, it's time for the band to wrap up, so we're down to the final few selections of the night. Before we play, we'd like to thank the Warrensburg-Latham homecoming committee for having us at tonight's dance," the band singer states enthusiastically. The crowd of students on the gym dance floor share applause for the cover band, including James and Jean. "We've had a great time playing for you. We're going to slow things down a little with a great tune called 'Cherish' by the Association. Hope you like it."

James takes Jean's waist as her hands lock around his neck. It takes little time for Jean to lose feeling in her arms due to James's height; instead, she opts to rest her hands on his biceps often. Holding each other close, the two share intense moments in their own world. James has a hard time hearing the music over his thoughts, let alone staying in time with it. Jean knows he will always have two left feet but feels his lack of coordination is part of his charm.

"Jean, when I saw you yesterday—" James starts, closing his eyes.

"Yes?" Jean removes her cheek from his tuxedo collar to look up.

"When I saw you playing last night, well, I'm not sure I can even describe what I was feeling, standing up there at the top of the bleachers. Seeing you felt like I could breathe again, and everything made sense. Life was in focus for me, and I felt like I was watching my future through you down there. I know I'm only nineteen, but I think smart people hold on to what they want and don't let go." James pans down to meet her gaze.

"What are you saying, James?"

"I'm saying I want you. Forever. I don't want to think about one second doubting my hold on you, so…" James takes a deep breath. "Will you marry me?"

Jean's heart skips an entire beat as the dancing ceases. Holding back the utter enthusiasm she feels inside, she miraculously manages to keep a clear head. "James, we're so young. I know you have plans to be an architect, and I want that for you more than anything."

"I want that too, Jean, but not as much as I want you. My whole heart is devoted to our future together. Being an architect would be nice, but my future means nothing without you in it. Nothing," James reassures, staring into her eyes.

"I don't know, James. What about our parents? What will they think?"

"Does it matter? I am more in love with you now after being apart than ever. My mother adores you, and you know every mother just tells their husband what to think in the end," James replies with a chuckle.

"That's true. My mother has talked my father out of some doozies."

"See? Please, Jean. It's all that I want. *You* are all I want. Please, marry me?"

Jean is still hesitant to accept, but her heart nearly explodes with joy. "Of course I'll marry you, James."

James beams with bountiful happiness before burying his face in her neck. Then he picks her up from underneath her arms and subtly sways her frame back and forth, nearly losing his unsure footing.

❦

"Good morning, Mom," James greets her happily, entering the kitchen to fetch a glass of milk. His mother stands in the kitchen in a pale-blue robe with her arms crossed, leaning against the side of the counter. She examines his face thoroughly, watching him move. James finishes his full glass of milk and rinses the glass out with water.

"Your breakfast is on the table." She nods toward the dining room as he glances over to see her face.

"Oh, you didn't have to make anything for me."

"I know, but I thought you could use a good meal after staying up last night. Plus, I don't get to cook for you much anymore."

James grabs the wooden frame of the chair, pulling it back. He sits down, looking over the meal containing cinnamon oatmeal, fresh cantaloupe, scrambled eggs, and orange juice. "Mom, this looks great. Thank you." James takes his spoon and digs into the oatmeal first.

"You're welcome. Well, tell me about last night. How was the dance?" She sits down across from James at the table.

"I had a really nice time. Jean looked beautiful as always. The dancing was bearable only because she was with me." James pauses briefly, allowing a slight chuckle. "She actually makes me feel like I can dance, like she personally gives me a sense of rhythm." James and his mother share a light laugh.

"Well, that's a relief. I'm afraid you are on the short end of your father's rhythm stick, if there even is one."

James quickly realizes the metaphor for his life in that moment before taking another bite: Jean makes him feel balanced, centered. He glares down at the white lace tablecloth for a number of moments.

"James? Anything you'd like to share with me?" James's mom questions with one raised eyebrow.

Shocked by his mother's perceptive nature, James finds reality quickly in time to answer her with his prepared response. He sets his spoon down into the bowl and looks up. "Mother, I've asked Jean to marry me, and she said yes," he states with complete confidence, still looking straight into her eyes.

Without dropping one beat of silence, James's mother smiles and stands, moving gently to take his hands in her own. A whole foot taller than her, James rises to accept his mother's congratulatory hug. She squeezes him tightly. "That is so wonderful, James. I really like Jean. She's absolutely perfect for you!"

"Thanks, Mom. It means so much to me that you approve." He loosens his hug.

"Approve of what?" James's father questions, entering the dining room unexpectedly. The expression on his face screams ill of his mood, no matter what the topic.

"Oh, nothing, dear," James's mother quickly replies. Sensing his mood, she did not want to bring up the news now.

"Horseshit! Tell me what's going on. Now."

"Dad, it's great news. Calm down," James replies gracefully.

"Don't you tell me to calm down. This is my house. My house, my rules! Tell me, or get out," he threatens.

James already feels his blood boiling. His forehead begins to crease. His father has taken this perfect morning and ruined it. Again. *How can one man be so angry?* James knows what he is doing, but he must keep his cool. Being just as stubborn as his father, there is only so much he can take before he explodes back. If he does, his dad wins. This is the game they have played since James was a boy, but back then James rarely escaped any of those situations without sustaining black-and-blue skin all over. His father found many excuses to beat him, all to no avail because James was an instigator. An ornery teenager even, but James is a man now, taller and stronger than his father. *I can't let him get to me.*

"James is right. It *is* great news," his mother states, trying to smooth out his cross temper.

James takes a moment to steady his breath with a sigh. "Dad, I love Jean more than anything. I asked her to marry me last night, and she has agreed to it," James delivers, standing up straighter.

"What did you do, son? Are you two in trouble? Huh?" His father starts crossing the dining room, preparing to come at James.

James knows what he is asking but is so shocked he would come to the conclusion that he cannot think straight momentarily. "No, nothing like that! Jean isn't like that at all. I love her, and she loves me. We just don't want to be apart. Isn't that enough?"

"It is enough. Enough to make you two wait until you're out of school at IIT. I'm not going to piss away all my money just for you to get sidetracked by some girl!"

"She isn't *some* girl. Jean's everything to me. Dad, haven't you noticed we've not argued once since I met her? She's the reason I've straightened myself out. Can't you see that?" James pleads with him through his eyes.

James's father misses one solitary moment, deliberating. "I can see that, son, but I will not invest in your education unless you wait until you're finished with school. You need to forget her for now. If it's meant to be, it'll be. Period."

James wants to hit his father, absolutely bash his face into the next room. Rather than do either, he steps around him to grab his keys to the Ford and books it outside to the car. He starts the Fairlane and peels out of his driveway. After the quick quarter mile to Highway 36, also known as Eldorado Street, he crosses the median bearing west, away from town. Heading this direction, his only goal is driving fast. With hardly anyone on the road on a Sunday morning, he is free. He pushes the pedal down as far as he can, reaching fifty miles per hour, then sixty. Quickly, the needle races up the speedometer. He breathes in a huff, beating the dashboard, the steering wheel, the seat, and the dash once more, injuring his hand. *I hate him! I hate him with all that I am! How could he do this to me? To us? I can't hurt her. I can't be without her. Dammit, why is he such a jerk?*

James contemplates his options. He sighs, attempting to bring his heart rate down. Realizing he is traveling ninety-five miles per hour, he thinks of Jean and slows down to sixty. Calming down, he ponders his actions. *Jean has to finish school this year. I'll try to ignore any wedding topics for as long as possible. I can keep myself busy at school, I'm certain. Jesus, I promised I'd see her before I left. I have to turn around. How will I face her now?*

At the next intersection U-turn, James slows down, putting on his left blinker to make the sharp turn in the opposite direction down the highway. Mike will be at his house to pick him up in just over an hour. James makes a left turn onto Wyckles Road from the highway. He passes farmland, flat wheat fields, and houses while en route to suburbia and Taylor Road. Suddenly, he is turning onto Doneta and Jean's driveway. She is already sitting on the porch, waiting. She smiles, beaming with excitement to see him. He turns off the engine while looking at her and sighs. He opens the door and steps out.

"I thought you'd never get here," Jean states with a genuine loving look while approaching.

"Yeah, sorry. My mom wanted to make me breakfast and chat."

"Well, that was nice. How's your mother?"

"She's great. Just misses me, I guess," James eyes a pebble on the ground, shoving his large hands in his jean pockets.

"She's not the only one." Jean shoves her hands in the tight opening under his arms. He stifles a brief chuckle, removing his hands from his pockets to hold her close.

"What's the matter?"

I'm doing a crappy job of this already. "Oh, I'm just sad to be leaving again. That's all."

"We'll see each other in a couple months, right? Thanksgiving, and then Christmas break will be here before you know it. You'll have so much time with me during your three weeks off, you'll be sick of me," she consoles, looking up at him with a witty grin.

James cannot stop his answering smile. He kisses her forehead and holds her tightly once more.

"I love you, James."

These words are like heaven to him, but he stifles his natural response, "Me too," and releases his hold. "I have to go. I haven't packed yet, and Mike will be at my house soon." He avoids looking at her disappointed face.

"W-well, okay, but my parents wanted to say hello to you. Can you stay one more minute?" Jean requests hesitantly, a look of confusion in her eyes.

"I'm sorry, Jean, but I can't keep Mike waiting. He went through the trouble of getting me here." James walks to the car door as Jean follows.

"Okay, have a safe trip."

"I will." He closes the door, starts the car, and rolls down the window. Jean reaches in for his hand, which he takes and quickly kisses. "Bye," he utters. James shifts to reverse and backs out of the drive.

"Bye," Jean responds softly while she waves. *Something's wrong. Very wrong.*

James returns home to pack. Mike cruises up the driveway just as James zips up his suitcase.

"Please don't worry about your father. I'll keep working on him," James's mother whispers to him in his attic bedroom.

"I know, Mom. I just don't want to hurt her. I'm sure she already senses a problem, but I care for her so much," James replies, sulking.

"Well, there's nothing to worry about then. You two will be just fine. I'm sure of it."

"Thanks, Mom. Sorry about this morning."

"It's not your fault. You did the right thing. Your father's a rare breed, James. He feels like he's got the best intentions, but he went about it the wrong way this morning. Don't worry. Everything's going to be just fine." James's mother speaks with confidence, patting his back. They exchange a final hug and descend the stairs.

James's father is waiting for him in the dining room. The two share a brief look, which James breaks away from first, turning toward the back door.

"Hey." His father speaks in a derogatory timbre. James hesitatingly turns back to his face. "You stay focused up there, you hear?"

"Yes, sir." James sighs.

"I don't want you coming back here until Christmas. We'll come up and get you."

"What about Thanksgiving?" James questions in shock.

"You don't need to be coming back those few days. Besides, I'm sure you'll have some studying to do for exams. Spend your time doing that instead."

James' mother opposes. "But, Hubert, I want to see my s—"

"*No* Thanksgiving!" He swiftly cuts her off in his loud tone with a chiseled look, gritting his teeth with downturned brows, creating a severe crease to his stone face. No one will dare argue with him now.

James sadly turns away from him and leaves. Defeated. Again.

CHAPTER

7

ean sits in her room at the desk, drafting a letter to James. Four days since he left, and she is feeling more lost than usual, trying to dissect the weight of the last twelve hours with him: a proposal followed by strange and distant behavior. *What could have happened at home?* Jean takes her pen and begins:

Dear James,   October 9, 1967

    I hope you were able to settle back into your dorm room quickly. It was such a surprise to see you. The best birthday gift anyone could ask for, truly.

    I noticed you were upset when you left. You know you can tell me anything, James. I won't judge you because I know your heart. Please, always tell me what is on your mind.

    I'll be here for you. Friends first, remember? I was just thinking about all our long talks in Fairview Park today. We could talk for hours about everything with ease.

    Please call or write soon. I miss you.

        All my love,
        Jean

Jean sits at her desk in a daze while peering down at the paper. Her eyes glaze over and blur. This is the shortest letter she has ever sent to James; it has also taken the longest amount of time to write. She feels a drop fall to her soft, smooth cheek, waking her from the trance. Realizing she is wasting time worrying about issues out of her control, Jean folds the letter, seals the envelope, and addresses it. She turns off her desk lamp and curls herself underneath the blankets of her twin bed.

James sits at his dormitory desk on Thanksgiving Day, debating the letter's content he is about to write to Jean. While attending school over the past month and a half, James has felt utmost inner turmoil, fearing Jean would side with his father's mandate and break up with him all together if she knew the truth. She supports his dreams so entirely and would never willingly detour him. Solemn and a serious case of depression is an understatement for his mood. James picks up the five letters she has sent since early October. He skims each one again, not needing to read as each one is memorized. *She knows. I'm doing a piss-poor job, even at over two hundred miles away.* He realizes his letters have conveyed little emotion and an exceeding amount of information on his studies. James focuses on his schoolwork at S. R. Crown Hall, drafting a massive design project for his Introduction to Architecture course due at the end of the semester. With it encompassing a majority of his time, he has barely a moment to complete the Freehand Drawing project due next week.

At present, he is thankful to be one of the few on campus working through the holiday, but he is also aching for Jean. He wants to pour his whole heart into the letter or reveal everything on the phone, but he is weak and refuses to cause her pain. Fearing the tone of her sweet voice could bring out the honesty he may not manage to control, he opts for writing another letter.

DEAR JEAN,   NOVEMBER 26, 1967

THANKS FOR YOUR LETTER THIS WEEK. I'M
SORRY I HAVEN'T BEEN ABLE TO WRITE AS MUCH
LATELY. I'VE BEEN WORKING REALLY HARD ON MY
PROJECTS, ALL DUE IN THE NEXT COUPLE WEEKS.
    I'M GLAD YOU AND JULIA HAVE BEEN HEADING
OUT FOR SOME FUN YOUR SENIOR YEAR. SHE'S
SO NICE, AND IT'S GREAT TO KNOW YOU HAVE A
FRIEND KEEPING YOU COMPANY WHILE I'M AWAY.
BE SAFE THOUGH.
    IT'S BEEN VERY QUIET ON CAMPUS THIS WEEK-
END. THE SNOW IS COMING DOWN STEADILY
HERE, AND I HOPE EVERYONE MAKES IT BACK TO
SCHOOL SAFELY ON SUNDAY. I WISH I COULD BE
THERE WITH YOU FOR THANKSGIVING. I MISS
YOU MORE THAN I CAN SAY. EVEN WHEN I'M IN
CLASS, NOT A MOMENT GOES BY I DON'T THINK
OF YOU, JEAN. I HOPE YOU KNOW HOW MUCH I
LOVE YOU.

    ALWAYS YOURS,
    JAMES

James tosses his pen onto the paper, feeling horrified at what
he is doing to Jean. Though every word is true in his letter, he
feels disgusted with the dishonesty of their engagement. *This is
what Jean wanted for me. I can do this. I'm not a quitter.* He folds
the letter and places it in the envelope to send off in the morning.

⁂

Christmas break arrives. James is relieved his parents reach campus to pick him up from his dormitory after completing his last
exam of the semester. Deep in the back of his mind, he thought
his father might decide to leave him but was certain his mother
would prevail in that argument after missing Thanksgiving.

Nervous about seeing Jean, James is uncertain he can remain unaffected by the weight of his father's words. He is unsure his father will allow him to see her without a hassle. James decides to wait out the long car ride before asking his mother's advice privately after dinner.

"Mom, I don't know what to do. I want to see Jean, but I'm afraid if I push it, Dad will go nuts and do something ridiculous," James whispers.

"I know. Let me think about this. He's headed to the store tomorrow morning. Why don't you call Jean to ask if you can see her while Dad's working? I'm certain he's working every day except Christmas. If he asks, I'll tell him I sent you out for something we needed."

"What would we need?"

"I'll think about it. Don't worry," James's mother whispers back soothingly.

James calls Jean the next morning to work out a schedule for visits. He avoids relaying his true apprehensions regarding his father but conveys the need to be home to help his mother with dinner each evening. Their first outing is to lunch and a movie.

"So I think I know the answer, but what was your favorite course this semester?" Jean is sitting across from James in a booth at his uncle's root beer stand and diner. Two empty plates lie smeared with leftover ketchup from the burger and fries meal for lunch. The clear soda bottles are nearly empty.

"Hmm, I actually enjoyed my drawing course more than I anticipated, but discovering all the history behind the world's architecture was extremely fascinating. I love history. In fact, if I were going to teach one subject, it would be that one."

"Why?" Jean questions, completely fixated on the blue eyes behind his thick-rim glasses.

"I suppose it's because the imagery in my head views each time frame with such detail that it creates a rise in me. It's like a movie playing up there. I'm excited by what I see," James responds. "Is that what you thought I would say?"

"Actually, not at all, but I'm glad I asked. I never thought about history that way." Jean smiles coyly behind her hands, now folded in front of her mouth on top of the table. James stares at the small fingers covering her lips. Moments of silence pass before Jean captures his attention. Without hesitation, she rests her hand down on the diner table, inviting him to accept. James follows the length of her arm up and swallows loudly to himself, debating the turmoil of what he feels versus what he knows is right. Jean reads his reluctance clearly before he swiftly takes her hand. At first, she feels relief. His skin is warm to the touch, but within seconds, Jean recognizes something she does not expect: a hollow and empty sensation of nothingness. The weight of the void crushes her inside. Anxiety then panic sends her mind racing. *Is it the pressure of classes? Has he really matured that much in five months? Maybe he doesn't want to be in a relationship right now. Or what if he's met someone else?* The next pull of air drags across her open mouth, catching tension in her gasp.

James sees her questioning eyes, and before she can muster up the courage, he pursues the opportunity for evasion. "Jean, my mother asked me to pick up something from the store before I head home. If I'm going to be back by dinner, we'd better go to the movie so I can get you home."

"Oh. Uh, sure," she replies, still taken aback by her revelation. "I'll get my coat." Jean takes the black peacoat at her side on the bench and stands, fidgeting with the sleeves as she finally pushes both arms through. With her back to James, the three large black buttons in front seem harder to handle than usual. Her hands start trembling violently enough to incapacitate her ability to maneuver. *Keep it together, Jean.* She lets out a deep puff of air and slides the last button through the hole, finally, and turns to face James with a smile. "Ready!"

James shows an involuntary half smile upon seeing her glowing cheerfulness, but grinds his teeth while turning to escort her toward the exit of the diner.

⚬⚭⚬

Just days prior to Christmas, it is surprisingly mild in temperature, allowing James the opportunity to drive the Fairlane after months without a car. Most midday outings with Jean consist of long drives while listening to music together. Seeing her only part of the day provides James a chance to regroup emotionally following hours spent exerting the energy to keep his distance.

Jean's older sisters require a majority of her parents' finances with both away in college, leaving Jean carless and without the ability to close the gap to James. Though her sisters are home for the holiday, the two conveniently claim a stake on their vehicles, catching up with old friends. Jean is accustomed to the distance apart, but it continues to place a heavy burden on her heart. James is everything she wants, but she feels genuinely helpless for the first time in her life. The independent spirit she once relished is compromised now as his hold permeates with a constant pull of gravity. Anxiety rips through her chest, seeping in at night when the hour is too late to practice her guitar. The calluses on her fingertips have never been thicker, but playing is her most important ally and friend post daily time spent with James. However, in the midst of her agony, Jean succeeds in outlining two original tunes for which she has no lyrics. She is optimistic words will come to her later and thankful for breaking down the barrier of her own creativity block for the first time.

Christmas Eve consists of time with close family at home. James feels encouraged by his father's good mood as it is his favorite holiday. The family attends midnight mass at St. Patrick's Catholic Church. James sits with his eyes closed for a bulk of the mass, reflecting on Jean's face. Agony for what he may lose hits him like a sledgehammer.

"Come on, James. Snap out of it," James's brother addresses, poking him to leave the pew for communion.

"Oh, sorry," James apologizes, rising from his knees. He proceeds to exit the row.

"You okay?"

"Yeah, sure," James whispers back, interlacing his fingers as he approaches the front of the sanctuary and priest. James and his brother, Eugene, are not close nor do the two share personal information with one another. James's ability to seriously taunt and torment his little brother from such a young age was consistent enough to cause a large rift between them. Eugene still feels slighted and understandably has a hard time forgiving his older brother's ornery behavior toward him. The brothers never shared a room growing up, so talking was always minimal. Lately, Eugene is stupefied by the absence of the usual attempts to humiliate or get him into trouble. He knows something is off but does not want nor care to pry.

"The body of Christ," the priest announces, holding up the host in front of James's face.

"Amen," he speaks automatically, opening his mouth to receive communion on his tongue. As James walks away, his head droops to gaze at the floor of the church.

After the service, the family rises after a mere seven hours of sleep, waking to open gifts and prepare for extended family in their home. James calls Jean after dinner.

"I know I made you promise not to get me anything for Christmas, but I have something for you," Jean claims over the phone.

"Jean, you weren't supposed to get me anything." He feels excessively awful at his thoughtlessness for at least not purchasing a Christmas card.

"I didn't!"

"What?" James is confused.

"I have something for you. Something I wrote. A song."

"You wrote a song?"

"Yes."

"Jean, that's amazing! I can't wait to hear it."

"Well, wait no more. I'm going to play it for you today since I can't see you."

"Oh. All right."

"Now it's not finished yet. I haven't got the lyrics down, but I'm working on it. This is for you. Merry Christmas."

"For me?" James's heart sinks down to his stomach.

"Yes, I hope you like it. I'm going to set the phone close to the sound hole so you can hear. Okay?"

"Okay." James breathes, hearing the receiver cord stretch over to where Jean sits with her guitar. He listens as she pauses briefly and begins. The first three notes start a beautiful melodic phrase on an offbeat in an arpeggio of glide picking, then a downward strum to accompany the first statement. The melody is intricately interlaced with each strum in a slow duple pattern and a simple descending bass line chord structure to warrant a sense of peace to the listener. She repeats the refrain at the top before changing direction for a short bridge, building tension and volume before the return of her gorgeous refrain once again. The last six notes are an elongated version of the melody played gently as overtones at the higher fret lines. The last harmonics resonate in a major triad, fading gently into the air over the phone.

James is speechless. Jean's song is easily the most beautiful piece of music he has ever heard. He feels a sudden thickness in his throat.

Jean picks up the receiver. "Well, what do you think?"

"Jean…I-I don't even know what to say," James breathes into the phone. "It's…really great. I can't even do it justice with words."

"You really like it?"

"I love it. Thank you so much."

"Good. That's all I wanted." Jean is genuinely pleased he is happy.

James feels the guilt run thick in his chest. His sense of evasion starts to kick him. "Jean, I'm sorry, but I have to go. We still have company downstairs."

"Oh, okay. Well, Merry Christmas, James," she offers calmly; the ache in her chest begins to creep up.

"Merry Christmas, Jean. I'll see you soon, and thank you, again."

"You're welcome. Love you."

"M-Me too. Good night."

"Good night," Jean returns hesitantly.

Both of them slowly hang up the phone in a state of shock.

Why didn't he say it? He always says it. "Me too?" I don't understand. Jean's mind races with all the possibilities she has gone over numerous times already.

James is likewise disturbed by his response. *Me too? What was I thinking? Why wouldn't I say it? Why* couldn't *I say it? She has to know something's wrong. What an idiot!* James sits on his bed upstairs, head in his hands for over ten minutes, letting each note of Jean's melody marinate in his head. Reflecting every sound he loves, he tries to not let the thickness in his throat win out tonight. Sighing, he stands and heads downstairs, floating through space along the way.

The next morning flows past nine o'clock without a phone call from James. Jean waits until ten and picks up her phone.

"Hello?"

"Oh, good morning! This is Jean."

"Hi, Jean. How are you this morning?" James's mother replies kindly.

"I'm doing really well. Thank you!"

"Did you have a nice Christmas?"

"I did. It was a little crowded in the house for the first time in a while, but everyone got along at least," Jean answers humorously.

"Oh, well, I guess that's good," she replies, gently laughing with Jean.

"Is James okay? He usually calls by now."

"You know, I haven't seen him come down just yet this morning. Why don't I go check on him?"

"Okay, thank you," she responds graciously. Jean waits for his mother to return to the phone, running her fingertips across the wooden desk in her room.

"Jean?"

"Yes?"

"I'm sorry, Jean, but he says he's not feeling well today. Says he thinks it's all the holiday food, but he's held up in his room right now."

"Oh, that's awful. Would you tell him I'm sorry he's not well? And to drink plenty of water and call when he feels better?"

"Sure. That's very sweet of you," his mother replies. "I'm sure he'll feel better tomorrow."

"All right, thank you."

"Have a nice day, Jean."

"You too. Good-bye!"

"Good-bye."

Jean has only known James to be sick one time in high school. He is rarely ill but knows the symptoms may last for days if it is stomach related. Jean is having serious cabin fever after the long holiday with family in the house. She needs to get out, if even for a walk. She picks up the phone and whips the circle dial around quickly seven times.

"Hello?"

"Hey, Julia. Can I come over?" Jean feels like she is drowning, asking her best friend to throw her a life preserver.

"Sure. You want me to meet you halfway off Taylor?" A savior; Jean is relieved.

"Yeah, that'd be great. Let's go for a walk too."

"Great, I've had way too much to eat the last two days." Julia chuckles into the phone.

"Same here," Jean concedes. "I'll throw on my tennis shoes and leave in about five minutes."

"See you soon." Julia departs.

The two friends share a pleasant three-mile walk in sunshine and forty-degree temperatures, conversing for over an hour, but return home when thick clouds quickly cover up the blue sky. Rain falls the remainder of the evening.

Early the next morning, the temperature suddenly drops in Decatur. The rain turns to sleet then into unrelenting giant snow-flakes before five o'clock. The snow piles up quickly. James turns on the radio to hear the weather report when he awakes. A massive snowstorm is sweeping down from the north over central Illinois. The motion of the storm is due to circle back up in a westward motion, centering itself in mass over much of the entire state, nearly the shape of a hurricane. The weatherman is predicting two to three feet of accumulation. James is due to call Jean around nine, but before he can, the phone lines stop working. Frustrated, he retreats to his room. He could risk driving over to her house, but his father would be furious if his car got stuck in the snow going to see Jean.

He heads across his attic room to his record player. *This is probably my penance for lying about being sick yesterday. Now I won't be able to see her for days.* He opens the lid and carefully drops the Doors onto the turntable. After he gently places the needle on the outside, "Break on Through (to the Other Side)" starts up. James escapes over to his desk, grabbing his whittling knife to continue detail on a crucifix he started when he returned home. With his feet, he slides his small tin trash can over to the side of his bed and sits down. He begins work on the shrouding cloth draped over the sides of the cross, puffing out air in frustration. *What the hell is wrong with me? Why didn't I want to see her? She wrote a song for me, and avoiding her is how I repay her? I'm no good. I'm never gonna be good enough for her.* His knife digs into the wood roughly now as he moves his blade quickly to etch out pleats in the shroud.

"Ouch! Son of a—!" he yells after skimming the top of his thumb with the blade, cutting it open. He swiftly walks across the room to his bathroom and runs ice-cold water over the wound in the sink. The blood stops running within minutes.

After thirty-six hours of straight snow, James, Eugene, and their father venture outside to start shoveling the three feet of accumulation from the driveway. James's father is homebound from working at his convenience store for three days until the clearing crews finally make it to Sunnyside. He orders his sons to work with him in the store on New Year's Eve to help with the backed-up restocking work from the weather closure.

The snowstorm disables phone services for five days, right up to New Year's Day. James is pleased to pick up the phone at nine o'clock and dial Jean's number for the first time since the snow hit. It rings longer than usual.

"Hello?"

"Jean?"

"No, this is Elaine."

"Oh, I'm sorry. You all sound so much alike," James comments.

"It's okay. People say that all the time," Elaine offers.

"Is Jean home?"

"Yes, she's here, but let me see if she can come to the phone. Just one minute, please."

"Sure." He wonders if Jean had the same problems with their phones since her neighborhood is across town. *Surely her phone was down too.*

"H-hello?" The voice at the other end is unclear and weak, barely recognizable to James and his acute understanding of Jean's vocal timbre.

"Jean? Are you all right?"

Jean pauses briefly in response to what she hears. "Oh. Sure, I'm okay." Jean tries to sound positive.

"Jean, you're not well. What's wrong?"

"It's nothing." Jean attempts clearing her throat. "I just, uh, haven't been sleeping well, and it's all just starting to catch up to me. That's all." She brushes it off, trying to sound more awake and cheerful. "How are you? Are you feeling better?" her voice manages to croak out.

"Oh, yeah, I was fine. I picked up the phone to call you that next day, but the lines were already dead. I'm really sorry," he says solemnly.

"James, I'm just so relieved you're okay. I considered hiring snow dogs to pull me over there to check on you. I was thinking the worst with your sickness and the storm, having nightmares about your parents not being able to get you to a hospital. Awful dreams."

"Aw, Jean, I'm sorry. I feel so bad. Are you going to be okay? Is your mom home to take care of you? Are your sisters helping?"

"I'm okay."

"You always say that."

"I know, but I am. I'll be fine, especially now that I know you're well," Jean admits.

James sighs in agony over what his lying has done to her now. He hates himself. "Jean, my father won't let me take my car out yet. He says it's still too dangerous to drive around the outer edges of town. I even offered to take Pershing Road over instead, but he got angry I even mentioned it. I'm afraid it may be a couple days before I can head out. He's been asking for help at the store as well."

"That's all right, James. It's not like we haven't been apart before. Just hearing your voice makes me stronger. I'm feeling better already," Jean says with a smile. "I'll be looking forward to seeing you in a few days though. In the meantime, we can still chat over the phone, right?"

"Sure," James replies.

"By the way, Happy New Year."

James lets out a puff in a smile, recalling how good Jean is at distractions, taking the attention away from herself when possible. "Happy New Year to you, Jean."

The couple catches up over the phone for an hour, relaying Christmas activities and New Year's plans with family.

James succumbs to his father's demands, working with him at the store the next two days. After a long afternoon at the store, James helps his mother with dinner while his father listens to the radio in his living room chair. They overhear the radio broadcaster reminding listeners about the Chicago blizzard just less than one year ago, dumping twenty-three inches of snow in roughly thirty-five hours. Businesses shut down for days, roofs collapsed, and some parts of the city were unreachable for an entire week.

"You get your ass packed and ready by Tuesday, you hear? I'm not taking any chances that you'll get stuck here in another snowstorm. We're taking you back early!" James's father yells toward him in the dining room while he sets the table for dinner.

"Dad, that's almost an entire week early. Please, can't I—" James is interrupted.

"You be ready by oh-six-hundred hours. Are we clear?" His father is aggressively stern from his favorite chair in the family room.

After a slight pause, James responds, "Yes, sir."

James understands his father's concern but senses that a storm like that rarely happens two years in a row. His return to IIT was set for Saturday the thirteenth, but he will have to return five days early now. Regardless, he has no other choice.

Decatur's weather takes a stable turn for better the following morning. In beautiful sunshine on January fourth, James is
ecstatic to be driving to get Jean after nearly two weeks of not
seeing her face. Though the cold is relentlessly brutal, the feel
of the steering wheel under his gloves creates warmth inside his
body. He makes the turn onto her driveway from Doneta, but
before he cuts the engine, Jean is making a short sprint for his
car from the shoveled walkway, wearing only her bell-bottoms, a
long-sleeved red sweater, and shoes. Her peacoat is absent. James
steps out of the Fairlane. "Jean, what are you doing? It's freezing!"

Beaming, she does not slow down but responds with a bear
hug, wrapping her arms over the top of his shoulders and around
his neck. Up on the tips of her toes, she squeezes him hard and
buries her face in his neck. "I've missed you," she whispers, still
hoarse from her lingering sinus cold.

"Mmm." James squeezes her tight, touching her dark hair
covering half of her back, smoothing it out of the way. "I've
missed you too," he returns. After several moments in his strong
embrace, she is barely touching the ground. "Let's get you inside
and warm." James sweeps Jean off the pavement, cradling his left
arm around her back with the other under her knees. She leaves
her arms around his neck while he walks toward the house.

James opens the door with the hand under Jean's knees, steps
over the threshold, and looks around into the quiet family room.
"Where is everyone?" He shuts the door behind him and looks
at Jean.

"Mom and Dad are working, and my older sisters took my
brother shopping."

"All alone?" James asks, shocked.

"For a while at least," Jean responds with a smile.

"Hmm, that's a first in a long time."

"Nice, isn't it?"

"Very," he says, moving toward the hallway to her room. With Jean still in his arms, he sidesteps down the narrow path to her bedroom, weaving inside the doorframe to the bed. He sets her gently onto her twin bed's comforter. She gazes up at him, waiting. "You should at least lie down while I'm visiting. You're still sick."

"I know, but would you lie next to me? Please?" Her eyes are still puffy with a subtle shade of mending circles underneath— sincerity in her plea.

"If there's room, I guess." James removes his letterman jacket and drapes it over the back of her wooden desk chair.

"Of course there's room, see?" Jean's petite frame takes up such a minimal portion of the bed as she lies on her side. James removes his boots and lies on his side, directly facing Jean. He folds his glasses before resting his head on her pillow then uses his right hand to help warm Jean, running it up and down her arm.

"That feels nice. Thank you."

"You shouldn't have run outside," James comments.

"It was worth it." Jean closes her eyes and exhales in a sigh, opening her lids slowly. James is staring straight into her blue eyes as he strokes her shoulder. Within the same second, the two realize what possibilities being alone might bring in this opportune time. Jean's heart starts to race when James stops moving his hand on her arm. His heart thuds in his ears. He moves his hand to the top of her head, tracing one finger along her long silky black bangs to gently pull the strands behind her ear. The feeling of his touch sends a shiver down Jean's spine. James takes the hair curled up in front of her shoulder and softly pulls it all back behind her neck, revealing the skin above her sweater line. James tenderly strokes her cheekbone with the back of his hand then cups his palm to softly shape to her face, gently using his thumb to caress the skin back and forth. Then he minutely moves his cupped hand down her face to her lips. Jean's breath drags through her mouth on the inhalation. She feels her bones tighten rigidly, but the muscles around them are on fire. Heat radiates through her whole body, feeling alive in unexpected places. The adrenaline races through her blood while James drags his thumb side to side along her full lower lip. Jean waits eagerly for his next move. She feels ready for whatever it might be as she gazes intensely into his eyes. She kisses his thumb slowly and gently, cupping her small hand atop his.

Does he know how much I love him? At times, she feels her heart is etched permanently onto her sleeve with neon signs pointing straight at the target. The moment she opened her heart to his love, her whole interior makeup changed. She did not abandon her will, independence, or individuality, but rather made an investment in a common and collective happiness, risking the possibility of adverse results at times. She is fully willing to accept those unfavorable conditions knowing she sees James not as the man she wants him to be, but instead as the man he envisions himself to become. Selfless love. Optimistic love. Jean's love.

God, I want to kiss her. I want to feel her against me. He nearly allows his actions to follow through before remembering what he must tell her today. James looks down on his inhale, stopping his hand in movement, then sighs while pulling away.

"What's wrong?" She questions, hurt.

"Jean, there's something I need to tell you. I know you'll be upset just like me."

Jean feels it coming; the kick to her gut cuts off all heat. Her body thaws suddenly, feeling the chill return from being outside. "What is it, James?"

He sits up on the bed, placing his feet on the floor away from Jean. "My dad wants to take me back to school early."

"How early?" She sits up on the bed.

James turns to face her. "I only have four days left. We leave first thing Tuesday morning."

Jean quickly calculates in her head. "Why? That's five days early."

"I know, but he's afraid Chicago will get hit with another blizzard and that I'll miss school if I'm not up there. You know there's no point to arguing with him."

"And there's not even talk of another blizzard on the news. Why can't he just wait to see what the weather will be?"

"He has to take off work, and Tuesday is the best day with the help he has to cover the store. And to top it off, he wants me to work at least one day before I go to help make up for his absence all day Tuesday."

Jean's head drops down, remembering she also starts back to school Monday as well. "So three days. That's all we have."

"Yes. I'm sorry."

Jean processes the information. "James, it's not your fault. We'll just have to make the best of it."

James shakes his head. "How do you do that?"

"Do what?" Jean asks in disbelief.

"Turn everything into sunshine and roses so quickly. We've spent almost this entire break apart, and you've already accepted the few days we have left." James is slightly annoyed with her ability to make light of every bad situation. "How do you do that? Because all I feel is misery right now."

"James." She places her hand over the top of his, immediately releasing his anger but revealing his sadness. "Are you pouting now?" She is shocked by the look on his face and somewhat amused. She smiles with a gentle scoff exactly when James turns to look. Now truly angry, he grabs his glasses and gets up from the bed. "James, relax. It's nothing we can't handle."

He shoves his hands in his pockets and begins pacing the short distance of hardwood available in her room. "How do you know what I can or can't handle? I feel like I've been in a constant state of turmoil since I left for school. And being back with ten minutes between us, knowing I still can't see you, it's even worse!"

"James, what you're feeling is exactly how I feel when you're away. I feel almost sick to my stomach when we're not together.

It's hard just to breathe, but the time we are together makes it okay. I savor all those moments when I close my eyes and picture you in front of me. The hurting and yearning is part of being in love."

"Jean, I don't want to hurt you. I won't do that. I can't do this anymore. It's just too hard. I-I need you too much. I can't focus in school." Speaking before thinking again, he realizes he never should have let the last part slip out and puts his head in his hands.

Jean feels the pain reappear in her chest, fear ripping through her stomach lining. Tears build up behind her eyes, thinking about what she needs to say. "You…can't focus in school?"

"You're in my every thought, Jean. Please forget I even said anything about school. Okay?"

"James, I can't mess with your future." Tears cloud her eyes and pour down over her cheeks.

Dammit, why did I mention school? She'll never let this go. James crosses the floor to sit directly in front of her on the bed. He takes her shoulders with his large hands, attempting to gain her attention. "Jean, look at me."

She closes her eyes and shakes her head slowly to the side. She refuses to look for fear her willpower may break.

"Jean, please. Look at me." He places the side of his finger under her chin, pulling it up. "Please?" He takes both his hands to cradle her face, wiping away overflowing tears. Jean slowly opens her eyes, sniffing and struggling to look up. "Jean, you are my future. Don't ever think for one second that's not true."

"But, James, just like you don't want to hurt me, I won't ruin your chances of being an architect. Don't you see?"

"See what?"

"If we stay together, we're both at risk."

"But you just said it's normal to feel this way."

"I did, but if I have to let you go to help you stay on track, then it's the right decision for both of us. I can't be happy knowing you're struggling, and I won't let you quit, James. We were friends first, remember? I know we can be friends again until you're done. It will take the pressure off, and you won't feel stressed by our engagement."

"H-how…when did I say I was feeling stressed?"

"You didn't have to. I just got the sense I shouldn't mention it to you. I haven't said anything to my family either, so don't worry, they won't be angry with you."

"Jean. No," James says fervently, staring into her eyes. "I won't let you go. Please. Don't do this to us. I'd rather feel the ache knowing you're there than not at all." James takes her hands and laces their fingers together, squeezing them gently. He brings both her hands up to the side of his face, kissing each one lovingly.

Jean starts to lose her resolve and glances away. She feels the same but cannot take a chance he will leave school for her. "James, you know I love you. Nothing will change how we feel about each other, but this is the best thing for us right now. We'll keep in touch, just not as often."

"Jean, I can't do that."

"Yes, you can. Plus, you've been distant since October, and I know the opportunity to take something off your plate will help you."

"Jean, I'm so sorry. You're right, I've been such an idiot. I just didn't want to hurt you, and I've failed miserably."

"No, you haven't failed. It's just the way our timing pans out right now in our lives. We'll be okay."

James shakes his head, disbelieving how optimistic she is all the time. No matter what the circumstance, she carries her own weather always. "I believe you, but it's just hard to picture my life moving forward without knowing you'll be there. Tell me you'll wait, Jean. Be patient for me. I won't make it if I don't hear you say the words."

Jean takes one hand away from his, reaching up to stroke his face. "Of course I'll wait for you, James." His eyes leave the bed, trailing up to meet her gaze. His free hand takes the back of hers, cradling it to his face.

"Please wait," he pleads, kissing her wrist.

"I will," Jean responds with a gentle grin.

James works at his father's store the next day, hardly able to hold himself up and focus. He understands the newness of the situation still stings but wonders how long he can handle the torture and agony. *If I couldn't focus with her in my life at school, how in the hell am I gonna focus without her?*

Jean did her best to encourage him before leaving the house yesterday, reminding him of her decision to stay in Decatur and commute to Springfield's Lincoln Land Community College until she finalizes her field of interest. The fact she will be close to home did make him feel slightly at ease, but he feels it a waste of her intelligence and talent to be attending a college without declaring music as her major. It seems obvious to him.

"James, time to leave, son," his dad calls. He glances up at the clock. Somehow between restocking and cleaning, he lapses ten hours of time. In a state of catatonic floating, comparisons of shell shock and posttraumatic stress run through his mind, thinking about his uncle Bobby.

Bobby returned home from the Korean War without one leg, unable to speak or hear, and with persistent ticks in his hands. Memories of dying soldiers all around him perpetually replays in his mind. He never sleeps, but when he does, the nightmares release night sweats and yelling on occasion. When Bobby returned, the family learned of his involvement in the Yalu River disaster, led by General MacArthur himself. He was the only surviving man in his platoon when China surprised the troops in North Korea, pushing them back toward the south. James cannot manage to separate his own despair today with the images of his uncle sitting in the recliner chair at his aunt's house and unresponsive to anyone who has ever loved him. Bobby will never function in society again, but James feels sympathetically lethargic enough to understand why.

Jean continues work on the lyrics to the music she wrote for James on Saturday morning. It seems like therapy for her to be at the guitar; a creative pull is apparent when her emotions appear on the surface. She cries frequently as she works but does not stop long. She is thankful school begins Monday but is anxious about her last visit with James that evening. Dinner will be at James's choice of restaurant, Monical's Pizza. The alpha and omega of his choice location does cross her mind, but she refuses to think that way for too long. *It's not the end, just a different way of thinking of us for a while.* She tries to soothe herself. James requested that she play the song she wrote for him in person after dinner at Julia's, who is hosting a small party.

Later, James picks Jean up at six o'clock for dinner. He makes his way slowly to Monical's with soft music in the background and only a few words spoken the length of the drive. Jean knows she will have to help the evening along with some positive energy to cheer up James.

Dinner is relatively quiet with small talk about schedules for the semester at IIT and what Jean's first summer of general education classes might consist of at Lincoln Land. Neither of them eat well, with half an unfinished pizza placed in a box to leave in James's trunk during Julia's party. The temperatures will likely take care of freezing the pizza for James until he can retrieve it at home later, though he will likely forget it altogether.

The party is already in motion by the time James and Jean arrive in Julia's basement. Punch and other desserts lay spread out on a square table in the corner with older worn couches and chairs throughout the room. All the places to sit are occupied, but Jean places her guitar case in the corner along with her black coat. The two make their way around the room, saying hello to friends.

James is surprised to see an old football friend in the crowd he befriended his senior year, a sophomore student named Ben, who transferred from St. Teresa. A junior now, Ben's eyes have been on Julia since he started school at Warrensburg.

"Jean, can I hear it now?" James is standing closer than expected as she turns to face him. She looks up into his eyes, still distraught.

"Um, sure. I just didn't want to be intrusive," she replies softly.

"Well, do you think we could go upstairs?" Julia's parents knew she was having a party but trusted her enough to leave the house and keep their own plans. The evening is still young at seven thirty.

"Yeah, I suppose," Jean replies, grabbing her guitar case from under her coat.

"Julia, we're going to head upstairs. Be back down soon," she states in her ear. Julia nods back, continuing her chat with Ben on the couch.

Jean places her guitar case on the floor in front of the family room couch, opens the latches, and checks the tuning. She sits down and invites James to sit beside her on the sofa. She begins the arpeggio of the melody, strumming the first chords once again. Halfway through the tune, the lyrics she drafted come into her thoughts as she plays through the refrain. She can feel the tears betray her and boil up to the surface. Jean tries to concentrate on finishing, focusing on the floor and her guitar so he does not notice her emotion. As she strokes the last of the upper frets to ring the ending overtones, tears begin to roll down her cheeks. James is overly aware of her every emotion since she started playing. He moves both his hands up to caress her cheekbones, wiping the tears aside with his thumbs.

"Jean," he breathes. "We don't have to do this," he reminds her.

Jean sniffs, determined to refocus her efforts for him. "Yes, we do."

James takes the neck of the guitar and sets it carefully behind her on the couch. He takes both of her hands, tugging her gently to stand with him. Pulling her in close to his body, he wraps his long arms around her small frame. He kisses the top of her hair and forehead while stroking her wavy curls down her back. They remain in each other's arms much of the evening, losing all sense of time.

⁘⟐⟐⟐⁘

James arrives to school safely and is the first student to return to his dormitory. The sun is shining while his mother and father depart to Decatur. He shakes his head, watching them leave. *It's just as well. I'd have been no good at home anyhow.*

Once settled back into his dorm room, he drafts a letter to Jean. He stares blankly at the paper, thinking of the things he wants to write versus the words he knows he should not. The farthest he gets is *Dear Jean* when the limit of his concentration is met for the evening. Somehow, he will follow through on his letter, but distractions are his only friend. He desperately needs less time to think about Jean.

James stands, agitated. He grabs his coat off the door hanger and slams the door closed behind him, unsure of where he is heading.

He quickly descends the stairway and pivots for the dorm foyer. The community board on the first floor reveals a number of activities and organizations to join on campus. It also advertises available jobs. The first sign James sees is a recent bulletin right at the center of the board. "Radio station needs part-time assistance." James stares at the flyer stamped by the Student Life office the twenty-second of December and tears it gently from the corkboard.

The next morning, James calls the station, not expecting an answer, but is pleasantly surprised. James and the station manager strike up a conversation about the position available and set up an interview for the same morning. After a quick discussion on

154

his musical tastes and previous work experience, he hires James on the spot and asks him to begin the next day. He must catalogue every album owned by the station, along with new records arriving daily. Since the previous assistant left school due to failing grades, the station also needs someone to shelve every pulled record at the end of the day using the created system. Though it appears to be mindless work, James agrees it is the best distraction he could ask for while at school.

CHAPTER

8

"**O**h, darling, you look absolutely amazing!" Jean's mother says.

"Thank you, Mother. I'm relieved graduation day is finally here," Jean mutters softly, looking down at her deep rust-red robe.

"It seems like your senior year just flew right on by us, honey," Jean's father adds with a smile. He realizes he forgot to grab his Nikon camera in the house and turns to open the door from the porch.

"Hmm, yeah."

"Have you heard from James at all?" her mother asks softly.

"Oh. Um, no. He's had exams, so I guess I didn't expect to."

"But it would have been nice of him to call," Jean's mother says, irritated, while pinning Jean's cap to her hair.

"Oh, Mom, he's also got an internship this summer. I forgot to tell you about the letter from April." *The very short letter*, Jean revises in her head.

"Well, that's nice. He must be very busy then," she consoles.

"Right," she affirms with a forced energetic smile for her mother.

"Okay, I've got the camera now." Jean's father steps out the front door.

"And that should do it." Her mother finishes pushing in the last pin.

"Thank you." Jean is genuine, looking into her mother's eyes.

"You're very welcome, sweetheart. You look beautiful."

"Jean, stand there in front of the rosebush. Those yellow buds just opened from all this heat," her father explains, fanning a draft to the inside of his suit coat. She moves to stand in the thick grass, posing for her father. "Smile big, Jean! All right, one, two, and three." He clicks the button, snapping the shot. "Okay, let's get one more beside the new car with your mother."

The two move to stand beside Jean's graduation present, a 1967 Dodge Dart with freshly washed and polished maroon finish.

"Sweetie, did you remember to mail in your course work selections for school yesterday?" her mother asks.

"Yes, I actually did that a few days ago."

"I knew you wouldn't forget," her mother compliments.

Jean sighs quickly to herself while standing in front of the automobile purchased to assist her in the long trips to Springfield for classes. Thankfully, one of her general education classes is being held close by at Stephen-Decatur High School twice per week in the evening. Jean is grateful she will avoid traveling those nights at least. Though the community college is the best decision for declaring undecided, she hopes her time there is short. With ease in science through school, the course she is eager to begin is biochemistry.

"All right, one more now. And here we go." Jean's father pushes the button for the shot.

Over the summer, Jean spends an absorbent amount of time on her course work, finding biochemistry to be an area of strength as she hoped. Jean learns a new song every week with her guitar but feels hollow with the outcome of her practicing. Her attempts to stay busy are successful, trying hard to be distracted and void of alone time aside from her homework.

The first and only summer letter from James arrives in August. He describes his internship experience with the local Chicago architecture firm Skidmore, Owings & Merrill as affirmation for his path in life. The radio station he works for also asked him to return his sophomore year. Stating only factual information, she is sad the tone of his writing is bitterly cold. It overwhelms her as she memorizes every word, savoring their sour taste. Though she would prefer more contact, she is confident that letting him go remains the correct decision for his focus.

After classes begin for the fall term, Jean writes a letter to James in early September. She describes her new courses for the semester and shares her news of making it onto the summer honor roll with straight A's. With a rigorous regime of course work for fall, Jean conveys her exhaustion by the end of the day with lack of time for guitar and uncertainty of remaining on the honor roll. She asks whether he would be traveling home for Thanksgiving, hoping his father would be more reasonable this year. She expresses an interest to meet while he is home for Christmas, suggesting pizza.

However, winter break arrives before Jean hears back from James. She has spent a year running through their last conversation and embrace at Julia's house in her mind. He begged her to wait, and she will continue to keep her promise. Jean assumes James will be home near his arrival date from last year, but he never calls. She places weight in possible relatives visiting for the holidays or spending time with friends. Jean decides to be patient, thinking he will call after Christmas. Julia is also home from college and creates a positive distraction as Jean waits, but no attempts are made after Christmas either.

Finally, Jean feels the pressure of the clock, placing a call over to James's house on the twenty-seventh. The phone rings.

"Hello?"

"Oh, good morning. This is Jean,"

"Oh, hi, Jean! How are you, dear?" James's mother asks, surprised and encouraged by her voice.

"I'm doing all right. How are you?" Jean asks politely.

"We're all doing well here."

"Oh, that's a relief to hear. I'm sorry to bother you, but is James home?"

"Oh, sweetheart. You're not bothering me at all, but James is working at the store. He's been working for his dad every day since he returned."

"Oh, all right. I'm sorry. I didn't know," Jean replies somberly.

"Jean, it's quite all right. James got back from school and seemed quite anxious to help his father out while he was home. Said he wanted to make a little extra money. It's quite unusual for him, but I'm so glad to hear from you," James's mother adds sweetly.

"Well, thank you so much. Would you let him know I called?"

"I will."

"Thank you."

"You are more than welcome," she responds. "Good-bye."

"Good-bye," Jean says softly into the phone. She takes the receiver and gently hangs up the phone. *I'll give him a few days to respond.*

Four days later on New Year's Eve morning, Jean ventures over to the convenience store where James works. She closes the door to her Dart, takes a deep breath, and about-faces to walk across the small lot to the front entrance. Her heart is pounding as she pushes the door open and looks around.

"Jean?"

Jean's heart palpitates briefly, turning to look at James. "Hi," she breathes slowly, seeing his wide bright-blue eyes.

"How are you?" The two echo each other's question in unison. Gazing into the eyes neither have seen in almost a year to the day, it takes both of them moments to realize the humor in their duel exchange. They laugh aloud briefly at the same time.

"Um, sorry," James offers, looking away.

"Me, too," Jean replies, smiling.

James remembers where he is and quickly looks around for his father. Jean sees his head snap out of the seemingly blissful state and watches him walk across the tile floor to the coat hook. He swipes his heavy wool-lined bomber coat and heads back out the front door. Swift and aggressive, James strides around the side of the building, glancing back to check she is following closely behind. Abruptly, James turns to stare in her deep-blue eyes from his tall stature. "Jean, I'm sorry. I just don't want my dad to get on me about not working," he lies easily, looking down at the loose gravel at his feet.

"Oh, I understand, and I'm sorry to bother you at work. I'm just wondering…whether you got my message?"

James traces a path up to her eyes slowly. He lingers there for a moment and begins to fidget, pulling his hands from his bell-bottom jeans and up to his inner coat pocket, searching. He finds purchase on a silver Zippo lighter and package of Marlboro cigarettes in his pocket. Without hesitation, he removes one cigarette and taps it on the outside of the lighter before placing it between his lips. He flips open the Zippo, pushes down the flint wheel, and lights his cigarette, taking in a long drag. His posture relaxes as he breathes out the smoke along the side of the store's brick wall. He looks up at Jean, who is in shock with her mouth dropped open. "Yeah, I got your message. I've been working a bunch."

Jean is trying to find the words to respond but is unsure which issue she is to address first. "When did you start smoking?"

"Oh, uh…Yeah, everyone does it in Crown Hall while they're working, and I guess the guys at the station all sort of got me hooked on the habit now. It helps to relax me a little too."

Jean just nods in reply. "Do you feel it's really helping? I mean, is it a long-term solution?"

"I don't know, Jean. Why do you ask?" James is slightly agitated.

"Well, I don't think it's good for you," Jean replies, confident.

"You're probably right," James takes another long drag from the end, a marginal squint as he inhales. "Neither is drinking, but you know I do that too."

"James, I didn't mean to upset you, but why are you acting this way?"

"What way?"

"Are you mad at me? I thought we decided this was best for you right now."

"You decided, Jean. Not me."

She lets out a scoff, irritated. "James, I'm sorry. You know this has been hard for both of us. Why are you so angry?"

"I don't know, Jean. Maybe I'm just feeling...I don't know. Maybe I'm just not cut out for this long-distance stuff." James flounders, trying to sum up his emotions.

Jean is beside herself with what she is about to inquire. She has to swallow before she begins, drawing her eyes down. "Is there someone else, James?"

James freezes. He stares into her eyes with shock coating his entire face. He slowly assembles his words. "How...how co—"

"You know I'll understand if that's the case. It would be hard, but I'm willing to accept it, if that's what you want." Jean refuses to look at him as she finishes the last of her words, holding back tears.

"Jean," James replies, flowing through a state of disbelief then back to anger. "I'm not sure what to say, but so long as I'm doing everything else wrong, then yeah, there's someone else," James takes another puff.

Jean hears each word slowly process, thankful she did not lock her knees. The wind from her lungs evades her body. Her whole life represents a floundering, flopping, and gasping fish stolen from sea. She is speechless, unable to move her mouth or tongue.

"I guess we should figure this out before wasting more time waiting, right?" James questions.

Jean's body starts to tremble beneath her peacoat. A nervous wave of shaking consumes her body; she loses all concentration.

"Right, Jean?"

"Sh-sure," Jean stutters softly.

"Isn't there anything else you want to ask or say to me?"

Jean hears him but is unable to respond.

"Okay, Jean, I have to get back to work," James relays, flicking his burning cigarette to the side parking lot, away from the store.

James initiates steps forward, walking past Jean, but she stands motionless as he passes.

"James?" she calls out to him, still facing away.

He stops, turning to look at her long black hair. "Yes?"

"Is she good to you?" The tears are budding over her lower lids now.

James lets out a sigh, pausing to reflect his answer. "Yeah, she's nice to me."

Jean simply nods, acknowledging his reply.

"Good-bye, Jean." James turns to head back into the store.

After a few moments, Jean whispers, "Good-bye" with tears streaming down her cheeks. She floats toward her car in the shell of the body she has left and no memory of her ride home.

⋅⋙⊙⋘⋅

"Come on, man. You gotta snap out of it! Let's go out and have some fun," Gary insists.

"You've been cooped up in this room far too long, man," Mike adds.

"You stayed here spring break all by yourself, now enough's enough. Come on!"

James lies on his bed motionless, staring down the length of his dormitory wall. He sighs and brushes his bangs away from his glasses. He looks up at Mike, contemplating.

"A few guys are meeting up tonight. They say they've got a plan for some real fun around campus later. Are you in?" Mike questions.

"What kind of fun?" James inquires.

"Some bad fun," Gary lingers on *bad*, a mischievous grin creasing his face. James looks at Gary, debating the seriousness of his tone.

"All right, I'm in." James stands up from his bed.

"Yes!" Mike exclaims, patting James's arm.

"Yeah, man!" Gary yells, raising his hands for dual high fives. James is consumed by the energy of the room, releasing the slightest smile as he smacks both hands in the air.

"Let's go!" Mike adds.

The group of men head out the dorm and travel to several house parties along the perimeter of campus. The beverages flow endlessly past midnight and into the morning hours.

"All right, it hasn't rained in about two weeks. The ground should be dry enough to move the dirt easily," Steve claims in a whisper, still slightly inebriated from the seventh beer he finished two hours earlier. The young men comprised of Gary, Mike, James, Steve, and four of his pals from various fields of study continue walking an adjacent path across Wabash, carrying shovels and large steel cylinders. Steve sneaks closely to the buildings across the grass, staying off the pavement near Thirty-Third Street. The campus is quiet at two forty-five in the morning, and as the dew sets in for the chilly April morning, the men see breath in front of their faces. Steve stops at the edge of Wishnick Hall, holding up his hand for the men to halt. He pokes his head around the corner to scope out the view, checking for any people or movement. He narrows in on the object of his concentration behind Hermann Hall and waves the men forward across the lawn and sidewalk.

"Hey, Mike, you be on watch. Everyone else, start digging in the shape we talked about," Steve whispers. "Gary, you got the cables ready?"

"Yeah, these are steel, man. We're good," Gary responds.

"Hey, James, have that first cylinder ready to go," Steve states.

"Yeah, sure," James responds apathetically. He watches two of Steve's friends dig a trench at the base of the massive rock. The known IIT landmark weighs between two and four tons and is made of nickel and traces of gold.

"Man, just imagine the expression on people's faces when they see this thing's been moved. They'll think they've gone crazy," Gary remarks as he locks the cable hooks together around the diameter of the rock.

"Jesus, guys, whose plan was this? This is never gonna work without some steel boards to center the rock over these cylinders or a solid track system. You guys should've started digging back here and tipped it," James comments, tracing his eyes to the smoother back side of the rock.

"What are you talking about? We went over this, and it'll be fine," Steve replies to James. He watches them shape the trench. Seeing the dimensions in person immediately changes his perspective on the spatial logic the men spoke of two hours ago, which also happened to be the time frame the entire group was entirely too intoxicated to form a proper sentence.

"You know what, guys? I gotta go," James states, setting down the cylinder.

"What the hell, James?" Gary states in shock.

"Quiet. Keep it down," Mike whispers.

"Come on, man. We need you," Steve pleads.

"Yeah, we need you," the other men echo softly.

"No, sorry. I've got to go, and this is never gonna work," James says, walking away from the stone. He heads toward the Thirty-

Third Street pavement to head back to his residence hall. *What in the hell am I doing?*

James finally falls asleep around four in the morning. After merely six hours of rest, he wakes and heads to the library to finish work on his physics paper. He ventures along his usual route back down Thirty-Third. Passing between Wishnick and Siegel Halls, he decides to peer right to see if Steve's crew was smart enough to quit, but the view is blocked. A crowd stands around the massive rock's normal resting place behind Hermann Hall. James cuts north to check out the damage.

"What were they trying to do?" A female student asks her friend, walking away.

"Whatever it was, they failed. Miserably," her friend replies.

James arrives at the base of the rock, which is now submerged in the earth with approximately 75 percent of its original mass in the dirt. The loosely packed soil sits evenly spread around the new diameter of the rock. "Holy sh—" James catches himself, noticing several professors conversing close by the landmark. *Idiots. Complete idiots.* James walks on to finish his work for the day.

⚜

James glances at the address of the invitation in his hand before turning the handle of Mike's new 1969 Plymouth Road Runner, complete with a V8 426 HEMI.

"Man, I can't believe your parents just had this waiting for you when you got home from IIT for the summer," James comments as he slides into the seat.

"I know, man! I was totally shocked, but you know the car I had wasn't cutting it, getting back and forth to school," Mike replies, shifting the car to reverse in James's driveway.

"You are the luckiest SOB I know," James comments. "You know where you're going?"

"I think so. Isn't it over off Main Street, toward the university?"

"Yeah, I've got the address here, though I could probably get you there blindfolded, truth be told."

"I'm sure you could. I didn't know you even knew Ben while you were at Warrensburg," Mike initiates.

"Yeah, he came over from St. Teresa and joined the football team. I'm pretty sure *he* chose to leave that school, unlike myself, but it is a small world. Not many upperclassmen think it's cool to hang with people who are younger," James remarks.

"Yeah, well, he lived pretty close to me until his parents moved over this way. If you ask me, I think his parents hosed him out of affording tuition to St. Teresa by moving. Look at these houses!" Mike exclaims. "Did you hear Frank Wright apparently designed a couple homes a few miles east of here before he ditched the US for Europe?"

"Well, they're not sure he finished the sketches before he left, and there've been rumors that workers in his firm had to finish the designs and oversee construction when he left," James adds. "After all, it's been sixty years. People make up whatever stories they want to suit their needs," James observes. "Take a right up here. Then it's just on your left," he instructs.

"Okay." Mike accelerates to the house James pointed out. The line of cars takes up nearly the entire street.

"Jesus, did his parents invite the whole town of Decatur proper?" James inquires.

"Nope, just about half," Mike adds, smiling. "I guess you only graduate high school once," he says while parking behind the tenth car from Ben's house.

Mike and James head up to the front porch of Ben's home. Mike knocks on the door, fanning his button-down shirt a few times to create a slight breeze on the warm June afternoon. Ben's mother greets the young men at the door. "Hello, Mike. My, you've grown up so much. Seems like just yesterday you and Ben were good buddies playing together in the old neighborhood," she comments.

"Yeah, time flies."

"And, James, it's good to see you again. Ben is excited you decided to come today. Well, come on in. The party's actually 'round back. We've got a nice barbeque going, so I hope you two are hungry."

"Thanks, and yes, we are definitely hungry," Mike claims. They make their way through the living room and straight back through the kitchen. Before reaching the sliding glass door, Ben enters the house.

"Hey, guys! Thanks for coming," he welcomes, reaching for their hands to shake. "It's really good of you to come. My mom's all about the parties and insisted on having one, so thanks."

"No problem, bud. Congratulations," James responds.

"Yeah, congrats, man," Mike adds, hearing the sliding glass open once again.

"Elliot! Hey, what are you doing here?" James asks, laying his hand out for a shake. "It's good to see you."

"It's great to see you too. How've you been?" Elliot asks James. Ben slides out the back door with Mike.

"Oh, getting along just fine. You?" James inquires.

"Well, my girlfriend and I are doing all right. I'm sure your mother filled you in, but we're trying to get ready for the baby now. I had some help finding a solid job over at the Caterpillar factory, so at least we feel a little more prepared now."

"Well, that's something then. You gonna marry her?"

"Yeah, we'll be sending out invitations here in the next week. A small August wedding…Can't get any hotter than that!" Elliot lightly chuckles.

"Huh, well, congrats, buddy. I'm guessing you'll need to trade in the motorcycle for a family car then?"

"Ah, man. I'm waiting until the last second. I just can't even think about departing with the Suzuki. That Hustler is the best," Elliot reflects.

"Yeah, I enjoyed test-driving it those times myself." James smiles.

"All right. Well, let's get some food," Elliot suggests. James turns to follow him out the door and hears music register in his ears as the glass slides left. He steps over the exterior threshold and immediately recognizes the chord changes: E minor to C major, back and forth. He scans the crowd, zeroing in on the center of the music. *She's here.* He hears her voice sing the second verse of "Eleanor Rigby," then the crowd joins in on each chorus. Part of James is screaming at him to turn around while the other part propels him slowly toward the back of the crowd on the lawn. He cannot miss the opportunity to see her, even if he no longer deserves the right to be in her presence. He inches forward as she finishes the last chorus.

The song ends, and the crowd erupts with applause around Jean. As they disperse, he sees her speaking with Julia and smiling in their close conversation. Jean is wearing a sleeveless lavender floral dress cut just above her knees. Her purple eye shadow accentuates her bright-blue eyes with dark lashes and hair to contrast. Even as she stands speaking and holding her guitar, she glows in the partial light. He feels drawn to her now, like the missing piece to an endless puzzle he has been searching for his entire life is found. When he reduces the gap down to five yards, he sees a tall figure near Jean turn around and drape his long arm around her shoulders. At the exact moment his arm drops to touch her body, Jean glances across the lawn, seeing James for the first time. The two share a gaze of shock and confusion lasting several seconds as Larry Patterson, former classmate, whispers in Jean's ear. Larry smiles but notices her frozen status and lack of response. When Larry looks up to see the direction of Jean's stare, he removes his arm immediately. Contorted and full of rage, James shares one final look with Jean and turns swiftly toward the back door of the house.

"Elliot! Keys! Now!" James yells to him on his way to the door. He opens the glass, not bothering to peer behind as Elliot follows him through the house to the front door.

"Uh, James? Come on. I know how you drive when you're upset, man. I've got a baby on the way," Elliot pleads with James.

"Elliot, now! I gotta get out of here," James puffs out aggressively.

"Okay, but please, just be careful." Elliot hesitantly hands James the keys to his black and chrome Suzuki X6 Hustler. James walks down the street to the motorcycle and mounts the near-three-hundred-pound bike. He grabs Elliot's cherry-red Bell helmet and straps it under his chin. His hand turns the key. He revs the engine, reacquainting himself with the rpm and mph instruments mounted near the headlamp. James peers over his shoulder checking for oncoming vehicles and takes off quickly down Wooddale Avenue. He rounds the corner at West Main Street heading east, ignoring the stop sign and accelerating to eighty miles an hour with no cars in sight. After moments of luxury, feeling the rush and knowing he could go faster, he respectfully slows to the speed limit as he reflects on Elliot's request. He is James's oldest friend and does not wish to ruin his chance for a solid trade-in for a new family car. He checks his current speed at thirty-five miles per hour and looks up. James catches a glimpse of a vehicle approaching in the opposite lane, slowing to turn left at the intersection at South McClellan Street only thirty yards ahead. The car's turn signal is on, but James sees that the driver is not stopping. Within ten yards now, the massive steel Oldsmobile pulls left, directly in front of James. He attempts to turn the bike into the opposing lane to avoid the hit, but the rear of the gray Ninety-Eight frame is excessively long. James relaxes as he hits the rear panel of the car with the bike, seeing the squared-off headlamp atop the handlebars while his body launches over the top of the car. His head hits the pavement first, cracking the helmet in two places, before his body rolls across the street like a rag doll. Upon contact, James loses hearing and consciousness. It was over in an instant.

CHAPTER

9

"James? Can you hear me, son? Squeeze my fingers if you can hear me." James moves his head slowly, eyes closed, toward his mother's voice. He sighs with a slight moan from the pain he feels in his head, moving less to avoid it now. "James?" He gently firms the muscles in his left hand, wrapping tightly around her soft fingers. James manages to open his eyes, blinking from the bright light in the hospital room. He continues to squint, sensitive to the morning sunshine. "Here," his mother says as she crosses the room to close the drapes. "Is that better?"

"Yeah," James whispers, slowly opening his lids all the way.

"Here's some water." She holds the cup up to his mouth and bends the straw gently toward his lips. He takes a strong pull of water, feeling the chill down his esophagus. His bed is inclined to easily take another pull from the straw. "You had everyone worried here at Decatur-Memorial. Lots of people were here to see you last night." His mother pauses. "As soon as somebody reported your accident at Ben's party, about half of them showed up," she adds with a smile.

While she finishes her statement, a flood of information pops back in his head. "Elliot! Oh, Jesus," he croaks out in a whisper, shifting in his bed to get up.

"Don't you worry about Elliot now. He's glad you're alive. Just relax. You've got a lot of mending to do yet." His mother taps the top of his knuckles wrapped in gauze.

"But I've gotta talk to him. I need to pay him back!"

"That won't be necessary."

"No, Mom. I have to make it right. You don't understand," he insists, more depth to his voice now.

"Elliot will be just fine. Now listen, I'll tell you what's happened, but you need to calm down and let me finish." She pauses, waiting for James to relax. "That man who pulled in front of you came here straight from the scene of the accident to check on you. Mr. Merriman is his name. He told the police officers what happened then came here asking about you. He felt extremely awful about the whole thing, as he should. In fact, when the police called your father, he was determined to give Mr. Merriman a piece of his mind before they filled him in on the half-inch glasses the man wears to see. It's no wonder this happened because he shouldn't be driving at all.

"As far as Elliot's concerned, a few of your friends told Mr. Merriman it was his bike you were on, so he offered to pay him full price to replace it. I think Elliot is meeting him this morning to get the money, in fact.

"He also wants to take care of all your medical expenses here and replace the clothes you were wearing. He sure is a nice old man, but I still hope they take away his license."

James sits staring at the white walls in front of him, processing all the information. "Hmm. Well, I guess all that's okay." James sighs. "Elliot's getting a better deal than he would've for a trade," he adds.

"James?" his mother states hesitantly. "There's one more thing I need to tell you. I'm afraid this is the bad news." She takes his hand once more.

"What is it?"

"Well, you hit your head real hard, hon. The doctors knew you suffered a bad concussion, but last night after midnight, they treated you for a massive seizure. They think it's from hitting your head at the angle you hit it. I saw your helmet, James. I can't believe that's supposed to be the best out there, but I always knew you were hardheaded." She attempts humor to reduce the crease forming on James's forehead.

"What does that mean, Mom?"

"Well, we're not sure of everything yet, but the doctors feel this may be a permanent situation. They're going to put you on some medication to eliminate the seizures, but it may take awhile to find the right one. I'm just happy you're home for the summer to figure this out."

"What about school?"

"School should be just fine, so long as we find the right medication first," she adds with confidence. "Don't you worry. You'll be just fine."

James sighs and looks over to the drapes, already loathing himself for insisting on taking Elliot's bike. *I could've run down the street. I could've gone west instead of east. Dammit.* Ten different scenarios play out in his head, and with each one, his anger intensifies. He closes his eyes, attempting to cope without mustering the tears he wants to shed.

James is held in the hospital for three long days. Doctors monitor his current seizure medication's effectiveness and ensure his movements are subtle enough to help reduce swelling in his brain. By the second day, James is dressing in his own clothes from home. His mother brings him fresh fruit along with a few books he brought home to read from school.

"Here you are, James. Fresh cantaloupe and pineapple for you."

"Thanks, Mom."

"I also have another surprise. Someone wants to see you," she adds.

"Mom, I really don't want to—" He cuts his statement short when he sees her in the doorway. "Jean." His eyes light up, and he shifts himself taller in the bed.

"Hi, James," she greets him with a tender smile. She is dressed in jean shorts and a red-and-white striped blouse.

"I'll leave you two to talk then." James's mother excuses herself from the room, a pleasant grin on her face.

"How are you?"

"Well, I think the better question is, how are *you*? You really had everyone worried."

"I'm fine. I just feel bad. You know I have a temper." He diverts his eyes while shaking his head. "I'm so stupid."

"Not stupid. Just stubborn," Jean comments with a humorous smirk.

"You know me well." He looks into her eyes.

She stares straight back and speaks fervently, "Yes, I do."

He stifles a chuckle.

"So, Larry Patterson, huh?" he suggests, looking at her expression. "I know. I've no right to ask you anything about your personal affairs. I was just surprised, that's all."

"You were surprised? About what, exactly?"

"Jean, come on. That boy's had a crush on you since you moved here. I saw his arm around you."

"And you thought I was with him because of his arm? James, I thought you were smarter than this."

"I'm smart enough to assume you've moved on with your life. I've ruined whatever chances we had left."

"Why do you always assume you know the answer before you've asked it? Huh?"

"Like you said, I'm stubborn," he replies, angry and fuming.

"James," she breathes, attempting to soothe him with her voice. The voice he loves unconditionally. She crosses the room to his bed.

"What," he responds, agitated.

"Do you really think it would be that easy for me?" Jean takes his scabbed-over left hand in her own.

He takes a moment to breathe calmly. "I don't know, Jean."

"Well, I suppose I may understand you better than you understand me then."

James is angry at the thought, his forehead creasing again. "So you're saying there's nothing going on with you and Larry," he states.

Jean sighs. "James, I have no interest in Larry."

"Well, he has interest in you."

"Yes, he's said as much, but I've made it clear I'm not interested."

"Good. He's not good enough for you anyway."

Jean smiles at his childlike pouting. "Okay."

"Jean, I've really missed you. I'm such an ass. I've been completely miserable and pathetic at school. Aside from my schoolwork, I just want to wipe the last two years from my memory altogether," he unloads in a sigh, squeezing her hand.

Jean stands there, stunned by his admissions. "But I thought you said there was someone else."

"Jean, I lied. I just didn't think it was fair to keep you hanging on when I couldn't be with you in the way you deserved. I'm sorry I hurt you."

"James, whatever made you th—" Jean is thrown into silence watching his face contort. His eyes roll back in his head as it falls lazily to the right side. James's body begins to flail on the bed, kneeing the tray, sending it crashing to the floor. "Help! Somebody help!" Jean gently holds his chest down and attempts to turn him onto his side.

"What's wrong, Jean?" James's mother rounds the corner, only needing one glance. She crosses the floor swiftly to help Jean hold onto James. Two nurses are right behind her. Jean steps back to let them work. The nurses angle his face down toward the pillow, allowing the jaw to relax, preventing mouth or tongue injury and keeping the saliva clear from his throat. Safe on the bed, the episode lasts nearly five minutes.

The neurology specialist walks in as his body calms to a still. He pulls his flashlight out of his pocket while crossing the floor, and the women all relax their light grip on James. The doctor checks his pupil dilation, heart rate, and breathing with his stethoscope then pulls the earpieces out.

"Well, I think it's safe to assume we need to try another medication now. When we find the right one, he won't have these problems, and he must be religious about taking it," the doctor insists.

"Yes, sir. He will be," James's mother responds. "I'll make sure of it."

"Would you excuse us? The nurses and I need to assess if there's been any more damage," the doctor adds, grabbing James's chart and a pen.

"Certainly. Come with me, Jean," she directs, opening her arm to Jean, who is still in shock. James's mother takes Jean around the shoulder and escorts her down to the waiting area on the floor. "Jean, sit down, honey." Jean obediently sits, a glazed-over expression on her face. "I suppose James didn't have a chance to tell you everything."

"I-I heard about his helmet, but I didn't know it was that bad." Jean places her head in her hands, tears welling up quickly. "Is he going to be okay? Can he still go to school?" she inquires through her sobbing.

"Jean, calm down. It's all right, dear. You know how stubbornly resilient James is. He'll be just fine. Like the doctor said, we just need to find the right medicine for him. Don't you worry now," she asserts, wrapping her hand around Jean's arm.

"This is all my fault," Jean states.

"What are you talking about?"

"He stormed off on that bike when he saw Larry's arm around me. He thought there was something going on, but there's not.

I didn't even see him at the party before he saw me. He was so angry. I could see it in his eyes." Jean's tears flow down into the cup of her hands.

"Jean, you know James. Always overreacting. He comes by it quite honestly straight from his father, but I'm afraid he gets his stubbornness from both of us. Now, please don't cry. James will be coming around soon after he sleeps off the lapse, and he won't want your pity. Come on. Wipe those tears. Here's a tissue." She hands her a few from the box atop the nearby table. Jean is a geyser of tears, thinking of her request for James to be careful and slow down on their first date. Her defensive fear of automotive tragedy is a force of distress never to subside. Maybe it is her fears propelling her to love and care so deeply altogether, which is a grim outlook for any individual to consider.

"Thank you. I'm sorry you have to see me this way." Jean wipes the snot from her nose.

"Don't even think of it. I know how much you care about my son. I know he's not a piece of cake to deal with either." James's mother smiles. "Are you okay to walk down the hall?"

"Yes, I'm fine. Just one more minute. I've got some makeup, which may help." Jean takes a few seconds to reapply her lipstick and ivory powder to hide the puffiness. "Okay, all ready."

The two walk side by side down the hall toward James's room. He is alert but tired after the ordeal. The nurses just finished cleaning the mess from the knocked-over tray as his mother and Jean round the corner to his room.

"Hi, how are you feeling, James?" his mother asks.

"Jean?" James is surprised. He looks around his mother to see her and sits up taller in his bed. "How are you?"

"I'm fine, James. Are you feeling better now?"

"Better? Were you here before?"

Jean looks at his mother, speechless.

"James, don't you remember speaking with Jean before your seizure?"

"No. I don't remember at all," he replies, now upset. He looks up into Jean's eyes, and then he truly sees her. He notices her puffy eyes and the disappointed and hurt look she is attempting to protect.

"Mom, would you excuse us please?" James asks in an assertive voice.

"Sure." She pats Jean's arm before leaving.

James looks away to the window, gathering his thoughts.

"James, we were having such a nice conversation before that happened. I wish you could remem—"

"Well, I can't!" James yells in her direction.

"I—I'm sorry." Jean is startled.

"Don't say you're sorry. I don't want your pity." James shoots a look straight in her eyes.

"James, it's not pity. Would you just let me tell you what was said?"

"No, I want you to go now. I don't want to see anyone. This is who I am now. I can deal with it on my own."

Every word stings inside Jean's chest. She stands there, seeing his anger for what it is in the grand picture. Suddenly, a rage bubbles under her skin, sending heated tears down her cheeks and a wave of angered gumption. "James, I know there was no one else at IIT now, so you listen to me. You get better and get it together because there's only so much I will tolerate!"

The astonished look on his face lingers. *What else did I tell her?* Before he finishes his thought, she is gone.

⋅⟋⟍⟋⟍⋅

During the next six weeks at home, James strikes out on three prescribed medications for his seizures. He spends all his spare time in isolation nearly the entire summer, refusing visitors and phone calls until his seizures are under control. By late July, he tries Dilantin and finds success. Monitored by his mother at

177

night and father during the day at the store, James feels relief to no longer need babysitting by August, especially when he is due to return to school in days.

On August 15, James heads back to IIT with Mike in his Road Runner. When he arrives at his dormitory, he finds a letter waiting for him from Jean. The postmark date reads August 1. He anxiously opens the envelope to read her words:

Dear James,   August 1, 1969

We made a few promises to each other before you went to school. I realize it's been more difficult than you or I could have imagined, and though we didn't establish any specific guidelines for our interactions as friends, I think it's time to talk about how we feel.

First, I need to address what was said at the hospital. I made it perfectly clear that while Larry may have interest in me, I have no interest in him. I can't control what you saw or how you reacted, but I feel an immense amount of guilt over the result just the same. It may be difficult to swallow, but I suppose this is a tough reminder to tame your temper and never assume.

James, it's also time to remember where we started and think about the conversations we had before you left. I understand time can change us in some ways, but our goals, needs, and emotions typically remain the same. Do you still love me? Your initial and first response to the question should guide your subsequent actions. Either way, make a decision and stay true to it.

All my best,
Jean

An overall taciturn letter, compared to previous communications. James sets the paper on his dormitory desk and walks away, reflecting on its contents.

⚜

"Did you hear the news, man?" Gary asks, pulling James out of the book he is reading outside the campus library.

"What news?" James inquires apathetically.

"Don't you work at the radio station still? I thought you'd be the first to know."

"Know what?" James inquires, clearly agitated.

"Mies died at Wesley Memorial last night," Gary answers.

"What?" James is alarmed.

"Mies van der Rohe died. They want to hold a memorial here for him on campus soon," Gary responds, knowing James heard him the first time.

"Hmm. That's a real shame." James sighs.

"Yeah, I know. What a genius, huh?"

"Wish I could've met him," James adds somberly, drifting his eyes to the dormitory wall where several snapshots of the prolific architect's buildings are lined up in black and white.

"Don't we all? Those bastards who went here twenty years ago don't know how good they had it learning from him," Gary mentions.

"Yeah, but they paved the way though, just like anything else."

In the days following his death, Mies's ashes are scattered in Chicago's Graceland Cemetery. Nearly every soul on campus plans to pay their respects at a special memorial service.

A week later, James opens the door to Crown Hall slowly, taking one step into the standing crowd of people gathered at the back of the memorial service. Even arriving ten minutes early, the chairs inside the large space are filled with faculty, alumni, and current students. People stand in every empty square inch.

James waits patiently for the ceremony to begin, watching a female cross the front of the hall carrying her cello. She sits opposite a portrait of Mies, and at the center is a podium with an attached microphone.

The last of the service organizers sit down, and the hall suddenly falls silent. The cellist brings her bow to the string with reverence and grace, striking the first D double stop to begin the sarabande from Bach's Cello Suite in D Minor. James watches her move with each phrase, embellishing baroque ornaments with exquisite passion. He watches how her breath follows the flow of the music, exuding vulnerable humanity in each note.

James reflects on the last time Jean played her guitar for him. His breath catches, briefly reliving the piece she composed and performed at Julia's house in his mind. The emotions of the evening overwhelm him while listening to the deep romanticism poured into this cello suite. Even sorting records at the radio station, he realizes his life has been void of music since that evening with Jean. His ears have regarded music as passive noise rather than an active listening experience with the purpose of creating a human response. He feels the vibration of each string now, as if the hair of the bow is cutting straight into the follicles of his ears and into the depths of his soul. The floodgates unleash an onslaught of sentiments withheld for over a year. The gorgeous performance acutely penetrates into his subconscious, and he gasps for air. James turns around, excuses himself, and opens the door to exit Crown Hall.

He sits down on the steps while his heart races. *Jean's right. It's time to make a move.*

Jean closes her political science textbook with a sigh. The time is five fifteen when she glances toward the clock on the wall. She packs her book bag with her notebooks, study cards, and pens lying atop the library desk and heads to her car in the parking lot of the Lincoln Land Community College library in Springfield. Exhausted after a full week of classes and hungry for supper, she yawns and turns the Dart's ignition, dreading her thirty-minute drive back to Decatur. She pops a piece of Wrigley's double-mint gum in her mouth to help from dozing along Highway 36.

Thankful for the long Labor Day weekend, Jean looks forward to playing her guitar. In the quiet drive home, she reflects that Monday is September first and exactly one month since she dropped her last correspondence to James in the mail. She attempts not to let the time lapse weaken, anger, or alter her mood before arriving home; however, her insecurities scream foul, propelling the doubts she feels toward his lack of affection.

Jean turns onto Doneta and her driveway when she recognizes the car sitting around her circle drive. *That's his mother's car. What's she doing here? Oh no!* Jean propels herself out of the car, shoving the heavy metal door closed. She moves quickly to the porch and front door, opening it swiftly to find James sitting on the couch, conversing casually with her mother and father. Three faces turn to look at Jean, now slightly flushed and panicked. Seeing James unhurt, she is relieved but cannot fathom why he is in her living room. He smiles warmly at her, as do her parents.

"Oh, Jean," her mother states as she crosses the living room with her arms out, palms up to take her daughter in a tight embrace. "This is quite a day!" Jean's brows angle downward into a complete look of astonishment as her mother squeezes her tighter than she has since her graduation ceremony finished.

"Mother, what—" Jean is interrupted.

"We'll just leave you two to talk, won't we?" her mother suggests with assertion to her husband.

"Oh, certainly," he responds, getting up from the couch. The couple retreats to the kitchen. Jean's eyes follow her parents, shocked by their willingness to oblige and more stunned as to the nature of her mother's greeting. Once out of sight, Jean looks to see James approaching her while looking straight into her eyes.

"Jean, first, let me start with an apology. I don't do this too often, and I'll likely get it wrong, but I've been the most unbelievable... Well, fill in any number of profane words and I'm it. I'm so sorry for what I've done to you, and us, over the past two years. I was too proud and afraid to tell you the truth. None of the excuses I could offer you even matter anymore. Nothing I say could ever lessen the enormous guilt I feel for putting you through so much, but I'm so sorry. Please...Say you'll forgive me?" James inflects his voice into a question.

Jean looks away, speechless. She opens her mouth to speak, takes a breath, but then closes it, looking away from his gaze. His presence douses a frozen layer of shock over her; she is unmoving but shudders from the nerves and sensation of false cold. Her teeth begin to chatter while her body registers pure fear. She attempts to clamp down her jaw, but her breathing then drags through her nose.

"Jean, are you okay?" James questions, placing his hands on her shoulders. "You're shaking."

"N-no. I'm fine," she stutters, fighting back the anxiety.

"Jean, here. Sit down." He leads her over to the sofa. "Here." He grabs the white cotton blanket draped over the back of the sofa arm, kneels down, and wraps it gently around her shoulders. He makes friction with his hands to warm her. "Is that better?"

Jean nods. "Why are you here?"

James stops his hand movement on her arms, looking up to read her facial cues. "I wanted to tell you all of that in person. Though I know you're too good for me, I figured I better go the extra mile to convey I am sincerely sorry. Please forgive me?"

"James, there's nothing to forgive," Jean says with pure conviction and strength in her voice.

He looks at her, confused by the quickness in her response. "There's everything to forgive, Jean. I made this much harder than it needed to be, and for that, I'm so sorry."

Jean laughs in response.

James looks at her in confusion and frustration. "Why are you laughing?"

"Because you actually thought I didn't know who you were before you left. Of course I knew you would make this harder than it needed to be. You always do, James. I'm shocked you felt we could scathe these college years without war wounds."

"But I spent so much time lying to you, ignoring the truth, and treating you so poorly," James offers.

"Yes, I know, but did you ever stop loving me or thinking about me?"

"No, but—"

"Then I forgive you."

"But I do—"

"It's in the past now, James. Let's move forward." She stares contently back at James, warm now from her revelation of his feelings. She shrugs out of the blanket and takes his hands.

James lets out a massive sigh, looking down toward the floor. "Jean, you're far better than I could ever manage to deserve."

"Hmm, I'm not certain about that," Jean replies with a smile.

He takes another large breath and brainstorms his next sentence. Now it is his heart beating irregularly.

"What's wrong, James?"

"There's something I want to say," James responds in hesitation.

"All right."

James shifts his weight to the opposite knee while reaching behind to his back pocket. "Jean, since the moment I saw you, I knew you were incredibly special. I didn't expect to ever deserve your affections in return, but I'm so thankful you see me for the man I yearn to be, and not necessarily the person you see floundering through his faults. You bring me a sense of peace at the end of the day, and I'm not sure I could ever survive this world without your beautiful and endless positive nature. You're the most wonderful person, and I'd be a fool not to ask you properly to please be my wife." James opens his hand to present a small half-karat diamond mounted on a thin gold band in his oversized rough fingers.

Jean places her cupped hands over her mouth in a gasp, tears immediately welling up in her eyes.

"Jean, would you make the happiest man on earth and marry me?"

Jean's fears completely subside, with tears in an endless flow down her cheeks. "Yes, I will marry you." She bypasses the ring for a genuine embrace. The sofa is close to the ground, and her knees hit the floor quickly as she wraps her short arms around his neck. Their bodies touch closely in a tight hold while kneeling on the floor together. James leans into her hair, taking in her scent; he wraps his long arms around her small waist. The two spend time retracing the curvature and contours of the other's torso for a number of moments. James pulls away to slowly slide the ring onto Jean's finger. She sees his hidden elation as he watches it slide perfectly into place.

"Jean, I want to let you know I've already asked your parents for permission."

"Oh. Well, by my mother's greeting, I'm guessing she gave her blessing?"

"Yes, she did, as did your father," he adds. "It's my father I'm worried about."

"Why?"

James sighs. "Do you remember the Sunday after the dance? I'm sure you noticed how distant I was before I left for school."

"Yes, I remember." At the same moment Jean responds, a lightbulb flashes inside her head. "He told you not to see me, didn't he?"

"Well, he approves of you, of course, but not the timing. He threatened to remove his financial support of my education at IIT if I kept seeing you."

Jean's expression was immediately sullen as his every action clicks together in full resolution.

"Jean, don't worry. I have a plan," he adds, excitement thick in his voice. Jean's eyes trail back up to his, waiting in anticipation. "I spoke with the dean of students at IIT who said if we marry, we will have special permission to live in Carman Hall, the apartment building on campus, next school year."

"Oh, wow," Jean replies in shock.

"I know it's a lot to take in at once, but I think we should plan to marry this summer. And...I want you to consider moving to Chicago with me while I finish school. With my experience interning at the architecture firm, I may even have a job as soon as I graduate, and you could continue your classes at the community college up there if you like. I've managed to save some money as well, so we'll be in good shape."

Jean's disposition seems positive. "Your dad, James. How will you stay in school if your dad doesn't support you?"

"Please don't worry about that, Jean. I will handle talking with my father. He won't be a problem, especially now that I've proven my worth and ability to focus. It will be okay. No worries," he claims, touching her cheek softly with the back of his hand. "Plus, I have my mother on my side," he adds with a smile.

Jean sighs, feeling relief again.

The following summer, the two are happily married at St. Patrick's Church in Decatur with both families present and supportive of the union. Jean moves to Chicago with James, and just as he predicts, the life he envisions starts to click into place. Jean begins work at a local bank near campus in August, receiving honorable awards in customer service and sales while continuing with business-oriented classes in the evenings. She is happy helping people and still spends one night per weekend performing at a local coffee shop on the outer edge of campus off Thirty-Fifth Street. Playing cover tunes for everyone to enjoy is the pinnacle of each week but also adds extra money to the savings account and assists in supporting living expenses. James never misses a performance despite all his homework and projects.

Graduating near the top of his class in the spring of 1971, James lands a position at the local architecture firm, Skidmore, Owings & Merrill, where he spent a summer interning after freshman year. A number of architects are hired to assist in the construction logistics of the Sears, Roebuck & Company Tower in downtown Chicago. The anticipated completion of the new skyscraper is spring of 1973. With James's involvement downtown, the two move into a spacious apartment complex just south of the construction the summer after graduation. The location is accessible by train, making their work commutes effortless.

The couple is also elated to learn their first child will arrive in the winter of 1971.

"It was a healthy baby…" Jean trails off as she realizes no one is at her side. "James?" She turns to look around, but she is alone on her padded patio bench outside in the garden. People continue walking past while the afternoon breeze sends a chill over her waxy pale skin.

PART 3

ELIZABETH

CHAPTER

10

I n the late morning, Elizabeth sits on the small sofa facing the black Steinway & Sons baby grand piano in the vast and beautifully decorated lobby adjacent to the lunchroom. She stares at the instrument, running her eyes up and down the ivory keys, hearing notes in her head as if playing a masterpiece. Afraid to embarrass herself, she never ventures over to the piano. She is alone in the room, but growing up without a piano disabled her chances of becoming a virtuoso.

"I could have been a great many things," she speaks in a soft tone. As a child and into adulthood, she loved to draw. With her father's sense of spatial logic came the joy of working with her hands in painting, chalking, or imitating images captured. She could have been an architect or an interior designer, using obsessive-compulsive tendencies in space, linear judgment, and precision. With both her parents' sense of passion, she may have been a politician, fighting intense battles for justice. From her mother also came an analytical eye. Independence drove her desire to explore diverse rocks, the stars, the moon, always studying the details of every facet intensely, trying to read more into the origin of each mineral or vast landscape of the star set.

What she really desired was to be a pianist, capable of sitting down to simply run her fingers across the keys, anticipating what would flow next. Elizabeth would dream about creating great piano works and compositions with the simple beauty of Chopin or Beethoven, but with the hands of Rachmaninoff or Liszt.

"Yes, but you are also beautiful just as you are," the unknown man claims. Still wearing his brown suit, he crosses the room to reach the piano in front of Elizabeth. He sits down on the shiny black bench facing her and expresses a breathtaking smile and wink before turning to the piano keys to play. She looks at him in shock. Elizabeth recognizes his talent within the first notes. Immediately, she knows the piece, but cannot recall its name. The piece is important, yet she cannot recall why. Her heart is racing in her chest while gazing at this man she knows but cannot place. *Who is he?* She is frustrated by her own question.

As the music continues on, Elizabeth relaxes and drifts with it, seeing vague scenes flash in her mind. Looking down at her soft, smooth hands, she notices the wedding ring on her ring finger and closes her eyes.

⁘ ❧❦❧ ⁘

Elizabeth is in her first week of school as a freshman music education major at a university just over two hours from home in the fall of 1990. "Ellie, are you coming to lunch?" Her new friends are waiting down the hall near the exit while she fumbles getting items placed into her locker in the music building. After only two days on campus, she was required to audition for a place in one of two concert bands that morning by the director of bands, Dr. Shore. Nervous to perform for anyone, Ellie is still trembling, needing hours to debrief from the ordeal.

"Yes, I'll be right there!" Ellie responds, taking the flute her father scraped money to purchase out of her bag. She loses grip on the soft case, watching it fall to the carpeted floor. "Oh, shoot!" She briskly bends down to pick up her instrument. Suddenly, her hand freezes. At the other end of her case, she sees a man's hand and traces his arm all the way up to meet a pair of piercing blue eyes. Ellie's breath catches, finding purchase on his lovely young face.

He stares back and speaks softly. "Please, allow me," he offers in a soothing voice.

"Thank you." She slowly stands with him, never losing eye contact. The two exchange a soft smile and glance away at the same time. The tall and slender gentleman hands her the flute case to place in the locker.

"I'm Robert," he says, placing both hands in the pockets of his beige wide-leg dress pants. His button-down silk sky-blue shirt enhances his eye color extraordinarily further. Robert's straight teeth are a brilliant white, which stand in contrast to his brown, smooth, and softly gelled hairstyle. His profile is stunning.

"I'm Elizabeth, but everyone calls me Ellie." She fidgets slightly with a strand of her golden hair. Her long bangs are pulled back straight in a silver barrette, but just past her shoulders her hair waves into large curls down to the middle of her back.

"It's wonderful to meet you, Ellie," Robert replies with a grin, looking into her blue eyes.

"Likewise, Robert." Her ivory cheeks flush a vibrant shade of pink to match the buttoned-down short-sleeve blouse she is wearing. The khaki skirt is cropped just above her knees and complements the lighter shade of her shirt.

"Ellie, we're waiting for you!" she hears her friends call from outside.

"Oh, I've got to be going," she says while opening her locker. Attempting to concentrate on the task of keeping her instrument safe, she closes the door and clamps down on the lock.

"I hope we will meet again soon, Ellie," Robert offers gently. Neither can stop glancing back while walking away. Ellie tries to put one foot in front of the other as she exits the music building.

As a freshman, Ellie is obsessed with organization her first week on campus. The orientation activities and inconsequential forced bonding seems to drag on forever, making her more eager to begin classes the following day. Her notebooks are all sorted with color-coordinated folders, already labeled for each course. The pens and pencils are lined up in her book bag with extra erasers, a calculator, and her assignment calendar. Books for each class are stacked neatly atop the desk in her dormitory, placed according to her schedule. Classes happen to begin on a Monday requiring she pack her bag for nearly a full day. Ellie's math textbook, language arts resources, university seminar notebooks, political science text, and music theory materials are added in her backpack. The weight of it might indicate a full day, but merely one hour of time will be her only break before heading to Wind Ensemble in the late afternoon. She is thankful her audition performance paid off, placing her in the higher-performing ensemble on campus. The other university band meets during her only slot available for lunch.

Though her morning of classes begins with math at eight o'clock, Ellie sets her alarm for six. Over the summer, she worked hard to establish an exercise routine of running roughly two miles every morning prior to breakfast. Breathing the summer air at sunrise allows Ellie further acclamation to the heat of the day, an energetic disposition with which to learn, and most importantly for her, a metabolism that will work in her favor.

Struggling with weight her entire childhood, the cruelty of children left a permanent scar on Ellie's spirit and remains in the seat of her subconscious and insecurities. Day one of kindergarten started with a group of slandering boys, and every subsequent year it was always someone else whispering, kids pointing, or others laughing. The peak of humility was in elementary school as the tallest girl in class. Several boys had major issues being shorter than a girl, but the insults continued as her weight ballooned in junior high. Stepping foot into school gave her anxiety up through high school, but the ownership, responsibility, and emotional freedom of making music brought her a sense of peace; being part of something larger than herself made her get up and keep trying every morning.

Always athletic as part of a softball team for ten years, coordination abounds. Reflexively solid with a long stride and strong legs, short-distance sprinting played in her favor against the skinnier students in school. Long distances never seemed possible to her with the knowledge of her heart murmur as a child. At times, it felt like a mental handicap every time fitness testing came around in gym class. One year in junior high, she shut down altogether and would not attempt to run the mile, barely finishing before the bell. Ellie recalls the failure to be her attitude and perspective making her last that day, not a lack of ability. She vowed never to be last again, providing her with a piece of the motivational puzzle she sees in herself when she wakes up to begin the day. With a focused mind-set, the summer routine left her fifty-five pounds lighter.

She puts her running shoes on the morning of her first day as a music education major in college and heads out her dormitory door.

Even though she has traveled in and out of the music building through orientation week to practice flute, she has not seen Robert. She has a hard time breathing when picturing the way he looked into her eyes. Chills run through her body, and butterflies fill her stomach; and so she welcomes the distraction of her large checklist of items to achieve by the day's end.

Exactly like every paranoid freshman, she leaves early for class, providing more than enough time to relax while waiting for the professor to enter the classroom. She selects a seat on the side closest to the exit, farthest against the wall, and several rows deep. Though Ellie is eager to learn, her mission in life throughout school has been discretion, preferring not to be seen nor heard, especially in math. Ellie is overly aware of her insecurities in the subject. Other than intelligent mathematicians and scientists, a number of people are wired two ways: those who are strong in geometry and those strong in algebra. Ellie senses the spatial logic in geometry and trigonometry with ease, but add a number next to a letter, and she is lost. Finite Mathematics is the only collegiate level math course she elects and covers a touch of everything; seeking extra help is inevitable.

The rest of the morning flies by effortlessly. She realizes her eleven o'clock class, American Political Systems, is going to leave her with a lack of appetite three days per week. Class discussions and debates are part of the curriculum, an aspect of human existence she truly loathes. In her mind, debates are a waste of oxygen requiring no actions, a pointless game and displacement of energy when people who want to change the world are doing it, not arguing over the best approach. It is utterly frustrating for her to listen as her relatives discuss world topics, politicians, and religious perspectives based on tertiary sources every holiday. Exiting this class may require a routine break back to the dorm room for lunch.

Ellie walks to the campus cafeteria for food, but looking at the offerings for the day she exits across the hall to the deli. A simple turkey and cheese sandwich with chips and water will help calm the nerves in her stomach. Ellie quickly walks back to her second-floor dorm room across the lot from the cafeteria and eats alone. The quiet peace of the space is lovely. Ginny, her roommate and a physical education major, befriended several people during orientation week, resulting in late returns home each night. She feels envious of her carefree nature but grateful to be more focused than Ginny.

Ellie shuffles her textbooks back in order atop her desk from the morning, resorts her book bag with items for Music Theory, and slings her flute gig bag over her shoulder. Heading outside to walk across campus, she feels relief to finally have a music class after her morning of none at all. She enters the room for Theory ten minutes early and sits off to the side again.

Students begin entering the room. "Hey, Ellie!"

"Hey, Beth. How are you?" Ellie replies energetically.

"I'm so nervous. Excited, but nervous. I'm a choir girl, and Theory scares me a little bit. My high school choir teacher didn't do the best job giving us all the information we needed to help out."

"Oh, I'm sorry. I'm sure you'll be great. Don't worry. I guess I was lucky being in both band and choir, so if you need anything at all, I can help you," Ellie encourages. "Do you want to sit by me?"

"Sure! Thanks, Ellie," Beth replies, consoled.

"Carolyn, how are you?" Beth asks while her friend walks through the door.

"Hey, Beth! Oh my gosh, I'm so happy to see you in here."

"Yeah, I'm happy you're in here too. Ellie, this is Carolyn. Carolyn, meet Ellie. We were in choir together back home," Beth finishes.

Ellie smiles up at Carolyn. "It's nice to meet you."

"You too, Ellie!"

"Carolyn is a cello player in addition to having an amazing soprano voice," Beth mentions to Ellie. She turns to look at Carolyn. "And Ellie is a flute player who is also a vocalist."

"Wonderful!" Carolyn responds. "So you chose instrumental, and I chose vocal, but we are multitalented ladies!" Her energy is vibrant.

Ellie chuckles. "I suppose so."

"I heard Dr. Gibbs is a really great teacher, but a bit on the frazzled side. I remember auditioning for my scholarship with her, and she is intimidating, to say the least," Carolyn mentions.

"Oh boy," Beth replies. "You guys…help." Beth breathes out her anxiety.

"It's okay, Beth. I told you I'd help you," Ellie reminds her.

Carolyn catches on to her tone. "Yes, Beth. We'll both help you. Ellie will rock the treble clef, and I'll rock the bass clef for you," Carolyn encourages, laughing.

"See? No worries," Ellie replies.

Dr. Gibbs enters the room; her frizzy and long blond hair is heaved up in a bun with round glasses covering much of her face. Wearing sandals and a printed dress cut off at midcalf, she hauls a stack of papers onto the upright piano at the front of the room. "Okay, remove all your books, binders, and folders from your desk. Take out your pencil with a good eraser and wait for further instructions. I am Dr. Gibbs, and I'll be handing out a pretest to see what you all already know from previous education."

Beth looks at Ellie with a troubled expression. Ellie mouths back to her in a whisper, "It's okay."

"You are to leave the packet facedown on the desk until I tell you to start. We all begin together as I will be paying close attention to who finishes each test first from now on, which will be the procedure for anything I hand out."

Ellie is one of the first to receive her pretest, another advantage to her seating selection. She can feel the pretest is at least three pages long.

"All right, you may begin," Dr. Gibbs instructs.

The first section is all key signature identification, onto ascending then descending intervals, scales, and mode identifications, and finally chord types. Within eight minutes, Ellie is checking her completed work. Seeing no errors, she is the first person to walk her paper up to Dr. Gibbs.

The professor watches Ellie approaching. "Are you positive all that is correct?"

She pauses before answering, now doubting herself. "Yes, ma'am. I believe it is correct," Ellie responds politely.

"What's your name?"

"Elizabeth, but I prefer Ellie. It's easier."

"Okay, Miss Ellie. Let's see how you did then."

Ellie hands her the packet and sits down.

"Hmm. Interesting." Dr. Gibbs turns to the second page of her pretest.

Ellie feels she is going to be sick, waiting for her next comment. She watches her skim the final page of her packet and set it down to continue monitoring the class. The next five minutes are torture, wondering what Dr. Gibbs is thinking until finally another person walks to the front. He hands her the packet with a look of defeat and sits down slowly.

The pretest takes roughly thirty minutes of the fifty-minute class. Beth is the last to turn in her packet, looking embarrassed as her tiny frame gracefully touches the back of the desk to sit down. Dr. Gibbs never mentions the pretest the rest of the hour. She teaches the grand staff and piano basics using the staff-lined chalkboard for reference and overhead projector. At one fifty she dismisses class, never declaring her findings to Ellie.

Ellie finds an obscure practice room upstairs in the music building to practice flute for an hour prior to heading to a ninety-minute rehearsal for Wind Ensemble. The rehearsal hall is in the performing arts building and adjacent to the School of Music. Ellie ventures over early to see where she needs to set up.

Dr. Shore, the director, is arranging chairs and helping students find their seats. He points Ellie to the chair on the second tier on the outside: perfect. Then he begins introductions. "Welcome, everybody. I hope you all had a relaxing summer. This year is going to be an exciting time to be involved with Wind Ensemble because we are planning a trip out of the country for a performance tour. Details on location and pricing will be announced in the coming weeks, but our time frame will be spring break. The university is really looking forward to a liaison we have the opportunity to establish as we venture out of the state and country.

"Speaking of a new liaison, our band manager, Vicki, is unable to assist us in setting up for rehearsals and concerts this year due to her other work schedule. Would anyone be interested in making some extra cash to help set up the hall every day for rehearsals and concerts onstage?" Dr. Shore's eyes sweep the ensemble, finding no volunteers until on his far right Ellie raises her hand. "Ellie, thank you for volunteering and for being willing to help. Stop by and see me before you leave today," he suggests, smiling at her from the podium.

She acknowledges his request with a grin and a nod.

As a music education major, Ellie's other course requirements include Ear Training to coincide with Music Theory, methods courses broken down by instrument and completion of two years of piano proficiency, for which she eagerly awaits. Since her parents could not afford a piano, a keyboard was supplemented where bad habits developed. She is tired of hacking away at the synthesized compositions in her head. Her creations sound decent, but she hopes to gain theoretical backing behind the music she writes as well. The notes of the piano are quite familiar, but she does not have the technical or sight-reading skills to pull her coordination together immediately.

After the eight thirty Ear Training class with Dr. Gibbs on Tuesday, followed by her Clarinet Methods course at ten, Ellie is thrilled to be en route to her first piano class. She finds the room number on the second floor of the music building and walks through the door. The rectangular room is filled with at least twenty electronic pianos and headsets draped over each attached music stand. She looks around the room amazed, having never seen so many pianos. Ellie quickly finds an empty piano bench along the side and sits down. She organizes her notebook, folder, and pencil on the music rack and turns in her bench to face the front of the room and the professor. She sees two tall people looking out at the students in class. She locks eyes with Robert immediately, also returning her gaze. Ellie barely notices the older woman standing next to him but does see a glare from her gold name tag with the inscribed university logo, obviously answering her question about who is in charge of class. Immediately, she glances at her schedule to be certain; Susan Cobalt is the name listed. She sighs in relief and looks up to see Robert gently chuckle in her direction, which she cannot help answering with a smile.

"Good afternoon, and welcome to Piano Level One. I am Professor Susan Cobalt, and this is Robert, our classroom assistant for the semester. Though Robert is a sophomore student, his piano performance skills began at the age of three. He is not only a prodigy but also a superior teacher as a piano performance major. The faculty has asked him to assist in your development as beginners this semester. Therefore, please allow him the same courtesies you would any other instructor. Now, let us begin."

Ellie hears the directives out of Professor Cobalt's mouth, performing the body and finger posture tasks as instructed for the next thirty-five minutes, but she feels as if her head is detached from her body. Her mind feels hollow on the inside, and yet she finds middle C with her thumb and places the subsequent right-hand fingers atop the correct ascending keys to practice the first primary drill of the day.

Fortunately for Ellie, Robert is at the opposite end when he begins floating around the room. Her heart pounds in her chest. Attempting to bury herself in the task at hand, she turns the headset volume up slightly and executes her first finger pattern on the weighted keys, drowning out the sound of her loud heart. Ellie is aware finger posture correction is inevitable from years of keyboard playing, but with an image learned from her conducting training, she quickly makes adjustments to alter the problem.

Robert continues looking around, analyzing levels of experience. Several students in class are having a difficult time looking at their music while playing with proper body and finger posture. He ventures toward the back of the room to see much of the same. When he turns toward Ellie, he stops. He is impressed. Not because he is enamored with her already, but because she is easily surpassing the rest of the class, which gives him a proud, satisfying feeling he cannot explain.

Robert makes eye contact with Professor Cobalt across the room, directing her attention to Ellie playing the given assignment at an allegro tempo with impeccable technique and ease with two hands. She looks at Ellie, acknowledging the progress, and gives him an affirming nod.

Robert pauses momentarily before gradually stepping to Ellie's side. She notices his presence and jumps, startled. She pulls her headphones off and covers her heart. "Oh my goodness, you scared me," she breathlessly half whispers with a smile.

Robert's tall stature bends down to speak softly. "I'm sorry I startled you," he says with a crooked grin.

"It's okay," she replies, still trying to slow her breathing down. "I guess I'm just a bit jumpy today." Ellie turns to slowly look into his eyes. Robert stares back, forgetting his next statement. The silence between the two is deafening, stretching over several moments. Ellie finally breaks, turning gently away and back to Robert. "Did you have something to tell me?"

"Oh, yes. I'm sorry, it's ju—"

"I'm sorry. I didn't grow up with a piano at home. I must be performing badly already. I will practice really hard, I promise," Ellie offers, apologetic.

Ellie's remarks snap Robert out of his daze quickly. "Ellie, actually, I was going to tell you I think you're the best in the class I've seen so far. Congratulations," he commends with a crooked smile.

"Really?" After the compliment sinks in, she is beaming.

"I'm surprised you haven't really played before."

"Oh, well, I've played, but it was always on a five-octave key-board at home. It was awful for my finger technique, but it worked for the simple compositions I wanted to write."

"You compose?"

"Well, yes, just little things. Contemporary style. Nothing of consequence," she minimalizes, looking down at her hands in her lap.

"I'd really like to hear them sometime," Robert offers.

"You would? Oh, they're really not that great. I'd be embarrassed, especially when I'm certain you are an amazing player."

"How did you just avoid all your finger technique fears? The way you were just playing didn't give me any sign you've developed improper habits," Robert insists.

"Oh. Well, in one of my conducting workshops for my first drum major camp, they taught us a little technique for rebounds by giving us an image to follow."

"Which was?"

"To pretend there are raindrops on each of your fingertips, which must be eloquently flicked away without moving the rest of your forearm." Ellie brings out her arms from her lap, palms down, and briefly demonstrates the technique. "From the way Professor Cobalt just described proper finger posture, I just figured the visual might work in this case."

"Hmm. In my fifteen years of playing, I've not once heard that analogy from any teacher, but it should work just fine."

Ellie quickly does the math in her head. "You're only eighteen?"

"Yes. Why?"

"You seem older. More mature."

"I suppose that's why I'm here to help. I've been accused of being old-fashioned because I still find it important to wear appropriate attire while attending university out of respect. My family wouldn't have me any other way as well."

"I think that's an admirable quality, Robert."

"Thank you," Robert says, looking down at his dress shoes.

"Well, I'm only seventeen, so it is true that age is relative. I think I have more maturity in my pinky than some of these fraternity boys, not to mention my roommate."

"Hah. Yes, you're right. You should be careful around those boys."

"A-hem." Professor Cobalt clears her throat to signal Robert to move on from Ellie. He stands quickly.

"Sorry," Ellie whispers while Robert turns to walk to the front of the class.

"The time is now eleven fifty. Your assignment for the week is on the top of the board, so please write it down. As I declared in the syllabus, you are expected to practice every day. This instrument will continue to be an imperative and integral part of your lives as musicians. See you Thursday." Professor Cobalt dismisses class.

Ellie gathers her materials, placing them in her backpack. Her new friend, Carolyn, comes up to her. "Ellie, I'm so glad you're in here with me. How did you do?"

"I think I did all right, but I'm sure it will get tough sooner than later," Ellie responds. She is ready to leave the class but apprehensive to wander away from Robert.

"Oh my gosh, putting our hands together is going to kill me," Carolyn says as they walk slowly out of the class. Ellie glances back to the front of the room while nearing the exit slowly with Carolyn. Robert and Professor Cobalt are speaking, but he manages one last look and soft smile before she leaves. Her heart races again with a blush, but she continues fluidly toward her busy day ahead. "Do you want to grab some lunch with me?" Carolyn trails off.

Following the same morning schedule as Tuesday, Ellie has lunch with Carolyn after piano again Thursday. She then heads back to the music building for her flute master class at one o'clock, followed by her first required recital at two in the afternoon. Every Thursday, music students perform prepared selections at the performing arts building for a recital. Student performers sign up in preparation for an upcoming individual recital to gain experience in front of an audience while others may have a studio requirement to fulfill as performance majors from their private instructors. Eighteen recitals is the minimum number music education students must attend per semester. It seems like an impossible feat, but as Ellie listens to the finest musicians on campus fill up the large hall singing opera and instrumental performances of concerto movements accompanied by pianists, she feels the requirement may not be enough. For the first time, Ellie listens in peace. No worries whether someone will sound sharp or flat, drop a beat, or forget a chunk from a memorized piece. She feels the margin of error for catastrophes significantly decrease while setting her discriminatory, sensory judgments to the side to take in beautiful music.

"Some of you may have met our last performer already in your piano course with Professor Cobalt," the dean for the School of Music introduces. She raises her hand, palm out, toward stage right and the black full grand Steinway piano sitting on the stage with the lid now completely open. "Robert is a sophomore piano performance major, and we welcome him as he performs Franz Liszt's *Liebesträume* this afternoon," she concludes. Robert walks out on stage while she finishes the last words. The audience applauds loudly in anticipation.

Ellie feels her stomach twisting in knots. A part of her yearns to run out of the aisle while the other is entranced with his entire presence. His pressed black slacks rest perfectly atop his polished black dress shoes before he takes a bow. The light-sage button-down shirt is an eloquent backdrop to the symmetrically patterned tie he wears to complement his black suit coat. He unbuttons it swiftly and smoothly as he sits down on the cushioned leather bench. The clapping subsides in preparation for his performance. She watches in awe. Robert drops his head and places his hands on the keys to begin.

The melodic line begins slowly in a delicate blend amid a wave of arpeggios in a flowing triple feel. His tender touch along the keys draws her eyes to his strong hands, then to the emotional expression in his gorgeous face as tension grows in the piece. He moves freely with the music back and forth. The power of Liszt's composition overwhelms Ellie through Robert's intense interpretation, gaining momentum and volume in one luscious modulation. The transition grows louder still, modulating up again with stacked octaves passionately accenting the higher descant, then falling like the trickling of rain down the side of a hill where the tender bridge then evolves into the recitative of the primary theme, winding through the upper octaves in an elongation. Finally, he spirals slowly and softly back into the middle of the keyboard, ending simply with a rolled chord in the home key of A flat.

Ellie is beside herself on the last chord. It takes several seconds for her to register that he is finished, even with the crowd erupting in a massive standing ovation for Robert. She remains astonished and stunned, rising slowly in a daze to clap for him. Robert bows, pausing for the standard two to three seconds, and exits stage right while the audience of students continues thunderous applause.

"Isn't he amazing?" Carolyn asks, coming up beside her. "And so good-looking too," she adds.

Ellie does not respond but snaps into reality hearing Carolyn's voice. Suddenly, she checks her watch. "Oh, shoot! I'm late for my flute lesson. Gotta run! See you later, Carolyn." Ellie exits out the auditorium door. She can hear the applause start to die off as she runs up the steps to the lobby.

The schedule for music education majors is intense. Ellie manages to sneak in a lunch three days per week, but life is in motion every hour of the day. Clarinet is her first methods class of many required in learning all the instruments of a standard orchestral setting within a semester's time. Her clarinet professor is brilliant but warns it is appropriate for students to practice their secondary instrument an hour every day. Since clarinet is only a temporary secondary, the flute must continue to be the bulk of her practice time. Ellie's private instructor relays that her practice schedule should begin with an hour warm-up, complete with long tones and technique drills on flute. Then she may move to her secondary instrument for an hour, followed by another hour on flute, practicing lesson repertoire and wind band music. She is to end practice time with her primary instrument to secure muscle memory and retention of literature. Add in the hour of piano practice, and it is a wonder how any music education majors sleep.

Even with the intensity of her rigid routine, Ellie understands she must also find another campus job. Logging an average of three hours per week at minimum wage to set up the rehearsal hall will not be enough to help relieve the financial burden of attending college for her parents. She never takes for granted one moment of time her father spends working in an attempt to keep her in school.

As the daughter of a blue-collar self-employed craftsman in the Midwest, Ellie understands the sacrifice he perpetually makes for her and her sister, Marie. Growing up, Ellie and Marie saw little of their father six days a week. His hardworking nature was as evident then as it is now, and she genuinely respects the rough, course, and often dirty hands he comes home with on a daily basis. Hence, even if it means a loss of sleep, Ellie will do what she can to eliminate the extra costs of food, books, and miscellaneous expenses while in school.

By early September, Ellie finds a balance between her practicing, studying, and social life. Since the start of school three weeks ago, she has only attended one party and returned home early. Determined to work hard and stay focused, she never manages to see Robert outside of her piano class, which makes her both sad and relieved, though she is not certain why. Her insecurities tell her Robert is *just a nice guy* and likely has a number of girlfriends calling him up; it is best for her if she not invest any thoughts over him. When she does have a moment to think of him, she feels frustrated. *Was I just imagining he felt the same energy?*

Ellie reflects on Robert's impeccable performance the first day of recitals as she lets her fingertips run up and down the ivory keys, drilling her two-handed five-note major finger patterns. She is playing in her favorite practice room on the third floor of the music building on a Friday evening, which is home to an old Steinway grand piano crafted from rosewood. The finish is a chocolate-russet color with a dark timbre, an older, authentic, and beautiful sound to the hammers and frame.

It is fairly quiet as she sits staring at the stained glass window opposite from the door, taking a brief break. Having opened the adjacent small window beforehand, she enjoys a soft cool breeze flowing in from outside. Ellie pauses a moment to fill her lungs with a clean deep breath, releasing the exhale slowly, content and thankful for all the blessings in her life.

Starting with C major and ascending up the scales, Ellie reaches F sharp major and stops, frustrated again. That particular five-note finger pattern starts on three black keys with the fourth finger moving to a white then back to black for the fifth. With the two white keys to choose from side by side, she cannot seem to get her muscle memory to hit the correct one the first time around. She lays her head on top of her arm, resting it on the piano frame underneath, attempting to conjure ways to trick her brain into doing it correctly before it becomes a bad habit.

Robert is observing through the door's glass window frame, waiting for an opportune time to interrupt or hopefully use an excuse to help Ellie. When her head drops, he assesses what he can do and gently knocks, startling her again. He enters the practice room. She stands up immediately, turning to see who is there, scared suddenly to be alone in the late hour. With her hand pressed to her pounding chest, she sees it is Robert and is both relieved and feeling sick. "You've got to stop doing that. You're going to give me a heart attack!" Ellie says breathlessly with a slight grin on her face.

Robert responds with a brilliant smile and a coy look in his eyes. "My apologies, Ellie. I just happened to finish my practice session and walked by your room on my way out. It seemed like you were upset?"

"Oh, it's nothing. I was just frustrated with myself. Nothing out of the ordinary," Ellie responds with embarrassment.

"I would really like to help. What is frustrating you? It sounded like you were working on the finger patterns."

"Yes, I'm just trying to trick my brain into remembering a few things, that's all. F sharp major needs to be crossed off the circle of fifths, apparently," she adds with a casual, tired chuckle.

Robert shares her musician's humor then offers, "You know, when I'm having trouble with something new, I try to remember that the most basic theory information is sometimes helpful. For example, your basic pattern of whole steps and half steps can be useful here." He pauses, motioning for her to sit back down on the bench. She looks at him with mild apprehension and disbelief over his presence in the room. Ellie tries to keep a clear head.

"Oh. Okay," she responds hesitantly.

"Did you notice that your fourth finger is nearly touching your third finger when you play these patterns?"

"I guess I haven't, no. I've just been thinking about the key signature and hitting the correct keys."

"Well, remember, your fourth pitch is always a half step apart from your third, so they will always be tighter together for these patterns," Robert offers.

"I never thought of it that simply before. I feel like an idiot now, having tried to overthink things so much." Ellie looks down at the keys.

"You are not an idiot. Quite intelligent, I think." Robert speaks gently, waiting for her large blue eyes to peer up. When she finally does look, they both lock into each other's gaze.

Robert reluctantly breaks away from the trance first. "W-why don't you start from C major to see if that helps?" He backs up to give her space.

"All right." Ellie aligns her posture and begins at an allegro tempo in eighth notes. She feels nervous as she moves up to C sharp then D major, fearing that her habitual blunder on F sharp major is imminent. When she arrives there, she is amazed to flow right past and onto G major. She is excited, wanting to stop and thank Robert, but encouraged to move on and finish the last five scales. Then she completes the exercise. "Wow. Thank you so much, Robert! That was it. I just needed to hear that in my head," she speaks, elated with her progress over the hump.

"You are very welcome. I'm glad I could help," he answers with a beautiful smile while brainstorming how he could capture even more time with her alone.

Ellie turns on her bench with a gracious grin but looks down again, attempting to avoid the oncoming blush of her cheeks.

"You know, one thing I did notice when you got to F sharp, possibly preventing some progress, is really a common problem with the black keys."

"Which is what?"

"I don't know if you've started focusing on finger posture as opposed to correct notes, but the tendency is to flatten out your fingers when playing back-to-back black keys," Robert says, approaching the back of the piano bench.

"Oh, like this?" Ellie starts on the F sharp pattern, pulling her wrists toward the white keys and flattening the shape of her curved fingertips.

"Yes." Robert leans down to gently reshape the curve of her fingers by placing his first finger underneath for an arch, but when he touches her, a strange energy current mixed with heat flows beneath their skin. Both catch their breath and gaze into each other's eyes in shock for the overwhelming feeling neither can deny. As Robert's face is only inches from Ellie's, a zing of electricity flows in the air. They feel propelled toward one another but restrain the sprinting, lively force in their bodies.

Without dropping any eye contact, Robert speaks directly to her with a sudden burst of confidence. "Would you have dinner with me tomorrow night?"

"Yes," Ellie responds without hesitation, remaining in shock from the previous transactions.

Robert beams. His heart takes off in a flutter while he forces himself back toward the door. Ellie returns his coyness with a shy crooked grin and looks down, still feeling the heat from his touch. He surprises himself by backing up into the closed door suddenly. Ellie chuckles then confines it, closing her mouth.

"Right. I should probably watch where I'm going," Robert comments comically.

"It might be helpful."

"I will call you tomorrow." He turns the handle to exit the practice room, regaining his composure. "Good night, Ellie."

"Good night, Robert," she replies softly.

"Carolyn! What was I thinking letting you talk me into buying this outfit? I can barely sit down!" Ellie's voice reaches higher frequencies, panicking over the new black skirt she is zipping up along her lumbar, which her friend encouraged her to purchase that morning.

"Ellie, you look amazing! Don't think anything of it. Trust me, Robert will love it." Carolyn adjusts Ellie's rose-colored top, a folded off-the-shoulder blouse, baring her defined collarbone, long neck, and shoulders. "Now sit down in this chair and let me work my magic," she insists with a smile. Ellie sinks down in her desk chair in front of the long mirror Carolyn brought from her dorm room, feeling like her personal life-size Barbie doll. Her massive workstation of makeup is scattered atop Ellie's desk, as if she came straight from a Mary Kay convention.

"Where's your pink Cadillac, Carolyn?" Ellie snickers.

"I let my mom drive it while I'm away at school." She holds a straight face for three seconds, then bursts into a giggle while shifting Ellie's long golden curls away from her neck.

"How do you know so much about this stuff anyway?"

"Well, my mom put me in a few pageants back home in Minnesota, so I learned a ton from those experiences."

"Wow, that's neat. Did you ever win?"

"Yes, actually. I'll show you my dorm sometime. I've got ribbons and trophies from a couple. I even have my old tiara from the pageant I won, which is cool."

"That is really great," Ellie compliments. She watches Carolyn cover her whole face with ivory foundation using a sponge. Then she picks up a gargantuan brush, dabs it in the powder, blows, and wisps it all around Ellie's face and neck. Ellie watches Carolyn's defined and pretty profile in the mirror while she works, wondering why Robert never asked her out. *She has such a beautiful complexion, steel-blue eyes, and smooth, silky hair, so why on earth would he ask me out? I'm a mess!*

"You know, you really do have pretty skin, Ellie," Carolyn commends.

"Oh. Uh, thank you," Ellie replies with uncertainty.

"Ellie, come on. You can do better than that." She stops applying her makeup.

"What?" Ellie is perplexed and turns to view her expression.

Carolyn sighs. "You really don't know, do you?" Carolyn shakes her head.

"Know what?" The crease in Ellie's forehead creates a canal of skin.

"That you're beautiful," Carolyn states gently, showing her perfect set of straight white teeth.

Ellie turns back around in her chair, looking at her reflection in the mirror. "No," she sighs, looking down. Ellie's chin starts to quiver as the tears pool behind her eyes. "No, I don't think so," she whispers.

"Ellie, don't cry," Carolyn encourages. "You don't want puffy eyes for your date, do you?" She reaches over to hand Ellie a tissue box from the shelf beside her bed. "Listen to me. Wipe your tears and look at yourself. You need to take a long, hard look. You should see yourself for who you are now and start believing that what is outside matches the inside." She looks down and away from her reflection. Carolyn takes the sides of her face from behind and pulls up, attempting to draw her eyes back to the mirror. "Look!"

Ellie's last tear falls as she stares back at her features in the mirror, still unwilling to yield or concede Carolyn's opinion. The bangs of her golden hair are pulled back at the top of her head in a barrette, coming down in large soft curls on either side of her exposed shoulders. Her blue eyes peer underneath gently arched brows and are symmetrically balanced over voluptuous lips and straight teeth. Her figure is full without being overweight and a bone structure exemplifying a certain grace in every long limb when she moves. Ellie stares into her own eyes, wondering if she will ever believe anything other than the horrible names she has been called her whole life. *What power those kids still have over me!* Ellie sighs, glancing away.

"Whether you believe it or not, you must start accepting compliments better, Ellie. A lack of confidence is not charming, not that one should be smug, but a woman exudes maturity and poise. Look people in the eyes and don't apologize all the time."

The deep indent in Ellie's forehead reappears. "How did y—" Ellie stops her question, seeing Carolyn's angry glare.

Carolyn begins to primp her hair back into place, taking the brush from her large kit on the desk. "Ellie, just trust me. Relax tonight, and know you look gorgeous."

"Easy for you to say." She is pleased with her simple rebuttal.

⟡

Ellie waits for Robert with Carolyn in the courtyard just across from her dormitory. The brick pathway leads directly in front of the university center, circling around the back of the primary instructional building on campus. Carolyn and Ellie sit on the black rod-iron bench across the drive and wait.

"What kind of car does he drive?" Carolyn asks.

"Well, he said it's a black two-door car."

Carolyn scoffs. "Well, that sums it up."

"Carolyn, I'm already nervous as it is."

"Oh, right. Sorry. Where is he taking you for dinner?"

"He asked me what my preference was when I listed American and Italian as my favorite foods, but I told him either would be nice. He said he would surprise me," she adds with a soft smile.

"That's exciting. What time did he say again?"

"He said six thirty, so he should be here any minute."

"Over five minutes late. Can't say I'm surprised. Are you?"

"Oh, a little, I guess. I think Robert's different, don't you?" Ellie finishes her last word when a small black convertible gradually rounds the corner and comes to a stop in front of the bench on the brick drive.

"Oh. My. Gosh. Are you kidding me?" Carolyn is exuberant and giddy as she stands, making a quick, lyrical giggle. Ellie realizes her own mouth is still gaping open, entranced by the stunning and shiny Porsche 911 Carrera 4 964 Series with the top down.

Robert smiles at Ellie through his window while placing the car in park and removes his sunglasses. Ellie realizes he is looking at her directly, snapping out of her current trance. He waves briefly, waiting for the top to finish closing. Anxiety fills her lungs, making it impossible to breath. "Carolyn," she whispers, attempting to find purchase on her hand but only grazing her arm. Carolyn turns, seeing Ellie's pale and nearly translucent color.

Carolyn bends over directly in front of her face to whisper, "Ellie, pull it together. Come on, breathe! Remember what I told you? Confidence, maturity, and poise." Carolyn grips her shoulder exactly when Ellie lets out a deep exhale, dragging the next clean intake through her locked jaw. "Here." Carolyn takes a few items out of her purse hanging at her side. "I hear these can help relax your stomach muscles. Take them." She offers two peppermint candies, placing them in her hand.

Ellie looks up at Carolyn. "Is that true?"

Carolyn smiles. "Does it matter?" Ellie returns a forced half smile and briefly runs over a movie plot from childhood in her mind: an elephant thinks he can fly after his tiny mouse friend hands him a magic feather. Ellie glances around her to see Robert rolling up the windows. The car is ready.

"Okay." Ellie stands to view Robert's approach, wearing pressed khaki slacks, a black short-sleeve polo, and matching black belt and dress shoes. She looks up at his smiling face. The setting sun reflects off his powder-blue eyes with minimal pupil exposure to obstruct the vibrant iris color. He looks down in a blush from his slender six-foot-three frame, sliding one hand into his pocket. She quickly feels another palpitation and breathes out.

"Hi, Robert," Carolyn welcomes, breaking the ice. He looks up in the final few steps of his stride to the bench.

"Hello, Carolyn. How are you?" Robert asks politely in his silky voice, directing his eyes briefly to her then back on Ellie.

"I'm doing quite well, thanks. All right, I should be on my way for dinner. You two have fun!" Carolyn gives Ellie a quick side hug and happily walks toward the front of the university center.

"And how are you, Ellie?" He takes a step toward her five-foot-eleven stature. She draws her eyes slowly from his defined chest to his pointed chin, past his perfect nose, and finally to his eyes. Spending most of her youth as the tall one in class and again among her group of friends, she feels relief to be this close and interested in a taller man who is not related or a teacher. His scent nearly makes her knees buckle with a subdued woodsy fragrance of oak moss, juniper, and lavender, a musk combination exuding masculinity.

"I'm doing well. Nervous, but good." She speaks with eloquent hesitation and a slight smile.

Robert laughs once through his nose. "You're not the only one, if that makes you feel better."

Ellie responds with a subtle blush and nods gently.

"Shall we?" He turns to gesture one open palm toward his Porsche while the other hand hovers behind Ellie's shoulder but does not touch.

"Sure." Ellie walks gracefully toward the car.

"I apologize I'm a few minutes late. I wanted to stop briefly to pick up something for you," he finishes, opening the passenger door. Ellie takes a step toward the rear of the vehicle, allowing him to reach inside and grab a deep-pink long-stem rose from the floor of the car. "This is for you, Ellie." He hands it over gently.

Ellie's heart drops one solitary beat. "Oh, thank you. It's beautiful." She graciously accepts the rose, pulling it slowly to her nose with a smile. She takes a moment to enjoy the sweet blossom scent, closing her eyes to appreciate it fully.

"You're very welcome." Robert looks on, seeing her delight in the simple gesture. "It is quite beautiful, though not nearly as beautiful as you."

Ellie looks up into Robert's eyes and smiles. Her heart takes off in a sprint while her cheeks flush to match the rose in her hand. Embarrassed by his compliment, she looks away but quickly remembers Carolyn's advice and looks back up to Robert. "Thank you," she enunciates with fervor.

Robert gazes into her eyes and welcomes her to enter the vehicle. Ellie nods in response, walking forward to slide onto the black leather seat. After both feet and her purse securely rest on the car floor, Robert gently shuts the door and walks to the driver's side. Ellie grabs hold of her seat belt and fastens it as Robert settles into the driver's seat. His belt clicks under his left hand at the same time he releases the break with his right. "Are you ready?" he asks with a bright smile.

"Definitely," Ellie answers energetically. Robert takes hold of the gearshift in his right hand and accelerates smoothly around the brick drive. The union of his foot-and-hand coordination shifting the manual transmission is flawless.

Ellie begins to register sound as he makes the turn onto the main road along campus. "I really like this music. What are we listening to?"

"This is Art Tatum. Have you heard of him?"

"I'm sorry. I don't believe so, and I'm sure that's appalling to you." Ellie tucks her chin down.

"Actually, not at all. I regret not coming into the world of jazz until extremely late in high school. Once I discovered all the facets that world offered, I was furious." Robert gestures at the stereo controls.

"Because you felt you'd missed out," Ellie finishes his thought.

"Yes, exactly. I'm trying to catch up now, but...How did you know?" Robert glances toward her, shocked and impressed.

"I feel the exact same way. I play flute, and though I grew up absorbing multiple styles of music from my family, the opportunity to actually play jazz was minimal. I learned a lot in high school listening to our jazz bands and attending my sister's jazz concerts, but even she suffered in areas like improvisation because of what instrument she played."

"What did she play?"

"Marie played upright string bass in orchestra from an early age, then in jazz band when styles of literature necessitated it. Electric bass was her main instrument for jazz band and in pit for marching band. She was an exceptional player and superior reader. I'd say even better than myself."

"What happened? Why did she stop?"

"Hmm." Ellie shakes her head back and forth slightly with a sigh. "Marie did go to college last year for music on a scholarship for both her skills as an orchestral player and jazz musician." Ellie pauses, debating her next word choice. "Let's just say that sometimes bigger universities can afford not to play fair when you're a girl who just might outperform everyone else."

"Oh no," Robert responds.

"Yes. She ended up quitting altogether after a semester of all the political and sexist nonsense. It was really a shame. Marie is tall, beautiful, incredibly intelligent, and never had to work for it. She's always been that way," Ellie reflects, lacing her fingers together in her lap.

"It sounds like you admire her a great deal," Robert suggests.

"I do. And honestly, without the experience she was unfortunate to suffer, I wouldn't have chosen a smaller school. I'm glad I did too." Ellie blushes, realizing her own double meaning.

Robert slides into a parking spot at the restaurant and smoothly pulls the break up to park. He looks over at Ellie, waiting until she finally peers up at him. "I'm really glad you did too," he affirms in a gentle, silky voice. Ellie returns his smile. "Are you ready to eat?" Robert opens his door.

"Yes." Ellie grips the handle to her door but stops upon seeing Robert's expression.

"Please. Allow me," he says tenderly with a crooked smile.

Ellie reminds herself to breathe while he walks around the back of the car.

Robert reaches her door, opening it gently. Ellie gracefully steps out, looking for a sign, and sees a logo of a tipped-over brown jug. "Where are we?"

"It's top secret." He pauses with a devious smile. "It happens to have the best steaks in town, however."

The two sit at a quaint square table in the corner with a small white burning candle lighting the darker interior. Stained glass windows reminiscent of a renaissance court celebration let in a colorful superficial glow from outside light posts. The room is filled with couples eating, remaining quiet with no children to liven up the pleasant romantic setting.

Robert orders a steak and a twice-baked potato, feeling pleased he is out from the blanket of regular campus food. Ellie remains conservative in her selections knowing an early morning run is imminent, ordering salad and the cheese soup.

The conversation remains void of any lull. Lively and charismatic to know one another, they share information about friendships from high school, the new people befriended since starting college, and their current teachers and schedules. Robert's schedule is busier in credit requirements than his freshman year as a performance major, coinciding with preparations for a sophomore spring recital. The composition by Liszt from the first student recital in August is one of a number of selections he is working on for the event.

Dinner is enjoyable with no delays or questionable presentation. When the waitress sets the tab down, Robert quickly removes the black leather folder, places his cash payment inside without looking away from Ellie at the bill, and returns it immediately to the table. He insists on paying when Ellie offers her half of the bill with cash and is genuinely uncomfortable at the thought, especially when she asks to help with the tip. Robert lays down the full weight of his gaze to finalize his wishes. Ellie appreciates his decisiveness and the gesture of treating a lady when initiating the desire to go on a date, even if she is extremely thankful he asked her out.

Robert escorts her to the car. "Ellie, how do you feel about bowling?" he inquires with one perfectly arched brow and a crooked grin while opening her car door.

"Hah! Excellent. Let's go!" Ellie smiles back as he shuts the door.

Robert avoids the bowling alley right next to campus, putting the couple in a position for maximum privacy at another location down the main highway. The evening takes on a friendly and comical banter due to their equal lack of skills in the art of bowling. Both are athletic but take turns missing the pins altogether. A tragedy, considering Ellie's mother averaged scores of over two fifty in leagues and her grandfather's near-three-hundred average. Ellie still manages to beat Robert's less-than-impressive scores twice, but by no more than ten points. The two leave the bowling alley laughing and head back to campus in the Porsche.

Robert parks in the lot closest to the music building, inviting Ellie out of the car. "I thought we might take a walk. Is that all right?" Robert asks politely.

The last thing Ellie wants is to end their amazing evening. "Yes. It's a beautiful night for a walk." She laces her hands behind her body, looking up briefly. Robert admires her profile from the side, watching her enjoy the air. The curvature of her long neck and accentuated collarbone stand out to him as one of her countless striking features.

"Beautiful indeed," Robert replies. Ellie glances in his direction but is taken aback by his gaze in return. Her heart races in her ears briefly. She focuses on placing one foot in front of the other, looking down to ensure balance and to avoid him noticing her blush. Safely, she begins another string of questions to distract her heart.

"I suppose I've not even asked you where exactly you grew up in Chicago."

"Well, our home is in Kenilworth, which is a northern suburb. It's farther away from the city than I'd like, but it's home and very nice."

"I'd love to see pictures some time. I went to Chicago on a choir trip once and really fell in love with the city, but wish I'd been able to see more," Ellie adds with a soft smile.

"You were in choir?" Robert stops and turns.

"Oh. Well, I guess I never mentioned that, but yes. I suppose I could give you the 'I've been singing since I could talk' cliché, but it really is true in this case." Ellie laughs through her nose once.

"What part did you sing?" Robert asks, amused.

"Since I'm a flute player, I'm sure it's obvious, but I sang soprano one. I've always been in choir."

"Interesting. I'd love to hear you sing." Robert looks at her square in the face with a devious twinkle in his eyes from the lights.

"Oh boy," Ellie responds, beginning a descent down the cement steps at the back of the campus chapel.

"What's wrong?" Robert follows her down the stairs, caring tension in his voice.

"Well, there's a reason I picked instrumental music."

"Are you doubting your vocal skills?" he questions, landing beside her on the sidewalk.

"No, I'm doubting my nerves. Even with years of forcing myself to sing in front of people in variety shows, musicals, festivals, family functions, or even caroling, I'm no entertainer, and I'm okay with that. I sing to teach, which is what I love and enjoy most, so long as I'm conducting with my back to the audience," she replies, chuckling under her breath.

"I think that's fair," Robert offers, continuing their walk. "But I'd still like to hear you sing."

"So where did you go to school?" Ellie poses.

"I attended St. Joseph's, a private Catholic school near our suburb. My parents felt it necessary to place my little sister and I in a quality-education setting while keeping us together."

"You have a little sister?" Ellie lights up.

Robert sees her joyful reaction and smiles. "Yes. Her name is Ashley."

"Oh, how old is she?"

"Ashley is a junior and full of curiosity. I'm certain with her rate of questioning every little detail since childhood, she'll end up a scientist or a doctor," Robert offers, amused.

"Is she also a musician?"

"Actually, yes. She plays Horn and quite well."

"She must have an exceptional ear," Ellie comments and pivots right alongside the men's dormitory.

"She does, but because she is such a drifter and spends her time asking why to everything, Ashley lacks the focus to practice. It still comes quite naturally to her, but I can only imagine her performance with a minute amount of motivation. How frustrating!" Robert exclaims with a humorous tone. Ellie shares a brief laugh with him.

"I know exactly what you mean. Did she also have private teachers then?" The two begin a steep ascent up the stairs alongside the university center.

"Yes. My parents sought out the best instruction, driving us down to the city every Saturday morning for lessons with members of the Civic Orchestra of Chicago and even principals for the Chicago Symphony Orchestra on occasion."

"Wow. Are you kidding?" Ellie stops to look at Robert, a crinkle forming between her eyes and her mouth dropping open.

"No." Robert shakes his head. "But starting at the age of three was the best thing. I knew music would always be a part of my daily life, even as a child. I don't resent my parents as most children do for being forced. I wanted to learn and loved practicing." Ellie and Robert continue up the last of the steps. "They also found summer nourishment opportunities for me as well, like at Interlochen. I'm sincerely thankful and indebted to them for everything," Robert remarks with a tender thick timbre.

"I can imagine." Ellie turns to view the back of Robert's head, peering in the opposite direction as they walk forward. Sensing the emotion in his voice, she is uncertain how to soothe him. Fearing she will sound ridiculous in her attempt or make him uncomfortable with a gentle pat on the shoulder, she opts for neither and remains silent. The pair ends up next to the bench where Robert picked her up earlier that evening. One linear line short of a rectangle, the two nearly made a full loop around the inner perimeter of campus.

Ellie sits down on the iron bench, feeling cold to the touch from the drop in temperature. Robert joins her, finally glancing in her direction after regaining his composure. "I'm sorry. Are you cold?"

"A little, but it's okay." Ellie rubs her hands together, trying to subtly use friction.

"That was so thoughtless of me to forget my jacket in the car. I knew you would probably need it." He shakes his head, embarrassed.

"Robert, it's okay. Thank you though. I should have opted for pants. In fact, since we are right next to my dorm, would you mind if I went in to change quickly?"

"Oh, please do. That would ease my guilt tremendously and make you more comfortable as well."

"Wait here. I'll be right back," she says with an exuberant smile.

"Absolutely," he returns with a warm expression and half a grin.

Ellie begins a quick pace to her dorm. Robert watches her gracefully and briskly head across the drive. "Oh no!" Ellie turns to face him. He immediately stands in response.

"What's wrong?"

"I left the rose in the car," she responds, walking back slowly. Robert smiles in relief. "It's so beautiful. I don't want it to wilt."

Robert walks toward her to close the gap. "Don't worry, Ellie. I can guarantee it won't be the last rose you receive from me, but I promise to get it to you."

Ellie pauses to catch her breath at his words. "Thank you. I'll be right back." She turns to resume her pace to the dorm.

Entering her room, it is unsurprisingly empty. With Ginny out and likely up to no good, changing is an easy process. She opts for a fresh coat of deodorant before donning her jeans, white undershirt, and a plain beige sweater. She slides into her running shoes and places a pale-pink windbreaker over the top. Stepping in front of the mirror, she notices strands of hair to tame back to the correct position along with the need to apply a quick facial touch-up. Upon finishing, she pops five to six Tic Tacs into her mouth at the same time. She closes her door, attempting to melt them down rapidly before reaching the exit downstairs. Robert is still forty yards away, but her heart sprints as he stands when seeing her approach. His smile is apparent even from a lengthy distance in the dim lighting.

Ellie closes the gap to the bench. "Thank you for waiting."

"Anytime. You look more comfortable and just as gorgeous as before. Now, I wonder how that works."

"Uh." Ellie lets out a breathy half laugh. "I'm not certain that's the case, but thank you," she replies with a blush, looking away.

"Would you prefer to sit or continue walking?" Robert uses his hands to gesture the options.

"Actually, let's sit. I have a question that's been on my mind since you picked me up." Ellie sits with Robert following suit, now closer to her on the bench. "This may sound like a forced question, and I don't mean to pry, but my curiosity is killing me."

"You want to know how it is I'm driving a Porsche, don't you?" Robert looks fractionally smug.

"Well, it is a very nice car. I'm interested, but I don't want to make you uncomfortable."

"It's okay. I want to tell you, and please, ask me anything you like."

Ellie nods in response.

"I tried to tell my father not to waste his money, but of course he insisted, and I didn't want to upset him further."

"Further?" Ellie questions.

Robert sighs, running his hand through his hair nervously. He pauses for several moments while pondering his thoughts. "Ellie, nearly two years ago my mother passed away from a massive coronary heart attack." Robert pauses briefly, allowing Ellie a chance to absorb the information. Her hands swiftly move to her mouth, covering her shocked response.

"She was feeling tired and short of breath for two weeks prior to the coronary, but she equated it to being under the weather. My little sister and I were her priority for sixteen years, and she was never ill. If she was sick, she never let it show. Her symptoms appeared over several days' time when I was a senior and Ashley was a freshman. We kissed Mom good-bye that morning in January, and I noticed she was particularly pale. I reminded her to call the doctor, as did my father, before we left, and I drove us to school.

"When we returned home, I called out for her, and she didn't answer." Robert pauses once again, recalling details he no longer wanted to relive.

"You found her," Ellie concludes in a whisper.

Robert's head dips down, his upper frame collapsing for the first time all evening. He rests his elbows atop his legs and runs his hands through his hair, pulling as he goes.

"Yes," he breathes.

"Robert," she exhales. Her tears easily run over the brims of her eyes. She continues cupping one hand over her mouth as the other travels involuntarily halfway to console him. She nearly makes it to his back before she stops, realizing he is likely tired of people feeling sorry for him. Ellie wipes her tears and takes a few moments to regroup. "I know you have probably grown to resent people saying how sorry they are, so I won't do that. I'd rather tell you…that if I were ever fortunate to have a son and he grew up to be half the man you've become, I would be *incredibly* proud."

Robert slowly sits up to turn toward Ellie, whose eyes are still sparkling from the tears. "Thank you, Ellie. That is so much better to hear, and it means more coming from you." He sees another tear escape down her cheek and wonders why. "Hey, I'm supposed to be the one crying. Please tell me what you're thinking," he requests in a smooth, soft voice.

"I'm sorry, I didn't mean to cry like this," she states, wiping her tears with the back of her sleeve. "I'm sure this doesn't help you," Ellie adds.

"Please think nothing of it," he replies while moving closer to her face to converse freely.

"I was assembling all the pieces in my head," Ellie answers. "I've suffered a contagion of losses in my life but cannot fathom losing a parent. I was thinking how selfish it feels to draw sadness and anxiety over deaths in *my* family when I've never suffered a loss like yours."

Robert looks down as he listens. "We all grieve in different ways, Ellie. How do you know my pain is worse than yours?" he interrupts gently.

"I suppose I don't, and you may be at peace with your faith enough to feel differently than I do about everything, but the void you carry for your mother is irreplaceable. I just can't imagine." Ellie turns her body to him at an angle, fidgeting with her hands as she compiles her next words. "And with this knowledge, I've realized something else about you that makes me both angry yet proud again." She sits up straighter and looks squarely at him.

"What's that?" Robert looks up into her eyes in anticipation.

"Robert, I'm quite certain you could have gone anywhere in the country on a full scholarship for piano. Namely Juilliard, for one. It's obvious you wanted to stay close enough to get home quickly to be there for your sister and father, but leave a large enough gap between you and Chicago to cope easier." Ellie pauses momentarily, watching his face. She then studies his upper and lower lips, now parted in shock. In between the silence and staring at his mouth, she ventures down an avenue of her imagination she knows she should abandon. She opts for breaking into his reflection. "Was I totally off? I'm sorry if I upset you."

"H-how…how do you do that?"

"Do what?"

"Take a stab in the dark and completely hit the nail on the head. How do you do it?"

"It's not something I do all the time. Trust me." Ellie half rolls her eyes and smiles crookedly, embarrassed by his assumption.

"I completely do. You must have psychic powers."

"No, not at all. I've just always felt my way through things. People seem easier to read when I place myself so deeply in their shoes. It's probably not the smartest thing to do, but I'm not sure people should lead with their head all the time. I'm 100 percent certain the world would be a better place if people thought with their heart instead of their head. It may not be as organized, but people would be more content with the honesty." Ellie breaks out of her rant to see Robert gazing into her eyes. "I'm sorry, I'm rambling," she admits quietly with a soft smile.

"No, Ellie. Don't apologize. I think you're brilliant." He pauses briefly to move closer. "If I were fortunate to have a daughter who loved half as much as you, I would be very proud. You should never apologize for saying what you feel because *that* is who you are, and it is beautiful. The root of your gifts is your heart." Ellie is drawn into his eyes and the words pouring out of his perfectly sculpted lips. The energy around the couple intensifies from a subdued glowing aura to burning magnetic cables, propelling them toward each other. Ellie fears she has nearly lost her will-power altogether.

Robert can barely contain his natural response, wanting to hold and kiss her deeply. Refusing to skip the proper steps, he breaks the connection of eye contact first, but before she considers any offense, Robert takes her hand.

A warm current zings underneath their skin, creating a sharp inhalation through Ellie's lips. Robert feels the surge just as in the practice room. The new sensation requires time for both to recover their thoughts; Robert makes soothing circles on the back of Ellie's hand. "That's going to take some getting used to," he comments with a coy smile.

Ellie laughs briefly. "Yes. I never realized..." She trails off, unwilling to give away her feelings too soon. Incredibly grateful for this moment with Robert, she looks down and away, shaking her head.

"You never realized that it could feel this way?"

"Not in the least."

"Hmm," Robert breathes, taking hold of her other hand. He delicately traces soothing circles on her hands. She feels World War III could break out, and she would never know the difference. They sit in silence, enjoying the feeling that permeates through their bodies.

"I suppose I never answered your original question," Robert reminds Ellie.

"Oh, I forgot as well," she responds lightly. "I gather you couldn't talk your father out of the car purchase under the circumstances."

"You gather correctly. He just wanted me to get back and forth from school safely and get to mass on Sundays. I've actually only had it for about six months."

"Interesting. What does your father do?"

"He is CEO for a biomedical research company in affiliation with Northwestern."

Ellie forces her mouth shut.

"Yes, my father is a smart engineer and businessman, but what's most impressive is that he was there for us. He never made it seem like we were his second priority. He made sure we understood he wanted to be there if he had to miss anything at all." Robert looks down at Ellie's hands.

"That's wonderful he supported you in that way considering everything on his plate for work." Ellie is genuinely happy for him.

"Yes, I'm incredibly lucky." Robert trails his eyes slowly back up. Ellie blushes from his intended meaning and looks away. "Ellie, may I see you tomorrow?"

"I'd like that."

"Perfect. There's a park near campus within walking distance. Can I meet you right here after lunch at twelve thirty?"

"That sounds nice," she replies warmly.

"Wonderful. I hope you had a nice time tonight."

"I had an amazing time. Thank you for everything."

Robert stands slowly while holding her hands. He pulls her up gently up to face him. Looking into her eyes, he brings the back of her right hand up to his lips. Deliberately and slowly, he kisses it, maintaining eye contact. "Good night, Ellie. Sweet dreams," he offers with his crooked smile. While lingering there with her right hand, he pulls up the left and kisses it as well.

Ellie is certain Robert can hear her heart accelerate like a propeller. "Sweet dreams to you, and thank you again, Robert." She takes a step toward her dorm feeling Robert's touch cling to her skin. Their arms stretch out as the gap widens between them.

"Good night."

"Good night," she replies softly. When the couple's fingertips finally release, both are left with the sudden reality of the current chill in the air.

Robert shoves his hands into his pockets and watches Ellie walk to her dorm. Once she is safely inside, he walks toward his car, glancing back frequently over his shoulder, wanting to remember this night always.

Ellie hears her phone ringing from down the hall and rushes to turn the key to her room, pushing it open. She sprints toward the other side where the phone rests on the mini refrigerator. "Hello?"

"So I want all the juicy details. What did you do? Where did he take you? Is he a good kisser? Come on, Ellie!"

"Carolyn, I could swear you're trying to live this out vicariously through me," she utters into the phone.

"Well, we do have similar tastes in men." She pauses. "All right, fine, I think Robert's a total fox. Would you pa-lease tell me now?"

"All right, all right." Ellie concedes as Carolyn giggles like a four-year-old.

CHAPTER

12

Ellie wakes to bright sunshine through her dorm window. She glances briefly at the alarm clock. *Seven thirty-eight? Ugh! I don't think I dozed off until after two.* She rolls onto her side, desperately wanting to fall back asleep before the alarm sounds at nine for her morning run and church. After speaking to Carolyn about her evening with Robert, she was too hyper for bed. Reminiscing every detail of her time with him, she feels it hopeless to even think she could go to sleep now. She turns to her left side to catch a glimpse of Ginny on her bed, passed out on top of the sheets with her shoes and clothes on from the previous night. Lying on her stomach with her mouth open and one leg hanging off the bed, her blond hair is still pulled up in a loose frazzled ponytail. *At least she made it to the pillow.* She chuckles to herself.

Ellie pops out of bed and assembles her exercise attire. After she heaves her thick hair into a ponytail, she laces up her running shoes and grabs her portable cassette player and headphones. She rewinds the Tracy Chapman cassette to the beginning, presses play, and uses the clip of the player to wedge it between her back and sports bra. *Someone really needs to invent an armband strap or something.*

After Ellie's run around campus and the track, she returns to shower and dress for church. Every Sunday, she sings in the choir at a Presbyterian church affiliated with campus. It is a perfect opportunity to keep singing while her rigid course and work schedules force her out of being in the university's stellar choral program.

While singing at church, every note pierces through Ellie's ears during the service, feeling hypersensitive to all she hears. Never more alive, she likens it to her time with Robert; the euphoric expression never disappears from her face. Carolyn glances at her in the choir loft often, making silly expressions associated with love; Ellie loses her grip on a straight face twice. However, as she listens to the sermon, she feels excessive peace. Her spirit is greatly exposed and raw inside, creating intense emotions of gratefulness and genuine humility for the blessings in her life.

After church, Ellie and Carolyn eat lunch at the campus café before heading back to the dorms. Carolyn invites Ellie back to her room to show her all of her old pageant ribbons and paraphernalia. She lets Ellie try on her tiara and shows her how to perform a proper pageant wave. It is more complicated than Ellie anticipates, joking that her dreams of becoming a contestant are now crushed.

Carolyn shows her trophies for horseback riding as well.

"I've never seen a riding competition before. That's so neat!"

"Horses are beautiful creatures, so graceful and gentle. When you look into their eyes and spend those initial moments breathing softly into their face to share your scent and touch their nose, it's like they can read your thoughts," Carolyn reflects.

"I bet you miss riding."

"I do. Very much," Carolyn adds, somberly letting the moments pass. Suddenly, she turns to look at the clock. "Oh, we've got to get you ready, girl! Let's go!" Carolyn gently pushes Ellie out of the door to walk over to her dorm.

Ellie walks out of the dormitory door at twelve thirty, seeing Robert waiting at *their* bench already. The acceleration of her heart immediately takes off as she approaches. Focusing on his eyes, she does not notice the two red roses in his hands. *Would it be awkward if I sprinted?* The gap between them closes, and without losing any momentum, she comes within inches of his body while staring into his eyes.

"Hello, Ellie." He smiles with a look of peace.

"Hi," she breathes sweetly, biting down on her lower lip coyly.

"How was your morning?"

"Peaceful. And yours?"

"Likewise. Is that a coincidence, you think?" His grin widens, lightly chuckling at his rhetorical question.

"If peace stems from happiness, you'd think I would sleep better." She lowers her eyes to his chest, fearing the dark circles are obvious.

He takes his free hand to pull her chin back up gently. His touch initiates the vigor and heat in her blood, making her breath catch. "I also couldn't sleep last night. I think part of being happy means you don't want to miss anything or any detail. The best moments of my time are spent retracing every second with you now," Robert admits.

Ellie knows exactly what he means; she feels her blood rush, standing close to his perfect face and mouth.

Robert comprehends a mere three inches separates him from touching her full lips to his own. He desperately wants to move forward. Without shifting his eyes from hers, he smoothly brings the roses up from his side. "For you, Ellie."

Ellie's eyes brighten upon focusing on the deep-red roses with unfolding gorgeous petals. "Oh, these are so perfect, Robert! Thank you," Ellie says slowly. She buries her nose near the top of both flowers. "I absolutely love roses."

"I'm glad you like them. Our gardens at home have tea roses scattered all throughout our landscape. The fragrance is so refreshing in the late spring and through the summer."

"Mm, I can imagine that's lovely," she ponders. "Okay, I've already lost one rose, so may I please go put these in water before our walk?"

"I promise your rose is still safe. Trust me. But yes, you should absolutely take them to your room."

"I'll need to find a vase, so I'll be as quick as I can."

"Take all the time you need."

"Thank you."

She has no vase. Noted, Robert reflects.

When Ellie returns, Robert escorts her through the center of campus at a diagonal path. They travel down a street along the outside perimeter, passing by three sorority houses along the way. The couple reaches the entrance to the grounds, which has an open iron-rod double gate. An old red-bricked street leads into the park but seamlessly transitions into a paved drive that stretches around the vast space.

Robert reaches his desired walking trail that loops around the entire park and includes a landscape of hundreds of beautiful old oak trees, a small lake, and rose gardens. When he feels at peace with their pace, he takes her hand.

"That feels so nice," Ellie speaks softly.

"Yes, it does," Robert agrees.

"I always thought these reactions were made up just for movies." Ellie chuckles lightly.

"It does seem rare. Have you ever been in a relationship?"

"Hah! No." She shakes her head, looking down at the ground.

Robert is confused by her response.

"You have to be asked out first to be in a relationship."

Robert halts abruptly, turning to look at her face with a slightly horrified expression. "No one ever asked you?"

Ellie pauses for a moment, rummaging through the words in the admission she is about to phrase. "Not one." She breaks briefly to hold back the emotions beginning to boil in her chest. "Just this past summer I lost a lot of weight. I suppose people from high school may not even recognize me now."

"You think you weren't asked out because of your weight?"

"Sadly, I don't think—I know. It's tough to be overweight, but even worse when it's accompanied by being tall. People can be quite cruel, especially when magazines give them a solid conception of *the norm*."

"It infuriates me to think of how shallow minded people behave, and typically when they're pressured to fit in cliques. It's a game of negativity, aiming at self-gratification and what people feel is humor. It makes me extremely angry knowing you suffered from that behavior," he consoles, squeezing her hand gently. They continue walking on the path.

"I wouldn't say it's something I ever got used to, but I became hyper aware and sensitive to my surroundings. Always worried about what people were thinking or what was being whispered. Being coordinated in sports helped a little because I wasn't completely without ability, but they focused on appearance."

"I take it you were unable to find someone worth liking under those circumstances then?"

"Well, no, actually." Ellie sighs. "I'm all too familiar with unrequited love." She pauses to look over at him as he memorizes her expressions. Puffing a touch of air through her nose to laugh at her thoughts, she gestures quickly to her chest with an index finger. "Big heart, remember?"

"Was it very hard for you? Did you ever tell him?"

"Yes, it was torture. That type of unanswered love is my idea of hell because what I have to give is wasted. I did tell him, but the whole 'I'm flattered, but I just want to be friends' answer seems to be a preprogrammed, robotic response."

"And are you still friends?"

"For now," she replies gently with a whimsical smile.

Robert lets out a lighthearted laugh. "You deserve to be upset. He's obviously a complete idiot."

"Hmm. He is tragically self-absorbed. Let's put it that way."

"Then you should know you are too good for him." Robert stops in the trail to take both her hands. She looks into his eyes as he unlaces one hand to pull back a strand of thin blond hair blowing across her face. The soft pattern he traces leaves a warm tingle along her nerves.

Will I ever get used to this? Ellie ponders.

"He doesn't deserve you," Robert says gently, slowly tucking the strand behind her ear. He lingers near her cheek with the back of his smooth hand, gracefully feeling the softness of her skin and rush of heat with his fingers and thumb. She moves her free hand to the back of his, exactly when he cups the side of her face. They stand unmoving, feeling the newness of their intensity together.

Robert sighs. "Hmm." He brushes her hair back, exposing her neck.

"What's wrong?"

"I'm beginning to understand now how difficult this is going to be," Robert says with a loving half smile.

"How difficult what is going to be?"

"To ever lose you," Robert replies, casting his eyes down.

"Robert," Ellie sighs. She takes the opportunity to follow her physical instincts for the first time. This perfect and incredibly sculpted face is inches away and open to explore. She gently places both her hands on the sides of his gorgeous smooth skin. The sunlight leaks through the windblown trees, making patterns dance along his face. Ellie strokes his cheeks with her thumbs, feeling the contour of his cheekbones with her fingertips. He closes his eyes to fully grasp the ardency in her touch. She ventures toward Robert's mouth and the sensitive natural crease of his smile. The tips of her thumbs then lightly trace over his lips, leaving him with an overwhelming sensation. He shivers, opening his eyes.

"Hey, guys, heads up! Bikers coming!" A biker zooms past Ellie and Robert just on the outside of the paved trail. Robert sees a pack of a dozen cyclists heading straight for them. He quickly pulls her off the trail by the hand and into his arms, embracing her around the shoulders. They watch the bikers pass quickly.

"Well, that was exciting." Robert chuckles. "And one way to get you into my arms."

Ellie laughs with him. "Don't worry. You don't need bikers to get me into your arms."

Robert releases his hold fractionally, sliding his hands down around the back of her waist, waiting for her to look into his eyes. "In that case, I'm never going to let you go." She trails up to meet his gaze, knowing he is completely dedicated to their relationship.

"Are you saying you want me to be your girlfriend officially?" Ellie asks with a coy, bright smile.

He returns her brilliant energy in kind. "Would you please do me the honor?"

"Hmm." Ellie prolongs a dramatic pause, toying with her response. "I'm not sure you're charming, sweet, intelligent, or talented enough. I'll have to think about it." Ellie snickers. Knowing he may jokingly take offense, she lets go of him to nonchalantly place herself behind a large oak, turning to smile at him.

"Oh, that's really funny. Come here!" He reaches out for her and misses. Ellie starts a dead run around the back of the tree and into an open pasture of Kentucky bluegrass. Robert follows with a long stride. She keeps a good lead on him with her fast sprint but knows she cannot keep the pace long. Ellie turns suddenly before reaching a small hill, laughing as he closes in on her. "You won't get away now," he smiles in a pant.

"How do you know I ever planned to?" she inquires breathlessly.

Robert lunges toward her, seeing her reflexively scoot to the side. "Do you have secret ninja moves too?" He moves forward and corners her in front of the hill again alongside a massive oak tree—cat and mouse.

"None that I'll show you. They're sec—" Ellie is cut off by Robert's quick lunge as they plummet into the low-grade slope. The two enjoy several moments of breathless laughter, waiting for their heart rates to slow down. Robert's hand is draped across her stomach while they rest side by side in the grass.

"Gotcha," Robert boasts, turning on his side to prop himself on his left elbow.

Ellie stares into his eyes as her chest continues its labored breathing. "You already did, Robert," she replies in a serious tone, with no trace of doubt in her voice.

Robert slowly traces a line with his fingertips down the side of her hairline, behind her right ear, to the base of her jaw, and the point of her chin. He opens his palm to feel the soft skin underneath his large hands, using his thumb to make soothing circles. Ellie places one hand on the side his face then runs her fingers through his soft wavy brown hair. Neither veers from the other's eyes, content to stay in the grass all afternoon.

"You know, I noticed in your list of attributes that *good-looking* wasn't mentioned," Robert comments with his crooked smile.

Ellie rolls her eyes. "Robert, come on."

"I'm just curious, that's all," he replies innocently.

"It's not my number one priority, and I'm sure you can understand why. You *know* you're gorgeous, but that's not why I'm here."

"You don't want to judge the way you feel people have judged you." Robert finishes her line of thinking.

"Exactly. It's wrong. I think more people should meet over the phone or through letters, but I'm not sure the world will ever change to be that selfless and perfect."

"Oh, I don't know." He pauses to tenderly lift her head under the seat of his bicep, pulling her onto his chest as he lies down. She rests her head below his left shoulder while he softly wraps his arms around her. "The world seems pretty perfect today."

"Yes," Ellie breathes. Moments pass as she ruminates over her next question. "So I'm genuinely curious now, but have you been in any relationships?"

"I've been in one, but it was a big mistake." Robert pauses briefly. "Freshman year, a good friend of mine decided we should go to a fall dance together just as friends. We went, we danced, and then at the end of the night, she thought it a good idea to start dating. I was naïve enough to think she was right since we got along so well. For six months, we were basically friends who held hands. No chemistry at all. Her new clique of high school girlfriends sifted through everything I said or wrote in letters. I felt like I was dating half the girls in school because they all knew our business."

"Did you ask her to stop?"

"No, I just ended it in the spring. I knew she wouldn't change. The clique she associated herself with absorbed her entire character by that point. Even if she were to change and step away from them, I already knew she wasn't for me. Not just that, but high school girls were not for me."

"You never wanted to date anyone else in high school after that? No one ever caught your eye?"

"No." He rubs Ellie's arm contently.

"I'm certain you had offers," Ellie assumes.

"Yes, and from a couple of nice girls. However, for good reason, no one ever swayed me," Robert comments, feeling sanguine.

"Interesting. All right, here's another crucial topic. Catholicism is important to you."

"Yes, my whole family attends mass every Sunday. Again, I'm fortunate enough to still feel attached to my faith that I want to get up and go."

Ellie sits up, her elbow propped, looking somber while she contemplates.

"What's the matter?"

"Robert, you know I'm not Catholic. I've always been interested in it, but I'm not sure I've found the right home for me yet. My parents just threw us into the closest church, hoping we'd learn something about morals. I've explored many avenues of Christianity in the last couple years, and the thing is, I can appreciate how each does it differently." Ellie dwells quickly on her next thoughts. "I don't ever want to get in the way of your faith. I can imagine your mother would be upset if she knew we didn't match in the most important way." She looks away to hide her gloomy disposition.

"Ellie, my mother was an amazing woman. We had some intriguing conversations in the last two years of her life. It's even strange to think how much we talked now in retrospect, as I'm certain it was God's way of providing us closure. For some reason or another, this topic did come up, and one thing she made me promise her was that I would love a woman for who she is, not how she celebrates her faith in God."

Ellie glances back at Robert, who is looking at her with a great sense of peace on his face. Even with the multitude of questions she wants to ask, instead, she lets the relief wash over her, seeing his arms open and ready to hold her again. She lies back down, snuggling against him. The warmth radiating through their skin is powerful. The force and passion of it overwhelms Ellie's emotions. A tear rolls down the corner of her eye. She sniffles quickly at the same instant Robert feels a tiny wet spot on his chest.

"I think I would have really liked your mother," Ellie admits.

"And she you, Ellie. I know for certain." He gently shifts the long golden curls away from her neck. "May I take you to dinner again?"

"I'd love that." She wraps her hand around his right arm for a slight squeeze.

Robert holds Ellie under the oak tree for two hours, content in both silence and intermittent talking. It is the perfect September afternoon with clear blue skies and a mild breeze to curve the tips of the grass. In their most peaceful silence, they even fall asleep for a brief time.

The couple returns to campus for an early dinner in the lower university center sub-and-grill café. After a delightful post-meal conversation, Robert takes Ellie for a short ride over to Dairy Queen. The evening air is calm while they enjoy their favorite Blizzards outside the music building's main entrance steps. Robert tosses the empty cups into the trash can and offers his hand to Ellie. He helps her off the step and nudges her to come inside the building. She follows willingly, wondering what he is up to. Ellie is escorted up the first flight of steps to the second floor, but Robert pulls her around again to ascend up the next flight of stairs to the third floor. Once at the top, he wraps his arm around her shoulders and guides her down the left hallway to her favorite practice room. He opens the door and motions for her to sit at the bench. She follows his lead but is confused as to why he wants her to practice right now.

"Please, Ellie, would you play one of your compositions for me?" Robert requests in an appealing, soothing voice.

"Oh no." Ellie stands up. "I haven't played through any of them in weeks!"

"You know as well as I do that it's just like riding a bike. No worries. How would I know if you ever made a mistake?"

"Easy. You'll be staring at my face the whole time, that's how."

"All right. I promise not to stare at your face. Is that acceptable?"

"My hands though. My technique is still so awful."

"I'll close my eyes, Ellie. Please?" Robert's plea behind his blue eyes sends a wave of heat through her icy veins.

Ellie sighs. "I can't believe you're making me do this." She shakes her head and sits back down to look over the black-and-white keys, debating which composition to play.

Robert bends down behind her and speaks at his lowest volume at the base of her right ear. "Ellie, just breathe." A shiver runs down her spine while placing her hands on the ivory keys as her mind slowly returns from dysfunctional intoxication.

She starts to hear the introduction in her head. *Key, tempo, dynamics, structure, phrasing, imagery...muscle memory. Go!* The music begins in the upper register with a six-note melody—an eerie slow tapping on a windowpane from the wind. A soft, tender theme elongates the melodic motif in a lower octave, accompanied by root, fifth, and octave ascending and descending arpeggios in the left hand. The pattern repeats again, establishing a sense of home to the listener. Then a pull of tension as the bridge develops deeper and lower with dissonance and louder dynamics, building a forceful transition into a grander, fuller version of the refrain. The melodic motif is played again with vigor. The music then softens into a transition into the next lowest octave. Quieter still, it spirals down to signal the closing of the window and the four final chimes like that of a retreating grandfather clock. Ellie's head drops, waiting for the last notes to dissipate completely while she pushes down the sustain pedal.

Ellie's ears begin to register sound, beginning with an intake of air from Robert behind the bench. She relaxes her hands in her lap from the keys only to have them quickly scooped up by Robert, who sits down beside her backward on the bench. He situates both her hands in his, interlacing their fingers, waiting for her eyes to move from the floor to him. He waits longer.

"I-I'm sorry. It probably sounds so simple and elementary to your trained ears." Ellie finally looks up, stunned to silence at what she sees. Robert's eyes are pink around the edges with one tear still flowing aside his nose. "Oh." She immediately unlaces one hand to tenderly touch underneath his left eye with her thumb, dabbing the wetness.

"Ellie...I don't have the words. I absolutely loved it. I know you probably believe I'm just saying this, but I'm truly not." Robert holds her hand to his cheek, caressing it.

"Really?"

"It made me think of my mother," he offers, returning their united hands back down to her lap. "Sometimes I see her in my dreams, and when I closed my eyes, I pictured the light of her spirit at my window at home. The music sounded almost like we were on an adventure around the world in one night's time, ending so perfectly with the imitation of the clock." Robert reflects further. "Why did you write this piece? What does it mean to you?" He glances up briefly then back down, somewhat embarrassed by his emotional state.

"Actually..." Ellie hesitates on her next statement. "I wrote this for my mother, Robert." His eyes pop up to her face. "It's called 'A Mother's Love.'"

He squeezes her hands slightly as she peers up quickly to read his face. "My mother taught me everything about affection. She was the only person who told me I was beautiful after a bad day at school. She held me as I cried." Ellie's tears run down her cheeks from the corner of her eyes.

Robert brushes the lose strands of hair away from her face and rests his large hand at the base of the back of her neck. He embraces her there, pulling her head softly forward as she looks down in shame from the tears. Their foreheads touch while his hand caresses her neck then travels to her upper back to make a slow soothing pattern.

"Quite the pair," Robert comments with a whimsical grin, laughing a puff of air through his nose. Ellie smiles back momentarily, her crying nearly ceasing.

The magnetism of their chemistry is overwhelming this close in proximity, but Robert subtly pulls back one-half inch. He removes his left hand from her fingers to lay it at the other side of her face. He gently nudges her chin up so she will gaze into his eyes. "I will never allow you to feel anything less than breathtaking. Everything about you is perfection to me, Ellie." Her lids gradually drop to cover her eyes, unwilling to accept his words—an innate and instinctual response.

"Ellie, look at me," he commands with gentle fervor. She proceeds to follow his wishes. "You *are* lovely." He brushes her cheeks with his thumbs, wiping away the final drops of water. With lips only centimeters apart, Robert begins to feel his self-control slip; the heated attraction is excessively forceful. He leans toward her, slowly closing his eyes as Ellie feels the natural progression of her next move. The initial touch of their lips sends rolling waves of electricity through their bodies. Neither can imagine ever wanting to stop the intimacy of their tender kissing. Both sets of hands are busy, delicately caressing the other's hair, neck, and face.

The couple cannot believe their strike of fortune in these personal moments of complete bliss. Robert and Ellie feels it a dream to be desired by the other, peeking from underneath the subtle creased opening of their eyelids to catch a glimpse at the perfection of one another's face.

The time in the practice room lapses quickly. Forehead to forehead as they stand now, Robert holds Ellie in his arms, knowing she has homework to finish. "I could hold you like this forever," he says, wrapping his hands around her back.

She returns his passionate embrace, squeezing his upper frame. "I know exactly what you mean."

"I know I need to get you back though."

"Oh. What time is it?" Ellie pulls back to question and looks for the stainless steel Rolex Submariner around his wrist.

"It's a little after nine," he replies gently. "I'll get you back."

"I'm sorry, Robert. I didn't intend to end the evening in a rush."

Robert chuckles slightly. "I'm certain neither of us would change one thing about our day, but schoolwork does dampen the mood slightly."

Ellie smiles at him, feeling the weight of his maturity in these moments.

"May I play something for you before we go?" Robert asks.

"Yes, please do. I love hearing you play. What is it?"

"It's a piece I'm working on for my recital. See if you can tell who composed it from what I have memorized so far." He sits down at the piano with perfect posture, placing his hands on the keys. The subtle, soft undulation of opening arpeggios starts in D flat major, and within a short number of counts, the melodic line begins. Simplicity inside the romanticism, the piece flows into a variation on the theme in stacked chords, creating a sense of a rolling ocean tide: forward then pulling back. Tenderly, the theme reappears, and grace notes outline an embellishment of the motif. Intensity builds now in preparation for a release, and on the resolve, he gently returns to the arms of the original theme again. The tension builds with dynamics and a quicker pace, flourishing in every direction possible, then retreating moderately in a spinning elongation and ascension up to heaven as if being set down softly to sleep on a cloud.

Robert breathes out a sigh, finally releasing the last dissipating chord by lifting the suspension pedal. The trance of his performance mode comes to a close within moments. He subtly clears his throat. "I didn't think I knew all of it yet," he admits in a smooth tone, staring at the piano in slight disbelief.

Ellie can barely stand. The spell she is under unravels gradually. "Robert, that was easily the most beautiful piece of music to ever grace my ears," she utters in shock. He turns to view her glowing face, genuine in all tender nature. Rising from the piano bench with ease, he stands directly in front of her. "Sadly, with no piano training or experience, I couldn't possibly know who wrote it, but—"

"I bet you could take a guess," Robert suggests with kind encouragement.

"Well, my guess would be Chopin."

"Yes!" Robert responds immediately.

"Really?"

"You're right. It's his Nocturne in D Flat Major, Opus 27. One of his most popular works, but also less traditional for a nocturne formula as well."

"It's an amazing piece," Ellie reflects, goose bumps running down her arms. "It seems like a work everyone should know, but feels almost too personal a treasure to share emotionally."

Robert steps forward while Ellie finishes her thoughts, mesmerized by the full contour of her moving lips. Ellie notices his closeness, engaging her heart's response. A short look determines the flow of one another's subsequent actions. Speaking is not an option for several minutes.

CHAPTER

13

I n the following weeks, the hours apart are incredibly long while the time together seems to vanish before it starts. Ellie is hired to work weekends at the campus deli but perpetually walks across campus with a spring under her feet, happily daydreaming of Robert in his classes. Having memorized one another's schedules, a sense of peace is assumed for their general well-being and safety while apart.

In mid-October, Ellie attempts to stifle a smile while walking to her least favorite course but fails when recalling the dinner conversation with Robert the previous evening. He posed the topics of marriage and children, conversation subjects she assumed off the menu until later in their relationship. *He must be thinking about it. "How many children do you want?" I can't believe he asked me that!*

She sits down with her notebook, textbook, calculator, and extra pencils at seven fifty-five. Her homework is complete, but she takes the minutes left to go over her probability answers a second time. The professor walks in quietly, sets his briefcase down, and writes the homework for the evening up on the chalkboard. Once complete, he opens the latches to his briefcase and begins distributing the graded quiz from Friday. While he floats around the room, his instructions are to hand in the assignment as he returns the quiz. Midway through the stack of nearly sixty student papers, Ellie's quiz is set down on her desk. Her reaction sends a roll of nausea and shock through her body. Immediately, she double-checks the name in the corner and cannot believe she sees the D+ written in red marker next to it.

"Many of you are performing quite well on these statistics concepts, while few of you continue to struggle. I'm happy to set up a time to assist you. My hours are on the course syllabus."

Ellie scrambles through her folder to find the window of time she must now use for extra help. Seven to seven forty-five on Monday, Wednesday, and Friday are the tutoring times. *I guess I won't be running those days anymore.* The professor begins his lecture, diving deeper into statistics that Ellie struggles to grasp with certainty. She tests well in numerous principles of mathematics, but the practice of varying possibilities and inductive reasoning brings out insecurities for how her concrete thinking is wired.

Class comes to a close. She eagerly asks to meet with her professor at seven o'clock Wednesday morning. He confirms his open conference time for the morning before she pencils it down on the planner in her bag.

⋅⦂⧉⦂⋅

"Robert, I just don't understand what I'm doing wrong. It's so frustrating to be challenged in this way. My father's practically a genius with these things, and I get geometry, but I just don't think this way. Ugh." She switches ears to throw her lunch meat back into the mini-fridge in her dormitory.

"All right, take a deep breath, Ellie. Remember that you've already done the hard part by requesting the professor's help. From what I hear, this teacher is all *doom and gloom* in class but is actually nice to those who help themselves." Ellie can feel the muscles in her shoulders relax slightly. His voice is incredibly soothing, even over the phone. "Try not to worry. You know I am happy to help you as well."

"Yes, which makes this all the more unnerving, by the way."

"Why's that?"

"Because you're so brilliant with everything."

"I don't know about that. Besides, I like to think of it as balancing out each other's weaknesses. I have no idea how to put a flute together." He chuckles into the phone.

"Very funny, Robert. Well, my main concern with that scenario is that I know you're so busy. I can't ask for your help when you've got enough on your plate as it stands." Ellie sits down on her bed, the uneaten turkey sandwich staring at her from the desk. Then the ensuing line of logic forces her appetite to dissipate all together. "Robert, maybe we're spending too much time together."

"Ellie, please don't think that way."

"I know. It's hard for me to even breathe out the words, but I'm trying to use my head here. I can't let my father down. I won't. He's working so hard to keep me in school. I can't possibly get distracted or do anything other than my best."

"And you are, Ellie. You're amazingly talented and smart."

"But I have to work for it, Robert. Incredibly hard."

"Listen. Go to the rest of your classes today, and try to relax before we meet for dinner tonight. I know things will be better after your first session with the professor. Do you believe me?"

Ellie reflects his positive nature. She loves how direct, yet gentle, he can be when her sense of reality is tainted. "Of course you're right."

"Good. I'll see you soon then."

"Sounds good."

"Have a nice afternoon," Robert offers sweetly.

"You too. Good-bye."

"Bye."

Ellie stands to hang up the phone on its base atop the mini-fridge. She turns to stare at her sandwich. Food no longer has an appeal while thinking of her father, who never eats lunch. She wraps her sandwich in plastic wrap and bends down slightly to toss it back into the fridge. "Ouch!" she gasps, feeling a ping of pain cut through her left deltoid. Ellie stands erect to massage the area below her collarbone where the pain originated, like a dagger piercing through the muscle. "What was that?" She rolls her shoulders back, anticipating the pain, but only feels a dull ache now. "Hmm." The crease in her forehead lingers while she picks up her flute and book bags for Music Theory, practice, and band rehearsal for the afternoon. She softly pulls both bags over her right shoulder and walks out the door.

⚜

The remainder of the fall semester passes quickly. Robert and Ellie barely have time to see one another the two weeks prior to finals due to projects and activities. Ellie's grade in Finite Math floats between an A- and B+, but the final exam will likely push the outcome to the latter. She hopes to make her father proud with all other grades resting in the A range.

Robert is making solid progress on his recital for the spring, having memorized another selection. Over winter break, he will have two private lessons with the principal pianist for the Chicago Symphony Orchestra to further refine the four pieces. The first time will be at the beginning of the month-long break and again at the end.

Ellie is sad to be packing up for the four weeks away from Robert. His Porsche is already loaded, fueled, and parked outside Ellie's dorm while she waits for her parents to arrive to take her home. In her room, Robert watches her place the number and address information he wrote down into her suitcase before zipping it up. The door is propped open while visiting, making it easier to carry the heavy suitcase and other items into the hall. Robert turns to see Ellie take the five-by-seven picture frame of them together off her bedside nightstand. She looks at it longingly, stroking the front glass before placing it in her pillowcase.

"Ellie, I'd like to come see you after Christmas. Would your parents be amiable to my visit?"

"Robert, we talked about this. Please don't feel like you have to come see me. It's a long drive."

"It's not that long, and I'm happy to travel however long it takes to be with you," Robert adds, slowly approaching Ellie. He pulls her into his chest, squeezing her gently while the heated current flows between them.

"That is so sweet of you," she utters into his shoulder with her heart racing. "I can't ask you to take the risk though. What if something happens on your way? Or the weather is bad? What about your family?"

"Ellie, it's all right. I'm not going anywhere. Where is all this worry coming from?" He releases his hold and places one hand on the right side of her face.

"I don't know," she says while caressing his hand. "I suppose it's just my anxieties with traveling. I do love to travel, but anything can happen, and I worry."

"Hmm." He moves his left hand up to embrace the entirety of her face, staring squarely into her blue eyes. "Do you truly think I would be careless with my own life now that I have you?" His thumb softly brushes over her lips before she has a chance to speak. She takes in a small breath of air to keep up with her palpitating heart when he pulls her closer to his body. Her head continues its jumbled quest to answer his original question, but she cannot recall what it is now. His chin lowers minutely to concentrate on her lips. Robert's open mouth grazes her cheek then down to the corner of her mouth, skimming past her lips and across to the other side. The scent of his body and touch of his hands takes over all Ellie's control. "Do you?" He barely sweeps by her lips once more with his own.

She cannot think. "Do I what?" she whispers back, biting her lower lip briefly while focusing on his mouth.

Robert smiles, knowing he is every bit as enamored. He tilts her head up one inch, leaning in gracefully to her open mouth.

Within the hour, Ellie's parents park in the circle entrance next to the dorm. She introduces Robert, who helps transport luggage to their vehicle, perpetually offering to carry items for Ellie's mother. Her mother and father are quick to assess his mannerisms in the short time frame of their meeting.

"I wonder whose Porsche is parked here," Ellie's father comments, loading the last bag.

"Oh. Well—" Ellie begins.

"It's a beautiful car," her mother adds.

"Well—" Ellie starts, but is cut off again.

"A 911. Not the fastest, but fast just the same," her father mentions.

"Oh, it's fast all right," Ellie comments with certainty. Both her parents shoot a shocked glare in her direction. "Actually, Robert is quite careful when I am around or in it at all."

"Yes, I make it a point to drive under the speed limit when Ellie is in the car," Robert chimes in with an innocent grin.

"That's your car?" Ellie's mother asks for confirmation.

"Yes, ma'am. I think my father bought it more for his own gratification than my own, but yes, I drive it."

"Huh," Ellie's father responds with surprise and an undercurrent of desire in his voice to ask more questions. He refuses for propriety. From his expression, Ellie can tell he is quite taken with Robert.

"I guess that's everything," Ellie looks apprehensively at Robert.

"Yep, time to go. Robert, it was nice meeting you." Ellie's father offers his hand. Robert smiles and smoothly crosses the short two yards to accept his handshake.

"Likewise, sir. I'm so happy to finally meet both of you. Ellie speaks highly of her parents all the time." Robert releases his firm grip and offers it softly to her mother. She takes his hand, squeezing slightly as affirmation of her approval.

"Nice to meet you too, Robert," Ellie's mother replies.

"Hey, do you mind if I run into the university center real fast to use the restroom before we go?" Ellie inquires, looking to her father. Robert turns and walks to her side.

"Sure, honey," her father responds.

"Bye, Robert." Her mother waves.

"Good-bye. I hope you all have a wonderful Christmas," he offers with a genuine smile and tender wave.

Ellie and Robert vanish out of her parents' view into the building. She grabs Robert's hand, leading him down the hall and around to the cafeteria. No one is in sight inside and around the corner. She stops and practically leaps into his arms one last time. The tears start to roll down her eyes as she squeezes his entire upper frame.

Robert feels the fire inside him burn with her body pressing against his chest. Holding her tightly, he takes in a deep breath, feeling full and complete. "Don't worry. I'm always with you, and you're a part of me." He gently pushes her shoulders back to view her face. He pulls her chin up, knowing she won't look at him easily in this state. "Ellie," he speaks softly. He slides one thumb underneath her wet eye to wipe away tears. "Ellie, look at me." She sniffs and begins slowly opening her lids upon the sound of his silky invitation. Her breathing staggers while taking in the beauty of his face. "I want you to know...I mean, surely you know already how much I truly love you, Ellie." Her eyes pop open in shock. "I suppose it may seem a bit early to be saying so, but something tells me we are the exception to any rules on proper timelines." Robert gazes at Ellie while he strokes her cheeks. She is quiet and engaged in every word he speaks. "Ellie, would you say something?" he asks with a crooked smile.

"I'm sorry. I'm just taking it all in." Her cheeks turn a light pink color. "Could you say that just one more time, please?"

Robert is thoroughly amused and delighted by her reaction. "Ellie, I am deeply in love with you." The words shoot directly into her veins, heating them up. She beams in happiness, thrilled to hear what she has felt since the beginning.

"I love you too, Robert," she replies tenderly. Her right hand latches around the back of his neck while the other rests on his left shoulder. "It feels nice to finally say it to you."

"I couldn't agree more." Robert leans in to her gorgeous lips once again. With an urgency for time, the pair attempts to keep their intensity in check for several minutes.

Standing still with their foreheads merely touching, Ellie knows she must leave now.

"I'm glad I was able to meet your parents. Now you need to convince them to let me visit."

"Oh, I don't think that will be a problem at all. I'm certain my mother is quite smitten with you already," Ellie adds with a giggle.

"Really?" Robert questions as the couple starts a slow walk out of the cafeteria.

"Robert, come on. And I think my dad wanted to have a serious car chat with you back there as well."

"Hmm, well, that sounds nice." He squeezes her hand. "Please call me when you arrive home safely?"

"Yes, I will. Drive carefully, and be safe too."

"No worries, Ellie," he reminds her.

"I'll try." She smiles back, now exiting the university center.

Over winter break, the couple writes letters and stays in touch with phone calls. After Christmas, Robert drives south for his promised visit. Marie's recent move into an apartment creates a vacant guest room across from Ellie's bedroom. Robert offers to find a hotel, but being open-minded parents, her mother and father insist he stay at their home, feeling it a waste of resources and money.

Ellie gives Robert the full tour around her hometown, complete with a visit to her alma mater, the popular hangouts, even taking him on night drives to catch quality views of the stars without light pollution.

"There's Polaris," Ellie mentions, pointing toward the end of the Ursa Minor constellation. She is bundled up in her winter coat atop Robert's Porsche hood. He is lying beside her with his head close to hers.

"The only one I truly know up there is Orion, I believe. What's the blue cluster again?"

"Well, since you mentioned Orion, I'll tell you a little more. See how Orion's belt points up to that cluster? That's how you can always find the Pleiades. They call them the seven sisters, but there are more than seven in the group out there."

"And because they are blue, that means...?" Robert pauses to let Ellie fill in the gaps.

"They are incredibly young stars, only born around our Prehistoric era, approximately."

"What are the proper terms for the Big and Little Dipper again?"

"That's Ursa Major and Minor. If you find Minor and travel down that line, you'll always find Polaris as well." She points, drawing a backwards arc.

"How do you know all this again?"

"I've always loved astronomy, and having a cool Earth Science teacher always helps. If it weren't for my mind block with chemistry, I might not be here with you right now," she comments with a chuckle.

"What do you mean?"

"I thought about majoring in geoscience at another college, but I'm glad it wasn't my calling," she says gently. "Maybe I could at least minor in astronomy or something."

"I think that's a fantastic idea, though I'm not sure what else you would learn." Robert sits up to look at her face.

"Oh, plenty. More formulas, I'm sure. Yuck." Ellie makes a sour look on her face.

Robert laughs. "I'd better get you out of the cold."

"Yes. Hot chocolate time!"

Walks, long hikes with multiple trails of diverse topography, and frequent jogs along Ellie's regular home route consumes the majority of time during Robert's stay.

On New Year's Eve and Robert's last night visiting, Ellie's parents play host to family members and friends at their home for a small gathering. Robert and Ellie naturally drift toward each other every spare moment, sensing the inevitable departure. Just before midnight, the whole party toasts with champagne, and at the stroke of twelve, gestures of love adorn the entire living room. Robert and Ellie excuse themselves to share a passionate, tender kiss in private just outside the house.

⋅⟨⟨⟩⟩⋅

The spring semester begins smoothly in mid-January. Ellie continues with a number of the same courses: Music Theory, Ear Training, Piano Level One, Wind Ensemble, lessons, and flute choir. New classes are in communications, language arts, and violin and viola will be her new secondary instruments for the semester. Upon Robert's encouragement, she opts to put singing back in her schedule as well, signing up for one of the university choral ensembles.

Ellie feels confident that picking a strings instrument up again will be easier after the three years she spent playing in elementary school. Though she spent ample time toying with her sister's bass the last seven years, mastering high strings in one semester will be impossible. She does take comfort, however, knowing she will not have to be in the rigorous routine of embouchure adjustments in daily practice. The warm-up and cool-down process for clarinet consumed an excessive, yet necessary, amount of time. No muscle memory accommodations are required for Ellie's transition this semester.

Ellie's practice and class routine is established with ease after the first two weeks. Into February, the balance of her studies, work, relationship with Robert, friendships, and other elements of collegiate life appears seamless. Her private teacher hands her the Mozart Concerto in G Major, a standard repertoire selection. She feels prepared for the challenge, having accomplished the Quantz Concerto in G as a junior in high school.

On a cold February afternoon, Ellie slips into her favorite practice room carrying her book bag, violin, and flute bag. She begins with piano first, ironing out a piece she will be tested on the following day.

Next, she opens her violin case, tightens and rosins her bow, slides the chin rest into place, and works through all her first-position scales. In the mirror, she glances frequently at her thumb and pinky's roundedness in the bow hold, along with her wrist underneath the fingerboard in an attempt to catch any habit-forming imperfections. She loosens the tension on her bow hair and sets the instrument down carefully atop the closed-lid piano.

Her flute comes out of the case, head joint first and wrapped in her polishing cloth, followed by the body, then finally the foot joint. Meticulously, she attempts to touch her flute little to avoid tarnishing the silver caused by the natural oils in the fingerprints. She checks to be certain her instrument is aligned properly with the tone hole, cutting a line straight through the body. Ellie sorts her exercises on the stand and brings the flute to her face. "Ouch!" She feels the unbearably painful dagger stabbing her in the left deltoid, and it is worse than ever. Ellie immediately sets her flute down on the piano and begins massaging the area with her right thumb, sitting on the piano bench. "What *is* that?" she speaks softly, a look of distress on her pale face.

The door to the room opens. "Ellie, what's wrong? Are you ill?" Robert questions, bending down on his knees to assess her needs. Ellie's stomach muscles tighten. She does not feel comfortable with him seeing her this way.

"Oh, I'm fine. It's just my shoulder. It's nothing," she mentions lightly, dropping her hand away from the pain.

"Ellie, don't do that."

"What?"

"You know you can't lie, so be honest," he urges. Ellie cannot be offended when he speaks the truth.

"It's just my shoulder. I'm sure it's nothing."

"If you're in pain, it's not nothing, sweetheart," he comments gently. "Can you lift your arms?"

"Sure. See?" Ellie lifts her arms out in front of her, palms down, and places them back in her lap.

"Okay, now lift them out over your sides."

"Robert," she says, irritated.

He silences her with one look of his eyes. She lifts them straight out again on either side, palms down. "See? I'm totally fine now. It's nothing."

"Wait."

"What, Robert?" She stands, and Robert follows suit, studying her face.

"I want you to lift them out to the sides again, palms up."

"Is this necessary?" Ellie sighs one last time but follows his instructions. Suddenly, she feels the sharp pain shoot through her left side. "Ah!" She drops her arms to grab onto the sore area, dragging air through her clenched teeth. He assists her gentle landing back onto the bench.

"Ellie, how long has this been going on?"

"Well, this is the first time I've not been able to play from it, but I guess it's been sore for a while."

"How long?"

Ellie's façade falters, then breaks. "I suppose the worst of it started in January. I wake up numb in my whole left arm or in pain at times."

"Ellie," he says with a sigh. "This is not the kind of thing you mess around with, especially as a musician, love. You need to see a doctor immediately."

"Robert," she replies, rolling her eyes. "Really?"

"Yes, Ellie. Really. Please trust me," Robert pleads.

"I do trust you."

"Then let's go. I'll help you with your things." He moves to place her books back into her bag.

"What can we do right now?"

"You need to call your mother and have her insurance company contact a specialist for you here in town."

"Then what?" she questions, placing her violin gently in the case.

"They will take x-rays and determine the problem so you can get better." He scoops up her bags and violin case.

Her large exhale indicates her distaste for attracting any attention. "Let's get this over with then." She follows him out the door, carrying only her flute.

.⁘⚬⚬⁘.

"Ellie, your joints are what we refer to as lax." Ellie looks to Robert briefly with a confused expression and back to the doctor. "Basically, your body has aligned itself improperly enough to cause irritation from movement. Nothing in your upper back, including your neck, is where it needs to be in order to lead a pain-free life, especially as a musician." He lets the information sink in as she contemplates her follow-up question.

"How...how did this happen? I've never even broken a bone before." She looks down and away, attempting to control her emotions.

"It's nothing you've knowingly done wrong, actually. You're tall. Most children who spike up in height at a young age, like yourself, never even notice the painful effects of poor posture alignment until later in life. Whether it's from insecurities in the way you carried yourself or always trying to shrink down to everyone else, the results are much the same."

"What do I do? I can't play like this for long, so how do I make the pain go away?" Robert takes Ellie's hand, which is clenched up in a ball from the tension, to relax her. Upon his tender touch, she releases her anxious posture with a slight sigh.

"I'm afraid there's no quick fix. It will take months of rehabilitation through physical therapy and diligent exercises to correct the issues. What's wonderful is that your body is strong, and you're into a routine of exercise already, but the therapist will ask that all these exercises be done three times a day. You'll have to make a commitment, and unfortunately, some of them will be painful. Emotionally, you'll be a bit more vulnerable and tired. It may even cause some depression," the doctor warns.

Ellie sits in silence while Robert makes soothing circles on the back of her hand with his thumb. A lone tear creates a path down the side of her cheek.

"When can she start, doctor? I can take her to therapy."

"No, Robert," Ellie whispers. "Your schedule's too full. I won't take your practice time from you."

"Ellie, you should start therapy this week, if possible. Here's the card for the rehab facility close to campus in affiliation with our hospital." The doctor hands her the information. "Just remember what I've said. The first month will be tough, but things will improve steadily as your therapy visits become less frequent."

"Thank you, doctor," she utters with a forced half smile.

"Thank you," Robert adds politely.

"It was nice to meet you both. Good luck now," the doctor comments before closing the patient-room door.

Ellie sits in the chair with puffy red eyes. She stares up at the x-rays of her shoulders, arms, and spine still up on the illuminator. She sees the physical discord in her bones he referred to; her disposition turns angry.

Robert sees the wheels turning in her mind without a spoken word. "Ellie, this is not your fault," he reminds her soothingly.

"Hmm." Ellie is disbelieving and irritated. "Robert, do you know how hard my father is working right now? On his hands and knees for me?" Ellie shakes her head. "And I couldn't have enough foresight to carry myself with better posture? I can't even imagine what he'll think when he finds out the expenses behind this one."

Robert lets her finish venting, allowing her to calm down before starting. "As a father, I'm sure he's thinking he just wants you to be better. He won't be worrying about anything else. I'm willing to bet my savings on it." He smiles from the chair at her side, then moves down to squat in front of her and look into her eyes. "Do you have any idea how to be selfish and try to focus on your own health?"

Ellie imagines such a reversal in thinking, unable to sit long in the thought. "No, I can't."

After a few seconds, she juts out her lower lip in an overly dramatic pout face created for his amusement. He laughs aloud at her picturesque and comically miserable expression. She starts chuckling with him. He turns his palms up as he stands, an invitation to assist her movement from the chair. She takes both his hands, standing to greet his eyes just above her line of sight.

"Wow," Robert says.

"What?"

"After all this therapy, you might be taller than me." He chuckles.

Ellie presses her lips in a hard line just before he kisses her forehead.

"Carolyn, do you think I could borrow your car while you're at choir rehearsal a couple days a week for therapy? I really don't want Robert to have to take me."

"Sure. No problem at all."

"You are a lifesaver. Thank you," she breathes.

"How are you two doing?"

"Well, with my extra exercises and therapy, we've not been able to meet for dinner hardly at all this week. Honestly, I think we're both feeling overwhelmed for good reason, which is why I want to get myself to therapy now."

"Things will get better, Ellie. I know all about recital preparation. I can't even tell you how many languages I'll be singing for mine in the spring."

"You know, I keep forgetting you're a year ahead of me. I suppose it's because of Theory class."

"I know. I just wanted to get all the general classes out of the way freshman year," Carolyn reminds her.

"Yea, I know what you mean. This communications project I'm working on is ridiculous."

"Just try to be confident and sell your presentation material," Carolyn suggests.

"You always give this advice like it's a piece of cake. I think I'm going to have to kick you."

Carolyn giggles into the phone, forcing Ellie to pull back on the receiver to avoid high-frequency hearing loss. The two wrap up logistics for the car and bid farewell.

During the next two weeks, Ellie drives to physical therapy, remaining dedicated to balancing her work and studies.

Ellie takes her seat in Communications class after delivering a persuasive speech on why people should use water filtration systems for their tap water. She feels confident in the research elements of her presentation but cannot remember one word she spoke to the audience. Her nerves boiled to the surface easily during the five-minute speech, nearly an eternity of time. The professor is busy scribbling down the last pieces of feedback on his rubric for Ellie. He appears to be taking longer to complete her paper than other student feedback forms in class.

Two others give their persuasive presentations before the end of the hour. Ellie's ears are still out of commission while other students speak, worrying about her own grade.

The professor hands the rubrics back to students before dismissal, and the reactions begin oozing out of the highest-scoring academic's mouths. Her teacher sets her rubric down on her desk and walks away. An 80 percent stares her in the face, etched in ballpoint hunter-green marker. Somehow, her reaction is not shock but complete indifference. She briefly skims over the assessment of the points taken away for delivery but is unchanged by the disappointment she feels in herself. A numb haze stretches itself out like a blanket over her whole body. The intense soreness she feels in her upper back even subsides underneath the veil of her self-defense mechanism. She folds the paper, tucks it into her bag, and walks in a daze to her next class. The entire day continues in the sanctity of the haze, all the way through lunch and dinnertime. She eats nothing in her dorm but completes her exercises with three repetitions each. Her body floats over to the coffeehouse on campus where she typically meets Robert after supper twice per week.

"Ellie?" She stops and turns to view Robert's outline, never meeting his eyes fully.

"Hey," she says softly.

"What's the matter? Are you hurt?"

"Heh, not technically," she replies sarcastically.

"Here." He pulls out a chair for her to sit down at the small table. "Tell me what happened."

Ellie slowly slides into the seat. "Oh, it's just that…my grades are suffering. I probably won't make the dean's list for the semester at this rate," Ellie explains with no emotional inflection in her voice. She does not make eye contact.

"Ellie, I told you I would help you," Robert offers.

"There's nothing you could possibly help me with, Robert. And I won't take time away from you."

"I know where you're going with this, Ellie. Don't think—"

"I can't see you anymore, Robert." She avoids peering up at the expressions contorting his breathtaking features, still gloriously appealing as his heart breaks at her words.

"Ellie, listen to me. This is a minor speed bump along our path. I admit we have more than enough going on, but remember what the doctor said? He said you were going to feel this way."

"But I'm not upset about the exercises. Sure, finding the time is rather difficult, but I just can't balance everything out, Robert. To overcommit my time now is to unpledge myself everywhere, and you don't deserve that either."

"Ellie, look at me," he requests in a soothing voice. Her eyes only drift to his chin and stop. "Look at me," he commands. She musters the will to make it up to his piercing blue eyes and nearly loses her resolve with his tender expression. He scoots his chair closer, leans in to rest his elbows on his knees, and takes both her hands. After months together, the electric zing they feel upon touching is not lost. Ellie's breath drags through her lips as her body is caught off guard by the powerful current. "Ellie, I know you feel that too," he whispers. "We are meant to be together. I don't know any other couple with such evidence to support their happiness as we have right here. I am completely in love with you, and I know you feel the same."

Ellie breaks away from contact with his eyes, tears now flowing down in droves. "I do love you, Robert, but I just can't be with you right now. I can't." She sniffs, taking a break. "I won't take any chances that my commitments negate all I've worked for and all my parents have done for me."

"But why is making a B in a class such a terrible thing, Ellie? It's not," he says, squeezing her hands.

"It is to me. You know that's who I am, Robert."

"No, Ellie. I think it *is* okay with you, but because others have those expectations, you feel the pressure to appease them."

"Whichever the case may be, that's how I feel. I'm so sorry." Ellie sobs harder. "I didn't intend to hurt you." She removes her hands from his hold and wipes her tears away with her fingers. Robert looks down at his empty and abruptly cold hands, forearms still resting on his lap. He sits back up, slowly drawing his eyes to Ellie. Contemplating.

"If you feel this is best for you, then I cannot argue. I am deeply hurt…more than I could possibly convey, but I love you enough to retreat." Robert pauses, attempting to keep his emotions together for another few moments. "Just remember, Ellie, *vous êtes ma raison d'être*," he speaks with gentle fluidity. He then quickly stands, grabs his coat, and walks out of the coffee shop.

From the years she spent in high school studying French, Ellie knows the underlying meaning behind his words with quick assimilation: *You are my reason for being.* Her tears flow harder now, disappointment in herself reigning over every other emotion. She gets up and walks out of the coffee shop. Once down the steps, she takes off running across the street in a sprint to her dorm. She feels her carelessness over hurting Robert sting every region of her chest as she crosses the quad on campus. She propels herself up the long stairs by the university center and up the short hill to pass her and Robert's bench in the circle drive. Her heart pounds fast in the dense winter air as she lunges toward the exterior door. She runs rapidly up the stairs taking two at a time, passing girls in the hall gawking at her pained expression. Ellie has the key ready, turns the knob, and flings herself onto her bed in the empty room as the door slams.

14

"Carolyn, I just don't feel like going out. I'm sorry," Ellie says over the cafeteria table at lunch.

"Ellie, come on. It's been, like, three weeks. It's nearly April! You didn't even call me over spring break when you got back from the band trip."

"I know, and I'm sorry." Ellie feels awful. "You know I didn't call anyone though. Marie even tried to take me out with some of her friends when I got back, but I didn't want to bring down the party. I felt miserable enough being in such a beautiful place like Dominican Republic with the band and not truly enjoying myself."

"It's so cool you were able to go though."

"Yeah, I'm glad I could make most of the payments myself. It really was a lovely place. The people and children we played for seemed genuinely happy about our presence, especially when we donated all the instruments. The kids were so sweet when we taught them how to hold and play each one."

"Aw, I bet that was neat."

"It was," Ellie replies, sipping her last drops of water.

"All right. I need to be honest. I'm trying to understand your logic here with the whole Robert thing, and I just don't get it. Tell me the hardest part about all this, Ellie. Do you regret breaking up with him?" Carolyn poses.

"I regret hurting him, of course. I still see him twice a week in piano class, which is extremely difficult. I try to ignore he is there, and he hasn't come over to help me at all, which is for the best. I love him, and I know he still loves me."

"How do you know? Has he tried to call you?"

"No." She drops her head with a slight grin. "But every Saturday morning, two long-stem red roses are left in front of my dormitory door."

"Oh, well, that's obvious then, but I wonder why two? I mean, why not more or just one?"

Ellie looks down, knowing the answer to his symbolic gesture. "Because two is the perfect pair and just enough. Every person deserves to have an equal match."

"Ellie, you belong together. You're wasting time ignoring that, and one day, you'll look back and kick yourself for not realizing it sooner."

"Well, I don't know about that. Besides, my grades have gone up, and my parents are happy I'm en route to stay on the dean's list, even with all the therapy happening."

"Are you still sore?"

"Nope! I feel better too. I still can't sleep on my left side, but it's no big deal. I'll be done with therapy in three weeks. I just have to continue the exercises once a day as part of my workout."

"That's awesome. You know, I can already tell a difference in your posture."

"Really?"

"Sure. I'm a former pageant queen, remember? I have a trained eye," she says with a wink and a giggly smile. Ellie chuckles with her friend.

"Come on. Let's get to Theory, goofball," Ellie suggests as she stands.

After class, Ellie stares at the recital announcement board in the foyer of the music building. All the April recitals are now listed with Carolyn's and Robert's one week apart. She is enraptured in the approaching date of Sunday, April 21, at two in the afternoon for his recital. Requiring no glance at her calendar, she knows she is free. Her heart reacts to this realization, but she stifles the yearning to imagine his intense and brilliant practice sessions. She begins to audiate the notes of his performance of Chopin's Nocturne in D Flat Major, Opus 27 and closes her eyes.

The loud accidental drop of a textbook from behind startles her into reality in the foyer. She walks down the hallway, back to her small practice room on the first floor to continue work on the Mozart concerto.

⋘☙⋙

In mid-April, Ellie snaps out of the beautiful dream of her and Robert under a massive weeping willow tree in an open barren pasture of green Kentucky grass. It is nearly four in the morning when she registers the intense wind zooming outside her window, along with a sheet of rain mixed in hail pinging against the glass. Suddenly, a droning loud siren breaks into the background of the symphony of rolling thunder.

"Everyone, quick! Downstairs!" The resident advisor, Lori, shouts from outside the hall, vigorously knocking on everyone's door. "Leave your doors open so I know you're out!"

Reflexively, Ellie bolts out of bed in the dark and attempts to wake Ginny immediately. She shakes her on the shoulder. "Ginny! Ginny, wake up!"

"What? What's going on?"

"There's a tornado on the ground. We have to move to the basement. Let's go!"

"Oh crap!" Ginny is still rubbing her eyes as she leaps out of bed with her tie-dye Grateful Dead shirt and nylon shorts from soccer the previous evening.

"Come on!" Ellie commands. They open the door to the dull glow from two emergency floodlights and fall into the flock of girls heading to the stairwell in a restrained panic. Ellie waits at the top of the stairs as everyone filters in, looking back down the hall to see Lori running to check every door. Ellie hears the storm intensify to a loud humming sound, like a moving train horn. Lori stops to pound on one unopened door.

"Girls! Are you out?" She continues to hit the door. "Girls!" Finally, it opens. "Oh, girls, come on! Tornado!" With Lori only one yard behind, they start a rapid sprint down the hall toward Ellie. She feels the vibration of both their feet running and the thrum of the cyclone. Suddenly, the window on the other side of the hall shatters. Ellie sees the end of a large tree trunk rapidly get sucked back out of the opening.

Ellie shouts to them, "Hurry! Don't look back!"

"Ellie, go!" Lori yells. As the two girls reach her, she swiftly turns and moves down the stairs, two flights of concrete steps to the basement. The entire dormitory of girls is huddled together in the center of the tiled floor. The building's foundation is immersed underground with no windows and is pitch-black. Ellie moves swiftly to join Ginny on the floor while Lori grabs her flashlight and clipboard hanging on the wall with a first-floor attendance check sheet. The other resident advisors are account-ing for their respective residents as well, panning the basement with their emergency flashlights. Lori finishes checking off each name on her clipboard, breathing a sigh of relief.

"I'm missing one. Oh god." The third-floor RA is in a panic.

Lori rapidly crosses over to her to find out the name of her missing resident. "Has anyone seen Sally Heedler today?" Lori speaks for the RA, who is in shock. The storm howls above the dorm. Ellie hears the ripping of the wind as the thrumming con-tinues. Every girl sits upright upon hearing the piercing sound of scraping steel screeching outside in the direction of the nearby circle drive. When it stops, Lori pauses and asks again, "Anyone?" The residents look around to see if someone will speak. "Carrie?"

"Yes?" A small voice echoes from the other side of the basement.

"You're her roommate. Was she in the room when you left?"

"No, I don't think she came home tonight though."

"Where do you think she might be?" Lori investigates.

"Well, she does have a boyfriend in one of the frats, so I guess she could be there."

"Okay, thank you," Lori replies. She continues to console the other RA from the third floor.

The wailing wind begins to subside after five minutes. Lori turns on the emergency antennae radio left purposely in the basement for these occasions as the sirens shut down. "Ladies, we must remain here until the residency director gives us the all clear. Sit tight. We've got some pillows and blankets coming soon because this can take awhile, especially if there is damage to other parts of campus."

Robert! Ellie feels the nausea roll in her stomach. She knows his dormitory has a safe basement, and though she has an odd sense he is unharmed, she wants to know for certain.

Three hours progress slowly, and by then, Ellie is the only one remaining upright, having offered her pillow and blanket to Ginny. With daylight illuminating the concrete stairs, she paces the floor around the cluster of resting women, sips at the water fountain from boredom, and sits back down multiple times.

Just after seven o'clock, a group of campus officials walk down the steps into the basement. Lori and the other RAs approach the team of people.

"Is everyone all right?" the resident director questions.

"Everyone is safe and accounted for except one," Lori replies gently. "Her name is Sally Heedler, and we believe she is at one of the frat houses with her boyfriend. At least that is our hope."

"I see," the director replies.

"Have the other residence halls been cleared?" Ellie is thankful Lori asks the most important question.

"The ones across the street have been." The director points in the direction of the newer dormitories. Ellie relaxes, knowing Robert is safe. "But we still have a few to go, and we have to assess the damage to every building first. You're the first building needing repair, but we fear it may get worse as we go along."

"How bad?"

"The roof is bad. The firemen are up there now to make sure things are safe. They will tarp it for now, and we will have people repairing it this afternoon, along with a few windows. Until then, you'll likely need to assign some first- and second-floor residents to host a number of third-floor girls."

"All right. We'll wait to get the room numbers from you."

The resident director invites several girls to spread out upstairs in the main lounge and lobby while they wait for instructions.

"Ellie, why don't you go grab one of the couches upstairs? You've been up all morning," Lori suggests.

Ellie nods and drags her feet up the steps with a blanket in hand to the lobby couch. She sits down and looks out the window to the circle drive, tucking her feet up on the couch to snuggle under the blanket. The chaos of the storm displaced branches and debris everywhere. Most of the damage is just west of campus, over by the park where she shared many walks with Robert. Ellie runs her fingers through her hair as she realizes their bench is not in its normal location. She rubs her eyes and glances across the lobby to the entrance.

In his jeans and plain white V-neck T-shirt, Robert stands, looking at Ellie. His gorgeous face is filled with both relief and tragedy, watching her from under ten yards away. Ellie's brows immediately arch, her forehead crinkling with relief for his safety. She leans forward to stand, desiring to speak with him desperately, but when she opens her mouth to talk, he turns to exit the dormitory. She is shocked, sad, and speechless from his exit but understands why he left.

Ellie reflects on every expression of Robert's while resting on the couch. Tears escape down her cheek before she falls asleep for over an hour, longing to restart the playing reverie cut short before the storm.

To be expected, campus classes are shut down for the day. Nearly every girl on Ellie's floor huddles around the large television in the lobby to hear the morning news. No deaths are reported from the storm at the university, including Sally Heedler, now destined to be the talk of the dorm, but people on the northwest side of town are not as fortunate. The tally is eight people estimated to be missing or dead at the hour. The path of the tornado was irregular, having the deadliest impact five miles northwest of campus in several residential areas. Ellie is concerned about an uncle and aunt who live straight west of campus. After one quick phone call, she is relieved to know they are safe but did not escape damage. The other dorms require no more than shingle repair and multiple windows replaced. Overall, Ellie can see the tangible evidence of a thankful campus after their close call as she looks around. Every student feels vulnerable, explaining why over half of the girls are still together on the lobby floor.

After grabbing a program on the music stand, Ellie descends five concrete steps from the lobby of the music building and touches the massive vertical iron handles adorning the large wooden doors to the building's intimate recital hall. She takes a deep breath before opening the door and proceeds immediately left and up the small incline toward the back of the room. She makes her seat location centered, taking her flute bag off to place on the gorgeous wood-finished floor. Ellie controls a small palpitation for what she is about to hear while gazing up at the black full-grand piano with lid raised high, shining under several stage lights against a wood-paneled backdrop to contrast.

Looking around the room, she identifies numerous professors and students, but toward the front rows there are faces of people she does not recognize. A tall middle-aged man with glasses is dressed in a three-piece suit standing next to a teenage girl with long golden-brown hair wearing a yellow sundress. Ellie assumes it is Robert's sister and father but cannot think of introducing herself now. *Of course his family looks completely wonderful. They must hate me now.* To distract her thoughts as students begin trickling heavily into the recital hall in the last two minutes, she begins to read the program notes for the performance.

Below his eloquent name and all the consequential information to mark the occasion is the list of selections. He will begin with Liszt's *Liebesträume*, the piece he feels most comfortable, having previously played it for the recital in August. Then onto Prelude in G minor, Opus 23 by Rachmaninoff to contrast the romantic selections between Liszt and Ellie's beloved third piece, Chopin's Nocturne No. 8, Opus 27, No. 2. The heat in her veins flush into her face and hands, thinking of that momentous day in the practice room. She reads on quickly to notice his last piece, Three Preludes for Piano by George Gershwin, creating another vivid flashback to their first date conversation about jazz. As she turns the paper over to read his program notes, she is elated for his persistence in creating an outlet to dabble in blue notes through Gershwin. She smiles to herself, ecstatic for his new-found skills to be presented today. *A romantically heavy program, but perfect for Robert's personality.* Since Robert's recital is elective as a sophomore, Ellie recalls his professor granting lenience in his selections.

She finishes the Gershwin program notes when the audience begins their applause for his entrance onto the stage, but not before she glances down at the dedication on the bottom: "This performance is dedicated to the memory of my beautiful mother and E." Ellie's heart sinks as she looks up to see Robert's exquisite reflection, smiling at the filled recital hall. His skin appears to glow under the lights against his black tuxedo suit coat with satin-facing lapel. The cut of his jacket fits his frame perfectly, accentuating his masculine yet slender physique. She watches him gracefully finish his approach to the front of the stage, take his three-second bow, and sit down on the leather piano bench. He unbuttons his coat swiftly and stares at the keys.

Still in a panic over the dedication on the program, Ellie grabs hold of the arms of her wooden seat. She ignores the overpowering desire to stand up and propel herself to the stage by squeezing her hands tightly around the armrests. The Liszt piece begins impossibly more beautiful than the first time it graced her ears. The intensity with which he pours his soul into the dynamic build through the middle section is heartbreaking to Ellie and incredibly powerful. The soft final chord fully dissipates; Robert stands with assertive eloquence to bow, smiling just before his exit through the wood-panel door at the back of the stage.

Within sixty seconds, he returns to the piano to perform the impressively difficult Rachmaninoff Prelude. Robert sits and quickly begins the low rumble of bass line chords; an exhibition of the composer's Russian heritage is heard within the exposition. His hands fly as he pounds the full sixteenth-note chords after a short diversion to a flowing duple against triple feel in the development. The piece ends with monumental variations in dynamic contrast in the recapitulation before ending whimsically on an ascending arpeggio up to a pianissimo G. The audience registers the humor of the ending with slight chuckles under their breath before monstrous applause erupts. Robert stands again with a wide smile on his face, and by the time he lowers his torso to bow, audience members begin an ovation for his superior performance. Robert notices their reception and pauses longer before his exit to show appreciation. Ellie is afraid she will come unglued if she lets go of the armrests and opts to stay seated.

Robert takes longer to resume before the next selection. Ellie notices the three-minute time lapse down to the second. His entrance onto the stage is remarkably altered from his exit with a facial expression equaling one of loss, though he hides it with a gorgeous half grin while bowing during applause. One hand is tucked subtly behind his lumbar while the other hangs freely. When he turns to sit down, his arm moves out from behind his back uncovering two long-stem red roses, which he places on the folded-down music rack of the piano with the blooms facing out. Robert sits down on the bench with perfect posture while Ellie sinks down in her chair, covering her blushing face with the program. No less than five music students turn to glance at Ellie, watching for the reaction she is attempting to hide. Robert places his hands on his lap for a number of moments, audiating his opening notes. The nocturne itself is not one of great difficulty for Robert, but he yearns to feel the presence and importance of every note today.

Robert places his hands on the keys and begins the soft flowing arpeggios. Every muscle in Ellie's body relaxes immediately as he floats into the tender melody. She watches his perfect profile, sensing each emotion as it filters from his gifted mind through his fingertips. He closes his eyes at moments of pure ecstasy within the movement of the music. She feels the same pivotal sentiments with him, allowing herself to finally release her tears. The passion in his performance is overwhelming, taking her back to the first time their lips touched with his long arms wrapped around her waist, holding her tightly against his sculpted chest. Seeing the strength of those hands now flying across the keys, she yearns to feel his touch but has no right to desire it. The tears come more fiercely now as he winds down into the last few measures. In her mind, the restrained sniffling and sobbing are entirely too noticeable for her to stay.

The audience bursts with clapping again on the release of his final chord. He opens his eyes and pauses briefly to gaze at the red roses in front of him before standing slowly to bow. The front rows begin an ovation with the rest of the crowd, rising to their feet in a matter of seconds. Robert continues to smile but scans the recital hall, subtly searching. Ellie applauds briefly from her seat, leans over to pick up her flute bag off the floor, and tucks it tightly to her chest. She glances up at Robert, who has just turned to exit the stage. "Excuse me," she whispers multiple times, cutting a path out of the row to the right. With the audience still standing, it is not difficult to sneak out. The crowd begins to relax back into their seats as Ellie reaches the end of the row. After five long seconds, she reaches the door to exit and pushes out. Relief and discomfort radiates through her body, standing now with her back to the opposite recital hall door; she pulls deep breaths of air while her tears flow. Ellie releases her flute bag gently on the floor and decides she must stay as the door shuts slowly.

Robert enters the stage for his last piece, immediately noticing the right-hand door to the hall close in his approach to bow. He smiles to accompany the bow then sits with his eyes on the red roses. His facial expression is peaceful as he starts the first of the three preludes.

Ellie hears the entrance of the single-line melodic riff. Lighthearted, quick, and fun, Robert's energy behind the driving rhythmic ostinato is apparent even through the thick wooden door. She rests her ear against it to feel the depth of the volume in the hall.

He pauses briefly when the first prelude finishes, resetting his frame of mind for the second movement. An ominous composition at the start immediately carries a lighter mood as the theme emerges above in the treble line in contrary motion. The piece alters and morphs into a sweet, tender deviation with only the style to unite the ending review of the beginning. The second prelude drifts off into the upper register with a mid- then low-range single note in closing.

Robert's break before the final prelude is shorter. The silence erupts with dynamic musical vigor, quickly quieting down to build speed and vivacity again. The piece spins in gyrating circles, energetically interlacing two melodies together in major and minor; fighting to the finish, the movement is just over one minute long. Robert finishes quick and strong, standing promptly on his last note to the left side of the bench, making a loop to turn back around. The audience explodes with accolades for his epic performance. Every person in the hall stands to cheer for him, several shouting "Bravo!" in his honor. He steps near the edge of stage to take his lengthy bow with a sigh and beaming smile of relief. Turning to exit the stage, the crowd is not ready to stop cheering. Robert waits twenty seconds behind the back of the stage and returns to give a second bow in appreciation of his audience. He lifts one hand for a small wave and single-head bow to the hall, a gesture of thanks for attending. He turns and swiftly grabs the red roses atop the piano then exits the stage.

Ellie listens to the massive applause from outside the door, feeling overwhelmingly proud of him for such an impeccable performance. She understands the distraction of stress she must have caused him in his preparations. The clapping subsides, and the door next to her shoulder swings open with fellow music students filtering out. Ellie swiftly picks up her flute bag and moves up the steps to exit the building out the front lobby.

⚬⚬⚬

Ellie sighs deeply while ascending the steep staircase to her second-floor piano class. It is her last lesson before students begin filing into the professor's office in one week to complete first-year proficiency exams. The teacher allotted Thursday's class time to practice independently.

Her heart beats fast from the combination of the vertical climb and primarily from the knowledge she will see Robert for the first time since his stellar performance on Sunday. Ellie is early to class as always but takes a moment at the top of the steps to slow down her heart rate. *Calm down, Ellie. In through the nose and out slowly through the mouth.* She attempts to self-soothe. Finally, she musters the strength to push herself through the doorway to the piano lab the last minute before class begins. Burying her head to her chest, she walks a direct path to her assigned electric piano at the back of the room. She removes her folder, book, and pencil from her bag and waits for instructions.

"Good morning, everyone." Ellie is surprised to hear Robert's silky voice; she then comprehends how much she misses it. "Professor Cobalt is ill today and has asked me to help you in any capacity prior to your proficiencies next week. I will be walking around the room to facilitate any assistance you may require." His perfect mannerisms are genuine and sincere. Ellie stares down at her book, fearing she may lose her ability to look away altogether if their eyes meet. She turns to the keys to prop her book against the music rack and places her headphones over her ears. She taps the power switch, selects the piano timbre she desires, and turns down the volume from the last user's settings.

Ellie diligently runs through all her required skills over the next half hour. Her scales are smooth, simple transposition elements are checked off, as well as rehearsing random sight-reading material in preparation for what Professor Cobalt may put in front of her for the exam. The only thing left is her chord progression formula of root, subdominant and dominant-seven chords, with proper voice leading using inversions. She begins in the key of C, fingers set to move steadily through the popular chord progression, then smoothly to her first and second inversions.

Up through the key of F, Ellie is sailing nicely. With focus as a band student, her mind is preset to be excessively at peace with the world of flats over sharps. Chromatically, she understands she should be thinking sharps as she travels up her chord formula, but G flat major stands a better chance in her head as opposed to F sharp. She hesitates briefly for the first inversion but halts all together on the second. Removing her hands from the keys, she brings one to her mouth in a panic. While everyone else struggled to achieve this formula in class for months, she perpetually breezed by with her solid and fast recall of key signatures.

Her fingers ought to know exactly where to go, but somehow her abilities are failing today.

"Try to start on F major again, Ellie." Robert appears behind her, speaking softly. Her heart takes off in a hard sprint, causing her lungs to keep up. Her chest rises and falls with his proximity. The rest of her body locks down. "Am I making you uncomfortable? I just thought you might want some help," he expresses quietly.

"Um, sure. Thank you," Ellie replies mildly. She moves her hands to set the F triad and moves through each inversion smoothly, then onto G flat major where her root position chords flow with eloquence. The first inversion is acceptable, but during the second her mind reaches a gap of uncertainty while executing the attempt. She places her fingers on the wrong keys and uses incorrect fingers.

"May I?" Robert gestures to the keyboard and Ellie's hands. Ellie weighs her decision quickly and nods for him to proceed. The heated energy builds in her blood as his body bends over to her side. Her hands brace for the touch, and every muscle stiffens to close off the sensations radiating in her skin. Then his fingers gently touch her right hand, sending waves of relaxation mixed with burning desire and passion throughout her entire frame. Robert observes her eyes close upon his touch. "Ellie, you know your key signatures extremely well. The hard part is over, but you are shifting your hand when it is not necessary, forcing you to miss the notes. Remember, the first finger and pinky veer away from one another the same distance within each dominant-seven progression. See?" Robert's beautiful and radiant hands enrapture the keys with his arms around Ellie's torso to demonstrate the consistent transition elements. After he begins the second inversion of G flat, he moves on to the rest of the keys to reiterate.

Ellie watches his hands while resting hers atop her lap, tracing over his arm as he plays. Dressed in his silk button-down powder-blue shirt and khaki slacks, her eyes glaze over the memory of their first meeting when he wore the same shirt. Her chest rises and falls unevenly now from the recollection, and the sound of the music is blocked from processing all comprehension through her hot ears. She resolves instinctively. Ellie can no longer evade him.

As he finishes the last chord, she wraps one palm around his defined forearm and squeezes gently while looking down. The tears begin flowing with the overwhelming surge of his touch once again.

Robert is stunned. He releases his hands from the piano keys and kneels down at her side. Seeing the turmoil on her face as she removes her headphones with one hand, he hopes he did not stress her further. "Ellie," he whispers. She weakens further at the sound of her name across his lips. "I'm sorry, I didn't mean to upset you." In a quick panic, he knows the fifty-minute class is complete, standing to make the announcement. "Class, please remember to turn off your pianos and return the headsets to the proper positions. Good luck on your exams!" The mass of students filter out quickly, less two stragglers paying no attention to Robert standing in the back of the room. After several tedious moments, he watches the last person exit. Immediately, he bends down to see Ellie wiping her tears.

"I'm sorry." Ellie weeps softly. "I just..." She cuts off her next thought.

"Ellie, please. Tell me what's wrong," he pleads. Robert waits while she struggles to find the right words. "Ellie, I know you were at my recital," he offers.

Ellie pops her head up in shock and looks into his eyes for the first time in months. "You do?"

"No one had to confirm you were there Sunday," he says with a genuine expression.

"How did you know?"

Robert pauses briefly before answering. "I just had a feeling," he admits. "A friend mentioned later that you left before the

Gershwin, which surprised me because I still felt the same in that performance."

After weeks of suffocation, Ellie's floodgates cease to function. "I was there the whole time, Robert. I couldn't bear leaving when you worked so hard. I listened through the door. After the nocturne, I felt like all my insides were scattered all over the place. You played it so beautifully that I couldn't hold myself together. I knew you were playing it for me, and I had to go."

"Ellie." His voice rings thick with sincerity as he moves closer to take her hands and hold them to his chest, one knee touching the carpeted floor. "I would play that piece for you a thousand times a day if you would just come back to me. Please, Ellie." He releases one hand and sweeps a thick golden strand away from the side of her face, lingering there to cup her soft cheek. "Come back to me," he beseeches once more.

Ellie moves her hand up to touch his cheek with the back of her fingers. He closes his eyes, feeling the sensation in their powerful connection. Looking at his breathtaking and gorgeous face, she knows their lives will never feel complete without each other. The music she creates in life will be meaningless unless Robert is at her side. Her sense of perfectionism and hard work ethic will never change by being with him, but without a sense of vulnerability and the will to open up, she will never reach the love she is capable of in life—the love Robert is undeniably worthy of. *Who is more deserving of my love than Robert? No one.*

"Robert," she whispers while caressing his cheek. "Of course I will."

His eyes open slightly at her words, and seeing her lips so close, he leans in swiftly for an emotional and powerful kiss—the first of numerous kisses.

Luckily, the lunch hour prevents others from bothering the couple in their sweet reunion. Ellie is content to be standing with Robert now, his arms wrapped around her waist. He kisses the top of her hair as he squeezes her frame once more. "I have something for you," he says, pulling away from her body.

"What?" He leaves the comforts of their embrace to retrieve his bag from across the room. "You have something for me with you right now?"

"Well, I carry it with me." He smiles back while unzipping the bag.

"Okay." She laughs fleetingly, honored by the gesture.

"All right, close your eyes," he requests with a mischievous grin.

"Really, Robert?" She stares back.

"Oh, absolutely. Close your eyes."

"Fine." She closes her eyes with her lips in a hard line.

He walks slowly back over to her. "I vowed I would not lose something very special, so I hope you will enjoy this gift. Open your eyes, Ellie." She opens her eyes to a thick five-by-seven-inch rosewood box frame. Encased behind the glass is the pressed deep-pink rose from their first date in perfect condition.

"Is this really the rose?" Ellie inquires with an astonished expression gracing her face.

"Yes. I promised you," he confirms while placing it in her hands.

"Wow, this is amazing." She pauses with a sigh, trying to hold back her tears. "Robert, thank you so much. It's the most wonderful gift I could ask for, truly."

"You are worth anything I can give you, Ellie. Don't forget that."

The happy couple shares a gesture silencing the remainder of their conversations for countless minutes.

For two years, Ellie and Robert never deviate from each other or their relationship. Robert graduates with his performance degree and is asked to be the university choral department's lead accompanist, attending every rehearsal for all five choir ensembles. His schedule is full between accompanying, the private students he teaches, preparations for voluntary recitals, and guest appearances with small orchestras in the Midwest. The apartment he rents is close to campus where he cooks and has Ellie over on weekends primarily. He manages to provide Ellie with all the support she needs in her last year as well.

In the final semester of Ellie's senior year and prior to the start of student teaching in January, she performs her senior flute recital. Because of the continuous cheers from the audience, which includes all of her family and Robert's father and sister, Ellie reenters the stage for a second bow. With her flute in hand, she sees Robert coming up the front steps on the opposite side of the stage. The audience quiets down quickly as Ellie looks at him in disbelief. *What is he doing?*

"I'm sorry, everyone. There's been a slight addendum to your program today." Robert projects his voice to the crowd. He turns to face Ellie in the exact moment she sees the red rose Robert is carrying in his left hand.

"Ellie, it feels as though my soul has waited an entire lifetime to be with you, and now that I've found you, I'll never let you go. Just being near you makes me happy and blessed to be living. You are my soul mate." He smoothly reaches into his suit pants pocket and bends down on one knee. Ellie's hands fly up to her face, realizing what is happening. He places a gold one-karat diamond ring band atop the red rose and continues. "And it is my privilege to ask you to do me the honor of becoming my wife. Will you marry me, Ellie?" Robert is beaming as he holds up the red rose for her to accept.

Ellie can barely see his handsome face through the tears coating her eyes. Her answer is simple. "Yes!" she happily replies through her tears. The audience cheers with rigor, hooting and whistling in congratulations as Robert stands quickly to slide the ring onto Ellie's left finger. He kisses her hand adoringly and sweeps her off her feet in a long embrace.

Ellie's eyes fly open to the present, seeing and hearing the man come to the end of a piece she can now recall from top to bottom: Chopin's gorgeous Nocturne No. 8 in D flat Major. Of course she knew it, and she knew the love of her life—her *true* love.

She stands and slowly walks toward the man across the room. She gently touches his shoulders, feeling the burst of magnetic energy through her veins from his body, tears streaming down her cheeks on the last chord. "Robert?"

Gracefully, he reaches up to hold one of her hands while turning to pick up the red rose from atop the piano. He looks up at her from the bench and stands, pulling her close to him from the waist. He takes one of her hands to cup his glorious face. "Yes, Ellie, my love. I'm here." She wraps her arms around him in triumph as he locks her in a tight embrace. The two kiss adoringly; she kisses his lips, face, and neck while gently running her fingers through the back of his hair. They both sigh in relief as they hold each other ardently.

After several minutes, Ellie realizes a number of things at once. "Where are the children? How are they?" As if anticipating her questions, Robert smiles and hands her the red rose, which she takes lovingly with an appreciative grin, pressing her nose into the petals. He brings one hand up to stroke the golden strands of her hair from her ear to her shoulder.

"They are both well and healthy," he replies. "Rose is finishing up her first year in college as a music performance major at Northwestern, and Liam is finishing his senior year in high school. He cannot wait to tell you where he has been accepted to begin his pre-medical school training at graduation. You'll be so proud!" Robert beams.

Ellie pauses to ponder, starting to see what her illness is leaving behind—a void for Robert. She loosens the grip of his arms and turns away from him slightly. "Robert, what will you do when Liam leaves?"

Robert's forehead creases with confusion. "Ellie, when Liam is in school, that will mean more time for us. I can be here all day with you then."

"Robert, you shouldn't waste your life on me." She takes a step away. "I want you to be happy. I'm never going to get better, so you should find someone else."

Robert sighs and steps around to look into her eyes. "Ellie, my happiness revolves completely around you. I could never be happy without you. We don't know that you won't get better, and with the research out there—"

"We've done the research, Robert!" Ellie's anger makes her blood begin to boil. "We've read through these cases together, and early onset is a dead end. Once the process begins, there is no going back." She walks back to the sofa and sits with her head in her hands to cry. Robert follows and sits next to her, making soothing circles on her back. "Why? Why does it have to ruin so many families? I did everything God told me to do. I fought for what He wanted, over and over again, despite all the roadblocks He put up, and now this? This is what I get? Why me, Robert? Why does it skip over people who've refused their purpose but claim the lives of those who've been submissive to His will? I mean, what was the point of it all, Robert? The fighting to be someone or something great, it was all for nothing now!" Ellie cups her face and softly sobs.

Robert allows her several moments, handing her tissues from the table beside him. He gently strokes her hair out of her face. "Ellie," he whispers. "We have hope, love, and God on our side. I've been doing some reading at home, and there is brand-new research out there."

"No, Robert. My hope ran out long ago when I decided to put myself in this place."

"Yes, and I begged you not to because I knew you would abandon your will to fight."

"Because having the will to fight won't help me here, Robert!" She raises her voice once again but relaxes amid her resolution. "This is a dead end. I am a dead end. So please, you need to go. Please, Robert," she begs with tears flowing down her cheeks. "Go start over. You deserve so much more than what I can give you, please!" Ellie stands, attempting to walk away. Robert catches her, taking hold of her shoulders to focus on her eyes.

"Ellie, listen to me. There is new research, and they are optimistic test runs will work at your age. You're not even forty, my love. The doctors won't attempt the new trial out on older cases, but they would for you. Think about it, Ellie. This is what we've been hoping and praying for!" he adds with animated optimism.

Ellie's eyes drop from his face and down to his chest. "It's too late, Robert. I can feel it down in the fabric of my bones. This is who I am now, so please...I'm begging you. Just let me go. Don't come back," she ends somberly. Ellie steps back and walks away, quickly heading outside to the courtyard.

Robert watches her exit and sits down on the sofa promptly before his knees fail. He remains seated nearly five minutes with his head in his hands. Repetitively running his fingers through his hair, he grips the follicles and squeezes. Then he stands abruptly and walks to the nurses' station.

"Excuse me, Patricia?" Robert speaks in a delicate tone.

"Yes, Mr. Eastman, how may I help you?" The lovely cocoa-skinned nurse replies tenderly. "Is Ellie having a bad day, sir?"

"I'm afraid so, but I wanted to give you advance notice that I may not be returning for some time as I have business to tend to on Ellie's behalf. I know you always do your best and you're so kind with her, but would you mind giving her some extra attention while I'm gone? I know her father and our son will be in more. However, it would bring me a better sense of peace knowing she has some additional care in my absence." Robert's mannerisms and piercing blue eyes work little to charm the slightest female acquaintance.

"I'll do everything I can to make her feel comfortable, Mr. Eastman."

"Thank you so much, Patricia." He breathes in relief.

"How long do you think you'll be away from St. Louis, sir?"

"As long as it takes," he replies, turning to leave the facility.

Ellie is outside pacing and starting to forget why she is crying when she sees Jean across the garden patio. Ellie is drawn to be near her. "Hello," she greets Jean while sitting down on the cushioned metal bench at her side.

"Hi, honey!" Jean replies back with loving excitement. The two enjoy the afternoon breeze and view of the roses across the pathway.

After four minutes, a nurse guides Mae to the garden in her wheelchair, locking her wheels after situating the chair directly next to Jean and Ellie sitting on the bench. Jean reaches instinctively for each of their hands—Mae on her left and Ellie on her right. Ellie takes Jean's right hand firmly, cupping it in both of her hands, while Mae loosely holds on to Jean's left-hand fingers, gently stroking them with her thumb in tiny circles.

Upon looking at one another with sincerity and love, they comprehend they are family, each fighting the same disease. Succinctly, each woman turns away in anger. In varying degrees of this realization, the loss of their past and future makes them grieve and mourn, wishing there was some way to help the other.

Still selfless.

Alone.

Lost.

With each generation, it comes earlier and earlier, looming and gene deep.

PART 4

ROBERT

CHAPTER

15

Robert returns home, tossing his keys on the small table in the foyer entrance with a sigh. His heels lightly drag on the hardwood floor while gracefully sauntering down the hall. He passes the line of picture frames and enters the master bedroom. Pausing for a moment, he registers the hollow and empty feeling of the space he used to covet; it holds no meaning for him without seeing her. He sits down on the edge of the bed and buries his head in his palms.

His tears are never for his own pain but rather the desperation from numerous roadblocks and not knowing where to begin. Clearly, he could venture back into the assisted-living building tomorrow, her possibly never knowing the difference; however, his spirit dangles by one lone thread. He lacks the fortitude to stand and endure her pushing him away another day. Robert worries for *his* Ellie every moment. The hollowness rips inside his chest at night when she is away from his arms, making it impossible to breathe.

Vague glimmers of a similar dark time creep to the forefront of his mind. Ellie forced them apart when the expectation of her performance as a student was at stake, but this time she feels justified by believing she will help Robert move on when nothing could erase the impact her love has made on his entire soul.

Robert retraces his steps during the months away from Ellie in college. The space apart he allowed was a torturous and depressing time for him. He thought the nights of insomnia and never grasping a full breath were over, and though the situation is different, the aftermath of what is ripping through his internal makeup is worse.

In college, students feel their lives are just beginning, and the unknown creates an endless pathway of wishes, dreams, and desires. Robert believed their long block of time together to be a guarantee. Their dreams have always intertwined, and at nearly forty years of age, she is not halfway done living.

He is completely dedicated to saving her and their life's happiness together, but how? Robert begins pondering the struggle Ellie suffered to finally teach in the place she desired, surrounded by the middle school students she connected with most because ironically, they were just as lost as she felt. He lets out a small chuckle and wipes the tears from his eyes briefly.

Before the early onset of Alzheimer's no longer allowed her the opportunity to change lives, she was a motivated band teacher for nearly eighteen years. She felt it was her duty to pay it forward and provide students with a superior music education, working hard to let each student know they owed it to themselves to reach their potential. However, when she felt defeated by her own high expectations, she stopped.

It's not fair. This life she only experienced a taste of. It's not fair! Robert vents, crying through his thoughts.

Ellie knew she wanted to teach since her sophomore year in high school. Long ago, she told Robert the exact moment she came to this realization of teaching. Ellie revealed she was awake in bed one evening, asking God what she should do with her life in prayer. Even with the underlying understanding for the power of the subconscious mind, she could not argue the booming response she heard from Him: *You will teach music.* She never before, nor again, experienced a response from God so profound, unable to fully describe the level of fervor in its intentions, even to Robert. No matter one's beliefs or general faith in life, an experience so remarkable has the power to alter destiny if one chooses to listen. For Ellie, the occurrence shaped her entire course, instilling the strong belief and validity her own life truly had meaningful purpose. Music was not just a gift to cherish, but rather to share and change lives.

Robert felt slightly envious of this facet because her endeavors were so tangible, the concerts and performances as direct evidence of student growth and achievement. Robert's path as a pianist, however, carried considerable intangible praise with verbal confirmation from people and music intellects regularly. Even after their 1994 wedding, the couple relocated to Chicago temporarily for Robert's graduate studies at Northwestern, where his highly respected professors attempted to instill a sense of confirmation for his performance abilities. Moreover, when crossing the country to perform with various professional orchestras, his audiences generically confessed how wonderful his playing was after a performance or that his interpretation of a particular work was inspiring, but he had no solid evidence he changed lives like Ellie. He admired her for it.

Robert continues to calm down and stiffens his tears. He sifts through every detail of Ellie's upbringing, attempting to find answers.

It took Ellie time to realize the sheer epiphany of her path in life based on her grandparents' human responses to music. As a child, she watched her grandma Mae sit down at the piano to play gorgeous embellishments of hymns, in addition to swing and rag tunes of her era. Mae always sang. Whether cooking, cleaning, or taking a stroll through a shopping department, music constantly permeated through her body. Ellie distinctly remembered the timbre of her beautiful voice, despite only hearing it in childhood. She naturally leaned into Mae's side at church to have a better listen. The memory of it was clear to Ellie until she could no longer remember the sound of her own voice. Ellie loved getting the saturation of old music from both Mae and her mother, Jean.

Musically, Jean did not fail Ellie either. She sang in abundance, played guitar by ear, and encouraged her daughters to sing to a fault. It was embarrassing to be brought to the center of attention by Jean, gathering around to harmonize the Andrews Sisters or sing miscellaneous tunes for family or friends. However, singing old songs brought back memories of Jean's own childhood and reminded her of Mae. *Jean...always the entertainer.* Robert lifts one corner of his mouth for a crooked grin and continues his reflections.

It was from this perpetual exposure that Ellie owed much of her own success. Certain traits had to come together on their own, such as determination and drive or time and place, but the passion of music and humanism behind her entire existence created the foundation for where her life stood. She could sing because her mother's mother sang to her as a child.

The more difficult question for Ellie became what type of music to study. Orchestral, wind band, and choral studies appealed to her equally for various reasons, but finances necessitated one avenue of pursuit. She knew if she overcommitted to all, then she may also suffer learning as much in one. The easy answer should have been singing, but unlike Jean, it was not a comfort zone for her, never wanting to be a star. When choosing flute in fifth grade, she found a band teacher who propelled her confidence and understanding of how far she could go with proper attitude. Band was a beautiful experience up through high school, especially when she found the art of conducting. She fell in love with it at the same time she experienced the high school's symphonic orchestra as a flautist, further fueling her dream of leading a symphony orchestra. Ellie felt an enormous passion for instrumental music. After realizing she could simply sing anywhere at anytime, the conclusion provided her with a final decision.

While searching for colleges to attend, she stumbled upon the original meeting place of her parents in Decatur, Illinois, home to Millikin University—a small private school with an excellent and established music program, but an education with a heavy price tag. Ellie assumed many loans on her own while her father drained every ounce of his pension to put her through, and he never said a word. Much of the savings he spent was from the time he worked in Chicago as an architect. After the Sears project completion, James and Jean moved to St. Louis with Marie to be closer to Jean's parents, who relocated near their first home in Manchester. The architectural job market was frozen and forced James into his hobby, carpentry. Using many of the skills attained from his coursework, he started with stair building and cabinetry, then on to trim detail while crafting elaborate and custom kitchen designs and decks. His plumbing and electrical knowledge expanded through experience until finally, any project was attainable. He became not just a carpenter but a true craftsman. His work was enjoyable, but Ellie hated imagining her father's body aching after an excessive amount of daily labor.

Merely two hours from St. Louis, Ellie did not know a soul entering college, and she rather preferred it that way. James's parents passed when Ellie was in elementary school, and though her uncle Eugene and other family members lived in town, she never burdened them with a call. She often visited the cemetery site just next to campus where her grandparents were buried. In prayer, she asked them for help and guidance finishing out each semester with grace and vigilance. Robert went with her on occasion, but losing her grandma Mary, James's mother, was something she never felt comfortable talking about, not even with him. She was irrevocably connected with her grandmother. The loss was Ellie's first funeral and an extremely traumatic experience.

Suddenly, Robert pauses midthought as his head snaps up, standing immediately in the middle of the bedroom. In his reflection, he realizes when exactly all this started for the three women he saw today.

In 2001, the whole family went through the stress propelling Mae's dementia forward. *That must be it!* Robert thinks through the timeline.

Katherine, Ellie's beloved cousin and friend, was amazingly brilliant, witty, and carried the energy of a hundred cheerleaders. As Mae's first grandchild and Jean's first niece, Katherine suffered from a brain tumor after she delivered her first child, Sydney, in the nineties. A natural delivery method left her petite body floundering along with forgetfulness and severe headaches. After a number of operations and treatments, she was given a clean bill of health. The family was exceedingly thankful for her recovery, and it created a stronger bond among them all.

Katherine married several years later and then learned she was pregnant again. She was thrilled and conveyed great happiness. Sadly, her symptoms returned in the second trimester. Never missing the beat of a joke, her wit and personality did not teeter one degree, but the family saw her disorientation and forgetfulness. Through Katherine's perpetual optimism, Ellie's eyes popped open to what was happening for the first time: Katherine was running in true martyr form by carrying her baby.

What torture that must have been as a parent! Robert reflects.

Her mother, Elaine, wanted Katherine to simply live and be well as any parent would but saw her perspective giving life to a baby her daughter already loved. Only a mother can understand the unconditional love felt within the womb, and Elaine instantly shared in Katherine's overwhelming adoration for her unborn grandchild.

The mass in her brain spread quickly. The doctors could no longer wait on her operation, and after seven months maturation, Miles was born two months premature. From one operating room to the next, a team of surgeons removed as much of the tumor as possible.

Katherine spent months in the hospital trying to heal, receiving treatments coupled with time for her new precious miracle. The whole family tried to see her often, but they believed she could overcome it again. She fought hard, but her body weakened as the months passed, and God needed her elsewhere.

Katherine's last public appearance was at her cousin's wedding before she was resigned to hospice care in Henry and Mae's home. Two weeks later, Katherine took her last breath with much of her extended family at her side, including Mae, Jean, and Ellie.

Robert tucks his hands in his pockets, remembering how Ellie found solace in her journal reflections that summer.

He moves across the room to open her top dresser drawer, a place he frequently stands to glance over what little jewelry Ellie acquired over the years. It is also the place she keeps her journals.

Robert pauses while holding his precious Ellie's diary in his soft hands. He gently turns the pages, finding the words dating back to those awful weeks following Katherine's funeral:

JULY 27, 2002

NO WORDS CAN DESCRIBE THE EXPERIENCE OF SEEING SOMEONE PASS. EVERY EMOTION RIPPLES THROUGH YOUR ENTIRE BODY, FROM ANGER TO WORTHLESSNESS, SHEER GRIEF TO NUMBNESS. WITNESSING THAT SPIRITUAL DEPARTURE CAN MAKE ONE FEEL NEVER SO CLOSE TO GOD AND SO FAR AWAY IN THE EXACT SAME MOMENT. KATHERINE ACTED AS CHRIST. HER SACRIFICE WAS THE MOST CHRISTLIKE ACT IMAGINABLE, AND THERE'S NO WAY I OR ANY OF THE FAMILY COULD EVER STOP TRYING TO LIVE A LIFE WITHOUT HER AS AN EXAMPLE. I ADMIRE KATHERINE'S COURAGE AND SELFLESSNESS FOR WHAT SHE DID, BUT THE LOSS IS SO PAINFUL. I MISS YOU, KATHERINE.

Robert considers the reality of what happened all those years ago and begins to move fast, tossing his socks, boxers, and undershirts into a small suitcase. As he flies back and forth around the master suite, he reflects on Mae.

Mae's symptoms began at seventy years old with a move to a new part of town. Even with the same furniture and memoirs, nothing appeared in the same place or position. Her children escorted her to the multitude of doctor's visits, but there was nothing to be done. No precautions to take. Losing her granddaughter in her own home was the ending blow to her stability. Katherine was Mae's sunshine, and when she passed, the last ounce of what Mae had left went with her. Mae was gone, and what was physically present was only an empty shell, floating along.

After a second move in a failed attempt to maintain better proximity with family, they moved a final time into a home Mae could have randomly recalled as it belonged to her mother-in-law. Again, the home was furnished with her own furniture and pictures, but nothing helped after Katherine passed. The family resorted to home nursing care to assist Mae with Alzheimer's, but when Henry became ill for a short time, Jean moved Mae into assisted living. Jean was only four years behind Mae.

Robert jets down the hallway to the main bathroom for a few travel toiletries. With long strides back to his master bath, he contemplates Jean's rapid deterioration in health.

With Mae in assisted living, Jean fought to remain in control for as long as possible. Because her siblings lived farther away, she held on to lucidity for her mother. An overt optimist, she rejected the belief it would happen to her, shoving aside worries and burying them deep, never to be considered plausible until too late. James refused to recognize Jean's symptoms as more than forgetfulness as well, but she would forget regularly. Not the major aspects of daily tasks at first, but few people could truly see it coming.

Ellie was scared for her mother while James hoped his life would be cut short like his parents to avoid the ailments Mae faced. He worked to close the gap between physical and mental inability. Every lever in James's mind turned freely, but his body ached liked an eighty-year-old man. He failed to realize one important thing, which Robert recalls Ellie citing in her diary as well:

JULY 31, 2002

DAD STILL SPENDS ENOUGH ON ALCOHOL AND CIGARETTES TO FEED A SMALL COUNTRY MANY TIMES OVER. GOD'S TIMING CANNOT BE ALTERED. NO MATTER HOW HARD YOU TRY TO DAMAGE YOURSELF OR YOUR BODY, IT IS JUST NOT UP TO US.

No determining whether James's parents may have possibly suffered the same fate as Mae, dying too young at age sixty. The nature of the disease feels sporadic as that of a tornado, picking and choosing who will strike out and carry the genetic disease.

Robert's mind begins to wonder whether Mae felt it coming. *Did she think about it when she was thirty, like Ellie? Was there anything she knew was for certain, or did it all seem like a dream in her mind?* For ten years, Mae suffered waking up in the morning, not remembering people, places, time, or memories of her life. She could recall a few faces on a good day.

And my sweet Ellie. Robert contemplates her struggle, refusing to be sidetracked with more tears.

Ellie fought to be there for her family and sister, her children, and most dearly, Robert. With awareness of the needs at home, she remained lucid until both children were nearly to college, but everything started slipping. Ellie dealt with death in abundance, taking on each fatality and loss. With her astonishing ability to empathize with every individual she encountered by placing herself in their situations, Ellie drained her energy worrying about the people she loved. Time seemed dear to her, and yet she felt complete while just observing her family's interactions, feeling the emotions in their voices. Her listening skills, even beyond musicianship, were impeccable.

Eventually, she started forgetting basic home-safety routines and ones at school that could have meant losing her job. Nothing could be done with the high efficiency she once mastered, and it scared her terribly, getting to the point where she could no longer multitask without forgetting essentials. She became a danger to herself and others.

After countless clinical exams, laboratory tests with blood work, MRIs, and a battery of neuropsychological testing—including attention span, coordination, memory, and problem-solving skills—Ellie was depressed. After weeks of arguing with Robert through the holidays, she checked herself into Gateway Assisted Living in January to be with Mae and Jean.

Robert's music brings Ellie back to full lucidity, convincing him that her mind is strong enough to fight.

Robert is done analyzing the pros, the cons, the expenses, the research, and the reasons behind it all; it is time to move.

Now.

Closing her journal swiftly, he moves to the phone sitting on a small round table between two accent chairs next to a row of tall bay windows. He removes the cordless phone from the base and dials seven digits rapidly.

"Hello?"

"Julia, it's Robert."

"Hi, Robert. How are y—"

"I'm sorry, Julia. I don't intend to be rude, but I'm in a bit of a rush. Would you mind staying with Liam for a length of time at our home? I'm asking on behalf of Ellie and myself. I'm going to do everything I can to help her, so I'm traveling out of town as soon as possible."

Julia deliberates briefly and responds, "Robert, are you certain he wouldn't be more comfortable here? I am right up the street from you, and it may help take his mind off things."

"I truly appreciate your offer, Julia, but Liam has a diligent homework routine with all he needs here to study. I would hate to compromise his efforts on the ACT next week as well. He's aiming to raise it one point to a perfect thirty-six."

"That makes sense. I'll pack a few things and be over this evening."

"Julia, thank you. Our family is exceedingly fortunate to have your friendship. You've been considerably helpful, especially after Ellie's sister moved away to accept that assistant professor position at Colorado College last year. Ellie was heartbroken, but you've been so helpful."

"You're welcome, and no need to thank me. Just keep playing that piano," she adds with a chuckle.

"Oh, I intend to. No worries. Before I go, I will contact Liam at school to explain my extended absence."

"Do you think there's anything to be done for her?" Julia inquires sincerely.

Robert sighs. "I have to believe so."

"I'll let you be on your way. Call my cell phone when you can so we know you're safe. I'll keep Liam informed."

"I will. Thank you so much," Robert replies fervently.

"Good luck," Julia encourages.

"Thank you. Good-bye for now."

"Bye, Robert."

⚜

"Dad, are you certain you want to do this? I mean, I'm just worried about your absence from Mom and what that will do to her."

"I know, son, but if I don't go now, it may be too late to help her altogether. She might never come back if I don't try."

"I understand. Please be safe," Liam extends to his father.

"I will. I've left enough cash for your meals at school, gas money, and a couple trips to the grocery store."

"I can take care of my gas, Dad. I do have a job," Liam responds with gentle maturity.

"All right. I'd like you to use the extra money I've left to take Julia out for a nice meal or two while I'm gone. She's doing us a great service, so be respectful and kind to her as she is Grandma Jean's best friend. Please remember how she loves to hear you play piano and indulge her motherly instincts to make her happy. She doesn't have any children of her own."

"I will."

"The school knows Julia is the primary contact while I'm away. Be sure you have all her information—" Robert is cut off.

"Dad, I'm weeks from being eighteen. I've got this, okay?"

Robert pauses, remembering his son is just that—his son, who is responsible, mature, respectful, and already a man. He thanks God every day for his healthy and exceedingly brilliant children, where test and readiness scores enabled a leap over first grade altogether in private school. "You're right. Good luck on your studies, Liam."

"Thanks, Dad. I love you," Liam offers.

"I love you too, son," Robert replies. "Talk to you soon."

"Bye, Dad."

Robert places the phone back on the base resting atop the bedroom table and returns to zip the lid of his suitcase. He walks down the long hallway of their home to the office and stands there a moment, glancing around the organized chaos. Across the room on a lengthy mahogany table is a number of stacked small booklets next to over thirty steno pads with notes written in casual disarray. In three elongated strides, he reaches the table where one booklet rests with scattered Post-its sticking to the pages. He folds over the front cover to reseal the crease and reads *Journal of Alzheimer's Disease, Volume 77, March 2012*, with the article entitled "Breakthrough in Early Onset Alzheimer's Treatment" by Dr. Scott Tresman. Robert takes the booklet in his hands, along with other references, steno pads, a large file with all of Ellie's medical information, and a photo of her from the nightstand and packs them into a carry-on briefcase with his laptop. With luggage in hand, Robert grabs his keys, wallet, and passport before closing the door.

CHAPTER

16

"**E**lizabeth, would you care to accompany me outside, sugar?" Patricia bends down to gain her attention. Ellie's eyes are focused on the black piano in front of her, attempting to remember the story of its importance. Once Patricia invades her line of sight with her thick-framed body, she snaps out of the trance, lifting her brow in surprise.

"Oh, I'd love to. Thank you, uh…" Ellie searches for the name tag on her white nurse's top.

"It's Patricia, honey," she says with a bright smile against her dark skin. She offers Ellie a hand to escort her out of the side patio glass doors to the courtyard.

"I'm sorry, Patricia. It's been a long day, I suppose."

"It's all right, sweetie. It happens every day," she replies with a chuckle, fanning her hand with glossy red fingernails to encourage forgiveness.

"It does? I usually have such a good memory for names. Sometimes I see three hundred students a day at multiple schools and do well with their names," Ellie reflects.

"Is that right?"

"Sure! Yesterday, I only hesitated a split second before calling on a boy with an older brother who looked just like him, but I got it right. My teachers did that to me because of Marie, and I hated it. I try to be accurate."

"I see." Patricia nods in kind. "How about we stroll around the whole lawn today, Miss Elizabeth?"

"Oh, well, Saturdays I usually just stop in to see my mother, but I wouldn't mind a little more exercise for sure."

"Okay then." Patricia looks away to crease her brows together. They stroll past the confines of the courtyard into the open lawn, home to a paved trail with a perimeter of tall English hemlocks covering up the security fencing in place. The vast area holds a number of old trees, azaleas, and rhododendrons in full bloom with greening cherry blossoms, redbuds, and crabapples. Before flanking left, Ellie sees a group of elderly patients standing to take turns rolling a large lighter mock bowling ball toward a group of pins on an assembled flat surface. A young male nurse assists in placing them back up every two turns. One pair is gently tossing a beach ball in close proximity, while another middle-aged man attempts a game of catch with his wheelchair-bound dad using an inflatable ball.

Ellie watches the people play as she walks. Patricia pulls out a handkerchief from her white pants pocket and wipes away a small layer of sweat from her forehead. "Sure is toasty warm today, isn't it?"

"Yes, but the subtle breeze feels nice. What is the date again? I'm not sure how it slipped my mind."

"It's May fifteenth, Miss Elizabeth."

"Wow. It feels like it was just Christmas. Time does seem to fly by."

"Yes, ma'am. I know your Liam will be graduating in a couple weeks now. You must be so proud of him."

"Graduating? Oh, you mean from middle school. Isn't it silly how we celebrate something we were expected to achieve when we were younger? It's so crazy to create all these ceremonies to glorify what should be the norm," Ellie speaks in a light tone, shaking her head with a grin.

"Yes, I suppose you're right, Miss Elizabeth," Patricia comments, looking on at her facial expressions from Ellie's profile. The worry of not knowing the date and the recollection of the day's events or understanding her purpose altogether for being where she is at present creeps into Ellie's eyes, slowing her steps as the reality of her nonreality clicks into place. The two ladies stroll around the half-mile pathway in silence a majority of the time.

"How is my mother...Patricia?" Ellie questions, stumbling over her name again. The couple rounds the halfway point in the far perimeter of the trail.

"Happy, like always. You know how she is, always one to brush off the heavy burdens. I know she'll be real happy to see Mr. Mason in here today, and Mr. Williams too." Patricia grins genuinely.

"Oh. Well, we better get back so I don't miss them either." Ellie's pace increases slightly in the final leg of the paved walkway. Patricia's heavy full-figured frame struggles to keep up.

"Mr. Mason and Mr. Williams have not arrived yet, Ellie. It's all right, honey. No need to rush," she encourages calmly. Ellie leads ahead of Patricia now, picking up her pace to a jog.

"It's okay, Patricia. I've got my running shoes on today. Time for some exercise! See you later," Ellie projects to Patricia while turning to jog toward the courtyard and main building.

The nurse shakes her head as she accelerates walking speed, her large chest panting with labored breathing. "Ooh, that girl is gonna give me a heart attack!" Patricia mutters to herself.

Meanwhile, Ellie's muscle memory kicks in as she treks in a calm pace along the flat pavement. Naturally, she remembers her limits as a runner with a murmur, taking air in through her nose at first, blowing back out the small shape of her circular lips. She feels the smooth glide of the rubber pounding against the concrete, the spring in the ball of her foot propelling her calves forward and in sync with the flow of her quadriceps and hamstrings. A muscle group in her arms frames the relaxed and open box surrounding her rib cage. Feeling the unease of her heart struggling to keep up with her lungs, the discomfort forces a drop in her jaw to take in a deep breath with her elbows out to allow further chest expansion. The perfect ebb and flow of her graceful body provides a feeling of happiness. The essence of imprisonment within her mind escapes her thought process temporarily. In these moments, she is free. With the breeze at her back, she accelerates comfortably. Her eyes grasp the beauty of the blooming shrubs, the greenery of the grass and trees, and the sweet sounds of birds chirping their song. She reaches the outer limits of the courtyard with an audience of geriatrics in her line of sight, staring as she quickly passes while playing their games. Entering the courtyard of stones, Ellie stops immediately seeing Jean stand with her nurse's assistance from her favorite bench.

"Mom?" Jean looks up to see Ellie's panting chest and wind-blown hair. Not wanting to alarm onlookers, Jean pretends to recall the tall middle-aged woman in front of her, avoiding her name.

"What's wrong, honey?" Jeans requests while attempting to walk toward Ellie; the nurse holds her back with one arm.

"Mom, I'm fine. I was just getting some exercise."

"Oh, that's nice. It is a beautiful day," Jean accounts with a genuine smile.

"Yes. I was just coming to see you. Where are you going?"

"Oh. Well, she was, uh…" Jean looks confused.

"I was just taking her to see her mother," the nurse replies.

"Oh, well, I'll come with you. I didn't get to see Grandma the last time I stopped by," Ellie says. She helps the nurse with Jean's other arm, assisting her balance. Jean's nurse looks over at Ellie, a large crease gracing her forehead in disbelief. Jean limps slowly across the courtyard. "Are your feet worse? I guess the diabetes has been tough on them."

"Sweetie, you know I'm just fine. Could always be worse, you know." Jean grins up at Ellie, still unsure of her daughter's name.

"Sure, Mom."

The three reach the edge of the main building, crossing the threshold into the open doors to the main lobby. Jean's fair-skinned young nurse with golden hair sees the object of her focus across the room. "Wait here just a moment," she requests sweetly. She moves swiftly to the other side of the lobby, retrieving Jean's wheelchair.

Jean sees her approaching and speaks gently to the nurse, "Oh, I don't need a wheelchair. I can walk, really. No problem at all."

"Ms. Mason, I've been given orders to have you sit as much as possible," she replies.

"Oh, well, I wouldn't want to get you in trouble then," Jean says while turning to place her hands on the arms of the wheelchair. She sits down carefully.

"Well, thank you, Jean. That's thoughtful of you." The nurse rolls her wheelchair over to the main nurses' station in the large T-shaped hallway. Ellie follows at her mother's side. "Wait here just a moment, ladies." The nurse ventures to the staff restrooms behind the desk.

Ellie plays with Jean's silky black hair while waiting, using her fingernails to smooth back the center of the thick mass. After two minutes, Ellie registers a soft conversation between three nurses. From the corner of her eye, she overhears Patricia and her mother's nurse, having returned from the restroom, along with a nurse she does not recognize whispering in the corner by the large desk. She continues heaving Jean's hair around while she listens.

"How am I supposed to tell them? I mean, what is it going to do them?" Jean's nurse poses.

"Mr. Eastman asked me to take care of Ellie, and this will surely set her into a spiral if we're not careful," Patricia states in worry.

"Ms. Williams has pneumonia, and you know what that means. We need to break it to them now before the shock does something worse altogether." Mae's nurse is adamant.

Jean's nurse sighs. "This is just...so hard. My training never prepared me for this situation," she sniffs, attempting to halt her tears.

"None of our training ever prepared us for this, honey," Patricia states.

"It's a completely rare and unique situation, but these women need us. Attempt to be as sincere and professional as possible over the next few days, and keep me informed of any changes. Bring them over, and we can all be there," Mae's nurse conveys assertively before taking her leave.

"You wipe those tears now," Patricia reminds Jean's nurse.

She follows Patricia's instructions, watching her walk around the large desk.

"Ms. Ellie, honey. Are you ready to see Grandma Mae?" Patricia's voice is in full volume now. Ellie continues stroking Jean's hair, unable to pull out of her internal state of despair. "Ellie?" Patricia beckons again.

Thankful to be given the answer today rather than embarrassment consume her thoughts, Jean now remembers her youngest daughter. "Honey, are you okay?" Jean's voice is heartfelt, opening her eyes now after the gentle pampering. "I know your ears are far better than mine, but didn't you hear her?"

Ellie clears her throat after deliberating a moment to speak. "Yes, we're ready," she replies, placing her hands on Jean's shoulders.

"May I?" Jean's nurse requests with her blue eyes beaming against a backdrop of sorrow.

"Sure," Ellie steps aside to let her push the wheelchair. The two nurses accompany mother and daughter down the hallway toward Mae's room. Ellie eases back behind Patricia in the procession, unwilling to see what is ahead.

"Run out all your energy, Ms. Ellie?" Patricia chuckles while walking past.

"Hm. I suppose so," she replies softly.

The women arrive at room 227. Patricia walks in front of the wheelchair to open the door. The nurse glides Jean's chair into the room with Ellie following behind slowly.

"Hi, honey," Henry greets Jean from Mae's bedside.

"Hi, Dad. How're you doing?" She is overly ecstatic to recall her father today.

"Oh, I'm all right." He grabs the sides of the cushioned chair, attempting to get up using his cane.

"No, Mr. Williams. You stay right there in your chair," his private nurse, Carol, states firmly while inching closer.

"Dad, don't try to get up. I'll sit right by you," Jean encourages. The two exchange a brief kiss on the cheek.

Henry pats down the smooth part in his thick hair, nervous to impress all the ladies in the room. "Hi, Ellie! Don't you look beautiful today, as always," he offers, opening his arms for a greeting.

Ellie looks hesitantly at his arms, not knowing the specific reason for her worry now.

"Hi, Grandpa. How are you?" Ellie bends over for a short hug.

"Oh, you know. I'm still breathing, so that's good." He chuckles, draining his last ounces of energy. Ellie breaks away to look at Mae, asleep in a hospital bed with the rails up. Henry turns to take Mae's right hand. "Grandma, on the other hand, is not so well." His voice thickens at the end of his sentence.

"We haven't told them yet, Mr. Williams. Would you like to, or shall I?" Mae's nurse asks gently.

"I'm not sure I'll get through it, so you go on ahead." Henry's chin dips down to his chest.

"Tell us what?" Jean asks.

Mae's nurse approaches the bed on the opposite side of Henry, Jean, and Ellie. Ellie backs up two steps in response. "Mae's body has started to shut down. She has lost the ability to swallow, which is the first in a succession of crucial functions she requires to survive. Because her brain won't cooperate due to the Alzheimer's, she's developed aspiration pneumonia and requires hospital treatment. The infection from her bedsore has also compromised her condition, so Mae is being transported today. I'm sorry to say Henry will have some difficult choices to make about the quality of her life." The nurse pauses briefly to give Jean a moment while tears run over the brim of her eyes.

Ellie takes another step back toward the door.

"How long?" Jean inquires in a whisper.

Patricia steps up to the rear of the bed. "Ms. Mason, when all these ailments begin challenging the immune system, there's not a whole lot the doctors can do. It could be as little as two days or as long as a week, I'm sorry to say. We're all *very* sorry to say," she finishes, glancing over at Ellie.

Ellie's enlarged eyes register the timeline of imminent loss. Her chest feels heavy and frail; her breathing staggers to accompany her pounding heartbeat in her ears—the only sound she can hear. The walls begin to slant at odd angles, blurring all the edges of her sight as oxygen escapes her mouth in a pant.

"Ms. Ellie?" Patricia asks in haste, moving closer to her patient. Ellie immediately backs into the door, grabbing the frame for balance. "Ms. Ellie, you need to sit down, honey. Please let us help you," Patricia pleads.

Ellie sees the outline of nurses approaching and stumbles into the hallway. She spots the clear shot down the hall and trips over her feet to begin a jogging pace. Ellie blocks the sounds of the nurses shouting for her to stop and the five Gateway residents staring at her body launching itself forward in graceful chaos. She refuses to slow down, rounding the corner at the nurses' station into the main lobby. She passes the piano and runs through the courtyard, gaining monumental glares from the geriatric patients and their visitors on the lawn. Ellie initiates a quick pace around the half-mile trail—too fast. Her heart beats loud and hard in her ears and chest. She gasps for air, taking in massive deep breaths through her mouth. The oxygen swims in her lungs but fails to fulfill the amount required to feed her heart's pumping valves.

Ellie thrusts her arms faster, forcing her elbows out in frustration. Her chest feels heavier now. The pressure tightens throughout her rib cage, squeezing her torso from every angle. Sharp pings jab her collarbone and underneath her ribs into her stomach, radiating agony as the lack of blood flow deprives her muscles of oxygen. In the warmth of the spring morning, Ellie can feel her fingertips and face tingle like icicles pricking her nerve endings, unaware of the purple discoloration consuming her skin. She continues on, fighting off her body's overdue demand to stop. Her balance weakens, the line of the pavement horizon wavering. Her throat clinches tighter amid the gasps for air just as her knees buckle with uncertainty. Ellie's feet stumble and shuffle from one side of the path to the other. She sees the grass just before her eyes shut closed.

Blackout.

❦

"Please. I need to see Dr. Tresman today. I've come all the way from St. Louis to speak with him," Robert pleads with the receptionist, exercising the ease of his charm mixed with underlying grief behind heartbroken eyes.

"Sir, Dr. Tresman is an incredibly busy man here at Banner. Do you know how many people, doctors even, have come into this medical facility with the same request?" The female receptionist is patient, smiling at him through frustration.

"I'm certain that is the case, ma'am. I'm so sorry to barge in, but I have no time left to spare. Please, my wife—" Robert's perfect face drops down to attempt the suppression of his emotions.

"Your wife?" The receptionist pauses, studying the outline of Robert's perfect features. Her guess at his current age is over an entire decade off.

"Yes, ma'am. She has early onset at just thirty-nine years old." He wipes the betraying tears with the back of his suit coat sleeve.

"Please. I'll wait here all day. I have every one of her files and all the background information he requires. I just need to see him."

The fifty-five-year-old receptionist feels a ping of gratefulness in her heart knowing her own sound and healthy genetic code is absent of the genes responsible for Alzheimer's. "The doctor is in trials with patients all afternoon, but I will see what I can do before he leaves today. Please have a seat in our waiting area."

Robert looks up with an elated expression he thought lost since Ellie's ill-fated diagnosis. "Thank you! This means everything. You have no idea." Robert glances at the nameplate on her desk. "Amelia! Thank you so much." He feels like a panicked schoolboy again, unable to contain his relief. He happily picks up his large laptop briefcase and strolls over to the waiting area.

Robert selects a number of chairs to assume residency. He removes his suit coat, folding it gently in the center from the collar, and places it on the back of a padded chair next to his seat.

Robert's sense of propriety and the distraction of his mission kept his mind off the Phoenix heat from the hotel walk just over a half mile away. In his focus of the task, he neglected the Continental breakfast offered.

He removes the wallet from his back pants pocket, finding singles to purchase a processed item from the machine—a last resort he truly loathes.

"Sir?" Amelia calls from down the hall.

"Yes?" he responds, approaching her slowly.

"We have a café just down the hall. The food selection is much better." Amelia points the opposite direction from her desk and the lobby.

"Thank you, Amelia. You've saved me again," he says with a smile, gathering his items.

"Don't worry about missing the doctor. He won't be available until the end of the day. Are you staying close to the Banner Institute?"

"Yes, thankfully, but I won't be leaving." His voice is tempered and soft now close to her desk.

"She must be very special," Amelia offers.

Robert puffs a sigh through his nose, a warm crooked smile accompanying his thoughts. "She is the most beautiful creature in every sense. Any amount of time lost is a loss for everyone."

"Hmm. I'm sure this has been difficult for you."

"I'm optimistic it's not too late. She's still there. I see it every day."

"I hope you're right," Amelia replies. "Every person who works for Banner feels the same. We all feel we're so close to answering crucial questions about the disease."

"Thank you. You've been monumentally gracious and kind, Amelia."

"You're welcome, sir."

Robert spends the bulk of his afternoon reviewing Ellie's medical files and history. In perfect recall, he knows the result of every blood test, biochemical biomarkers, brain scans—including the magnetic resonance images, computed tomography, and positron-emission tomography scans—along with each answer from her neuropsychology tests and clinical interviews. He can recite facts surrounding her regular eating habits, exercise regime, and sleep patterns. Robert knows the exact dates of her first episodes of mild cognitive impairment, maintaining a calendar of each incident thereafter. In his notes are the prescription doses for donepezil and memantine Ellie refused to begin until she drove to the wrong building for school last spring. Donepezil helped her memory to amplify synapse connections and replenish the chemical acteylcholine, a key ingredient for nerve cell communication. Memantine increased her functional skills, regulating excess glutamate, which disrupts and kills nerve cells involved in memory and learning.

He peruses the research journals on Alzheimer's for the last year, accustomed to the common terminology associated with each acronym. He can recall every doctor, each trial in progress, and the institute responsible for the succession of breakthroughs over the last ten years. Robert understands the odds are not in his favor; he must try.

Beginning at five o'clock, he glances at his watch every five minutes, afraid the doctor will forget, ironically, or be called away before seeing him.

Five thirty-five. His internal sense of pulse and timing knows exactly how sixty beats per minute feels, needing no reference to his watch.

Five forty.

"Mr. Eastman?" A deep voice echoes through the follicles of Robert's ear canal from the lobby. Robert stands immediately in response.

"Yes."

"Good evening, I'm Dr. Tresman." The doctor walks halfway to meet Robert with an open hand, towering four inches over him at six foot seven.

Robert takes hold for a firm handshake. "Dr. Tresman, I can't thank you enough for your willingness to meet with me."

"At Banner, every case is important and may help us unlock answers. I have to tell you, however, that I don't think we can possibly help based on what Amelia mentioned."

"I know the odds are not in my favor, but—"

"You had to try." Dr. Tresman finishes his thought.

"Yes. Ellie means everything to me. We have a connection impossible to describe, 'like a fairy tale,' she would say. Every moment we've shared together, every detail of her life and who she is, appears to be locked inside."

"Hmm. Well, bring your things with you. Let's head to my office."

"Thank you," Robert breathes. He quickly gathers his suit coat, scoops up all the files, and slings his briefcase over his shoulder. The two walk through the lobby in the direction of a long hallway.

"You seem familiar to me. Where are you from?"

"My wife and I live in the suburbs of St. Louis County where she was raised, and I'm from Chicago."

Dr. Tresman opens a tall door to escort Robert down another hall. "I take it you met in college."

"Yes, sir, as undergraduate students."

"What did she do for a living?"

"She was a fine band director."

"Ah, a musician. How sad to lose an educator of music," he replies.

"Are you a musician?"

"I used to play piano through high school. I love it still, attending concerts frequently."

"Wonderful."

"The Phoenix Symphony Orchestra hasn't exactly been in existence half as long as the fine St. Louis orchestra, but it's nice to appreciate and listen to great works live."

"Indeed."

"And what do you do, Mr. Eastman?" Dr. Tresman opens the door to his office, inviting Robert to sit down in front of the massive U-shaped desk as he walks around to his chair.

"I am a concert pianist, but I also teach privately and freelance."

"You're Robert Eastman!" the doctor exclaims energetically. Robert smiles in response, sitting down with a subtle shade of surprised confusion in his expression.

"Yes."

"You've played with the orchestra here before. I saw you perform years ago, and you were amazing!"

"Thank you, sir." Robert naturally diverts his eyes, humbled by his enthusiasm.

"Your interpretation of the second Rachmaninoff concerto was brilliant, so intense and vivacious! After hearing your rendition of that, along with the Shostakovich encore, I was sold. I bought your CDs and make everyone listen to them in the lab."

"That's...Wow, that is something," Robert stammers graciously.

"Efficiency levels appear to be higher when I play your recordings for them."

"Is that so?" Robert feels a strange sense of purpose for the first time in his career and, unbelievably, in the most crucial circumstance.

"Absolutely. No question."

"Thank you for that." Robert is beside himself with emotions of self-worth.

"Well, what a great surprise, though I'm sorry it's under these circumstances. May I?" Dr. Tresman opens his palms out toward the files in Robert's hands.

"Certainly." He hands him the elongated medical records and scans.

"I'm just curious, but what did you mean when you said every memory appears to be 'locked inside'?" The doctor looks straight into his eyes.

"I visit her every morning. Ellie's entire life unfolds before her when I play the eighth Chopin nocturne, which was *our* piece. Her episodic and semantic explicit memory is completely intact. She understands every autobiographical decision she ever made down to each detail, including the one she made to put herself in assisted living."

The doctor gently contemplates the wording for his next thoughts. "If I were in her place, Chopin as a trigger would be quite acceptable."

Robert nods with his eyes down, understanding his position on the delicate matter.

Dr. Tresman opens the thin paper file from the side and retrieves the DICOM disc first, quickly loading it into his computer. While the software loads the images, he removes the complete radiology and physician's reports to read. Robert is quiet as the doctor reviews the multiple pages of reports for five minutes.

He turns to open the files on his computer, analyzing the results and the accuracy of what he has read thus far.

"It would appear you took your wife to some of the finest neurologists in St. Louis. I'm well-acquainted with the doctors and clinical research there at Washington University." Dr. Tresman continues reading the scans. "I'm assuming she was denied for the major familial early onset study due to her mother and grandmother's sporadic onset?" Robert pretends not to understand the direction of his accurate assumption. Though Jean's symptoms began in her fifties, Mae's mild cognitive impairment did not appear until her seventies. With the highly irregular family history, Ellie does not fit into any specific category for treatment. At thirty-nine, the side effects of trial medications may be severe and life threatening.

Robert deliberates momentarily. "I can provide you with any information you need about Ellie. Anything above and beyond what is in her medical files if need be." Robert's voice sounds confident.

The doctor drops his posture to the tall back of the leather office chair and crosses his arms with a sigh; this is the look Robert feared from day one.

"Mr. Eastman. You're a highly intelligent, educated man, and I'm quite certain you already know what I have to say—"

"Please. I'll do anything for her. We're willing to try anything. I know about your trial. Can she do it?"

"We are still looking for patients, but the drug we are testing is for the prevention of the disease in families with the mutation, not reversal. You know that. I'm sorry, but she's surpassed the age requirement."

"No!" Robert stands immediately in anger, pacing to the back of the large office. "It's not too late! It can't be." Robert presses his fist to his forehead, pushing firmly from frustration.

"I'll never understand how hard this must be for you, having to cope with this at such a young age. It's not fair."

"Dr. Tresman, my wife changed lives. Every day! Completely and incandescently euphoric in her work and purpose, she *chose* to step away when she could not give 100 percent of herself to the students. And when she couldn't give her best to her family, she forced her way into that home so she wouldn't burden me." He pauses to shake his head in disbelief. "She was concerned she would *bother* me. Are you even familiar with that level of selflessness?" Robert inflects his voice in subtle panic.

"She sounds like a beautiful human being, Mr. Eastman. This disease is hurting millions of people and their caregivers every minute. I understand, but I am bound by my oath, to my own bosses, and the people we represent to set limitations for these trials."

"Screw your limitations! My wife deserves a better life." Robert looks at his face, every emotion ripping through his wet blue eyes. He turns again to the back of the room, crossing his arms as he gathers his thoughts. He breathes deeply for many moments to calm his rare temper.

"Are you married, Dr. Tresman?" Robert's voice is soft and weary.

"Yes, twenty-five years this summer."

"Can you imagine a connection with someone so intense, so strong, that it physically transfixes every nerve in your body?" Robert pauses to reiterate his thoughts further. "A magnetic influence so real and powerful in touch that it's impossible to deny? Have you ever known such a feeling?"

"I regret not, though doctors in other fields would argue your romantic reactions to be vaguely behavioralist in nature when not given all the information, but I see your point."

Robert turns around to look at his face. "I know it seems far-fetched or cliché to you, believe me, but the only explanations I deem worthy of description are *soul mates*, *true love*, or *destiny*. How many people have that kind of physical evidence? This isn't some movie fantasy. Our bond is beyond comprehension, and I know I can save her."

Dr. Tresman crosses his arms, looking down at the large files he has yet to dissect completely. He sighs as he contemplates. "Do you have all her blood work here?"

"Yes."

"And what about her grandmother's and mother's blood work? Do you have access to that information?"

"You're curious about the genetic mutations." It was not a question.

"Most patients have them, and depending on which mutation she carries, I can't help you. Early-onset familial Alzheimer's is not something anyone could help you with now that she is symptomatic. The trials in Colombia are for preventative treatments, as I'm sure you're aware." The doctor holds his breath momentarily. "The circumstances would be exceedingly rare, but if she does not have the mutation, there may be an option."

"Which is...?" Robert waits.

"The likelihood that she does not have it is exceedingly low, according to her family history, but I'll have to take these files home to look. Meet me here first thing tomorrow morning. Speaking of love, I'm late for a dinner date with my wife."

"Thank you for the effort you're making for Ellie. As you know, St. Louis has a plethora of resources and neurologists specializing in Alzheimer's, but due to her unique situation, we ran into several roadblocks."

"Mr. Eastman, every case has subtle variations, and it is in many of these cases that we unlock answers, along with more questions. I understand your wife is special, but I'm intrigued why three generations acquired such a drastic turn of symptoms within a relatively short time frame, especially if there is no mutation."

"I have a theory, and I'll let you get to your wife," Robert politely offers as Dr. Tresman gathers the files into his laptop briefcase.

"Get some rest. I'll see you at eight o'clock," he says while removing his lab coat, replacing it with a black suit coat to match his slacks. Robert also gathers his suit coat and laptop.

"Thank you again, sir." Robert's heartbeat begins to calm.

"You're welcome."

⸻❦⸻

"Miss Elizabeth? Can you hear me, honey?" Patricia touches her forearm, tapping it gently. She watches Ellie's eyes flutter; her head turns slowly to the side as it rests on the pillow of the bed in her room.

"Mm," Ellie moans. A small cry erupts within her throat as she registers pain, both internal and external. Tears flow down the side of her face freely before her eyes open.

"Oh, Miss Ellie, it's all right," Patricia consoles. The nurse reaches over to a small end table near the bed and presses play on the iPod dock boom box. Robert's recorded performance of Prelude No. 15 by Chopin begins. Ellie's ears perceive the sound while her eyes remain closed. The crinkle of pain surrounding her face disappears instantly. Her head gravitates to the left softly as she slowly opens her lids to the morning daylight through her curtains. An eight-by-ten photograph rests on the nightstand in her line of sight. The picture displays a man and woman on their wedding day, face-to-face in preparation for a kiss. She reaches instinctively for the frame, moving too quickly.

"Ah-ow!" Ellie whimpers out.

"Be still, Miss Ellie. You hurt your neck and back real bad yesterday in your fall. Try to be still now," Patricia encourages. Ellie turns to look at her face.

"W-what happened?" her voice croaks. The nurse gets up to retrieve the picture around the opposite side of the bed. Ellie's eyes follow her figure around the room. Patricia places the picture frame in her hands.

"Well, I suppose you probably did hit your head against that tree you rolled into. You don't remember feeling overly energetic yesterday?" Ellie's forehead crinkles in confusion. "I guess not." Patricia sighs. "Miss Ellie, your heart couldn't keep up with your sprinting yesterday. You'd think you were trying to qualify for the Olympics!"

"Oh." Ellie relaxes with understanding. "Did anyone else get hurt?"

"Just you, honey. You gave us all quite a scare."

"Sorry." She is disappointed and embarrassed.

"Here, you need to drink some water." Patricia tucks a smaller pillow gently behind her head before handing her a full cup. "Here's your medicine too and some toast and fruit to start you off."

"Thank you"—Ellie glances at her name tag—"Patricia."

"You're welcome." She watches Ellie take three sips before observing her wash down the medications. Patricia refills her cup from the pitcher resting on the rolling tray at the side of her bed.

Ellie sets down the cup and looks at the picture in her hands, perceiving the music again. Her fingertips gently stroke the glass. She ponders momentarily, tugging at the periphery of her autobiographical memories. Seemingly, the blow to her head, coupled with the picture in her hands, creates a direct pathway to every detail in her mind today. A solid confrontation with each decision greets her, knocking her breathless. *Robert.*

Patricia sits back down next to her, seeing her near the brink of breakdown. A patient's good day for memory can be a double-edged sword, mixed in a nasty cocktail for depression. "Miss Ellie," Patricia says lightly. "Please, let me get the wheelchair. Maybe we can head outside and enjoy the nice weather while it lasts? It's supposed to rain tomorrow."

"No, thank you," Ellie replies quickly.

"I'd love to see you take a bite of that toast." Patricia is enthusiastic.

"I'm not hungry, Patricia."

"Oh, come now. You haven't eaten since yester—"

"No, thank you. I'd like to be alone, please," Ellie retorts while staring at the photo, touching Robert's face through the glass.

"All right, Miss Ellie. I'll come check on you in a little while now," she states compassionately. Glancing at her disposition on the way out, she worryingly exits the door of Ellie's large and elegantly furnished suite.

"Dad, you need to get back here. I saw Mom this morning, and she's not well. The morning after you left, she had a bad fall outside."

"What?" Robert is panicked through his cell phone. He stands and paces around Dr. Tresman's office.

"Yeah, she took off running too fast and blacked out. She suffered some bad bruising, but no broken bones."

"Why didn't they call me?"

"Patricia called Grandpa James because she didn't think you were reachable. Grandpa told me and Julia, but no one had a chance to call you yet."

"I understand everyone's busy, but they should have called. On the other hand, I'm certain Grandpa didn't want to worry me while I'm away."

"And he's worried about Grandma now that Grandma Mae is away at the hospital."

"What?"

"She has pneumonia, and they can't feed her anymore."

"Did your mother find this out?"

"Yeah, right before she took off."

"Jesus." Robert registers further evidence for his theory. "I'm sorry, Liam. I'm sorry you're dealing with all this without me."

"Dad, I am worried, but have you talked to Rose? She's so stressed at school with her exams and performance juries that she's considered asking for extensions from her professors. I told her to stay focused and hang in there, but she's freaking out about Mom."

"I'll call her as soon as I'm off the phone. I'm going to call Grandpa Eastman too."

"Good. When are you coming home?"

"As soon as I can. The doctor has been contacting his colleagues all over the world with specialized research teams to analyze Mom, Grandma Jean, and Mae's genetic files. The doctors are intrigued with their case, so I have to believe we're getting close, son. I'm also attending a conference with Dr. Tresman out of the country this week, but I promise I'll be back for graduation."

"Okay, be careful. I'll talk to you soon," Liam states in closing.

"Give your mother an extra hug for me, and I'll see you soon. Love you." Robert ends the phone call with one button.

"I suppose it's a good fathering practice to shelter his worry," Dr. Tresman comments from his desk. "Even if we hit a wall and crash here."

"I'm optimistic we can at least buy his mother more time. He deserves it, as does my daughter."

"What does Liam want to do when he graduates?"

Robert puffs out a smile. "He's been accepted to a number of fine institutions, including Cornell, Brown, and Johns Hopkins, but like Rose, Northwestern seems to be close to his heart and a little closer to home."

"All top premed schools. I'm sensing an underlying mission in development here."

"You sense correctly. Liam will be a fine neurologist, I'm sure. If not in our lifetime, I hope the research he conducts in his generation sees the end of this disease."

"I have to believe with the substantial strides we've made in just the last ten years that we are close."

Robert nods in agreement with a sigh. He picks up his iPhone and opens the recent contacts. The phone rings three times.

"Hello?"

"Dad, it's Robert."

"Robert, how are you, son?"

"I am doing well, but I'm afraid I need to make this brief. I need your help."

"What's wrong? Is it Ellie?" His voice is thick with concern.

"Yes, but it's more complicated. Are you able to get away earlier for Liam's graduation?"

"I'm sure I can rearrange my golf schedule, Robert. You know you're always more important than my strenuous retirement activities," his father adds sarcastically.

"Thank you, Dad. I appreciate it. Have you spoken with Ashley?"

"She'll be there for Liam's graduation, but she has a heavy travel schedule right now with all her biomedical presentations. She's on a flight back from a clinic in China as we speak."

"Okay, you or I can speak with her later then."

"What's going on?"

"I'm in Phoenix right now at the Banner Alzheimer's Institute."

"With Dr. Tresman?"

"Yes. I need you to check in on Rose for me. I'd like you to accompany her home immediately following her exams this week. She desperately wants to see her mother."

"I'll book our flight today then." His father is confident.

"Dad, I think Ellie's condition is exacerbated by stress and grief. I'm afraid of what my absence is doing to her, even though that is what she wanted."

"We'll get down there as soon as we can then, Robert."

"Thank you. I'll call Rose. I'm sure she'll be relieved."

"Tell the doctor 'thank you' for all of us."

"I will, though I know he's sick of hearing it."

Patricia wheels Ellie down to the lobby, over the threshold, and into the courtyard gardens. Even after three days of rest, her back is still tender from the fall. With stretching, her neck has gained mobility but pings in pain when extending movement beyond her shoulders.

"I'm glad the rain finally stopped," Patricia comments.

Ellie does not respond.

"Here's your mother now, Ellie. That's sure to make you feel better." She rolls her wheelchair over to Jean's bench near the rosebushes.

Jean looks up. "Hi, sweetie!" Ellie briefly glances up at her mother, remaining unemotional and somber. "What's wrong?"

No response.

Jean takes Ellie's hand. "Are you all right?" Jean is confused. She looks up at Patricia. "What's wrong with her?"

"She's just having a real hard time right now is all, Ms. Jean. She won't talk to me none either," the nurse replies.

Jean looks at her near-catatonic daughter. "It'll be okay, sweetie. Whatever it is, it'll all work out. Don't you worry!" Jean is charismatic, as usual, even on days she is unable to recall her daughter's name.

Ellie, who is quite lucid today, recalls a memory from age six when Jean was tucking her into bed one evening:

> "Mommy, when you're a hundred years old, you won't be my mommy anymore," Ellie says on the verge of tears.

> "Oh, sweetheart. I'll always be your mommy, but I may not be here on earth. I'll be up in heaven waiting for you." Jean can tell she is concerned about mortality, perceptive at such a young age. "But no worries now. I'm right here, and no matter what, I'll always love you." Ellie pulls her onto her small chest, hugging and squeezing her tightly to hide the escaping tears.

"Here's your dad now, Ellie," Patricia states, snapping Ellie out of her recollection.

"Hey," James greets everyone, carrying a tray of plants and a small bucket of gardening items. He sets them down on the bench next to Jean, who stands for a hug and kiss. James turns to see Patricia and Ellie.

"Good morning, Mr. Mason," Patricia declares.

"Morning. How are you?"

"I'm just fine, sir."

"How are you feeling, Ellie? Still sore?" He bends down to kiss her on the cheek.

No response. She looks down with a squint from the sun poking out from the clouds.

James directs his attention to Patricia, searching for an answer to his confused expression.

She shrugs. "Ever since her fall, Mr. Mason. She hasn't spoken to me, and she's not eating real well."

James contemplates the right combination of words for his daughter. "Honey, I know you can hear me." James bends over to speak. He slowly lowers onto one knee, attempting to seek her eyes and attention. "Ellie, look at me."

He waits.

Nothing.

"Ellie, look at me." His voice is fuller and more demanding. Her eyes move up fractionally but do not reach his face. "Ellie, you need to eat. Robert will be back soon, and you have two children who love you. You need to take care of yourself. For them." He lets the information resonate.

James struggles to stand after years of abuse to his knees as a craftsman. Patricia takes his arm to assist. "Thank you, Patricia. She should be better now. I know my daughter. Her sense of responsibility runs thick. When someone else's well-being is on the line, she'll do what it takes. Even this disease can't destroy who she is at heart right now." James speaks with assured confidence.

"Thank you, Mr. Mason. Good to know," Patricia replies.

James turns to Jean. "I've got a surprise for you today." He reaches into the bucket and takes out his kneepads while gesturing to the small palette of flowers.

"Oh, how pretty. Thank you!" Jean is exuberant.

"I'll put them right underneath your rosebush over here. It was looking a little barren."

"You sure do a great job with these plants, Mr. Mason. I know the staff appreciates all the pruning and weeding you do," Patricia compliments.

"It's good for Jean to see me every day, and it's great for the garden."

"And good exercise too," she adds with buoyancy.

"That too."

"Now that's what I call multitasking." Patricia laughs as James smiles.

Ellie spends the next hour watching her father's outline plant flowers across from Jean, gazing blankly with unfocused vision at his repetitive actions. James waters the plants, removes the kneepads, and wipes excess soil from his hands. He leaves briefly to wash up, and when he returns, James bends down in front of his wife and kisses her hands in her lap. Looking up at Jean's beaming smile, he moves to sit beside her on the bench to enjoy the new additions together. He wraps his arm around her shoulders, sharing thoughts about work and other news.

From where Ellie sits, she sees the affection and love her parents still share. Though Jean requires constant supervision James cannot provide, she knows he still loves her as much today as the day of their wedding.

"I think they need to come today," Henry states evenly to Patricia.

"I don't know, Mr. Williams. Ellie finally started eating again yesterday after Mr. Mason spoke to her. It's been quite an emotional roller coaster for her lately, and I've got to consider her health."

"They put Mae on morphine this morning. I was hesitant to even leave, but I think she's waiting for them."

Patricia sighs and shakes her head. "I don't know, sir. It's going to be risky transporting them over there. If Ellie responds badly and takes off again, I can't keep up."

"Neither can I, Henry," his nurse, Carol, comments.

"I understand. I'll talk to James," Henry replies.

"He's with Jean in the courtyard, of course."

"Thank you." Henry crosses the lobby using his cane with Carol on his other arm.

"Let me go get him from here, Henry. We don't need you falling too."

"Very well," he answers.

Carol reappears two minutes later with James and Jean, holding on to each other and moving slowly. The nurse briefly explains the situation on the approach to Henry.

"Patricia offered to go," Henry comments to James.

"I understand. Liam's on his way here with Julia. He's strong. Why don't I ask Patricia to accompany them along, and I'll take Julia with Jean and I?"

"Thank you, James. I know they would want to say their farewells to Mae."

"Yeah, you're right. Too bad Marie can't be here. Her schedule's all tied up in Colorado until June. She's devastated she's not here."

"Tell her how sorry I am to hear that. I requested they put Mae on a ventilator until our return. Her vitals were dropping quickly." Henry's eyes divert down as he turns the opposite direction into the lobby.

"All right, let's head on out then." James is somber.

Liam arrives, pulling up to the covered circle drive with the assumption he would be escorting his mother to the park. When he steps out, James greets him with the news and plan for transportation. Within five minutes, Liam is driving Ellie and Patricia to the nearby hospital. He exits the car at the main entrance and is met by volunteers, who provide a wheelchair for Ellie. Patricia waits to move Ellie until after Liam parks the vehicle in a space. When he returns, they travel up the elevator to Mae's floor.

Henry sits in the bedside hospital chair at Mae's right, stroking the fingertips of her purple bruised hands from the onslaught of intravenous needles. Jean is at her left side with James, accompanied by her older sister, who is praying in the corner, and Jean's younger brother, peacefully gazing at his mother. Elaine, the second oldest twin daughter, is sadly out of town after weeks in St. Louis bidding adieu to her mother. The sound of Mae's heartbeat through the monitor, along with the mundane pumping of oxygen into her body, are the only sounds in the room.

Parked just outside the hallway, Patricia grips the handles of Ellie's wheelchair facing the hallway while Liam stands across watching her frustrated expression. Ellie halted the progression of the wheelchair, stomping one tennis shoe down, before entering the room. She refused to cross the threshold and would not say a word.

Liam moves to bend down in front of his mother, speaking softly. "Mom, I know you understand why you're here. You love Grandma, so please go say good-bye. She waited for you." Ellie's facial response is chiseled and hard while contemplating an answer.

"I don't want to be here, Liam," she whispers, looking away.

"Okay, Mom. I hope you don't regret leaving here then. I'll tell Grandpa."

When Liam rises to bid farewell, two male doctors and one female nurse arrives at the opening to the door, excusing themselves gently. Henry sees their entrance; his chin quivers. Jean takes James's hand at her shoulder.

"Mr. Williams, please pardon us. The nurse said you were ready, but if you need more time, by all means," the doctor speaks compassionately.

Henry wipes his tears quickly and grabs hold of Mae's hand again. "No, I think we're ready," he replies with a croaky voice. "She's ready to go home now."

Jean takes Mae's left hand and stands slowly from her chair. She bends over to place a tender kiss on Mae's forehead, smoothing back the soft curls of her silver hair with her hand. "Goodbye, Mother. Sing happy songs until we meet again. I love you." Jean gradually turns to James, who is flushed red with emotion, and walks forward into his waiting arms.

Jean's sister floats closer to pray over Mae while her brother gently kisses his mother's cheek, whispering words of love in her ear. Mae's oldest daughter then places a final kiss above her brow and removes herself back to the corner to continue praying.

Henry flexes his leg muscles to stand, bending over to Mae's warm cheek to tenderly and adoringly touch her with his lips. "So long, doll. My beautiful bride. We'll dance together soon." He caresses her cheek with the back of his hand, lingering to her warmth. "You wander down the lane and far away, leaving me a song that will not die. Love is now the stardust of yesterday, the music of the years…gone by." Henry struggles to finish singing the last words of their song. He weeps, remembering a perfect evening with Mae long ago.

One of the doctors takes the initial step, moving smoothly toward the ventilator machine buttons. Once in front of it, his fingers reach out to initialize shut down.

"Wait!" Ellie shouts from the hallway. The entire gathering turns to watch her rise from the wheelchair; slowly and gracefully she crosses the room. Her eyes focus on Mae but carry the burden of shock for her own presence in a foreign space. The frame of her body shakes, erupting with uneven bursts of air through her lungs.

Henry moves slightly to allow Ellie space. She gazes at her grandmother, superficially filled with oxygen from a machine, feeling emotions from anger to resentment and then wonder. *Is she dreaming? Is there a light? Can she see Katherine and all our loved ones?* All the questions build further angst for what truly burdens her heart: she must bid her farewell. She bends down to whisper in Mae's ear, soft enough for no one to hear her words. "Grandma...Thank you. Thank you for living a beautiful life filled with love, laughter, dancing, and music. I thank God for your voice. Without it, none of us would be here. I pray for your peace, Grandma."

She gazes up at Mae's profile, stroking her hair back as tears roll down her cheeks now. She leans back down to her ear one last time. "Please look after all those who suffer in this way, Grandma. Let them remember their way home. I love you." She lays her cheek at the side of Mae's forehead, resting it there for a moment. A solitary tear falls down atop Mae's head before she stands and turns the opposite direction. Ellie returns to the wheelchair, wiping her tears with the tissues Patricia places in her lap.

Henry resumes holding Mae's hand at her bedside. He gives the doctor a nod to proceed. The doctor acknowledges Henry, the other resident and nurse, then initializes shut down on the ventilator machine. The last flow of oxygen runs through the equipment as the second resident removes the tube placed on Mae's mouth. The heart monitor seems louder without the noise from the ventilator, cutting through their ear canals. Within two minutes, Ellie registers the slowing of Mae's heartbeats per minute without turning to see the screen. She waits outside the room, gazing off in a daze. Sixty beats per minute, a pulse engrained from years of music training, echoes through the room, followed by fifty-four beats per minute for eighty seconds. Mae's breathing catches with two swift pulls of air through her wrinkled lips. Her pulse falls to forty-two beats quickly, then thirty-five. Moments pass at the same heart rate but drops suddenly to eighteen when the agonal rhythm progresses quickly to asystole. The flat line from the monitor rings out a solid ping of sound just before the nurse shuts down the volume. Tears flow gently and quietly throughout the room while Mae's spirit drifts away.

The doctors watch the monitor for over a minute before one travels forward slowly to physically test Mae's pulse with a stethoscope, followed by an assessment of her pupils with his light. "Time of death is 2:22 p.m.," the doctor declares. The resident beside him writes down the pertinent information in the chart while the nurse shuts down all the equipment softly. "I'm deeply sorry for your loss, everyone," the doctor speaks soothingly. He turns to address Henry. "Mr. Williams, please take all the time you need, sir. The nurse will notify me before you leave to assist you in any way possible." The three of them exit the room in silence.

Ellie looks halfway up to Patricia, still sobbing. "Can we go now? I'd like to be alone, please," she states softly.

"Yes, Miss Ellie. We can go on back now. Liam?" She looks to him for affirmation.

"Yeah, Mom. Let's get you back. I'll just say good-bye quickly." Liam walks into the room solemnly. Jean and James hug their grandson tightly, as do his great-aunt and great-uncle. Henry remains hunched over, holding his head in his hands, motionless and tranquilized by his loss. Liam beseeches Carol to deliver a message. "Would you tell Grandpa how much I love him? My mom is overwhelmed, and I don't want to disturb him now," Liam says in a whisper.

"Certainly, honey. I'm so sorry about your great-grandma," Carol replies quietly.

He drops his head in a silent nod. "Someday this disease won't exist if there's anything I can do about it." His thick brows angle down in frustration.

"That sounds like quite an undertaking, but if anyone can achieve that, it's you."

Liam simply nods in thanks for her kindness. He waves one last time while subtly exiting the door. Patricia holds the back handles of Ellie's wheelchair, pushing her through the hospital hallway.

*

The day of the visitation, Rose arrives home accompanied by Robert's father via airplane. In a rush to see her mother, she and her grandfather spend little time freshening up before leaving for Gateway to see Ellie. Liam arrives home from work in time to escort the two in Ellie's rarely used sedan sitting in the garage.

"Liam, have you heard from Dad today?" Rose asks with concern from the backseat.

"No. Not for a few days, actually." Liam focuses on the road.

"Oh," she states in disappointment.

"You two needn't worry about your father. He's doing everything beyond all limitations or restrictions placed before him to help your mother. He'll return when he succeeds."

"If he succeeds," Liam replies.

"Remember who raised your father, Liam. Just as he knows you, I also know my son. I hope you two find great love and the one person worth risking everything to save."

Rose sighs. "They do have a rare love. I hope you're right, Grandpa."

"Okay, we're here." Liam turns off the engine and exits the car. The three venture toward the main entrance foyer to be checked in as visitors. "Now remember, Mom may or may not be actually talking today. If she shows you any kind of reaction at all, then cherish it. Try not to react, no matter how shocking it may be."

Rose nods, nervous and emotional to see her own mother after months away. The trio signs in and walks around the corner to the large lobby with the piano. Ellie sits alone, staring blankly at the keys; her black flowing dress has a chiffon overlay of soft white flowers in patches ending at her midcalf. The flattering dress swoops down in a V-neck with two long thick straps tied in a bow just under her lowest left rib. Her golden hair is pulled back with a large black barrette, and waves of soft curls flowing down her torso. The glow from her makeup gives her an angelic appearance, taking Rose's breath away. She gasps, holding her hand to her chest. Liam watches his sister and grabs her shoulder to spin her about before Ellie catches the reaction. "I'm sorry," Rose whispers. "I'll pull it together, I promise." Rose speaks respectfully to her brother, even though he is a year younger.

Liam gently pats her shoulders. "Deep breaths, Rose."

Within sixty seconds, the three visitors advance into the lobby. "Hi, Mom!" Liam approaches his mother first. "Look who I brought with me." Ellie looks up from her daze at the sound of his voice as he steps to the side to show his guests. She immediately beams upon seeing his face, standing to greet him, but is stunned at the sight of her daughter. "Rose is home from school for the summer, Mom. Isn't that great?" Liam encourages her to speak, but she is still in shock.

"Rose." Ellie's voice is stuck between resonance and a whisper having not spoken for days. She approaches her daughter slowly as if seeing her for the first time. Her hands reach out to stroke her smooth face. "You're so beautiful," she breathes, looking into her daughter's eyes. Rose can no longer contain her emotions, cupping her mother's loving hands to her face while tears fall down her soft cheeks. Consumed with a multitude of rushing feelings, Ellie draws Rose's forehead to her own to share a lovely reunion.

Held in a tight embrace, Ellie pulls away gently with a bright smile gracing her face to look at her children. "I am so happy you're both here."

"We're happy to be here with you too, Mom." Liam wraps his long arms around his sister and mother. His grandfather looks on at the family with a sense of peace.

"Mom, Grandpa's here too." Rose backs up to remind her of his presence. Ellie focuses in on her father-in-law, seeing the familiar attributes of his face mirrored in her children's features.

"Hello," Ellie whispers, veering her eyes down while leaning forward to give a gentle hug.

"Hi, Ellie. You look wonderful as always," he compliments with a grin.

"Oh, I'm sure I'm a mess now, but thank you," Ellie states, still unwilling to accept a compliment in totality.

"Guess what, Mom? I spoke with Aunt Marie this morning, and she'll be in for a visit the first of June. She can't wait to see you." Rose is excited to relay the news.

"Oh, that will be nice, sweetheart." Ellie feels comfort hearing her sister's name.

"And Ashley will be here for Liam's graduation too. She has missed you as well," Ellie's father-in-law adds with a smile.

"How wonderful," Ellie replies in a soft voice, unable to pull an image of Ashley to her mind.

"Mom, do you have your purse? I can help you freshen up before we go," Rose offers.

"Go where, honey?" Ellie questions in confusion; the three guests pause in surprise.

Liam, always ready for any circumstance with his mother, responds maturely, "Mom, we're on our way to Grandma Mae's visitation. Do you want to freshen up before we leave?"

Ellie's face turns white, recalling the progression of her thoughts the last three weeks. She takes hold of Liam's arm for balance, looking down to hide the despair on her face.

"Are you all right? Do you need to sit down?" Rose questions.

"I'm—" she whispers. Her eyebrows arch up, sorrow ripping through her chest.

"Come with me, Mom. Let's go to the ladies' room." Rose holds out her arm, wrapping it underneath and around her mother's waist for the walk to the restroom.

Rose helps Ellie touch up her mother's foundation powder under her eyes, reapplies blush and a soft coat of mascara, followed by a layer of shimmering lip gloss in the restroom. Ellie's body and mind shut down to autopilot, casting her attention away from Rose's beautiful appearance as she launches back into a catatonic daze.

"Mom, I've missed you so much," Rose offers. "It's been hard to be away at school."

Ellie hears her daughter but cannot muster the strength to speak. She nods in response, acknowledging her emotions by gently squeezing Rose's arms. Rose hugs her mother again before they exit the bathroom.

• ⚬⚬⚬ •

Mae's visitation and funeral are well attended, filled with a plethora of extended family members and friends. For the funeral, Ellie sits beside James and Jean near the front row. Rose and Liam begin the ceremony with a gorgeous and emotive performance of Rachmaninoff's Vocalise Opus 34, a six-minute prelude for cello and piano. They return to Ellie's side for the bulk of the service but exit briefly to lead two of Mae's favorite hymnals, "Just a Closer Walk with Thee" and "The Old Rugged Cross." The ceremony is beautifully crafted to commemorate Mae's withstanding musical influence over their lives.

Ellie swims alone in her thoughts, diving deeper into despair over the loss as she copes with death again. At the nearby professionally eloquent funeral home where several loved ones were seen for the last time, including Katherine, her tears come in unrelenting waves now as she sits in silence. Jean, however, often smiles in denial of her sense of sadness, wiping away leaking water before it flows down her face.

For two days, the nearby conversations of close family and friends regarding Ellie's and Jean's rapid deteriorating status escapes their conscious minds. Questions regarding Robert's whereabouts are posed, explained, and met with abundant hope for his success.

Upon returning to Gateway, Ellie remains in a daze and suffers for days. She is visited daily by Rose, Liam, and her father-in-law but cannot seem to crawl her way out of the dark and unresponsive state of depression. Rose perpetually holds her mother close, kissing her on the cheek often, and plays her favorite cello pieces. Liam plays for his mother as well but has admittedly not mastered the emotional finesse of the Chopin nocturnes like his father, refusing to perform those selections. Rose and Liam worry whether their performances are helping Ellie's current condition.

"Grandpa, I'm just not certain we should play for her anymore. She cries so much already and even more when we play," Rose mentions over dinner at home one evening.

"Rose, music registers in various parts of the brain, but in an Alzheimer's patient, the medial prefrontal cortex is the portion that can help access memories through music and also the last area affected by the disease. When your mother hears you play, it helps her remember autobiographical information. We are doing everything we can to keep you, your brother, and your father at the forefront of her mind in the most literal way. Stopping would be the worst thing for her right now."

Rose considers his explanation as truth. From her understanding, it is exceedingly difficult for doctors to correctly diagnose patients with this disease, which is why her mother went through a surmountable number of tests. Due to the overlapping gray areas in all seven stages, actions and memories may be completely random from one minute to the next. "I bet that's why she's so sad. A piece of her is missing without Dad here."

"I'm sure much of that is the case, sweetheart."

"I hope he gets back soon and in time for Liam's graduation on Friday."

"Me too."

⚜

Ellie wakes to the light of a glorious sunrise followed by clear blue skies. Patricia assists her wardrobe selection for the day in preparation for Liam's graduation ceremony in the late afternoon. Ellie slips a long deep-purple flowing dress over her head. The top is supported by one-inch straps with material cutting down in a wide low V across her chest in front and back, accentuating her neck, collarbone, and shoulders. She adds a bracelet and necklace with touches of lavender, purple, and silver to match her outfit, leaving the diamond stud earrings from Robert in place as always. She applies her makeup, choosing shades of purple and lavender eye shadow to highlight the color of her blue eyes. Her beautiful blond hair falls freely in soft curls around her shoulders and back.

Desiring the warmth of the sunshine on her skin, Ellie grabs her wide-brim hat and white silk shawl and heads for the courtyard. She walks freely through the open lobby doors. Across the pathway outside, Jean is sitting on her favorite bench, watching James weed the gardens. Ellie gracefully crosses the stone walkway to sit next to her mother. Jean expresses surprise by the visitor at her side, smiling at Ellie's brilliant and beautiful glow.

"Good morning, honey." James turns around to greet his daughter. Ellie smiles kindly at her father, never looking up to meet his eyes. "You look really nice," he adds, turning back around to his work. She crosses her ankles, tucking them under the bench to the side, and wraps the shawl around her shoulders to avoid sunburn.

The next half hour passes peacefully as Ellie enjoys the slight breeze mixed with the sweet fragrance from the roses while holding her mother's hand now. Suddenly, her ears register the sound of the piano coming from the lobby. She instinctively stands, letting go of Jean's hand. With a confused look on her face, her next move is uncertain.

James hears the music and rises up, turning to see his daughter's mind at work as she attempts to assemble the puzzle pieces. "Go on, Ellie," he says softly.

Her eyes lock on his, acknowledging his directive. He nods to her with further encouragement. "Go." His voice is filled with sincerity and an edge of anticipation.

Ellie walks slowly across the courtyard, clutching onto her shawl with nervousness. When she crosses the threshold, she sees a man in a black suit sitting at the piano. She removes her large hat, tossing it onto the loveseat just to the left without looking. Ellie's heart is in flight as her ears take in the beauty of the performance. She takes one step forward, then another. A solitary red rose rests on the edge of the closed music stand next to a small yellow bulky package on the opposite side. A memory tugs at the perimeter of her mind, but she cannot grab onto it entirely. She moves closer to the man, feeling drawn to him and sensing the music's importance.

Patricia and several other nurses are gathered at the counter across from the lobby, stunned while watching Ellie's sudden interest in the man playing piano. The catatonic qualities of the last three weeks have vanished within seconds from her body and face.

Ellie pauses, staring at the back of the piano player's head. She knows him but cannot recall how. Regardless, she glides closer, holding out one hand while slowly progressing. She hesitates once more, ignoring her audience. Apprehensive of whether to keep moving the last step, she is within inches of his back. Reaching forward, she feels a forceful magnetic pull from the ends of her fingertips to his body. Her heartbeat races faster, feeling heat in every fiber of her body's frame; she finally propels herself to touch his shoulder.

She notices an immediate release as his posture relaxes with an exhaled sigh of relief. He drops his head while playing the last chord of Chopin's Nocturne in D Flat Major then places his left hand delicately atop her fingers. Electricity flows through Ellie's nerves as her blood boils and the wave of memories flood her mind. Overwhelming emotion graces her face. She gasps, taking in every moment of her past with Robert as it unfolds within seconds, like a movie in fast-forward. Her eyes immediately fill with water watching him turn to slowly rise while taking the red rose in his right hand. He meets her gaze for the first time in weeks with a smile and moves her hand to his cheek, cradling it there gently. One tear escapes down his smooth face, then more follow. She glances down briefly to accept the red rose he places in her hand before their eyes meet again. "Robert," she breathes, pulling closer to him now.

Robert moves his hands to tenderly stroke her golden hair back and away from her face. She closes her eyes briefly in response to his delicate touch and opens her lids to see every attribute of his breathtaking face. "Yes, my love. I'm here, and I will never leave you again. And you… will never leave *us* ever again." The fervor in his voice pulls their faces together, closing the gap of their bodies quickly. Robert and Ellie embrace, kissing adoringly and passionately. The time grows long enough to disregard the place, any sense of propriety, or the growing audience of their magnificent reunification. Ellie touches Robert's gorgeous face with her fingertips, making the circuit several times, kissing around the corners of his lips, his cheeks, knowing with absolute certainty he is speaking the truth. She is somehow as confident about his statement as she is of her love for him; their love will never fade with distance or time. With Robert, she is finally safe from herself.

Liam and Rose arrive at Gateway thirty minutes later, elated to hear the news of their parents' reunion from Patricia. Ellie and Robert are still standing next to the piano, holding one another, speaking in close proximity, when their son and daughter approach.

"Liam! Rose!" Robert is elated. He opens his arms for a massive embrace of his two children together.

"Dad, I've missed you," Rose speaks through her tears.

"I've missed you too. I missed everyone." He turns back to look at Ellie as he holds his kids tightly, kissing the tops of their heads. Robert holds out the side of his hand, inviting his wife to come forward. He releases Liam and Rose slowly to wrap his arms around Ellie. "Your mother's going to be coming home."

"For how long?" Liam questions with skepticism.

"Forever," Robert replies with assured conviction as he stares lovingly at his wife.

"How?" Liam asks.

"Did you find someone to help her?" Rose questions.

"Yes. Your mother's going to continue her current medications but will add new ones to help reverse the amyloid buildup in her brain. If the amyloid theory is correct, the molecules will separate and allow her the ability to fight off the plaque. It won't reverse the damage to the brain cells, but we hope this will halt the progression."

"So she doesn't have the mutation?" Robert's father enters the lobby to speak to his son escorted by his daughter, Ashley, having picked her up from the airport.

"Aunt Ashley!" Rose and Liam speak in unison, rushing to her side for a hug.

"Hi, Ashley. It's so nice to see you." Robert walks over to hug his sister, as does Ellie.

"Hi, everyone. Looks like I'm just in time," Ashley states with a cheerful disposition and clings to Ellie's waist after their hug.

She looks at Robert. "I'm sorry, you were saying?" Ashley cues her brother to answer.

"She does not have familial Alzheimer's, thankfully, but it's a rather complicated and rare form in an early enough stage that may be helped by this new trial medication. Her memory has also been compromised by the extra cortisol being released from stress, shutting off the communication between the cells."

"Her hippocampus is smaller," Robert's father concludes.

"Yes."

"Excess grieving created higher cortisol levels," Liam adds.

"Yes." Robert looks at his son, amazed and grateful for the knowledge gained from the advanced courses in anatomy, physiology, and biomedical sciences offered at his high school.

"I love this kid." Ashley walks over to Liam, playfully nuzzling his dark hair. "If I didn't know any better, I'd think you were my nephew being that smart." She laughs. Liam smiles in elation by her comment.

"As happy as I am for my daughter, I want to know about Jean," a resonant deep voice questions from the back of the lobby. The group turns to see James sluggishly approaching Robert with a solemn expression, bracing for impact as he tucks his hands into his jean pockets.

Robert prepared for this reply on the return flight back, knowing this moment was imminent; however, he did not imagine it so public. "I'm sorry, sir. I didn't intend for all this to come out in front of everyone, but I suppose now is the time." Robert and James both divert their eyes from each other. "Ellie's situation is exceedingly rare and considered a sporadic form of the disease. The key was the specific variation she carries on the apolipoprotein E gene on chromosome nineteen. APOE instructs the building of a protein that carries cholesterol and other fats through the bloodstream but is thought to be associated with creating excess plaque in the brain. The other factor was the cortisol, exacerbating her symptoms. She's young and active, which created the specific avenue for this trial's pertinence in the very early stages. The medication will only work to buy more time under specific requirements and by following the prescribed dosage within this age and stage of development. If all the factors don't line up, it won't work." Robert's eyes are genuine and soft with compassion for his father-in-law.

"I see," James replies simply.

"James, I'm so sorry," Robert's father speaks with sincerity. "It's one step at a time right now for these researchers."

"I understand." James is defeated.

"Sir, both Jean and Ellie still have the power to help others. I've already registered Ellie, but I hope you'll consider registering Jean for one of the Alzheimer's genetics studies conducted here in St. Louis."

"What are those?"

"They are trying to investigate families affected by tracking their physical and mental evolution. Since the brain can show changes as early as twenty years prior to symptoms, they need help from anyone who thinks they might carry the genes or descendants of family members having suffered. They assess those registered every one to three years depending on age. In time, they hope to stop its development." Robert is animated.

James considers the new information. "You just said Ellie doesn't have the gene, so how can they help if neither of them have it?"

"The mission is also to create a database to help track the progression of the mutation, should it occur, before it happens and to create a comparison or control group in certain studies. Other genetic researchers want family volunteers with two or more members having suffered from late onset, which is information that could possibly help *all* of Mae's descendants, including your own grandchildren." Robert holds his hand up in Rose's and Liam's general direction, standing beside their aunt Ashley.

James looks at his beautiful grandchildren, feeling an opportunity to help defeat these horrific odds for the first time to save his grandkids. "Would you set that up for us, Robert?"

"Absolutely. I'll call first thing Monday morning." Robert steps over to wrap his arm around Ellie once more, kissing her forehead tenderly.

"So how will this play out differently for Mom this time, Dad?" Liam asks.

"She'll take her meds, we will exercise together every day, avoid stress, see a nutritionist, and in time, she could possibly even teach lessons from home again if all goes well." Robert caresses Ellie's arm as he gazes into her blue eyes and strokes her cheek with his opposite hand, pulling his forehead to hers. The entire room is grateful for Robert's return, but none happier than Ellie, whose heart is complete and full of hope for the first time in years.

⚜

Ellie's dreams of returning to teaching in a private-lesson capacity are filled within two years. She rarely suffers a bad day while home with Robert as he is constantly in her line of sight, never leaving her alone to question any burdening perspective she held from the past. The cortisol-reducing medication increases her sense of euphoria, coupled with the natural release Robert provides just by being near her; she is elated to awake and start the day with him.

Rose receives her undergraduate performance degree from Northwestern, followed by a master's in performance from Eastman all within six years of study. She is one of the youngest professional musicians to be offered and accept a post with the St. Louis Symphony Orchestra as a full-time cellist, also working with private students where time permits. She visits with her mother frequently during the week.

After several years in medical school, Liam takes a position to continue neurological research of Alzheimer's in affiliation with Washington University close to his parents, attempting to produce an optional streamline test to check for the molecules responsible for the disease while in infancy. After a multitude of breakthroughs in research and trials, he wants to prevent families from dealing with this terrifying ordeal though treatment earlier in life.

Nothing makes Ellie happier than having her family close to home. It is the most important aspect of living in her world. The music, however, connects her to pathways on the highest level and to information and emotions she could never attain through visual cue or by verbal explanation.

The road she continues to fight for and walk down, reaching students in the most meaningful way and possibly changing their life's path, is of utmost significance and the work of a greater power. Her entanglement in children's lives is a purpose created for Ellie, giving her much to live for and happiness in life.

EPILOGUE

"What time is it, Robert?" Ellie questions.

"It's six twenty-seven. Sarah should be arriving any moment. Do you have all your lesson materials prepared?" His voice is calm and pleasant.

"I believe so," she replies, opening Sarah's file folder in her lap. Ellie pauses to review Robert's notes from the previous week's flute lesson with her student. Her eyes peruse the information quickly and efficiently, recalling glimmers of her time with Sarah. She closes the file to briefly memorize the printed digital snapshot of Sarah on the front cover. After her second lesson over three years ago, Robert requested permission to capture Sarah's picture along with two other students Ellie teaches once per week.

Following two years of regimented dedication to Ellie's health and further progress in clinical research, Robert felt her ready to return to teaching under his supervision. His six thirty slot for piano instruction is devoted to shadowing flute lessons three nights per week following dinner. With five years of observing and absorbing woodwind technique, Robert could perhaps earn an honorary degree for pedagogy in flute performance but still lacks the application elements.

Robert's schedule is full during the day between practice and a steady stream of private students of all ages. When he must travel for special orchestral appearances or play for special occasions in St. Louis, Ellie accompanies him. Before her symptoms began, she remained at home during his trips. She genuinely enjoys excursions with Robert now, but her primary euphoria and lucidity stems from his presence alone. Even as he teaches lessons, Ellie swims in the sweet timbre of his soothing voice. After breakfast every day, he happily plays a Chopin nocturne or any selection of her choosing. She attempts to focus on crosswords, sudoku, or reading throughout his lessons but is often sidetracked to a fault as their connection never waivers.

He happily glides into his brown leather chair positioned in the far corner of the massive living room with vaulted ceilings. The dark hardwood flooring is home to several large area rugs, one of which is underneath two Steinway & Sons baby grand pianos set close together.

Ellie answers the door amiably while Robert dates the top of the yellow steno pad paper on his lap. The buoyant penmanship he exudes follows a beautiful day with his loving wife. *One of her best days all around*, Robert reflects. However, *random* is a common descriptor word associated with those suffering from the disease; within minutes or an hour, the circumstances of their reality may change.

"Okay, Sarah. Did you have a chance to prepare everything from last week's lesson?" Ellie questions. She grabs her assembled flute from the floor stand resting beside the piano and turns to watch Sarah put her instrument together from the leather bench.

"I did…for the most part." She smiles at Ellie with traces of guilt in her eyes. Ellie laughs lightly in response to her hesitation. "I'm sorry. I had three tests this week at school, so it was super hard to find time."

"I understand. It's tough to balance everything out. I remember. Let's just see where we're at this evening."

"Okay." Sarah feels the weight of her guilt lift slightly from her shoulders. She blows hot air through the tone hole, warming up the inside of the solid silver chamber.

"Did you warm up with long tones at home already?" Ellie starts sorting the exercises onto the music stand.

"Yes! I did do that," Sarah speaks energetically.

"Perfect, then we will start with scales. Yay!" Ellie playfully mocks her own excitement. Every musician understands the necessity of scales, but typically their mastery is approached with as much pleasure as eating a solid diet of green vegetables. Scales are crucial to your health as a performer, but require an enormous amount of time and patience to master initially. As a sophomore and third year student, Sarah is ready to extend her scale knowledge by tackling melodic minor forms. "I know you're super excited. Don't deny it." Ellie laughs openly.

Sarah chuckles at her humor.

"Last week we worked on E flat major and C minor, correct?"

"Yes."

"And, how are those? Smooth yet?"

"Umm…I can play them in sixteenth notes and slurred, but probably not at the goal tempo."

"Okay. Off we go!" Ellie sets the metronome on the stand at sixty beats per minute, slower than the eighty beats mastered the previous week. The clicks begin before Sarah and Ellie raise their flutes. "One, two, three-ee-and-a four," Ellie counts off. Two octaves of slurred sixteenth notes ring perfectly in sync, both ascending and descending the E flat major scale.

"Good, Sarah. I know it's our first scale of the evening, but let's do it again. This time, play fuller and louder on the last few notes. Really try to pull the edge and squeeze the juice out of the lower register. Your air must be warm. It exits quickly with an open relaxed embouchure, as you know. Get rid of all the air. All right?"

Sarah nods in understanding. Ellie counts off once more and plays to the end with Sarah, whose tone is now darker, rich, and full. "Excellent, Sarah! That's it. You know what I always say. Tone is everything, right? Playing fast won't matter at all without a quality sound. When you make tone a priority in your practice, it will follow you in every passage. People will want to hear it too, so play out down low!"

Robert acknowledges Ellie's positive energy with a smile.

Ellie bumps the metronome up ten clicks for E flat major, then another ten, which Sarah masters alone with a full tone in warm-up. He takes note of her exercise on the steno paper before she moves onto C melodic minor. Ellie repeats the same process, reducing the metronome speed to sixty and gradually speeding it up. Within five minutes, Sarah meets her goal tempo for the week for both scales.

"Okay, time to introduce another major-minor combination." Ellie bumps the metronome back to forty and mutes it temporarily. She smiles, knowing Sarah is likely cursing antagonistic thoughts at Ellie in her head right now. "It's not that bad, though, because you've already played A flat major, right?" Ellie pauses briefly to confirm and wait for Sarah's nod. "So we will just be speeding it up. The related minor for A flat is F melodic minor right here." Ellie points to the next scale down on her printout. "It will be a piece of cake for you."

"Sure," Sarah manages to utter sans confidence.

"All right, here's A flat major." Ellie points to the high notes. "Have you been playing your chromatic every day in three octaves?"

"Mostly. Yes," she replies.

"Well, look at your highest note here." Ellie points to the ledger lines. "A flat, of course, and it is completely accessible if you already go past that up to high C, right?"

"Right, but I can never remember the notes when I'm reading that high. I'm blanking on how to even finger the high A flat right now."

"Oh. Well…" Ellie hesitates. "How did I used to describe that fingering to help my students? Or am I thinking of another note?"

Robert's eyes pop up to Ellie, a crease rising between his brows. He clears his throat in the silence. "I believe you gave her the laminated amended fingering chart when she first started lessons with all the information."

"Thank you, Robert. I can't believe I forgot that trick. Strange," Ellie notes while tracking down the fingering chart for Sarah's reference. She hands her the paper to glance at before circling the two new scales. "We're not going to have time to play these tonight after all, but take a look at them at home. Let's move on to your primary repertoire for now since it's still brand-new. Continue working on your études though, and I'll listen to those next week as well. Okay?"

"Sounds good," Sarah replies, not noticing Ellie's hiccup in flow.

Robert gazes intently across the room, watching Ellie sift through the music folder on the stand.

"Here we go," she pulls out Three Romances, Opus 94 by Robert Schumann and edited by Rampal. "You've played the first movement, which is a contradiction to the simple and heartfelt second movement introduction here. I love this piece because it forces you to stretch yourself musically. Technically, it is not above you and only a real fingering challenge in a couple areas, but musically, it is a minefield of work. You must play this with vulnerability and an openness and willingness to make honest music. Sing it through your instrument, and play from your heart."

"I'll try," Sarah responds sweetly.

"Good," Ellie comments softly. She adjusts the metronome and pushes the mute button for 120 beats per minute. "Whenever you're ready," she announces to Sarah. She brings her flute to her mouth, sets her embouchure, and begins the pickup notes on count 3 after a deep breath. The sweet melody leaps and flows within a comfortable, effortless range of notes. Sarah attempts to play the first phrase softly to contradict the repeated and similar second phrase at a louder dynamic. The constant shifting of volume abounds in the romantic setting for the tune. Arriving at the third line of music, accidentals and symbol markings altering the original key signature flourishes, creating colorful chromaticism and a short development section in the music. The recapitulation of the second movement's introduction is performed softly, reminding the listener of the initial phrase before the piece leaps atop a mountain for the highest note then falls back gracefully to the tonal center in the key of A.

"Wait." Ellie pauses. "First, the opening line and a half was wonderful. You truly shaped the phrase beautifully, down to the shimmering vibrato and dynamic contrast we spoke of last week. Well done. Let's just take a look at the third line quickly." Ellie's brows arch down. She leans forward to have a closer look at the notes, analyzing the dark shapes on the page. "I believe you played a wrong note in here, but I'm trying to figure out where. I think it was in the third line here," Ellie ponders.

Robert is stunned. He has never heard Ellie say "I think" during a lesson, let alone witness the questioning of her error-detection skills to describe the precise location of wrong notes in a performance. If not for Robert's rare perfect pitch, her auditory capabilities would admittedly surpass his own.

"Let's just start from here and play it again." Ellie points to the third line.

"Okay." Sarah brings her flute to her chin. She begins the third line and plays nearly to the end of the fourth line.

"Wait. Stop. You're playing a wrong note," Ellie says once more.

"Which one?" Sarah asks.

Robert sees Ellie studying the page, her finger moving back and forth along the lines. The silence begins to linger on while Ellie's expression becomes panicked.

Ellie looks at the music with the same symbols marked down the page. Suddenly, none of them make sense. Three sharps indicating the key signature, the treble clef, and the C at the beginning for the time signature are just empty symbols. She is frozen, unable to tell her student what note was played or how to correct it. Her grieving blue eyes are covered in horror.

"Umm…I…" Ellie stutters.

Robert sees her expression, swiftly rising to graciously walk over to Ellie's side. "My apologies, Sarah. Mrs. Eastman is not feeling well today." He arrives behind Ellie and invites her to sit on the musician's chair close to the piano with a gesture. Once sitting, he leans down in front of her, takes her shoulders in his arms, and awakens her body with his touch. Her blank look of terror turns to worry while gazing deeply into his eyes. He cups her face tenderly before turning to attend to Sarah. Robert walks around the opposite side of the piano and shifts the leather piano benches into alignment with Ellie's chair. "Here's a chair for you. I'll sit on the piano bench on your other side so we can all view the music."

"Thank you, Mr. Eastman," Sarah speaks in a polite tone, sitting down on the bench.

"At one point, I believe you played a C natural when it should remain C sharp from the key. If I remember correctly, C sharp can be, ironically, quite a sharp pitch if you don't adjust your embouchure, which is possibly what Mrs. Eastman was hearing, but let's try it again, shall we?"

Sarah brings the instrument back to her mouth, takes a deep breath, and begins line three, playing to the end without error. Robert teaches the remaining five minutes of the lesson.

Ellie sits quietly, staring blankly at the black-and-white colorless page.

Nothing.

AUTHOR'S NOTE

My reason for writing this novel comes down to one word: Hope. Everyone has a hope for something... The hope to find a job, a hope for strength in trying times, to end war and crime, or a hope to find love. My intuition believes that every human being now knows or is acquainted with an individual affected by some type of debilitating disease or cancer, whether family or close friend. Consquently, it is apparent to consider that every adult, or even child, has hoped for a cure for someone they know, knew, or cared about at one point in time.

My grandma Sarah suffered with late-onset Alzheimer's disease (LOAD) for ten years. My hope is to bring awareness to this terrible epidemic through these love stories and tales of optimism. Though the plot resolution of this particular story may be farfetched or outside the realm of possibility in the medical profession right now, my prayer is that more clinical trials lead to answers; otherwise, a staggering 16 million are estimated to be affected by 2050, up from the 5.4 million in 2012, according to the *Alzheimer's Association* (www.alz.org, 2012). By raising money for research, we can allow people the opportunity to simply *remember*. I can imagine nothing worse than losing the ability to think clearly, which some patients suffer in developing sporadic early-onset AD or familial AD (EOAD or eFAD) with symptoms potentially presenting as early as the low thirties. How cruel to have the ability to run for miles but not the memory capacity to recall how to get home. It's a tragic disease.

Options for testing. Would you want to know? Even if you choose not to learn whether you have a genetic mutation responsible for the disease, you can help. Please find out how to get involved by visiting the websites found on the next page.

The medial prefrontal cortex is an area of the brain responsible for autobiographical memories and connecting emotions to music. It also happens to be the last portion affected by AD. Music appears to be a gateway to patients' lucidity, if only for moments, through the end of one's life. It is my plea, along with thousands of colleagues in music education across the world, that we continue traditions of music excellence in our schools to ensure connections to our families, their thoughts, and their minds until the end of natural life.

If music be the food of love, play on!

GET INVOLVED

(Information courtesy of the
National Institute on Aging [www.nia.nih.gov])

Alzheimer's Association
225 North Michigan Avenue, Floor 17
Chicago, IL 60601-7633
1-800-272-3900 (toll-free)
1-866-403-3073 (TTY/toll-free)
www.alz.org

Alzheimer's Disease Education and Referral (ADEAR) Center
PO Box 8250
Silver Spring, MD 20907-8250
1-800-438-4380 (toll free)
www.nia.nih.gov/alzheimers

The National Institute on Aging's ADEAR Center offers information and publications for families, caregivers, and professionals on diagnosis, treatment, patient care, caregiver needs, long-term care, education and training, and research related to Alzheimer's disease. Staff members answer telephone, e-mail, and written requests and make referrals to local and national resources. The ADEAR website provides free online publications in English and Spanish, e-mail alerts, a clinical trials database, the Alzheimer's Disease Library database, and more.

Additional information about genetics in health and disease is available from the National Human Genome Research Institute (NHGRI), part of the National Institutes of Health. Visit the NHGRI website at www.genome.gov.

The National Library of Medicine's National Center for Biotechnology Information also provides genetics information at www.ncbi.nlm.nih.gov.

- The Alzheimer's Disease Genetics Study is gathering and analyzing genetic and other information from one thousand or more families in the United States with two or more members who have late-onset Alzheimer's.

- The Alzheimer's Disease Genetics Consortium is a collaborative effort of geneticists to collect and conduct GWAS with more than ten thousand samples from thousands of families around the world with members who do and do not have late-onset Alzheimer's.

- The Dominantly Inherited Alzheimer Network (DIAN) is an international research partnership studying early-onset familial Alzheimer's disease in biological adult children of a parent with a mutated gene.

- The National Cell Repository for Alzheimer's Disease (NCRAD) is a national resource where clinical information and DNA samples are stored and made available for analysis by qualified researchers.

To learn more about the Alzheimer's Disease Genetics Study or to volunteer, contact NCRAD toll-free at 1-800-526-2839 or visit www.ncrad.org.

YOUNG ADULT
DISCUSSION QUESTIONS

1. Are the three women's stories actually what happened or fabrications of their memories?

2. Is life too easy when growing up or seem perfect when you're younger? Does everything really go your way?

3. Would you want to know if you had a gene responsible for AD? Why or why not?

4. How would you change your actions today if you could prevent AD from happening to you?

5. If you could do something to help someone else with your skills or talents, what would it be?

6. If you had to choose between your mind or your body functioning to the end of your life, which would you pick? Why?

7. Do you know someone with AD? If so, what symptoms have you witnessed? If not, how would you handle speaking with a person you believe afflicted with the disease?

8. How do you cherish your family's precious memories?

9. If you could pick one aspect or time period of the novel to explore further, when would it be? Why?

10. What do you do to relieve stress in your life?

11. What are examples of tough decisions you might make for your parents at an older age?

12. Is it harder to lose someone you love quickly or over a long time? Does your answer change when considering the symptoms of Alzheimer's? Why or why not?

Alzheimer's Myths and Untruths

Information courtesy of the Alzheimer's Association website, December 2012. http://www.alz.org/alzheimers_disease_myths_about_alzheimers.asp

1. Memory loss is a natural part of aging.

2. Alzheimer's disease is not fatal.

3. Only older people can get Alzheimer's.

4. Drinking out of aluminum cans or cooking in aluminum pots and pans can cause Alzheimer's disease.

5. Aspartame causes memory loss.

6. Flu shots increase risk of Alzheimer's disease.

7. Silver dental fillings increase risk of Alzheimer's disease.

8. There are treatments available to stop the progression of Alzheimer's disease.

ACKNOWLEDGEMENTS

Alzheimer's Association – St. Louis Chapter

Jan McGillick, MA (SW), LNHA–Education Director, St. Louis Chapter of Alzheimer's Association

John C. Morris, MD – Distinguished Professor of Neurology, Professor of Pathology and Immunology, Professor of Physical Therapy, and Professor of Occupational Therapy at Washington University School of Medicine; Director, Knight Alzheimer's Disease Research Center, Washington University School of Medicine

Randall J. Bateman, MD – Distinguished Professor of Neurology, Washington University in St. Louis

Eric M. Reiman, MD – Executive Director, Banner Alzheimer's Institute; CEO, Banner Research; Director, Arizona Alzheimer's Consortium

Special thanks to the following:

My friends: Thank you for encouraging me to write this novel, and to one friend in particular, who reminded me not to be afraid to put my name on it. To all my proofers, I am forever and deeply grateful.

My former teachers/professors: I tell a story to my students every year about a 10-year-old girl who overheard her parents discussing their financial problems one evening while she was lying awake in bed. The girl wanted to help her parents desperately but had nothing to sell or give up, except one thing. Having rented an instrument for her to participate in band as a fifth grader, it was the only thing the girl could do to ease her parent's burden going into sixth grade. The next morning she presented a letter to her band teacher saying she could no longer participate in band. She sat back down in her seat, appeased to have helped, but heartbroken to give up her love for playing. Then, something miraculous happened. The band director called her into the hall from class and asked her one question: "Do you want to play the flute?" She answered, "Yes, with all my heart." His response was the most important of her life: "Then, I will find you a flute. Let's go to band." He patted her on the shoulder and saved her life that day...

Dr. Eric D. Knost: Words cannot express my gratitude, but as you know, *where words fail, music speaks*. Simply stated, I would not be here without you. Thank you for your words of encouragement and believing in that 10-year-old kid with glasses and braces.

My colleagues: Thank you for all your support and kindness in my tenure, especially Mark McHale. I admire you all so much, and I absolutely love teaching every day!

My sisters, Jennifer and Natalie: Thanks to Jenn for reminding me I have a voice and I should write; your pushy encouragement and support have made all the difference in this journey. Thanks to Natalie for keeping my feet on the ground and being the reader in the family, pointing us to great books. Our strong emotional connection is something I'll cherish forever. As a family, let us continue to fight this disease together for Grandma Sarah and those who continue to suffer from Alzheimer's.

My parents, Carl and Gloria Elam: Thank you for everything you did or didn't do in my life to get me exactly where I am today. I know the sacrifices now, though times are different, and what it takes to raise loving children. Your love for me is irreplaceable and perfection to me. I love you so much.

My children, Lana and Luke: Thank you for showing me the greatest love and affection of all–for you both love so deeply because I felt such love from Grandma and Papa. You two have been so patient with me, even when I took time away to write on occasion. I hope you know how much I love you always. Every parent wants health and happiness for their children. It is for this reason that I started this book, with pure faith and hope that you will never have to deal with this disease in your lifetime. If you do, continue praying for a cure, and do what you can to help a worthy cause like AD. Remember to work hard for your dreams for talent is not born in you; you must take the opportunity to create and become something more than *average*. I believe in you both with every fiber of my being.

Lance: Thank you for putting up with my late nights, my irritable days of no sleep, and for taking our loving children on many adventures so I could write. Your selfless actions and positive spirit make you the best father imaginable and a sincerely wonderful person.

God: There's no question I believe in the power of His will, especially having experienced some of the most meaningful and spiritual moments in my life through music. The palette of emotions one feels when listening to music can only be explained by a greater presence at times. Jesus, thank you for guiding my life's work, conveying my mission in education through prayer, and providing my entire reason for living. Through You, I find love and happiness every day.